Athenian Steel

Book One of the Hellennium

by

P.K. Lentz

PROLOGUE: Longing for Oblivion

"Geneva, I'm sure there's a reasonable explanation for this," said Lyka, an unwelcome presence hovering over the pilot's controls in the hardliner's steering chamber, "but it looks as if we're in the wrong layer. It's Severed. There's no way back. We're trapped here."

Lyka did not seem particularly alarmed, but then Lyka was old, much older than her two crewmates, even if she did not look it, and was perhaps less prone to fits of excitement than other fighters of the Veta Caliate.

Eight seconds later, Lyka's severed head floated free in the zero-grav, haloed by a cloud of tiny globules which burst into flat red flowers on contact with the chamber's smooth surfaces.

The head drifted gently past the small room's only hatch, which presently opened at the approach of the third and final individual aboard the hardliner *Longing for Oblivion*.

Eden had certainly overheard Lyka's observation. Now her eyes went wide at the sight of her slaughtered crewmate. At her pilot's console, Geneva triggered a control to quickly seal the hatch. Four fingers of Eden's hand were pulped in the closing orifice as she tried, and utterly failed, to hold it open. She did not scream.

"*Geneva!*" she instead howled in rage at the fibresteel door. "You're dead, traitor!"

Alone in the steering chamber but for the two wayward parts of the nominal superior she had just killed, Geneva ignored Eden's promise and the stream of stinging insults which followed it. She double-checked her instruments. This was the right layer. Not the one on their mission manifest, of course, but the right one. *His* layer. That was *his* Earth directly ahead.

Pre-industrial, which was good. And the hardliner's current course would land it somewhere in the western hemisphere, which was also good.

Their landing would be less a landing than a fiery disintegration in this Earth's atmosphere. But it was vital that *Longing* not survive, and for that reason Geneva had overridden those elements of the liner's systems which enabled it to transition between void and atmosphere, gravity and none. The hardliner would break up on entry, and the three crew aboard would make landfall, or seafall, separately from their vessel and each other, and with no protection but their voidsuits. All three would surely sustain catastrophic damage. But they would heal. They would survive. Geneva had hoped to be able to destroy her companions utterly before reaching her destination, but that was far from a simple task, the tools for which were not typically present on a hardliner.

No, her sabotage had not gone quite as planned, but then plans only worked in perfect worlds, and perfect worlds did not exist. For that reason, Geneva had few certainties concerning what she would do when she got groundside. Rather, she trusted in her ability to take advantage of whatever opportunities might arise to work toward the achievement of her aim.

Her final aim. Her last mission.

She knew what she would *not* do. She had no interest in ruling this world or in depopulating it by the thousands, both of which were available options. One way or another, her existence would end in this endeavor, and she would have the luxury of taking her time at it, since Caliate pursuit seemed unlikely. She could live a life here. Many lifetimes. Primitive ones, but surely enjoyable.

Maybe her two companions would even unwittingly help. Neither bifurcated Lyka nor furious Eden, pounding uselessly on the hatch with one hand and one freshly made stump, had any inkling as to why they were doomed. They were Geneva's siblings, of a sort. Two of thousands, most of whom called her vile names behind her back, if not to her face, and who only grudgingly trusted her because Magdalen told them they must. Magdalen was wrong after all, it seemed: wayward Geneva had been a traitor to the Caliate once before, and now, with this act, she became one again. Betrayal was easier the second time.

They hit atmosphere. Instruments showed the steering chamber getting very hot very fast. Eden's pounding stopped, and she screamed a few last words in the moments before the hardliner *Longing for Oblivion* achieved its eponymous wish.

"I will find you, bitch!"

Staring blankly at the instrument panel, Geneva paid her no heed.

Above the clouds, and far above the square sails of wooden ships crewed by mariners to whom the sea on which they fished and traded and made war was the center of the world in more ways than one, a strange vessel's long journey met its catastrophic end. Three of the many small, burning fragments into which the vessel shattered had once been alive, and would live again.

PART 1

PYLOS

1. Strange Flotsam

Ninth day of Metageitnion in the archonship of Stratokles (August 425 BCE)

By moonlight the Helot rowed his tiny boat, its hull patched and rotten, toward the shore of the mountainous island that dominated Pylos harbor. Sphakteria, it was called, an ugly name for an ugly lump of rock. Windswept waves from the Ionian Sea poured relentlessly through the narrow channel between island and mainland and threatened to swamp his little craft, a fleck of chaff on Poseidon's vast domain. But such were the only conditions in which this voyage might be made, for in daylight and when the weather was fair, Pylos harbor was watched over by Athenian triremes, the crews of which would halt and slaughter any who tried to run their blockade.

But what was the risk of death to one enslaved by birth to men whose sons hunted and killed his kind as practice for the killing of better men? Ever had that been the lot of Messenians, at least since their ancient conquest by Sparta, to toil in servitude as Helots whose highest hopes in life were to meet a natural death and leave behind a few sons to inherit their hard lot. Until now, that was. Now there was cause to dream of more, for the Spartan forces besieged on Sphakteria had promised to make rich men of any who could smuggle them food, and free men of any Helots who did the same. Yes, the risk of this short excursion was high, but so was the reward—freedom, an unthinkable thing for one upon whose people Sparta renewed annually her declaration of war, in order that a Helot's murder might cause his killer no ritual impurity.

Now the Spartans were embroiled in a war more pressing than the perennial one against their slaves. In six years of war with Athens, Sparta's ancient hegemony over the Peloponnese, her own backyard, had gone unchallenged—until this summer, when out of nowhere the Athenian general Demosthenes had landed at Pylos and built a fort. Thinking Demosthenes their deliverer, Pylos's Messenian population had gone over to him, yielding the city to Athenian control. A Spartan army, recalled from its annual siege of Athens, had descended swiftly on Pylos from its landward side, whilst even more troops were brought in by sea for a naval assault.

Either Demosthenes was favored by his city's gods or the Spartans had angered theirs, for when the desert dust had settled and the tide had rinsed the shore clean of blood, the Athenians remained in place. The Lakedaemonian army still held the surrounding plains, but Athenian ships controlled the harbor where sat the isle of Sphakteria, on which Sparta, confident as ever in eventual triumph, had stationed a garrison before the battle.

Now those men were trapped. When Sparta's attempts to negotiate their release were met in far-off Athens with scorn, the proclamation had gone forth: freedom to any Helot who risked bringing the trapped men provisions. It was an offer only a fool could refuse, but Pylos, it seemed, was a city of fools, for instead of seeing that the Athenians cared nothing for their welfare, but only for humiliating their enemy, Messenians had flocked in even greater numbers to Demosthenes. Did they not realize that the moment Athens' aims here were achieved, her forces would abandon Pylos to the mercy of its once and future masters? And those masters knew no mercy. When the last Athenian ship had sailed and their shortsighted local allies fell, as surely they would, the punishment for those Helots who had turned, along with many who hadn't, was sure to be swift and brutal.

This Helot, though, was no fool. He saw what the future

held, and so he rowed on through the crashing waves. He cast a backward glance over one shoulder at his destination and saw Sphakteria rising from the silvered water like the spine of a great black serpent bathing in the harbor. In silhouette the island's shore did not look treacherous, but it was, so much so that his decrepit little boat was unlikely to survive the landing. No matter. It needed only to get him ashore along with the precious cargo that would make him a free man.

Land came unexpectedly in the form of jagged black teeth jutting from the water. The sea around the boat frothed white on the rocks, pelting the Helot's face with chill, salty droplets. Squinting down the darkened shore he picked out a spot where the rocks seemed fewer and less rugged, and he hunkered down and pulled harder on the oars. A swell thrust the boat's prow into the air, and as it slammed down, the oar in his right hand snagged between two rocks and snapped in two.

No cause for panic, he told himself. The current, choppy as it was, was bearing him toward his chosen landing. He gripped the remaining oar with both hands and put it to use as a pole to ward off sharp rocks.

About halfway there, a pale shape in the surf caught his eye. It poked out from behind some black rocks a few oar-lengths shoreward, rising and falling gently in a tangle of undulating seaweed. Craning his neck for the few seconds that he could safely divert his attention, he made out curled fingers attached to a forearm.

A corpse. The sight was no surprise, for the summer's naval battle had consigned a great many bodies to the depths. Poor men, their shades would drift inconsolable for eternity, denied entry into Hades' hall.

The Helot had seen his share of corpses in his lifetime, but never a drowned one, and so as his progress past the rocks gradually brought more of it into view, he couldn't help but steal a glance when caution allowed. Someone had told him once that a body left at sea bloated up like a fatted pig and turned just as pale, yet this corpse's skin had pigment yet, or at least it seemed so in the moonlight. And it was thin, slighter even than the average man would be in life.

When at last the wave-tossed corpse stood revealed from head to waist the Helot gaped in amazement, for this was no sailor, but a woman. A scrap of black cloth covered one of her sea-girt breasts, but the other stood bare, its nipple a dark crown on a mound of silver-blue flesh. Tendrils of hair writhed about her face in a black corona. He could not make out the features clearly, but they appeared sharp and serene, hardly misshapen by violence or bloated by drowning.

Tempted as he was to stare, especially upon discovering that her lower half too was bare, he tore his attention away and focused on the nearby beach. Only a few more rocks were left to navigate, little danger by the look of them, and he would come aground.

A wicked thought occurred to him, swatted down as swiftly as it arose, that if he were careful he might pick a path back over the rocks by foot from shore and search the corpse for jewelry. But no, he had come to Sphakteria for his freedom, not trinkets of silver and bronze, not even gold. Were he to be caught plundering the dead, he might spend his first day as a free man awaiting execution. No, he would simply tell the Spartan garrison what he had seen and be done with the matter.

At last he ran his little boat aground on the rocky shore, holing its hull in the process, and thoughts of the woman fled his mind. He was alive and soon would be free. Throwing his body ashore, he scooped pebbles from the beach and pressed them to his lips, but he wasted little time in that enterprise. He had to unload his cargo quickly, lest the tide come in suddenly and sweep it away. There were too many canvas sacks for him to carry all at once and so he made three trips, piling them at the top of the beach. While he was doing this, a voice boomed over the rush of the breaking surf.

"You there!"

Startled, the Helot looked up to see a lone figure approaching down the shoreline. Moonglow turned the man's bare chest blue, his long hair fell in a cascade over his broad shoulders, and his dark beard was wild and untrimmed. "You bring us provision?"

"Aye, lord!"

Even in the dim light, wearing a coarse cloak of undyed wool, the speaker was unmistakably a Spartiate, an Equal, born to fight and kill, just as Helots were born to serve. Wearing their armor of leather and bronze, bearing eight-foot ash spears with blades of sharpened iron, Spartiates were Stygian beasts who struck fear into the hearts of all men. Naked but for his cloak, this one proved that Equals needed no such trappings to inspire terror.

The Helot waited with two sacks piled on his back while the Spartiate closed the remaining distance across the beach, crouched, and thrust a gnarled hand into one of the sacks on the ground. It came out with a barley cake, which he examined in the low light before replacing. No doubt he was starving, but discipline forbade him from partaking before his share had been allotted, even when the sole witness was a Helot whose word was worthless against his.

"You'll have your freedom for this," the giant Equal said. He hefted the remaining three sacks and balanced them on sinewy shoulders.

"Thank you, my lord!" Blood pounded a triumphal march in the Helot's ears, a wave of euphoria imparting fresh strength to tired limbs. As he began to walk behind the master whose name he did not know, he remembered what he had seen on his approach to the island and mustered the courage to raise the matter.

"Lord!" the Helot called out. He bore only two sacks to his master's three, yet he practically had to run to keep pace with the far-striding Equal. "I saw a body washed up on the rocks!"

"That's common enough," the soldier said without stopping. "We'll send someone."

"But lord, this was a woman!"

Now the Spartan halted and turned. Even bent beneath his greater burden, he stood taller than the Helot, at whom he gazed down curiously from the shadowed pits of his eyes. "A woman?"

"Aye, lord. She looks... fresh."

The Spartiate sighed, shrugging the sacks from his back onto the rocky sand. "Show me."

2. The Dead Arise

Forever had the men of Lakedaemon, descendants of Herakles, been a superstitious lot, and never more so than in times of great success or deep misfortune. Currently, for the over four hundred Spartiates and as many Helot shield-bearers trapped on barren Sphakteria, it was decidedly the latter.

One of those Spartiates, Styphon, son of Pharax, who presently walked down from a mountainous lookout post, was perhaps less inclined than most to fret over omens. That quality, he liked to think, helped to make him a good *phylarch*. One day, if he lived, it might serve him well at higher ranks. Yet even the fiercest of skeptics, which he was not, would have had difficulty denying an omen such as the one facing them today, a sign that had sent the twenty long-haired Spartans under Styphon's command scrambling to prostrate themselves in prayer.

The omen was a woman. Persian, by the look of her, and despite being stone dead and cold to the touch she had golden skin as pure and unblemished as that of any aristocrat's freshly bathed virgin daughter. She was everywhere depilated from the neck down in the manner of whores and Athenians, which made her, in Styphon's mind, more likely than not some man's mistress drowned to keep her quiet. But then it was possible that all Persians plucked. It seemed probable enough, given that even their men were womanly. Spartan women sure didn't go smooth, and their men were glad for it.

Princess or slave, Persian or Greek, her presence was an ill omen, and ill omens sapped men's confidence, which in turn made them more likely to die. Already the Helot who'd discovered the corpse in the surf had suffered a slit throat in the night, and hungry as they were, the soldiers had decided to burn as an offering to Zeus and Artemis a third of the good barley cakes the unlucky slave had brought.

In that impractical action the men had been unanimous, but they were split on whether to bury the woman's body properly or cast it back into the sea. Until the matter could be decided, it sat on the ground outside the bounds of their encampment. Helots had been assigned to watch over it and keep the crows away, but strangely they had not been forced to cast a single stone, for no crows came. This was seen among the ranks as an even worse omen, notwithstanding that crows themselves were harbingers of doom. Still, Helots continued to watch the body in case any birds did come, not so much for the sake of preserving the corpse, but because birds could be cooked and eaten.

Styphon rounded a great stone outcropping on his descent of the mountain and caught first sight of the moss-encrusted stone fort which was the camp under his command. Its roof had long ago collapsed, making the structure more stockade than fort. The walls that remained were hardly the height of a man. It was said that old Nestor had built the thing, and perhaps he really had, but whoever had put it there had positioned it sensibly on the highest part of the island where the sheer cliffs were impassible on three sides. Should the worst come to pass, Epitadas, the *pentekoster* in charge of the island and currently commanding the main body of troops at the island's center, had designated Nestor's fort as the site of their final stand.

Whatever fate lay ahead for the Spartans besieged on Sphakteria, victory or death, it would surely arrive soon, for atop the mount which he now descended, Styphon had witnessed a sight which made it all but certain: seventeen Athenian heavy triremes spilling fresh troops onto the beach at Pylos. A runner would bear the news on to Epitadas, who would say something on the order of, "Let them come."

Indeed, let them, Styphon agreed. Far better to face one's fate head-on than to sit hammered by the sun against an anvil of barren stone, sipping brackish water by the handful, breathing clouds of oily soot and forever waiting. Sphakteria by now would have broken a less disciplined force. The womanly Athenians wouldn't have lasted a week, let alone three months at the height of summer's scorching heat.

Before Styphon completed the trek into camp, a scream reverberated over the rocks. The screamer appeared below, a Helot running toward the camp from the south. Styphon quickened his pace, hurtling over loose rocks and flirting with a neck-breaking spill while in his pounding ears rang the mad Helot's persistent shrieking. Hardly a minute later, Styphon arrived at the rear wall of Nestor's fort, nearly slamming into it, then raced around the corner to where the camp's entire population, forty men and slaves in all, dressed like Styphon in ragged chitons that clung with sweat to their chests and sunburned thighs, had gathered around the wild-eyed screamer.

Styphon penetrated the human curtain just as another Spartiate belted the Helot in the face, silencing his crazed shouts and sending him sprawling. When the slave managed to drag his head upright, it was to cry out, face twisted in terror, "*She moved!*"

There was no need to ask who, for there was only one female on this cursed rock, and she was stone dead. Knowing that, the twenty Spartiates who had just been grumbling or laughing at the slave's fright fell instantly to silence.

"Someone is playing a trick on you, donkey!" Styphon hissed.

The look of terror on the Messenian's face did not fade. He insisted again in a whisper, "*She moved...*"

Styphon was drawing back a sandaled foot to kick the man in the head when he froze and realized in the same instant as did his comrades that the slave had not lied at all. If trick this was, it was an elaborate one, for there at the crest of the ridge, not thirty paces off, the woman stood, naked but for a scrap of black cloth over her left breast.

Staggering, she fell hard onto her knees, set one hand on the earth and rose again. The men gasped and invoked the names of gods, and Styphon barked at them, without taking his eyes from the risen corpse, "Spartans, are you men or little girls!?"

The woman, or shade, or whatever it was, having regained its feet, stood swaying gently, arms held out in a search for balance. Its head was bowed, tangled dark hair hiding its face.

Some citizen or slave whispered, "We must leave this place."

Styphon bellowed, "Lashes and demotion for any Spartiate who runs!"

The warning was meant for his men, but theirs were not the only ears to hear it. Up on the ridge, the dead thing picked up its head and turned eyes toward them. A score of grown Spartan citizens, death dealers all, gasped. Styphon himself, whose faith in the creatures of legend was not strong, half expected to see under the black hair a grinning skull or harpy's beak, but there was only a face. Its expression could not be read from this distance, but Styphon sensed on it an emotion he had witnessed many times before and knew well. *Fear*. The shade was afraid.

Styphon ordered over the muttered prayers of others, "Catch her!"

As if she had heard, which perhaps she did, the corpse-woman turned and made to flee the camp. She stumbled, knee striking the rocky soil, but she bounced to her feet again in a flash and ran.

Still, no Spartan moved. No wonder, since neither had their leader. Styphon remedied the lapse by taking off at a full run. As he went, he pointed and shouted out the names of his men in small groups and told each where to go. For a moment they all stood bewildered, but soon enough they became Spartans again. A superior had spoken and could not be disobeyed. The hunt was on, its aim to prevent their quarry from reaching the wall of trees (blackened stumps, mostly, since the cursed Athenians had lately set fire to the island) which marked the arbitrary southern boundary of their mountain encampment. In the end it could hardly matter if she made it there, of course, for there was no true escape to be had for anyone on tiny, besieged Sphakteria. *If only*.

Stumbling every five steps, the corpse-woman proved easy to catch. Rather, she proved easy to surround; after that, no man was willing to go near her. Thus what resulted was a sort of moving cordon, within which the prey was free to move about as it wished.

After some minutes at this impasse, Styphon called out, "Kneel and let us approach!"

The she-thing's head whipped round to face him. Hardly a spear-length away, Styphon looked straight into eyes that were the pale blue of a winter sky and deeply frightened. Her bare female form seemed a delicate thing, with slender limbs and nary a dimple of excess fat, but when she moved, muscles rippled under skin the color of summer barley. The features of her oval face were finely wrought, from pointed chin to wide, dark lips to thin brows arching over those pale eyes. Many men, in vastly different circumstances, and if their tastes ran to the exotic (which Styphon's, like those of most Spartans, did not) would have counted her as attractive.

Her lips made an omicron shape in Styphon's direction, but if she had been about to speak nothing came of the effort, for before any sound could emerge, her well-formed legs buckled, sending her once more to the rocky ground. She raised a bare arm with palm open and fingers spread wide in a warding sign. Styphon saw her limbs subtly tense like those of a runner on a starting line, saw that the fear in her eyes had faded and become calculation. He gleaned her intent and cried to his men, "Back! Back!"

Too late. The animated corpse whirled and lunged like an animal at a man standing opposite Styphon in the cordon. Her chosen target backpedaled, but the undead assailant was too swift and succeeded in her aim of snatching his shield.

None of the men in camp had been armed at the time the woman appeared, yet during the chase some had managed to grab a short sword or hoplon, and because of that, now their quarry had a shield, too. She crouched behind the stolen, bowl-shaped barrier in the center of the cordon, turning every few seconds to present the hoplon's crimson lambda blazon in a new direction. The icy eyes that peered over its rim issued silent challenge which none were inclined to accept.

Styphon stepped forward, unarmed, open palms upraised. The she-thing faced him. Stopping well out of her reach, he met her gaze steadily, endeavoring to betray no trace of the unease which the gods knew he felt.

"Who are you?" he demanded. He held his breath for a moment to listen intently, and in doing so he noticed that the woman's own breath was inaudible, even after the considerable exertion of her flight.

"What do you want?" Styphon tried next, but again there came no reply. Perhaps she could not speak, or spoke only the tongue of some far-off homeland. "We do not mean to harm you," he offered anyway.

That reassurance, spoken in slow, clear syllables, won him a reaction of sorts. Her blue eyes flicked away from him to left and right, scanning the audience of soldiers and Helots that watched in rapt silence. Styphon squatted to bring his face level with hers. Her knuckles remained white on either side of the shield rim, but her eyes had calmed.

"I command these men," Styphon said, "and I swear you will come to no harm by them."

Until Epitadas orders it, he thought but opted not to add.

The woman's gaze sank groundward and for a moment appeared empty, like that of some old man whose body was sound but whose mind had gone to pasture. She maintained that attitude for a few beats, looked up again, and spoke at last. Her voice was not the cackling of a harpy or the moan of a restless shade. In fact it was barely a voice at all, more like the croaking of a tiny frog or the last rush of air from the lips of the dying.

"Lak—" the woman said, and choked. "Lak...e...dai...mon?"

No doubt she had recognized the crimson lambda emblazoned on their shields. That didn't mean much, for one could scour the land between Babylon and the Pillars of Herakles and hardly find a place where that symbol was not known and feared.

"Yes," Styphon confirmed. "We are men of Lakedaimon. Spartans. I am Styphon. Where is your home?" She stared. "What is your name and who is your lord?"

No hint of understanding lit her pale eyes. Styphon's hope for a reply was waning when the woman surprised him.

"In the name of... Zeus Hikesios..." she said in her raking voice, proving that she knew at least a little Greek.

"I have no power to accept you as a suppliant," Styphon answered. "The pledge already given will have to suffice.

What say you lay down the shield?"

Very slowly, with much hesitation on her part and patience on Styphon's, she lowered the hoplon. Only then did Styphon remember that behind it she was stark naked.

"Bring a cloak!" he called to any Helot. Shortly a tattered red garment was placed in his waiting hand. He held it open and advanced cautiously on the corpse-woman, whose wary eyes held fast to him the whole way. Reaching her, he draped it over her bare, golden shoulders before stepping back and addressing the dumbstruck wall of flesh surrounding them.

"She is not a shade or a *daimon*! Any man who does her wrong will answer to me!"

At length the soldiers muttered their assent, if reluctantly. If there had been any doubt as to whether the sudden appearance of a woman's corpse on the island was an ill omen, now that said corpse walked and talked, all doubt was erased.

"Disperse," Styphon commanded. Picking up the stolen hoplon (on most days, he would punish the man who had lost it, but not today), he faced the she-thing. "The gods and I must know who it is I am bound to protect," he said.

She croaked three strange, harsh syllables which Styphon presumed must comprise her name. "Geneva."

3. Sea-thing

A curtain of rags was hung in the rear of Nestor's fort to afford the risen corpse, a lone female in the company of men, a modicum of privacy. Behind it she had sat all morning, muttering rapidly in what seemed to be Greek, even if the words were too swift and her voice too soft to allow for proper eavesdropping. From her tone, she seemed to be conversing idly with herself, or else with spirits.

It had been a year at least since the softness of a woman's voice had last filled Styphon's ear. His wife Alkmena had died long enough ago that even though he had loved her in his youth, the sting of her absence had dulled to vanishing. Strangely, this female made him think of Alkmena for the first time in an age, even though the two were as different as day was from night. His present company was the prettier by far, in spite of her foreign complexion, but Styphon would never choose her, even had he not seen her rise from the dead. There was some repellent aspect to this creature's perfection.

The woman was mumbling softly as Styphon pushed the veil aside and entered her feeble sanctuary. On seeing him, she fell silent and looked up from the bed of leaves on which she sat, legs hugged to bare breasts inside the encompassing cloak. Her delicate foreign features were relaxed, sky-colored eyes devoid of fright. She had raked fingers through the black, salt-stiffened hair that fell barely past the nape of her flawless neck. A Spartan woman's hair would only be so short after she had cut in mourning, or after her wedding night, of course, when she symbolically mourned the loss of her maidenhead.

The look she gave Styphon as he knelt to come level with her was, like his own, a measuring one. Pale, cold eyes made him all but forget why he had come. Summoning his will, he shook himself free of their enchantment and found voice with which to deliver his message.

"Our commander has ordered you thrown from the cliffs."

The heights in question dominated the northern sky. The woman's head half-turned to direct a casual glance in their direction, and then her eyes were again an unwelcome burden on Styphon. The unearthly creature asked, in a feminine voice very different from the dry rasp it had been earlier, "You are... to agreeing with he?"

"It is not my place to agree," Styphon said, understanding in spite of her broken Greek. He hardened his black eyes. "Only to obey."

Shockingly, her thin lips pressed together in a tight smile. "You come now for taking me to cliff?"

The Greek which the creature spoke (if only just) was Attic in dialect. That was not unusual for foreigners who had not known the language from birth but rather been compelled to adopt it, usually through slavery. Even if her grammar was imperfect, sounds dripped from the tip of her tongue like the very honey which lent its color to her flesh.

"No," Styphon said. "Only to inform you, so that you might—" He cut himself short, unable to finish for embarrassment.

"Might what?" It seemed more idle curiosity than real concern.

With a scowl Styphon admitted the thinking that had driven him here. "Our commander was not witness to your... *rising*. He assumes we are mistaken and that you are a mortal woman. But an Equal is familiar with death before he can walk, and you were *dead*. I am no superstitious fool, but I thought that if you knew his intention, you might... return of your own accord to..." Styphon grit his teeth in displeasure at being forced to speak such nonsense. He forced himself to finish, "...to wherever it is you came from."

The men had reached consensus on where that was, but Styphon had little regard for their baseless conjecture. The name for her that had stuck around camp was *Sea-thing*.

Her thin brows arched in... amusement? "That is many kindness of you." She glanced around her. "This place am Sphakteria."

It was not quite a question, but Styphon answered it anyway. "Yes."

"How much days you have been here?"

"Seventy, give or take."

Sea-thing's lips pursed as if in thought, and she asked next, "You have seen Athenian refin... *reinforcements* come?"

"This morning." He shook his head. "Why should any of this concern you?"

She chewed her lip briefly before answering, "I only wish to be knowing how long before falls the hammer."

"Hammer?" Styphon echoed. "What do you mean by that?"

"Sorry, maybe you are not having that expression." She lapsed into a pensive silence, during which one hand rose slowly up from inside her cloak and toyed with a tendril of her tangled hair.

"*What do you mean?*" Styphon repeated.

Sea-thing's gaze rose and met his. "Styphon," she said heavily, "how do you wish for your name to be remembered?"

It seemed a strange thing to say, but then she had said nothing thus far which was not strange. Anyway, the answer was simple enough. "I would have said of me what any Equal would. *He died in battle*."

Sea-thing leveled a grave look. "I do not knowing how you die, but I do know one thing about you, Styphon, son of Pharax. In two days' time, when the Athenians invade this island, you will surrender to them and make every Equal here an apricot."

Seeing Styphon's heavy brow furrow, she chuckled humorlessly.

"I'm sorry," she amended. "Wrong word. After what I've been through, I am very hungry. I meant *prisoner*."

4. Thalassia

Styphon stared at her, stunned. When his wits returned a moment later, he said, "Not only would that action be an affront to all I believe, I lack the power to make such a choice."

"At present," she said. "But you would have it if Epitadas and Hippagretas were to falling. Which they will."

With this, her latest in a string of impudent remarks, the frustration welling in Styphon's breast suddenly exploded into his sword arm, which lashed out at the speaker's flawless mouth.

The blow never landed. Instead, Styphon's fist stopped inches from Sea-thing's cheek, held there fast in a set of swift-moving golden fingers which might as well have been iron rods. Thus did a Spartan Equal, peerless among the fighters of Hellas for strength of limb, find himself at the mercy of a barbarian female. He struggled in vain, while from behind the binding hand, pale blue eyes watched with no sign of strain. Only when Styphon let the tensed muscles of his arm go slack did the grip holding it ease.

To block his attack, Sea-thing's right hand had shot out from inside the tattered red cloak in which she huddled. Now, adder-like, it slithered back into hiding.

Pride was a possession of limitless value to a Spartan, and those who would wound it did so at grave risk, for once he was locked in battle, a Spartan's pride would not permit him to yield. But Spartans also had minds and were capable of knowing when to pause and contemplate before leaping over certain thresholds.

Seated before him, Styphon saw just such a threshold.

Still, pride did not let him rub the hand that she had squeezed or meet her pale eyes. Staring at a patch of moss blooming between the ancient wall-stones of Nestor's fort,

Styphon asked in a humbled whisper, "What are you?"

She asked as softly, "What do you think I am?"

Styphon sneered. Spartans had little taste for such verbal games as philosophers and Athenians liked to play. "I know not," he muttered.

"What do the others think I am?"

He informed her of the consensus reached by the men of the camp. "A Nereid."

"They are right," she said. "That is what I am."

Styphon stared at the stones. At length, he dragged his gaze back up to the self-proclaimed sea nymph.

She smiled and said, "You don't believe me."

"You are no more a daughter of Nereus than I am."

"Tsk," the thing's pink tongue chided him. "You wouldn't want to anger my Father so soon before a battle. Speaking of which," she said with sudden gravity, "I have given you priceless information. I possess much more. What you choose to do with it could have lasting consequences."

Styphon shook his head. He was trying, short of clapping hands over ears, to block out her voice.

"I don't think Sparta breeds stupid men," were the next words to flow from her honeyed tongue. "Look at the evidence. I rose from the dead. I am stronger than you. If you didn't notice, I knew your father's name. So if I also tell you that I am an oracle, I dare say you have cause to take me seriously."

She was right that the Lykurgan *agoge* did not turn out brainless fools, no matter how loudly and often Sparta's enemies made the opposite claim. And she was right that it would be the height of idiocy to take less than seriously such a being as she.

Styphon treated her to a resentful glare and grated, "It is no mortal's place to know the future!"

"What mortals know is for immortals to decide," she said. The creature's once-broken Greek was by now nearly flawless, if still strangely accented. "And one now has chosen to tell you that before dawn on the day after next, the Athenians will assault this island, disguising their movements as the regular changing of patrol ships. Your two commanders will be among the fallen, and you, Styphon son of Pharax, will consign to irons all the Equals who survive."

"Why tell me this?" Styphon growled. He might have roared it were he not conscious of the need for discretion. His men were in easy earshot and doubtless curious about the goings-on behind the curtain. "The threads of Fate bind me no less for knowing that I am to disgrace myself!"

The red-cloaked oracle frowned. "The threads of Fate are threads, not chains," she said, "and as easily snapped. Knowing of the attack, you might thwart it. Failing that, instead of yielding you could choose to die with hon—"

"I have heard enough!" Styphon hissed. "I will take you to Epitadas. You may give him your oracles."

"You mean the man who ordered me thrown from a cliff? No, I choose you. Tell me, Styphon, does Pharax yet live?"

His mouth was already open to insist that she meet Epitadas, but his protest died as he realized she could tell the *pentekoster* anything she liked, easily making Styphon look the fool. Instead he just answered her question. "No."

"How did he die?"

"In battle." With resignation, Styphon began to sense the direction of her argument.

"Good for him," Sea-thing said. "Do you have a family of your own?"

By now Styphon was responding blankly, mechanically, wishing he were elsewhere, but unable to leave. "Only a daughter. Andrea."

"There's nothing *only* about a daughter," she reprimanded him, then asked, "What will happen to Andrea if you are declared a *trembler*?"

Styphon's eyes followed the snakes of bright green moss that filled the gaps between the black stones of the fort's crumbling wall, and his mind followed the unpleasant course of Sea-thing's thinking. Were he to disgrace himself here, his daughter would suffer a lonely life of misery and shame. No Equal would ever wed her, for who would wish to plant his seed in a womb through which flowed a coward's blood?

Perhaps those piercing eyes could see inside his mind, for Sea-thing said next, quietly, "That is what Fate has in store, unless you choose to make it otherwise."

"How?" Styphon asked hopelessly. "Epitadas is the only one who can act on your warning, and you refuse to speak to him."

A hand emerged from her crimson shroud to point at the battered copper horn which hung from the belt of Styphon's chiton. The horn had gone unused these long months, but remained always by his side, lest it not be at hand the moment it finally was needed.

"That is an alarm, is it not?" she said. "You need but sound it when the time comes."

Styphon's hand fell to the horn and clutched it tightly. "You said you do not think Spartans stupid, yet you would have me do something only a fool would do: stand against Fate."

The creature sighed a feminine, nasal sigh of exasperation. It reminded Styphon of Alkmena at times when she had found him too bull-headed to be swayed by her wise counsel.

"I cannot make the choice for you," Sea-thing conceded.

"You can serve Fate and live a life of lasting shame... or serve Sparta, and live or die with some glory that might anger the gods a little. I know what I would choose. But then I like making gods angry."

Mind reeling, Styphon realized his fingers were white around the neck of the copper horn. He released his grip. "I know not your reason for wishing me to do this thing," he said. "But it hardly matters. Now that you have cursed me with this knowledge, I cannot stand by and watch disaster claim the lives of my countrymen. I will warn Epitadas, on the slim chance he might listen. If he does not... I will consider what to do." Meeting the eyes of the Sea-thing, whatever she was, he swallowed dust and steeled himself. "But I would ask something in return."

The corners of her expressive mouth turned earthward. "You want more? More than the chance to escape doom for Sparta and disgrace for yourself?" She scoffed lightly. "Fine. Ask, and we'll see."

"I would see my daughter spared from the consequences of my actions," Styphon said. "Whatever course I take, if I should wind up in dishonor, take Andrea from Sparta and find her a new home. A temple of Artemis or some other place where she will learn to honor the gods. And tell her that her father was no coward, but only tried to do what was best."

Where Styphon had hoped to find some measure of sympathy light the creature's pale eyes as he finished, he found only hard calculation. "I could do that..." she answered, ominously, "but you would owe me another favor."

Styphon's heart went cold at the thought of enslaving himself to this creature. Better an Athenian prison, with bars and walls which could be seen and touched, than the invisible cages so often used by human women and inhuman creatures of legend.

She must have seen the horror on his face, for Sea-thing's features softened. She reassured him, "I may never collect. But when one is new to a world and poor of possessions, it rarely hurts to gather favors."

Styphon wanted to believe that he would never see her again, that she would never call in his debt. Somehow he doubted it, but it offered a shred of hope to which he might cling as he nodded his assent to the black bargain.

"I agree," he said. "But I have forgotten your name." She had uttered it just once, in the raking voice with which she had first awakened, and its syllables had been ugly and barbarian besides.

The raven-haired being whose corpse the ravens would not touch smiled. "I've overheard your men talking about me. They call me *Thalassia*," she said. "*Thing from the sea*." Styphon nodded the truth of it. "That will do," she said. "Now, I'm really very hungry, if you could spare some provisions. Something with honey, preferably. You won't likely be needing food much longer."

5. Horn of Fate

Styphon gave the men of the camp the story that Thalassia was in fact a priestess of Artemis, whom they dared not harm for fear of bringing down the wrath of the one she served. Though Epitadas' order to kill her was common knowledge by now, the men all concurred, at least outwardly, with Styphon's choice to defy it. Even if some few of them thought it was better to be rid of a woman's unlucky presence, none wished to bear the ritual impurity of having done the deed himself.

Not that any five of them combined would necessarily be capable of killing her, only Styphon knew. But he did not tell them that, for such a claim would rightly cause them to question his grip on reality. And so Thalassia lived, sitting in seclusion behind her curtain and devouring barley cakes as quickly as Styphon could sneak them to her from the store of rations which, if she was to be believed, would soon be unneeded. Another day passed and another night fell, a night that to all but one Spartan on Sphakteria was no different then the seventy before it. To that one, who knew this night to be their last, little sleep came, and when it did it was plagued by dreams of vengeful gods, and monsters from the mists of legend.

Early the next morning, Styphon heard by way of messenger that the Athenians had sent to the island with a demand for surrender in exchange for mild treatment of all prisoners until such time as a general settlement could be reached between their cities. Thalassia had foretold that just such an offer would be made. Naturally, as no powers of oracle were needed to foresee, Epitadas refused. Styphon chose that moment to send his own messenger from Nestor's fort to the main body of troops at the island's center with the suggestion that the demand for surrender, coming so soon on top of the arrival of reinforcements, erased all doubt that an attack was imminent. The runner returned Epitadas' terse reply: "The *phylarch*'s opinion is noted."

Night fell on the second day since Thalassia's arrival, and the gods and glittering stars looked down upon Sphakteria and dared a mere mortal man to stand alone against their divine order. Laying on his back on the cold earth, Styphon gazed up with heavy eyes and heavier heart. As night wore on, meager rations combined with lack of sleep caused his thoughts to meander. In his visions he saw Alkmena, smelled the scent of sage in her dark curls and looked down upon the shallow white depression in the small of her bare back as she lay face-down on their marital bed, awaiting him

He saw Alkmena's grave, white as her skin but far colder, a block of stone set atop a mound of distant Lakonian earth, watered with women's tears. As Alkmena hadn't died in childbirth, her stone was unmarked, as any man's would be if he died outside the battlefield.

Realizing he was drifting off, he roused himself. His hand went instinctively to his waist in search of the copper horn which tonight was to be Fate's unlikely instrument.

It was gone. He sat bolt upright and searched around him in the darkness, palms frantically brushing the rocky soil, but to no avail. There was nothing around but the scattered bodies of slumbering Spartans, dark hulks barely distinguishable from the weathered rocks which jutted up all over camp. Rising, Styphon picked a path through both sets of obstacles in the direction of Nestor's fort. Sleep fled his limbs, and he moved with the speed and urgency of a man certain of his destination.

Seconds later, he thrust back the curtain of rags. Behind

it, wrapped in her cloak, Thalassia perched owl-like on a fallen wall stone, all of her weight on the ash-coated toes that peered out from beneath the crimson cloth's tattered edge.

Sudden as his arrival had been, he failed to surprise her. Not only that, she knew why he was there, and proved it by opening the cloak and exposing a hand blue-tinged by moonlight. In it was clutched the copper horn.

"Give it to me!" Styphon lunged at her. To his surprise, Thalassia made no effort to thwart him, allowing him to snatch the instrument from her open palm. She might as well have been part of the ancient masonry for all that the flurry of motion affected her balance.

"Why?" Styphon demanded in a harsh whisper.

"It's time." Thalassia's face was expressionless in the moonlight. "Blow it."

Anger fled Styphon. "Just a little longer," he said. "If the men wake and see nothing, how will I explain? Let me climb to the heights and look for myself."

Even as he spoke, he knew it was only an excuse to delay the his first step down an irreversible course, the defiance of Fate.

"By then, it will be too late," Thalassia said. She reached down into a corner of her sanctuary, where Styphon now noted the presence of provisions in excess of what he had brought her. She must have crept through the camp, stealing food. From a pile large enough to feed three men for three days, she plucked two cakes of honey and poppy seed and pushed them one after the other into her mouth.

"You have told me how this siege is meant to end," Styphon said, ignoring her breach of the common good. "But what of the war? We are but a few hundred, of no significance. If we fall today, what becomes of our city? "

Thalassia finished chewing and hung her head. "I could

lie to you," she said. "If you were a less decent man, I would. But the truth is... you'll win. Twenty years from now, and at such terrible cost that other cities will eclipse yours within a generation."

Styphon's heart, briefly stilled, took halting and tentative flight. "But Sparta will be victorious?" he asked in disbelief.

"Yes." Her admission was reluctant. "Barely. Only barbarians benefit when Greeks slaughter each other. A victory here might shorten the war and—."

"'*Might*'?" Styphon echoed, receiving in reply only a dismissive flick of Thalassia's starlit features.

Thalassia groaned. "With my help, victory will be all but certain. I can give you ideas, weapons, that will put you far beyond any who might challenge you. I *am* a weapon," she added with sudden ferocity. "The most dangerous fucking weapon on this earth, and you sit there looking at me like—"

She drew a sharp, calming breath, and smiled.

"Never mind," she said sweetly. "Just blow the horn like we agreed. You won't regret it."

"I will not," Styphon said. He had seen and heard enough. The glimpse of rage he had just witnessed escape through Thalassia's carefully controlled facade made him even more certain what his decision must be. Yes, this creature was dangerous, he was sure of that. She would be the ruin of every man who came in contact with her.

Styphon pulled the horn from his belt, drew back and hurled it into the darkness over the fort's half-crumbled wall.

Thalassia's head hung once more. When she looked up, she said calmly, "I was afraid you might do that. That's why I climbed the heights a while ago and a had a chat with your watchmen. They're much more superstitious than you."

Breathless, Styphon demanded, "What have you done?"

Instead of answering, she craned her neck to the north

and up to the crown of the heights which loomed black against the nighttime sky. Styphon followed her gaze and saw what she saw: a spark of light, a thin finger of smoke cutting the cloudless sky. It was the watchmen's flame, the signal of an Athenian assault.

Her pale eyes returned to him, and Thalassia said, tauntingly, "If you don't sound the alarm now, you'll be shirking your duty, no?"

"You bitch..." Styphon said, but there was little fire in his voice. She was right, of course. The warning beacon having been lit, it was his responsibility to raise the alarm.

He knitted the fingers of one hand into his long, unkempt locks and tugged them in frustration before clambering over the wall to hunt for the horn.

To a Spartan, duty trumped even Fate.

6. Invasion

Well before dawn's glow obscured the dome of stars over Pylos harbor, four red-beaked, angry-eyed Athenian triremes churned black water in innocuous maneuvers meant to disguise their true, less innocuous intent: attack.

The island was still a black shape in the distance when a low, clear wail split the air from the direction of the island. Demosthenes, son of Alkisthenes, standing on the deck of one of the four Athenian ships, loosed a bitter curse. How had the Spartans known?

It mattered not. The invasion would go forward regardless; it just would not be the one-sided slaughter for which he'd hoped.

"*Auloi!*" Demosthenes cried. *Spear-points*.

To the soldiers cramming the triremes' decks, it was the code which meant their landing would be contested. Athenians would only set foot on Sphakteria behind the lowered points of their spears. He repeated the cry, and his voice competed with a second blast of the Spartans' alarm.

Shifting his weight constantly against the tossing of the trireme that had him, like all the closely packed men aboard, constantly bouncing off shoulders and shields and rails, he gazed out over the prow. On the moonlit beach of the island's southern shore, dark blots were already darting about: Spartan soldiers spotting the long-awaited invasion and hurrying to arm. A Helot runner would be on his way inland by now, bringing word to the main body of Spartan troops, probably somewhere near the island's center, where sat Sphakteria's sole source of water, the one thing which which kept the tenacious enemy alive. Demosthenes had stared out over the harbor at the ugly island all summer from his quarters on the acropolis of Pylos, and he had dreamed of the day he would capture it. Today.

The four triremes drove for shore, while on the beach fully armed Spartans trickled out from the tree line. The polished iron blades of their tall spears caught the moonlight. From this distance, in the dark of night, their shields were dark circles, but soon enough the feared crimson lambda would show.

Rather than forming up in the conventional wall of shields, the Spartans spread across the beach in loose clusters, poised to descend on the ships as they beached. That was just how his own force had repulsed the Spartan marine assault on the city of Pylos months ago, their attempt to recapture the city, the very engagement which had left this Spartan force trapped on Sphakteria.

Three of the four ships in the first wave were loaded with Athenian citizens in full hoplite panoplies of helmet, round shield, bronze breastplate and leg-greaves. Demosthenes stood among the hoplites on the deck of his own ship, *Leuke,* but unlike the men around him he had yet to don his helmet. Its cheek pieces gave wide enough berth to his mouth that his voice could escape it unimpeded, but the bronze covered his ears, erasing any hope of hearing a reply. The sea wind whipped his head of sand-colored curls, a feature as distinctive as the red crest of rank adorning his helmet. In youth, boys had mocked him for the 'womanly' attribute, along with his wide, brown doe-eyes, but no longer. Not to his face, anyway.

"*Atraktoi!*" Demosthenes yelled in the direction of the fourth trireme. That ship held bowmen, and the word meant *Spindles*. It was the derisive term by which the Spartans referred to arrows. Why not use it as his command to fire, Demosthenes had decided. Since Athens maintained no formal force of archers, the bowmen were Ionians from cities that paid tribute to Athens. The Ionian captain heard Demosthenes' shouted command, and seconds later his men loosed a volley at the beach.

Not much could be expected of archers firing in darkness from the swaying deck of a ship, and sure enough, not one of the spear-wielding shadows on the shore crumpled to the beach or wailed in pain. But the bowmen, and soon the targeteers, too, with their iron-tipped javelins, would keep up a hail of missiles until the melee began and the risk became too great of their missiles lodging in friendly backs.

Demosthenes vessel *Leuke* was not the first to reach the shore. The chance currents of the harbor bestowed that honor on another ship, *Habra*. Her hull ground up on the pebbly beach and pivoted sharply to starboard, the rowers shipped the oars on that side, and hoplites began vaulting the topstrake to plunge six feet into the breaking surf. Most failed to land on their feet and had to scramble upright in the knee-deep waters by frantically digging spear-shafts and shields into the sand, even as ten or more Spartans, about a quarter of the total number waiting on the beach, bore down on them at a full run, man-skewering spears held high. The rest hung back to await the arrival of the other ships, lest one be allowed to land unchallenged.

The first handful of Athenians from *Habra,* those who had managed to keep their footing against the tide, waded onto Sphakteria. Water still lapped their greaves when the defenders, who by now had gathered considerable momentum, slammed into them. The two sides converged, battle roars going up from both sides alike, and the invasion began in earnest. The fighters became black shapes engaged in a frenzied dance of flashing moonlit spear blades and splashing seawater. For some seconds there was utter chaos, a suspended moment in which Demosthenes and forty other watchers held their collective breath—and then the result became clear: the defenders had got the better of the initial clash. Most of the sharp death groans that pierced the night came from Athenians, whose silent corpses soon rocked back and forth on the breakers.

The Spartans fell back and regrouped in a line on the shore to meet the next challenge, for *Habra* was not yet done disgorging her marines. But Demosthenes could not watch what befell those men, for now it was *Leuke*'s turn to hit the beach. At the prow, Demosthenes pulled his crested helmet onto his skull, turned and exhorted his men, "I know you are afraid. These are true Spartans, bred to kill. But look at them! They can hardly stand from hunger, and they come from a city that's too poor to even equip them properly. Instead of helmets they wear metal hats that leave their necks and faces exposed!"

These things were true, but if they'd yet caused Sparta to lose a battle, Demosthenes did not know of it. Some even said the uncovered faces of modern Spartiates were more intimidating than the encompassing faceplates of bronze their fathers had worn. But this was an exhortation to battle, and it needed not take such details into account.

"Do not hold back!" Demosthenes continued. "The sooner this island is ours the sooner we put this cursed desert city behind us! There is much Spartan blood in the harbor already. Let us fill it with more!"

He raised his hoplon of bronze-sheathed wood, with its Pegasos blazon, and a cheer erupted from the sea of brazen helms that their wearers had coated with pitch to prevent them catching moonlight, a stealth measure of no use now. Likewise, to avoid the glinting of their blades, not to mention accidents on the wave-tossed ships, the Athenians' heavy spears had been stowed in a bundle on the deck. While

Demosthenes spoke, the spears were distributed, and by the time *Leuke* began her broadside pivot into the surf, the hoplites aboard were fully armed and waiting to leap the rails, five by five, into the surf. One of the waiting clusters of Spartiates raced down the beach in Leuke's direction, spears raised over long tresses that bobbed under the rims of their cheap bronze pilos caps.

As the shore approached, Demosthenes spared a swift glance down the shore to where *Habra* had landed. He had no time to discern detail, but the fight there did not seem to be going well, for it was still taking place in the surf. The Spartans further back, meanwhile, seemed to have lost a man or two to the archers' white-fletched arrows, and now javelins, as the Ionians' ship drew nearer.

"*Pallas!*"

Screaming the name of the goddess, Demosthenes went first over the rail. He plunged for a stomach-churning second, then his sandaled feet struck wet sand with a jarring force that buckled his knees and might have toppled him were it not for the spear whose butt-spike he drove hard into the ground for balance. He sprang up and ran, barely conscious of his fellow fighters splashing down to his left and right and following, if their feet stayed beneath them. Screaming, he went to meet an onrushing foe doing its level best to make Sphakteria's invaders unwelcome. He went straight for the foremost Spartan, who even in the dark could not have missed the red crest adorning the helmet of his opponent. A general. Here was his chance to be a hero, he would be thinking.

The chance was lost, for Demosthenes braced his left foot abruptly in the shifting pebbles, pushed off to his right and slashed his spear in a wide arc that tore out the Spartan's throat, sending his body headlong to the rocks and his shade into the mist-cloaked fields of asphodel. Two of the dead man's countrymen were right behind. Twisting and ducking behind his hoplon, Demosthenes took the first of them in the groin. Another Athenian fresh from the surf took the second in his bare thigh, which gouted black blood onto the beach. He shrieked in agony, but only for as long as it took Demosthenes drive his spear's butt-spike, the lizard-killer, as some called it, down the man's throat.

By now Demosthenes was flanked by at least three of his countrymen, perhaps more, with others close behind, judging by their piercing wails. They had a chance of success, but only if they survived the imminent arrival of a half-dozen more Equals just paces behind their fallen brothers.

"Hold fast!" Demosthenes said left and right to whomever was there to hear. He crouched behind his shield and dug in his heels just in time. One of the charging defenders, slowing in his full-tilt run to avoid collision, brought his own spear blade down in an overhead attack which Demosthenes deflected with the rim of his shield before trading back a short jab with his own spear. The enemy dodged, but was unprepared when Demosthenes, seeing he was in no danger from left or right, let go of his spear and launched his body forward, putting all his weight behind the bowl-shaped hoplon on his left arm.

Their two shields glanced off one another, but it was the Spartan's which was flung aside. Demosthenes' shield struck him a body blow, and as he fell back the Spartan's right hand lost its grip on his own spear, which scythed away to clatter on the pebble beach. Atop his foe, Demosthenes yanked his short sword free from the scabbard on his hip and drove it sidewise up and under the Spartan's leather breastplate. The man still lived, flopping about on the ground and screeching like a stuck boar, but he was out of the fight. Demosthenes worked his blade free and readied it for the next challenger.

None came. The absence inspired a moment's triumphant exhilaration, after which Demosthenes turned and went to the aid of a comrade by stabbing his opponent in the spine. He cut another down behind the knees, and within moments the only men standing in the corpse-littered stretch of shore were Athenians. More were coming up behind every moment, while not far off, the men of *Habra* were relieved by the arrival of marines from the third and fourth ships, finally overwhelming the beach's defenders.

Soon Kleon, Demosthenes' distasteful partner in this venture, would arrive with a second wave of troops to take advantage of the foothold just gained. But this was no time for self-congratulation or even for taking count of the fallen, those silent or groaning lumps on the dark earth. It was no time even to wonder how the Spartans had seen through what had seemed so clever a ruse. There were plenty of Equals left, eager to avenge those who'd just died, and more killing yet to be done before Sphakteria was taken.

7. Dirty

By mid-morning, Helot runners bore word of defeat to Nestor's fort. First, defeat on the island's southern tip, the outpost there slaughtered to the last man, just as Thalassia had warned.

Fate could run its course, it seemed, without regard for the blowing of a horn.

Hours later, defeat came at the isle's center. The Athenians were refusing to do battle like men and instead relied on weapons which killed from afar and drew no line between brave men and cowards. By all accounts, the island was now flooded with bowmen and targeteers whose stock of spindles seemed unending.

Looking south from atop the front wall of Nestor's roofless fort, Styphon watched the volleys arc up and over the distant, fire-ravaged landscape of the island, hang momentarily in the air and then slash earthward, vanishing into the great cloud of gray ash kicked up by the heels of Epitadas' main force of Equals as it shuffled this way and that, advancing and falling back in a desperate effort to engage its elusive, womanly foe.

No, to call the Athenians womanly was an offense to women. Spartan women would never behave thus in love or in war.

A Spartiate's leather breastplate could only half the time could stop an arrow, and even less often a javelin. The bronze pilos caps were little better. The elders of Sparta said 'the poorer the equipment the braver the man,' to justify the melting down of the old heavy Corinthian helms, now only worn by officers. Whatever truth there was to that adage, it could scarcely be put to the test against an enemy which refused to stand face-to-face.

Only the lambda-blazoned shields of Lakedaimon had never changed, and today more than ever, beneath a rain of missiles, the lives of Spartans would depend on their round shields. All that any of the twenty Equals at Nestor's fort could do now was pray that under cover of the great ash cloud Epitadas would make some brilliant move which would catch the too-clever Athenians by surprise and drive them back into the sea they loved so much. But all knew, none better than Styphon, that such hope was in vain. Discipline forbade any Equal from saying so, but all knew that the best they could hope for now was that some number of their comrades would succeed in falling back to the fort rather than dying where they stood and leaving twenty alone to face a thousand. A Spartiate might say that such odds sounded good, but he'd only be boasting to cheer his fellows' spirits for the imminent trek to Haides.

It was past noon when a fresh Helot runner burst out of the line of charred trees. Panting and sweating in the space below Styphon's perch atop the roofless fort's south-facing wall, he shouted up his report.

"Epitadas comes with three hundred!" the Helot said, and Styphon's spirits sank, for even though he knew this must be counted as good news, he had secretly harbored hope for a better showing. "Hippagretas is among the fallen."

The death made Styphon second-in-command on the island. It was one more thread thus woven on Fate's vast loom, leaving only Epitadas standing in her inexorable path, one life separating a *phylarch* from the curse of command. It seemed that the song sung by Fate as she worked was an angry and pompous march, not some quiet lamentation so delicate as to be thrown off tune by the single misplaced note of a copper horn.

Dismissing the Helot, Styphon addressed the men

arrayed in a defensive line ten paces in front of the fort. The rears of their inadequate helms gleamed in the late morning sun, so many times had their bored owners and Helot shield-bearers polished them with mud and sand over the last seventy days.

"Battle comes at last!" Styphon cried. The hoplites knew better than to turn their backs on the distant enemy in order to look at him. "It is battle such as the feeble Athenians know it, but mark my words, they'll run out of spindles before we run out of blood. If you keep your shields high and heads down, then before this day is done we'll have our chance to show these fucking sons of whores how real men fight!"

The Spartiates answered with a chorus of roars, pretending they believed the empty words any more than did their speaker. The exhortation given, Styphon dismounted the stockade wall and crossed over the scattered stones of the fallen interior walls on a straight path for the fort's rear corner, where dwelt, assuming she'd not flitted away on whatever current had brought her, Thalassia. He threw back her rag curtain and found her still there.

"Could you defeat the Athenians?" Styphon demanded without preface.

Thalassia reclined with her back against the corner, one bare arm resting on a bent knee just as bare. Her scarlet cloak hung open, only just obscuring her femininity. Judging by her open posture, which changed not a bit on account of Styphon's entrance, she didn't much care about what was covered and what wasn't. In that, at least, she reminded him of a Spartan woman. Scattered around her were kernels of barley and clusters of honeyed poppy seed, the shrapnel of her bestial, daylong rampage through what was left of the camp's provisions.

She raised her head from the stone and looked up with

interest. Styphon hung on the movement of dark lips that stood pregnant with promise.

When finally they moved, their speech disappointed.

"Possibly..." Thalassia said. "Probably. But there would be no honor in that for Sparta, would there? And if I'm going to continue helping you, that's not how it will work. I can't do everything myself."

It was just as well, Styphon thought. He had felt shame in even asking, having been driven to it by the desperation of seeing defeat looming so near. Who knew, anyway, if she really could fight an army? She might claim so, but then laughter-loving Aphrodite had joined battle on the plains of Troy only to swiftly wing her way back to Olympos in tears.

"But you can still win," Thalassia said.

Styphon tried not to let hope swell in his breast. Like Thalassia's every promise, he knew it could not but come with some heavy price attached.

Still, he could not help but ask, "How?"

"Fight dirty," she said matter-of-factly. "Ask the Athenians for a truce, then use it to find and slaughter their archers. Agree to meet with their generals, and when you get close to them, cut their throats."

Were Styphon's mouth not bone dry, he might have spat. Instead he hissed his disgust through clenched teeth. But in truth, he wondered. Instinctively, such a course was repellent, but Spartans were not above, as Thalassia put it, fighting dirty. Had not Kleomenes burned a sacred grove when thousands of fleeing Argives took refuge there, with no harm done to his reputation? But then Styphon was no king and had no other glorious deeds to his name to overshadow the inglorious.

The choice between being remembered as the first Equal ever to consign his comrades to chains and one who had dishonored a sacred truce to assassinate enemy generals was not a particularly hard one. Yet questions of Fate muddied that water. A battle was not a war. Could Sparta win this day, instead of losing, as Fate demanded, but still emerge victorious in the greater conflict? Thalassia might claim to know, but only the gods did.

If Styphon could be certain of just one thing when it came to this creature before him, this golden-skinned bitch that the sea had belched up, it was this: she was no fucking goddess.

"Whatever happens, do not forget the thing you have promised," Styphon reminded her. "Andrea. She dwells with the widow of her mother's brother."

"I will not," Thalassia said. "But if you make good choices today, there will be no need."

She suddenly looked up over the low inner wall of the ancient fort. Styphon did likewise and saw nothing, but soon heard the shouts of greeting which told him Epitadas and the survivors of the rout at the island's center had come.

"Fight dirty," Thalassia urged one last time.

8. The Goddess's Wrath

Epitadas' men came in their hundreds, shuffling and limping from the tree line, mixing with and vastly outnumbering the polished inhabitants of Nestor's fort. The forlorn retreating force's mood was grim, its lips tight, its shields bristling with arrows. Some men walked with white-fletched shafts lodged in their backs or breasts, and almost all leaned heavily on their spears. Reaching the stockade, Helot attendants among them slumped to their knees against walls to grab a moment's rest before being kicked or spat upon by masters in a mood to inflict harm on someone, anyone. Behind them all, somewhere invisible as yet in the distance, an inexorable tide of death was surging north up the island's length to swallow the men of Lakedaimon, shields and all.

It did not take long for the new arrivals to begin taking note of Thalassia's presence. Soon a cluster of ash-encrusted refugees had gathered at the curtain of rags, and they pushed it back, revealing her. Styphon knew some of the men as close confidantes of Epitadas, and their grumbled words and black expressions bespoke displeasure at this proof that the *pentekoster*'s command had gone ignored. Styphon inserted himself between those men and the red-cloaked Thalassia, whose perfect, foreign features remained placid.

"She is a priestess of Artemis," Styphon lied. "Killing her would turn the goddess against us."

Largely, if not only, because Styphon outranked them, the men yielded. But they were still whispering their dissatisfaction when a deep voice bellowed in rage from somewhere behind. "*Styphon!*"

It was Epitadas. An inbuilt instinct to obey made of Styphon's spine an iron rod. The crowd of battered hoplites which had swamped the fort parted to reveal Epitadas stalking up in his old-style Corinthian helmet, its red horsehair crest bouncing with every emphatic step of the his sandaled feet. Behind him walked a retinue of ten or more hoplites who looked like stone statues come to life, all dull gray ash marbled with dark blood. Flanked by these ghosts, the *pentekoster* drew up face-to-face with his field-promoted second-in-command. He inclined his bronze-clad skull over Styphon's shoulder.

"Why does that *bitch* yet live?" The metallic voice might have belonged to the helmet itself.

In spite the midday summer sun, Styphon's skin went cold inside its shell of stiffened leather. "She is a priestess of Artemis, *pentekoster*," he lied plain-faced to his superior, a punishable offense. "We dared not bring down the goddess's wrath."

A sharp laugh emerged from Epitadas' mouth, a pink hole framed by an overgrown black beard and the bronze cheek pieces of his encompassing helmet. "*We?*" he mocked. "Who commands here? And it is true that you have 'dared not'!" He waved an arm at the arrow-riddled army of the half-dead behind him. "Here are the ones who have *dared*!"

Though Styphon knew that he and his men could hardly be chastised for having remained at their assigned posts, he held his tongue and accepted the rebuke.

Epitadas drew a short sword, the blade of which still shone brightly in contrast to the rest of him. There was little chance the weapon had seen use this day, given the way the enemy fought. The sword's tip came to rest on Styphon's breast, at his heart, daring him to move.

"You!" the *pentekoster* barked at Thalassia. "Come forward! Remove that cloak! You haven't earned the right to bleed in it!"

From behind him Styphon heard a soft rustle, and

seconds later, Thalassia stood at his left arm. She must have understood that she'd been summoned to her death, but for reasons that could be obvious to no other than Styphon, she seemed unafraid.

The sword point rapped the stiff leather of Styphon's breastplate. "The sea brought us this cunt," Epitadas said forcefully, "and then it brought us the Athenians with their spindles. By defying my command to throw her back, son of Pharax, you brought us doom, and for that"—he tried to spit in Styphon's face, but since he'd been breathing soot all day, no moisture flew—"you are demoted. As for you, whore," he faced Thalassia, "I told you to remove that cloak!"

Epitadas shifted his sword-point to Thalassia, who neither flinched nor stepped back so much as a hair's breadth. Pale blue eyes unworried, she obeyed. The fingers which had been holding the crimson cloak in place at her neck opened, and it slid from her shoulders to the rock-strewn earth, revealing her nymph-like form in all its golden splendor.

Spartiates were nothing at all if not disciplined in their public displays, having been trained not even to cheer a victory, since victory was to be expected rather than celebrated. Still, more than one Equal now could be heard to gasp on the fall of that cloak. Brazen-faced Epitadas was not among them. His blade went to the hollow of Thalassia's supple neck, where it would take him less effort than was required to swat a fly to soak the earth with her lifeblood. Still, his victim's hard eyes still showed no fear.

"*Pentekoster*, she is beloved by Artemis," Styphon pleaded. His intent was not to save Thalassia's life but that of Epitadas. "I beg you, reconsider."

Epitadas snorted. Around him, the members of his blood- and ash-caked retinue eyed Styphon with hands ready on their own sword handles, daring a demoted *phylarch* to interfere.

It was at that moment, with sharp bronze poised to open the throat of a woman who was no mortal woman at all, that the first brutal shower of Athenian arrows fell on Nestor's fort.

The tip of one of those countless white-fletched shafts, unshakable in their lust to return to the earth whence they came, found the unshielded flesh at the back of Epitadas's neck. Pierced between the skirt of his Corinthian helm and the upper edge of his leather corselet, the pentekoster spasmed. His sword swiped wildly and flew from his hand, bouncing off a moss-covered wall to land spinning on the stones of the uneven floor. The blade's movement only ceased when the body of Epitadas crumpled to one side and fell atop it.

The only move Thalassia made was to take a single step backward to remove her bare feet from the path of Epitadas' crashing head. The soiled red crest of the fallen leader's helmet brushed her knees.

Dumbstruck, the onlookers raised shields belatedly, distractedly, against the incoming Athenian barrage. Styphon didn't bother, entrusting his life instead to Fate and a few paltry layers of stiffened leather. "*Goddess...*" he whispered.

He was alone in finding the breath with which to speak, and alone in one other thing, too: the knowledge that Epitadas had not been laid low by the Athenians or even by Thalassia, but by Fate, whose unbreakable chains bound fast even the eternal gods. To the rest, it was clear that their leader had been struck down by the Delighter in Arrows, the virgin huntress Queen Artemis herself.

Believing their own goddess against them, no man, not even those closest to Epitadas, objected when Styphon—demotion forgotten, since it had been issued in furtherance of a sacrilege—voiced his intent to ask the Athenians for a truce.

***

Word had come. The Spartans, driven back to a final redoubt at Sphakteria's north, wished to talk. Demosthenes was inclined to listen. He stood now at the the edge of a charred forest at the fore of fluid Athenian lines which had only just coalesced in the wake of the enemy's wholesale retreat. The Equal coming to parley was named Styphon, a lower-ranking officer to whom command of the Spartan force evidently had fallen. That was good news, for it meant Epitadas lay among the fallen.

Would that Demosthenes waited alone for Styphon, but beside him, chewing olives three at a time and spitting their stones to the earth, was his co-commander, Kleon. Technically, Kleon was his superior, but in truth he was a tag-along: a leader from the rear, a man whose fiercest blade was his tongue. Kleon's detractors in Athens (who comprised virtually all of the aristocracy) had coined a new term to describe him: *demagogos*, a leader of the masses.

His always-red cheeks were purple with delight as he chattered on about the impending humiliation of his rival Nikias in the Assembly: "Sure, he made me look the fool for a moment, but who will look the fool on my return? I promised them Sphakteria in twenty days, and how many will it have been on my return? Five, including the journey! Ha! And I'll come with hundreds of Equals in chains to boot! Men have said there'll be birdsong in Tartaros before Spartiates condemn themselves to chains. Bah!" He cupped greasy fingers behind his ear. "Do you hear that? *Tweet, tweet!*"

Demosthenes let the petty ranting of the politician go unanswered. Looking sidelong at Kleon, still wearing the brightly polished, ivory-inlaid breastplate which would scarcely need cleaning after the battle, Demosthenes failed to see the appeal. Sure, Kleon's rival, leader of the so-called

Peace party, Nikias, had let the siege of Pylos drag on all summer, unnecessarily, out of conservatism or even jealousy that seizing the city hadn't been his own idea. Nonetheless, Demosthenes thought, one Nikias was worth three Kleons. Maybe more.

After too long, a lone figure appeared from out of the burned wood and trudged across the field of ash in a steady, unhurried gait. The man was Kleon's height, which was to say short, and approximately equal in mass, but this man wore his girth in his chest, where Kleon's was in the middle. Like all Equals, the man wore his black hair long, a deliberate disadvantage in close combat meant as a display of contempt for the enemy. No helm covered it, and the leather breastplate was clean of the ash which clung to his legs, greaves, and trailing edge of his faded scarlet cloak.

The man, presumably Styphon, carried no shield or weapon in hand, but his short sword bounced in its scabbard on his thigh. His left hand rested on its hilt as he drew to a halt within sword's reach of both his enemies. Demosthenes' hand fell casually, involuntarily to his own blade. Contempt showed in the black eyes which rested between Styphon's heavy brow and at least once-broken nose. He said nothing for some seconds.

Kleon spit an olive pit, waved an arm, urged, "Well, out with it!"

Demosthenes failed to stifle a frown. The Spartan's black eyes, formerly shifting between the two, now selected him as the one more worthy of address, if only by a hair. Eyes fixed, Styphon's right hand crossed his body and its fingers wrapped around the handle of his sword. Resisting the urge to take a step back, an urge to which Kleon succumbed, Demosthenes mirrored the Spartiate's move. He'd never known the Spartans to blatantly violate a ceasefire, but then they weren't prone to surrender, either.

Styphon drew his sword. The move was ponderous and as such conveyed little threat, and so Demosthenes let his blade remain sheathed while the Spartan shifted his grip to his sword's neck and held the weapon aloft horizontally. It hovered for a moment in the space between the three leaders, while over it intersected the narrow, black gaze of a Spartan and that of the Athenian mockingly called 'Doe Eyes' in his youth.

The sword plunged groundward, landing with a feeble thud in the ash at the sandaled feet of the day's victors. Its owner followed the symbolically dropped blade with a gob of spit—or he tried anyway, but his cracked lips failed to produce enough moisture.

"Fate is on your side today, preeners," Styphon grated. "Next time, we shall see."

Demosthenes nodded grimly, Kleon cackled, and the hours which followed were consumed by the dispatching of messengers to and from the Spartan force besieging Pylos as Styphon sought and received permission from that force's commander to turn the truce into surrender. There were to be no conditions, but one strange request was made. Among the trapped Equals was a priestess of Artemis whose return to Sparta they wished to arrange.

"A priestess fights with them!" Kleon scoffed. "Sparta is harder up than we thought!"

9. False Priestess

Just after dawn, Demosthenes left his headquarters in the squat, crumbling citadel perched atop the acropolis of Pylos and descended into the town. The priestess captured on Sphakteria had requested an audience with him. He could come up with no reasonable explanation for why any woman, priestess or otherwise, should have been present on the island. It was laughable to think the Spartans might have brought her there deliberately. Why then had she come, and for how long had she been among them? Her request for audience suited Demosthenes well enough to consent to it, if for no better reason than to satisfy idle curiosity.

The streets he walked were narrow and winding. Until recently, Pylos had been a city of slaves, and it showed. The roofs of the Messenian Helots' modest homes were thatched, the temple columns made of porous stone or even wood, and there was scarcely a public garden to be found. Even at this early hour Demosthenes was accosted at every turn by men and women rushing up and shouting barely coherent praise. Potters, weavers, carpenters, jewelers, sandal-makers and hawkers of every ware emerged from their stalls as he passed, offering up second-rate goods as gifts of thanks to the man they called Liberator.

Diplomatically refusing, Demosthenes managed to lose the fawning crowds and reach his destination, a little whitewashed cottage on a quiet side street of a southern neighborhood. It was of fresher construction than most in Pylos, with a terra cotta roof and a small but parched garden in front. A Messenian guard by the entrance offered him a cheerful greeting then rapped on the wooden door. It swung inward, and a mousy girl appeared.

“I would see your mistress,” Demosthenes said.

The Messenian girl answered with eyes downcast, "Perhaps you might wait until she has taken her breakfast, my lord."

Demosthenes smiled impatiently. "She is the one who sought audience with me. I promise not long to delay her."

Probably accustomed to serving harsher masters, and unwilling to risk further offense in protecting her lady's privacy, the girl stepped aside, and Demosthenes passed within. The cottage's main room was furnished with a low couch and a scattered assortment of cushions in gaudy hues. The soot-blackened corner hearth, gently aglow, was well stocked with bronze cooking pots and utensils. The Messenian girl vanished through a faded turquoise curtain into the rear of the house and spoke some words in an urgent whisper. A second female voice answered curtly, and the curtain was shoved aside.

"Welcome, lord general," said the second voice's owner, an older woman who bowed her head in servile Helot fashion, beckoning Demosthenes in.

Smiling gratitude, he ducked under the doorway's low lintel. The rectangular inner room, decorated with a woven rug and a pair of matching wall tapestries, was well lit by a north-facing window. Against the leftmost wall was a neatly made sleeping mat, while to the right sat a low wooden table flanked on either side by long sitting-cushions. At the table, seated on a cushion and facing Demosthenes over a breakfast of bread soaked in dark wine, was the priestess. Behind her knelt a third young Messenian girl who was focused intently on an effort to craft some elaborate hairstyle out of the priestess's dark hair, in which effort she appeared to be hampered by the insufficient length of said hair, the ends of which barely grazed the preistess's shoulders.

"Leave us, please," Demosthenes said.

The frustrated hairdresser loosed a petulant sigh, but followed the two older maids out of the chamber. The curtain fell behind them, swaying gently.

Demosthenes' subordinates had seen to the priestess's removal from the island, and so the present encounter marked the first time he had laid eyes upon her. Her eyes were cool and pale like the surface of a mountain lake, and they fixed him with a measuring stare. Above them were perched delicate brows and freshly washed black hair descending from a central part in two lustrous waves that ended in a collection of loose curls around the nape of her neck. Her skin was of a light gold complexion, the Eastern hue which Greeks called 'dark' but which in reality was lighter than that of most sun-blasted Greek islanders. Her features were harder to place. Certainly she was pleasing to behold, her jawline delicate, small nose tapering to a point. Since her capture, the Messenian girls assigned to her service had bathed her and dressed her in a finely pleated, floor-length chiton of light orange gathered under the breast with a braided rope.

The fact of this woman's physical perfection was impossible to deny, even less to ignore. Hers was the sort of beauty which seemed to transcend reality, that which inspired the tongues of poets and twisted those of other men.

Demosthenes had never been a poet.

The palely intense eyes never left him as he took a seat across the table from her. "Don't let me interrupt your breakfast," he managed to say. "I hope you find our hospitality sufficient."

The lower half of her face formed a smile, patently false, whilst higher up, her pale eyes observed him with guarded interest. She seemed not yet to have touched the food on the terracotta charger, and made no move to start. Something about the fast-fading smile, and not least those pale eyes, filled Demosthenes with disquiet. Why should that be?

He purged his unease in a chuckle, though he felt no amusement. "If you've no wish to exchange pleasantries, I suppose it's up to me. You must know my name, since you asked to see me. You, I am told, are called Thalassia." His laughter was as forced as her smile had been. "Where I come from that is how we refer to a piece of driftwood. Not exactly a name many men would give to their daughters. Of course, we pronounce it with a double-tau, Thalattia, where you use the Doric sigma."

He realized he was babbling, and the priestess's slightly bemused look suggested the fact was not lost on her either. He sank into silence, after a moment of which he found himself forced to avert his eyes from hers. He had walked into this room a conquering general of Athens, Liberator of Pylos, a man who, as of yesterday, had achieved what no other had in history, compelling Spartans to consign themselves to irons. Yet now he sat cowed by some barbarian female, exquisite as she was, who had yet to speak a word to him.

Something was not right about her. He could not think what it might be, but it made him long for a swift departure from her presence. Since pride did not allow for flight, he instead lifted his gaze and started the encounter over with a fresh resolve to dispense with chatter.

"The Spartans have agreed to your ransom," he declared. "As soon as they produce the agreed sum, you shall be on your way."

"I don't wish to be ransomed," Thalassia said. This, her first utterance, was no plea. Her tone matched his own in authority. It also served to revealed that she spoke with an accent, no surprise given her appearance.

Her eyes were hard. Demosthenes looked into them and wondered if he had yet witnessed them blink. He certainly was blinking now, rapidly, in surprise at what she had said.

He laughed, nervously. *What was it about her?* "I fear that is for men to decide, not you."

Amusement betrayed itself in a corner of Thalassia's thin, dark lips. A golden hand appeared and set a scrap of black cloth upon the tabletop.

"Take it," she said.

Frowning, Demosthenes knelt on the cushion opposite her and did as she requested. The black fabric was as soft and supple as silk in his hands, but when he pulled it taut, it stretched like no textile he had touched before. When the tension was eased, it snapped back to its former shape and size.

"An intriguing novelty," he said, "but—"

Thalassia pushed toward him a bronze table knife. "Cut it."

"I am not here to play games." The unexplained current of unease welling in his stomach kept Demosthenes' tone mild.

"It's no game," she returned. "You'll see. Just cut it."

Demosthenes sighed. That it seemed more of an invitation than an order allowed him to indulge her with pride undented. Taking knife in one hand and fabric in the other, he brought the two together. As it had done in his hands, the cloth stretched around the blade. He pushed and pushed, and then gathered the fabric at the edges and tugged hard on it.

Strange. No matter how much force he applied, not even the tiniest trace of the bronze blade's point emerged from the other side. He adjusted his grip and tried again, but with no more success. It was as though some blacksmith and his wife had together learned the secret of spinning bronze into thread and weaving it on a loom. Conceding failure, he set both objects down on the table.

"I admit I have never felt its like. I see the value in it, priestess, but—"

"I am no priestess," Thalassia interrupted in an unwomanly, unyielding tone that proved she could command a room with more than just her appearance.

Demosthenes folded arms in front of him before recalling the advice of his boyhood tutors in rhetoric, who maintained that such a posture betrayed insecurity. Swiftly he undid the move.

He put on a false, condescending smile. "Then what are you?"

Of course, her answer would bear on her ransom value, and so might also be of immediate, practical interest.

"A prophet," she said confidently.

Demosthenes scoffed.

"Would you like to know your future, son of Alkisthenes?" Her pale, intense eyes gripped his.

Demosthenes swallowed hard and fought to suppress a chill. He stood abruptly and backed away from the low table. "If you wish to spout lies," he said in disgust, "in a few hours, you can go spout them at the Spartans."

"In the eighteenth year of this war that Athens is doomed to lose," she went on regardless, "you will die. On your knees. In a ditch. In Sicily. You will be chased down like a dog and executed. You will be forgotten. The Athenians who will be remembered for their parts in this war are Kleon, Nikias, Thucydides, Alkibiades. Many more. But not you."

Demosthenes had been determined to leave, but her words hit the mark. He was not an overly superstitious man, filling his house with charms and such like some did, but he was respectful enough of those immortal forces which governed men's lives to know that such oracular utterances as these were not to be dismissed out of hand. She had spoken of his death, the duration and outcome of the war—momentous things, but for some reason it was the very last word of her oracle which struck him. A name.

Her inclusion of Alkibiades, ward of dead Perikles, was strange. Being under thirty, the youth had led no armies and would remain ineligible to do so for years to come. He had distinguished himself in a few battles, but his present fame had largely been won in the back rooms and bedchambers of Athens, and did not extend far beyond the bounds of Attica.

Demosthenes resumed his seat at the table with renewed, if fragile, confidence. "We Athenians are lovers of beauty," he said reflectively. "I would hate to be compelled to mar yours with the lash in order to arrive at that other thing which we Athenians love, which is the truth. You will speak plainly, and truly."

Thalassia eyed him in silence for several beats with an unchanging look. Then she faintly shook her head.

"The lash could be fun," she said. "But we'll have to try it another day. I apologize in advance for what I'm about to do. You're not leaving me much choice."

With that she sprang across the table in a blur of pale orange linen. Before Demosthenes could get to his feet or even cry out, her fingers were clamped around his throat. His hand went instinctively to the offending wrist. Though it was thin and its flesh soft, the muscle and bone underneath might as well have been marble.

Thalassia forced him to rise. She walked him to the room's east-facing wall and pressed his back against it. He fought for air but found none, succeeding only in emitting clicks and gurgles. His head grew hot, eyes bursting from their sockets. All the time he pulled and pulled at the hand and single arm which held him utterly helpless, an arm which clearly contained in it more power than any champion pentathlete could boast of possessing in all four limbs.

But he refused to give this woman, this *creature,* the pleasure of hearing him beg for his life. If he could even get the words out. And so after some moments of frantic struggle, Demosthenes fell limp and readied himself to pass the black gates. At least he might bear with him on this coldest of journeys some comfort just as cold: that his instinct to fear Thalassia had been dead right.

10. The Third Thing

Only when it seemed too late did Thalassia open her hand. Demosthenes' linen-covered back slid down the rough plaster wall, and he settled on the floor, hands flying to throat, chest heaving with precious, life-giving breaths. He gazed through a pain- and terror-induced mental fog at his attacker as she squatted to come level with him.

"Again, I'm sorry," she said. "I don't have an endless supply of patience. You seemed to be taking the long path to acceptance."

"Acceptance?" he coughed. "Of what?"

The curtain at the small room's entrance fluttered, and the face of the eldest Messenian maid appeared wearing a look of concern.

"Fuck off!" Thalassia said. The curtain fell abruptly back into place, swinging gently. Her pale eyes turned back to Demosthenes. "What should you accept? Let's say, for now, three things. First, I understand that you may be used to treating women like pets, but you will treat me as an *equal*. Second, nothing I say is to be taken lightly." She half-shrugged. "Unless it's a joke, in which case laughter is appreciated, but not mandatory. I do have a wonderful sense of humor. But rest assured I am deadly serious when I tell you the third thing which you need to wrap your head around."

She extended a hand toward Demosthenes' face. Involuntarily, he flinched, but the hand only settled under his chin and pushed upward with just enough pressure to discourage any attempt to remove the back of his head from the wall. Thalassia waited for Demosthenes' eyes to settle into hers, and then she told him in a bare whisper, an inhuman flash lighting her pale eyes, "I am not of your world."

With an iron hand mere inches from the exposed neck

which already burned hot with its mark, Demosthenes dared to laugh. The act hurt his throat and threatened to drown him in a fit of coughing, but he kept it up, out of spite, whilst looking down his nose and a golden skinned forearm into Thalassia's hard eyes.

Momentarily, those eyes softened. The tight downward curl of her lips reversed—and then opened in a breathy laugh that mirrored his own.

Thalassia did not laugh for long, and when she stopped, Demosthenes saw the wisdom in doing likewise. Her fingers fell from his chin, and she sighed a nasal, feminine sigh.

"I know it may not seem like it right now, but I respect you, Demosthenes. That's why I asked to see you. We are going to have a civilized conversation, you and I, and if you're as smart as I suspect, it will go well. But I'm going to tell you right now how it ends, and that is with you agreeing to take me to Athens. Understood?"

Clearly, she was no ordinary woman. Just as clearly, she could kill him if she wished. But under no circumstances could he simply yield to her threats. Still, there was no point provoking her with outright refusal.

"If I am to treat you as an equal," he said instead, rubbing his throat, "should we not both be on our feet?"

Fierceness gone from her features, Thalassia offered an open hand to help him rise. When Demosthenes clasped it, she pulled him up as easily as a man might hoist a cup of wine. For a moment after he rose, he could not help staring at her. Thalassia's arms were perhaps athletic but hardly Titan-like, her shoulder curved with a sculptor's perfection. A scrolled bronze pin nestled in the shallow dip of her collarbone, from which point her pale orange chiton descended in pleats that surmounted a smallish breast before plunging to the floor. His eyes lingered on her golden neck, not because he wished to admire it, worthy as it was of such, but rather only to forestall meeting her eyes. Some men might have got lost in the hollow of that throat, but not he, not after what he had seen and heard, and at any rate, now was hardly the time. And so, collecting himself, he looked into Thalassia's face, which, owing to the fact that her height matched his almost to an inch, stood at his eye level.

On it was, surprisingly, a look of patience.

"Sit down if you'd like," she invited him after they had stared at one another for the space of a few breaths. "Take my breakfast. I ate on the island. With luck it will be a long while before I'm hungry again."

Full understanding of her words eluded Demosthenes, but he ignored that. "Actually," he ventured, "I would prefer we continue our talk in public, where you might be marginally less inclined to, ahem, kill me."

Thalassia shook her head. "I'll stay here until it's time to sail. I won't kill you."

Demosthenes moved toward the curtain; Thalassia did not follow. "That is of some comfort," he said. "But my throat still insists on witnesses."

"Wouldn't getting strangled by a woman only be more embarrassing with witnesses?"

Demosthenes looked at her sharply. "Who is looking for you?"

"No one." Her insistence was rather too forceful.

"You wish to stay indoors. You want passage to Athens. You are a fugitive."

As Demosthenes spoke, his eyes fell on the scrap of spun bronze on the table. He moved to retrieve it. Thalassia did not stop him, and he tucked it into the pocket formed by the roll of his chiton over his belt.

When it seemed a glare was to be her only answer, he

offered, "I could escort you to the citadel, assuming that my protection is of any use to you. Conversation will have to wait until later, though. If our fleet is to depart tomorrow—with or *without* you aboard," he added pointedly, "then there is yet much work to be done today." He took a step toward the exit where, although his confidence was returning, he paused and asked with only a minimum of irony in his tone, "Am I free to leave?"

Thalassia said nothing, and Demosthenes passed through the curtain into the dwelling's front room, where the three Messenian maids had gathered in a far corner. Who knew what ideas they had about what they had just overheard behind the curtain? Demosthenes caught at least one set of eyes lingering on his neck, which undoubtedly still glowed red.

"All is well," Demosthenes reassured them with a smile. "You are dismissed, with many thanks for your service."

Eyeing him warily, they departed. Following them to the door, Demosthenes next sent away the guard, then turned and found Thalassia hanging back in the curtained inner doorway.

"Will you come?" he asked.

She frowned and made a show of reluctance before joining him. He stepped outside, and she followed, throwing glances left and right as they walked side-by-side through the parched garden under a rapidly warming desert sky. Looking down, Demosthenes saw that she carried the table knife in partial concealment in her right hand, projecting upward with the flat of the six-inch bronze blade pressed to her wrist.

As they turned together onto the dusty street, Thalassia tugged a pleat of her orange chiton. "You couldn't have picked a less conspicuous color?"

"Believe it or not, your wardrobe was not selected by a general."

"You're not a general," Thalassia returned. Her watchful gaze was everywhere but on him.

Demosthenes halted mid-stride. "Why do you say that?"

She spared him a brief look. "Sorry. Sensitive issue?" Then, irritably, "Can we please keep moving?"

Obliging, Demosthenes resumed. "Since you knew those other things you said, I suppose it's no wonder you'd know that I missed the last elections to the Board of Ten."

She nodded. "In hiding after your defeat in Aetolia."

Demosthenes stopped again and whirled on her. "A defeat for which I redeemed myself and then some, against the Acarnanians!"

Remembering himself, he calmed and began moving again. The acropolis of Pylos rose in the distance to the north, and crowning it was the ancient whitewashed citadel which was their destination. There were few souls abroad in this neighborhood of the city's fringe. Most would be out toiling at their jobs, even the women, the rest in the agora.

"No need to defend yourself to me," Thalassia said innocently, scanning the low rooftops on either side of the street. "You will be elected general again, even without my help."

"Even without..." Demosthenes echoed, and then became lost for words with which to rebut such an insult.

Thalassia took a break from her surveillance to lay eyes on him briefly. "I don't mean to imply you're anything less than competent," she said, resuming her watch. "The opposite. But your city does need me. If you want her to win, that is."

He had not forgotten—how could he?—Thalassia's baleful words inside the house, that Athens was doomed to defeat in the this war. But she had said much else, too, and nearly strangled him besides, leaving his mind cluttered and his tongue confounded.

Demosthenes tried, aloud, to sort some things out. "First," he began, "I accept that you are more than what you appear to be. But when you say Athens is doomed, why should I believe you? Across that harbor, three hundred Spartan Equals sit in chains. To recover them, their leaders will come begging us for a treaty. We are nearer to victory than ever we have been."

"Oh, there will be a treaty," Thalassia conceded. "But tell me this: what's a treaty worth among Greeks?"

Demosthenes gave no answer, for he knew the shameful truth. Treaties were worth very little. Few ever lasted out their set duration.

"This war will not end in exchanges and envoys," she said with confidence. "It will end in total victory. Sparta's. But, lucky you, you won't have to live to see it." The road split, and Demosthenes pointed down the leftward branch they were to take. Several steps down it, Thalassia correctly observed, "This way is not the most direct."

"It avoids the *agora*," Demosthenes said. "I am not unknown here. I'll be accosted."

"I thought you wanted witnesses."

He shrugged. "And you are clearly a fugitive. You tell me, do I need to be seen more than you need not to be?"

Fingering the handle of her palmed knife, Thalassia proceeded up the deserted route Demosthenes had chosen for her sake.

"Why Sicily?" he asked as they got underway, recalling the prophecy of inglorious death Thalassia had earlier thrown so casually at him across the table.

"Does it matter? It's more than ten years away." Her watchful, wintry eyes flashed a conspiratorial look. "A lot could happen before then... if the right alliance were made.

This war could be over in, let's say, two years?"

"Alliance?" he asked with interest. "With what city?"

"No city," she said. "You and me. Us. We win the war for Athens."

The path increased in grade, and Thalassia began to get ahead of him, her fine, high-laced sandals crunching an unflagging rhythm on the dry road. On either side of them stood a series of decrepit buildings which were among those abandoned earlier in the summer, when thousands of frightened Messenians had chosen to flee the city rather than risk suffering reprisals when the Spartans—as was inevitable in their minds—returned.

"Ally with *you*?" Demosthenes said scornfully. "I do not even know what you are."

Thalassia looked over her shoulder at him and smiled. "I'm a good luck charm," she said.

When again she faced the road ahead, she halted suddenly. Twenty paces in front of them stood a woman. She wore a gray traveling *chlamys*, its hood thrown back to reveal long, golden hair tied in a single braid which fell over one shoulder. At her waist, their hilts peeking out from behind the cloak, hung not one but two sheathed short swords.

An unwomanly word passed Thalassia's lips as Demosthenes drew up beside her.

"Fuck."

11. Fury

"Who is she?" Demosthenes asked. He put hand to sword, strange as such action felt when facing a female. He could not recall ever having seen a woman bear a sword; it was a sight he surely would recall.

"Eden," Thalassia said loudly. It was less an answer to his question than a chill greeting directed at the other.

The woman returned a short, harsh string of syllables in a foreign tongue. Her tone was less cold, but the ghost of a smile which touched her lips more than compensated. She spoke a few more fluid, non-Greek words, then glanced at Demosthenes. Her smile reappeared, and she continued in an accented Attic similar to Thalassia's, "—or perhaps we should converse in Greek for the benefit of your new friend. No doubt you have told him many lies. Perhaps he will learn something."

She turned her eyes upon Demosthenes. If Thalassia's eyes were the color of a winter sky, this newcomer's were that of summer: a rich indigo that seemed deeper still for being set in a pale, aristocratic face.

"For instance, do you know, Athenian, that you presently stand beside one of the universe's most vile traitors?" Eden's gaze swept back to Thalassia, and Demosthenes was glad for it, for this woman's look had frozen the breath in his chest. "For reasons beyond me," she continued, "and beyond all who ever knew her, Geneva was forgiven. Yet the moment she resumed her place of trust—"

"Get out of our way, Eden," Thalassia said evenly.

"Why did you do it?" Eden said, and she addressed Thalassia again by the same harsh, alien word she had first spoken on their meeting. It was a word that seemed subtly to sting Thalassia, if Demosthenes judged correctly. "Explain to me why you brought us here, to this shit layer nowhere near our objective and *blew up our fucking ship in the atmosphere!"* By the time Eden finished, she was speaking through clenched teeth that were as white as frost. *"Tell me why!"*

"Get out of our way," Thalassia repeated.

Eden chuckled, coldly. "Or what? You know I am superior to you. I will not let you pass. Nadir exists on this earth. Lyka has gone there. Her beacon is active—as yours was until two days ago—so you know that. You and I will follow her, await extraction and return to Sprial. I trust Magdalen will not forgive you a second time." She lifted a snowy brow. "I may suggest a few punishments."

Thalassia's demeanor remained outwardly calm, but Demosthenes knew it for what it was: the sort of calm that one adopts when cornered by a salivating wolf.

"You know nothing, Eden," Thalassia said. "Go. Follow Lyka. Sleep and wait for rescue. I will never trouble you again. I'm sorry for stranding you here. If there had been any other way—"

Eden scoffed and lifted a long, pale finger. "There is one small problem with your suggestion... and that is that *you serve the Worm*!"

She smiled, reining in the simmering anger she had briefly allowed to surface. These two women were more alike than they would ever admit, Demosthenes silently concluded. He had caught a glimpse of Thalassia's temper, could still feel its mark on his neck.

"I serve Magdalen," Thalassia asserted.

"Bullshit!" the other screamed. She set eyes once more on Demosthenes and asked, "Has Geneva told you what she is called by her own people, women and men who were once her friends but now are loathe to speak her name? It is the name I have been calling her by. Let me see if it translates..."

Eden smiled a spiteful smile. "*Wormwhore*. Yes, I think that serves."

"I do not serve him," Thalassia asserted plainly. "I hate him more than you do. Now get out of our way."

Unsurprisingly, as with the previous two iterations of Thalassia's request, Eden showed no sign of complying. "What say you, Athenian?" she asked next of Demosthenes with a smirk. "Surely you know respect for such things as law and loyalty. What do you think must happen?"

Suddenly, Demosthenes found himself the object of both women's attention. He could see in Thalassia's pale eyes, in the mouth drawn into a tight line, that she dearly hoped he would take her side. If one of the two women repelled him more than the other, it was doubtless Eden, yet... more than that, he wished to see them both ushered out of his life by the swiftest possible means. In just this one morning, the hard-fought victory which he had every right to savor had been all but soured.

"I think..." he began, and cleared his throat. He addressed Thalassia without looking directly at her. "I think that... perhaps it might be best if you went with her."

Eden grinned. "A credit to his city," she said. "Come, Whore. For the moment, I am still willing to let you walk. But if I must cut you to pieces and carry you away in a bloody sack instead, so be it."

While Demosthenes' mouth hung agape in uncertainty as to whether this threat might be a literal one, he caught a sidelong glance from Thalassia in which she made abundantly clear the depth of her disappointment in him. Then, suddenly, moving as quickly as he had seen her do one time before, she was upon her enemy.

Eden foresaw the attack and had time to draw one of her two swords, but only just. Thalassia avoided its first swing.

The table knife flashed in the palm of Thalassia's raised right hand, on course for Eden's face, but Eden's free hand shot up and blocked it while she brought her own blade back for a second swing. Thalassia twisted, and the blade missed her head by a hair's breadth—and then the wrist of Eden's sword arm was locked in Thalassia's iron grip, the same grip that still felt fresh on the skin of Demosthenes' neck. The two took to grappling, each trying yet unable to drive her blade into her opponent's flesh. They whirled together in a swift, deadly dance of whipping dark and golden locks, of gray cloak and pale orange dress.

The dance ended as few others did, with one of the partners, Eden, slamming her forehead into the other's nose, a headbutt which left her forehead streaked with Thalassia's blood. She tried to land another, but Thalassia dragged the woman's sword arm up between their faces, obstructing the blow.

Three paces away, Demosthenes stood unsure whether to intervene. Apart from temple friezes of Amazons, never before had he seen such a sight as this, of women locked in fierce combat. And even in the friezes, the women's opponents were male.

"Ladies, surely there is a better way..." he said feebly.

By choice of one or the other of the women, their struggle went to the ground, where they rolled in the dust with legs entangled. The orange linen restricting Thalassia's lower body rode up, exposing her thighs, while the other's paler legs were already bare under a high-hemmed slave chiton. Somehow Thalassia came out with the advantage, slamming her attacker's sword hand repeatedly against a rock embedded in the roadside. The rock grew slick and dark with blood, and Eden's sword fell free, clattering on the ground. Thalassia went for it, but the other woman's injured hand clapped onto Thalassia's forearm, stopping her. Their other hands meanwhile fought over Thalassia's table knife, the point of which Eden had managed to turn toward its wielder's face, its tip biting Thalassia's cheek.

As the sword flew free, Demosthenes' wits and his instincts, briefly absent, returned. He moved in long strides toward the sword and kicked it out of either woman's reach, then drew his own blade and leveled it at the combatants on the ground.

"Stop!" he cried—not too loud, lest he draw onlookers. Again, when they didn't desist: "*Stop this madness, now!*"

They rolled, and Thalassia came out on top with one hand free. Consequently, Eden had a free hand, as well, and she sent it toward her waist where her second sword awaited. Thalassia's hand, meantime, grasped a smooth stone half-buried in the earth, wrenched it free and hefted it over Eden's head.

Demosthenes watched in horror as, without hesitation, Thalassia brought the stone down with tremendous force into her opponent's face, smashing the skull. Eden's hand flew from her half-drawn sword and came up, too late, to block the blow. Thalassia wrenched her knife hand free of Eden's grip and stabbed Eden's blocking arm in the wrist, clearing a path that the blood-smeared stone might find its way for a second time into Eden's half-crushed face. Blood and brain matter smeared cloak and dress and skin and ground, yet incredibly Eden's limbs fought on. Of her two deep blue eyes, the one which was not buried in gore stayed open and retained the spark of life.

Straddling her beaten foe, Thalassia struck Eden a third time in the head before reaching for the half-drawn sword at Eden's hip. Statue-like, his own sword still pointed ineffectually at the pair, Demosthenes watched aghast as

Thalassia plunged the short sword over and over into her victim's neck and face, so hard that the tip could be heard scraping ground underneath. Blood splashed from each new wound like libations poured on an altar to some dark god.

Seeing the savage fury which lit Thalassia's face, Demosthenes knew he had to act, had to end this. He took two long steps forward, and reaching the scene of battle, he thrust his sword with all the force he could muster into mad, golden-skinned Thalassia's back. It slid between her ribs, grating on bone, through her heart, and out the other side, under her left breast.

Thalassia's head whipped round, dark tendrils of shoulder length hair partly obscuring the crazed, unearthly eyes, knit brows and bared teeth which came together in a look not of surprise or pain, but of undiluted rage. She hissed, and then ignored him, turning her crazed attention back upon her victim.

Demosthenes backed slowly away, leaving his sword embedded in Thalassia's torso. He saw that the single eye within that mutilated head on the ground stood open still, and not just with the empty stare of a corpse. This mutilated being was alive and fighting, and it did not let the momentary distraction offered by Demosthenes' interference go to waste. One of Eden's blood covered hands found the very rock which had caved in her skull, picked it up and hurled it at Thalassia, who was forced to raise an arm to ward it off.

The respite thus achieved was brief, but it was enough to let Eden slip free. Having done so, the scrambling, blood-covered thing which had moments ago been a woman had but one clear goal in mind: *escape*. Getting her feet under her, the near-headless Eden ran off at speed, gray cloak and blood-soaked braid trailing behind her. She ran west to where, beyond two or three rows of houses, the land fell off sharply into the sea.

Leaping to her feet, Thalassia ran after. As she went, she reached around behind her, grabbed the handle of Demosthenes' blade and slid it from her chest to wield it as though she had just drawn it from a scabbard. Two swords in hand, showing no sign of flagging in spite of her fatal wound, she vanished around the back of a row of empty houses.

Both women ran at exceptionally high speed. Even were Demosthenes so lacking in good judgment as to attempt chase, he could not have kept up, much less overtaken them. Left alone, he stood silent and frozen, watching the place where they had vanished. Slowly his gaze went to the blood pooled in the road, proof that what he had just witnessed was no delusion. He looked down at his hands and found them trembling, glanced around to see if anyone else was near. Thankfully, no one was.

Should he flee? He quickly decided there was no point. If her spun bronze and iron grip had failed to convince him entirely of the truth of Thalassia's claim not to be of this world, now there was no room for doubt. If a being such as she judged that he had to die, there was no escaping it. Better to face his fate like a man than run away and be hounded to his death by a seething Fury while hoping in vain for some merciful god to step down from the heavens and save him.

He steadied himself, spoke a few words aloud to Pallas, and he waited for judgment.

Within a few minutes Thalassia reappeared, walking slowly with just one sword in her right hand. In the left was what looked like a fat, bent branch. A bright red stain covered nearly the entire midsection of Thalassia's orange dress, centered on the wound Demosthenes had inflicted on her, and her golden skin was everywhere spattered with blood. She was as something stepped straight from the depths of

Tartaros, and her icy stare, like her slow but inexorable march, had but one object: Demosthenes.

Without breaking her gaze on him, Thalassia stopped five paces away and threw down the bent branch, which landed with a strange, soggy flop.

It was no branch. It was her defeated adversary's arm, severed midway between shoulder and elbow.

There was no time to stare in fresh horror at that sight, for Thalassia raised the sword's tip and aimed it at Demosthenes. "Stay."

She did not bother to imbue the word with any tone of command. None was needed.

Dropping to her knees before the severed arm, she clasped its wrist in her free hand and plunged her sword's tip into its bicep. From there she proceeded to slice down its length, opening the flesh from one end to the other, cutting down to the bone, as if gutting a fish. When that was done, she set down the sword and used her fingers to peel back flesh and muscle and sinew. She worked methodically, going from wrist to bicep, digging through the bloody mess as if... *searching* it.

The sight forced Demosthenes to put the back of one hand to his lips against a stream of acid rising from his stomach. Thalassia glanced up and delivered a malign smirk before resuming her bloody endeavor.

"Fuck!" she cursed when her fingers had traveled from one end of the severed limb to the other and back again, leaving it an unrecognizable mass of meat at the center of a dark red pool.

Would that she had found whatever she was seeking, for it was now in an even fouler mood that she retrieved her sword in blood-covered hand, rose to her sandaled feet and approached the object of her anger. She gazed down her tapered nose at Demosthenes and said nothing for a time, only eyed him with the kind of look a judge might give a defendant accused of patricide or some other unspeakable blood-crime. Demosthenes did his best to meet the look unflinchingly.

At length, Thalassia exhaled loudly and declined her chin.

"Are you fucking serious?" she asked. "Did you really just stab me instead of her? What the fuck is wrong with you? What do you have for brains? An *olive*?" Her blade cut an invisible line back and forth between them. "I thought we had a connection!" she lamented.

Suddenly baring gritted teeth, Thalassia balled her left hand into a fist with which she made to strike Demosthenes. But she held back as if in deliberation.

"I'm sorry to have to do this," she concluded. Then, with an almost apologetic look, she punched Demosthenes square in the stomach, doubling him over. "You *dumb...*"—a linen-veiled knee connected with his sternum—"*dumb...*"—her foot hooked behind his calves, sweeping his legs out from under him—"*fucking...*"—he fell hard into the dirt, where Thalassia screamed a final, made-up word into in his face —"*FUCKWIT!*"

Knowing it futile, he chose not to defend himself. Leaning down, the raven-haired Fury gripped a handful of sandy curls at the back of his head and pulled, forcing him to face her.

"I could have destroyed her," she grated. "Instead, she escaped into the sea, and all I got was an arm. That's your fault." She released her grip on his hair and with the same hand began to stroke it. "But you know what? I forgive you. Why? Because we're friends, aren't we, and you're going to take me to Athens...*right?*"

"R-right," Demosthenes said between labored breaths.

Helping him up, Thalassia presented to him the gore-coated sword—his own, which had pierced her—handle-first. He took it, and she set to straightening and brushing off his chiton.

When she was done, she warned him darkly, upraised finger in his face, "Don't you ever, *ever* stab me again. Understood?"

12. Gash

Demosthenes cleaned his blood-smeared sword the best he could on a nearby tuft of tall grass before sheathing it. "You can't be seen in town looking like that," he observed to the woman whom he now viewed less as his prisoner and more as a captor.

Looking down at her utterly ruined dress, Thalassia frowned. "True. We'll separate. I'll meet you tonight at the fort."

Before dashing off down a deserted alley, she gave Demosthenes a look with her pale eyes which promised the appointment would be kept whether he wished it or not.

He nodded as though he had a choice.

***

As he resumed his day's duties, Demosthenes tried to put out of mind Thalassia's imminent return, as well as the appetite-stealing sights of one woman mutilating another and butchering her severed limb. Not surprisingly, he failed. Still, he accomplished what had to be done: loading the prisoners and the spoils of war onto the ships, overseeing the construction of a trophy on Sphakteria, helping the city's Messenian leaders and their cousins of Naupaktos plan how best to preserve Pylos' newly-earned freedom, and enduring the political prattling of the demagogue Kleon, who made clear his intention to claim all the credit for the victory just won upon their return to Athens.

By the time the sun sank and he retired to his private chamber in the citadel, Demosthenes had arrived at a quiet, reluctant admission. He believed Thalassia. After what he had seen, how could he not? What to do about her proved more elusive...

She did not keep him waiting. As the first stars made

their appearance in his window on the fort's third story, so did she, via the same aperture. Climbing in cat-like, Thalassia stood against the wall in the light of an oil lamp.

"Hello again," she said. Her manner was subdued, her head hanging at an angle of humility heretofore unseen. Before he could wonder why, she explained.

"I'm sorry about earlier," she said. "I should not have..." She searched for words and gave up. "I just shouldn't have. I'll try not to do it again."

Demosthenes sat on a stool facing her across the wool- and reed-stuffed mattress of his simple timber bed. "*Try?*"

"*Try,*" she repeated with a self-deprecating smirk.

She advanced toward the bed, got on it, crawled to its center and settled back onto her haunches. She still wore her tattered orange gown, but she appeared to have washed it in the sea, since around the faded bloodstains, in swirls like the tendrils of a sea creature, were lines of dried salt.

"I have given much thought to the things you said... and did." Demosthenes told her.

"And?"

"Lacking any other explanation, I am forced to take you at your word. More or less."

"Good." Bringing one leg out from underneath her, Thalassia began unlacing her sandal. "Part of me thought that when I came here, you'd have twenty armed men waiting for me. I'm glad you didn't."

"What would have happened?"

"Twenty dead men," she said plainly. She tossed the sandal on the floor and started removing the other. She flashed him a cold look and amended, "Twenty-one."

"I stand here willing to believe," Demosthenes said. "Can we not dispense with threats?"

She smiled. "Yes. Yes, you're right. As we come to trust

one another, I'm sure I'll stop that."

"If I am to trust you, I must know more. Not only scraps that you see fit to throw to me, as though I am some dog lapping at your heels, but *everything* worth knowing. I will not ally myself with an enigma, nor will I stake my city's future on one."

Thalassia's look was one of disappointment. She shrugged and said, "So ask me something."

There were many questions in Demosthenes' mind, a roiling sea of them, all begging answer, but if forced to choose but one...

"How do you know these things?" he asked. "About the war's outcome? About..."–it was hard to say aloud–"my death."

"That's easy," Thalassia answered. "Well, perhaps it is, depending on... never mind, we'll soon find out. Imagine that every bit of recorded knowledge from every city you have ever heard of could be compressed to fit on the head of a pin. All the literature, art, music, speeches, civil records, land deeds, account books–everything, all of it. And then the pin could be stuck into your flesh where you would have all of that information at your disposal, to access as quickly as you can think about it. Are you with me?"

"I... I suppose so."

"You're half lying, but I'll go on anyway. Now imagine that the knowledge on that pin was recorded not today but fifty years from now. A hundred years. A thousand years. Ten thousand years. From where you stand, the people who inscribed the pin are not yet born. To them, what happens here today, what happens tomorrow and every day for the rest of your life, including how you die, is–"

"History," Demosthenes finished for her.

Thalassia rewarded him with a pleased nod.

"And you have such a... *pin* inside of you?"

"So to speak."

"Where are you from that such things are possible?"

Thalassia blew a huge sigh and flopped back on Demosthenes' bed. "I realize you feel a need to know these things, but must we do it now?" she asked petulantly. "I can't explain to you in a few minutes how the universe works. It's much more complex and fluid than you can imagine. It's much more complex than even I could have imagined before... never mind. Later. For now, what's important is that I know what the Spartans will do even before they do." She propped her head up on one elbow and arched a brow at Demosthenes. "Do you think that might be useful?"

Demosthenes scoffed. "I see that wherever it is you come from, they have knowledge of the *rhetorical question*." He leaned forward on his stool, fixing the too-casual Thalassia with a serious glare. "I do not 'feel a need to know' these things, I *do* need to know them. And you will tell me, if not today then soon. But perhaps there is a more important question to be answered than where you came from, and that is what interest does someone like you have in seeing one Greek city triumph over another?"

"Does it matter?" Thalassia dragged herself back into a seated position, hands resting on ankles, bare arms framing the blood-stained hole in her dress, and presumably the body under it. "Victory is victory."

"You know that to be a lie," Demosthenes chided. "Victory, too, is a 'complex and fluid' thing. So tell me, what do you care about our war? Does this *Magdalen* person wish for us to win, whoever that is? Or... the *Worm*?"

Thalassia bowed her head. Demosthenes sensed in her reaction, a momentary look in her eyes–there one instant, gone the next–the truth of something she had said to Eden.

She did hate this man or creature they called the Worm. The name caused her pain, and shame, too, if Demosthenes was not mistaken. Perhaps it was made worse by knowing, as surely she did, that its speaking now could not help but cause a second word to spring to mind: *Whore.*

He would not dare speak aloud to Thalassia the name which Eden had translated into Greek for his benefit, the vulgar epithet she claimed that Thalassia's treachery had earned her. He would not say the name, but neither could he let Thalassia fail to explain why Eden and others called her by it.

"Why?" Demosthenes pressed when she did not answer immediately. "If you cannot even answer that, then I must demand that you leave. Even if it costs me my life."

She thought for a moment, sighed, answered, "I'm sure you'll have no trouble grasping that the outcome of one day shapes the events of the next. Had your invasion failed yesterday, your day today would have been very different, correct? You might even be dead. Do you have children, Demosthenes?"

"Do you not know? You know all else about me."

"I only know what people of your time thought worth recording."

Taking a beat to recover from that blow, Demosthenes answered, "No. No, I do not."

"But surely you intend to. If you had died on the island, any children you might one day have fathered would never exist, would they? Nor their children's children, or their children, and so on. So... suppose I knew that some one of your descendants not yet born would become my enemy," Thalassia continued. "What might I do to destroy him?"

"You could... kill me," Demosthenes said, feeling suddenly ill at ease with the topic.

"And what if I didn't know that my enemy was *your* descendant, but just... someone's, somewhere?"

Demosthenes considered. He did not like where his thoughts took him. "If you were devoid of conscience, if you were a *monster*," he said, "then I suppose you might kill a great many people, in the hope that the right one was among them."

Thalassia rolled her eyes, dismissing his judgment. "Or," she began emphatically, "one could simply change the courses of events so that *different* people died, and *different* ones were born. Not more or fewer, necessarily, just *different*. Instead of a hundred Athenians lying dead on a certain battlefield, a hundred Spartans do. Your aims are served, and so are mine."

"Whose line is it that you would see wiped out?" Demosthenes asked quietly.

From her place on the bed, Thalassia fixed him with a glare of an intensity he had only previously observed in the moments before she had attacked him. "You know," she said. "If I wasn't wrong to choose you, then you already know."

"The Worm," Demosthenes declared with confidence. "What did he do to you?"

Lips tight, Thalassia shook her head. "One day you can ask me that and I'll answer... but not today." Rolling forward, she crawled closer to him and settled on the corner of the bed. She said with mischief in her cool eyes, "Today... was a bad day. I got attacked. *Stabbed*."

She slipped first one shoulder and then the other out of her trashed chiton. The garment settled onto her thighs, but remained there but a moment before she shifted her legs to remove it entirely. Kneeling on the bed, she reached out and set a hand on Demosthenes' knee.

"I would very much like to end it," she said, "...in a *better* way."

She must have bathed herself in the sea along with her

garment, for her honey-colored skin was covered all over with a fine tracery of brine. Her breasts would have served Praxiteles fine as models for those of a nymph carved in Parian marble, but Demosthenes' eye was drawn to the raw, black gash just underneath them. The half-day-old wound was covered by a scab and surrounded by a faint pink halo and clinging flecks of dried blood.

Demosthenes dragged his eyes to a random wrinkle in the bedclothes. He said nothing, for he was not entirely sure how best to reject woman who would smash her enemies' skulls and hack off their limbs, or else wipe them and their lines from existence entirely.

Thalassia sighed, withdrawing her hand. "I understand," she said. "You're Athenian. You like boys, don't you?"

"I.. I like women just fine," Demosthenes returned. He was unsure where to focus his gaze, and so it flitted around even while powerful base instincts urged it back to Thalassia's body. "But I prefer women who do not have a history of assaulting me. And, for that matter, ones who... lack stab wounds."

"Pfft, you gave me that," she said. "But fine, I'll wrap it so you won't even notice. It's not like you have to stick your cock in it. Unless you want to, I guess. As for the other thing... I said I was sorry."

"I know, but... still."

Thalassia scoffed, settling back into a casual pose which left her legs parted shamelessly. Her body had not a wisp of hair upon it below the neck, Demosthenes could not help but note before he shifted his gaze even farther from her, onto the patterned plaster floor.

"If you think this isn't my real body," she assured him, "it is. I haven't got tentacles, talons, feathers, snakes for hair, or anything like that. This is really how I look. I'm as human as you... only better."

"It is not that." This much was true. Had not the physical forms of deadly Medea, bewitching Kirke, treacherous Klytaimnestra and a hundred other women, mortal and demigoddess alike, been those of pleasing females? Not all dangerous women had claws.

"What, then?" Irritation edged Thalassia's voice.

Demosthenes searched for gentle words with which to voice the thinking that kept his cock firmly in check... or rather kept it unfirm. He failed to find them quickly enough.

"Our brief history leaves me hesitant to speak any ill of you," he admitted.

With a sigh, Thalassia levered her splayed thighs shut. "No," she said resignedly. "Speak freely. I won't hurt you, I promise."

"Very well..."

Still, what to say? In spite of her promise, he could hardly risk speaking the undiluted truth, which was that based on the few hours of their acquaintance, he had found Thalassia to be an opportunistic, foul-mouthed, ill-tempered butcher, possibly a traitor, possessed of neither modesty nor morals.

She was, in short, everything a good woman should not be.

Just in time, Demosthenes' straining mind produced an excuse which was equally true, yet less likely to provoke.

"If you would have me enter into partnership with you," he said, "I would prefer my judgment not be clouded by the pleasures of your flesh... which, doubtless are... significant." She struck him as one susceptible to a well-placed compliment, and this was no lie.

He finished and held his breath while Thalassia's pale eyes appraised him. At length, her hard expression broke into a half smile. "I thought you said Athenians loved the truth."

Demosthenes released his held breath and drew another with which to speak, but found himself lost for a plausible denial.

"You can't lie to me," she said, thankfully without a hint of remonstration. "My senses are far better than yours. Your skin, your breath, your heartbeat give you away. Give me the real reason. I can take it."

Feeling defeated, but at the same time reassured, Demosthenes resolved to oblige her. Still, he spoke in terms rather milder than he might have. "It is... not only a repellent outer form which makes a monster," he said.

"Hmmh," Thalassia intoned. "A pretty monster, am I?" She shrugged and clicked her tongue. "That's fine. I've been called..."

She hesitated, and Demosthenes knew why. *Traitor. Wormwhore...*

"...worse," she finished. "It's your loss. Where I come from, men aren't so afraid of women."

"It is not fear that–" Demosthenes began to object. Then he said instead, in anger, "This is my world. I have no obligation to defend it, or myself, against your criticism."

"Fine." Thalassia sat on the bed with legs tightly crossed, frowning down at a naked thigh which she tapped absently with the tip of one finger. "If you change your mind soon," she said, "the invitation stands. But as your ally, I should warn you that if you don't... and maybe even if you do... I'll find someone else."

They sat for some seconds in a silence which Demosthenes recognized as awkward. Whether Thalassia thought the same, he could scarcely know or tell.

"So this place you come from that is full of braver men than I," Demosthenes asked to break the silence, "what is it called?"

With a groan, Thalassia flopped back on the bed. "I'm sick of talking. But if we have to do that instead of having fun, at least come lie next to me. I'm cold."

Demosthenes touched hand to brow; it came away moist with sweat. "Even were it not high summer, I would have trouble believing that a draft causes you discomfort where a blade between the ribs does not."

"All right, then I'm lonely. Just get over here."

Seeing no immediate harm in it, Demosthenes rose from his stool and crawled onto the bed beside naked Thalassia. As soon as he was in place, she laid her cheek on his shoulder, her soft hair tickling his neck. A warm hand settled onto his chest.

It was of no concern.... His mind and his will were strong. He was no animal or barbarian, enslaved to the body's baser instincts. Thalassia's touch, in fact, far from exciting him, caused his flesh to recoil, so long as he kept at the forefront of his mind the grim vision of what those soft hands had done to Eden.

"You were going to tell me where you came from," Demosthenes prompted when she seemed content to just lie there.

"The *Veta Caliate,*" she finally said. "It's not a place so much as a thing. An army, of sorts, led by Magdalen. We are recruited from throughout time and space. Mostly women, but not entirely."

"An army of women," Demosthenes mused. It was an idea far removed from the realm of the possible in Athens, indeed anywhere in the civilized world. "For what purpose?"

"Magdalen's," Thalassia answered. "No one but she sees more than a fraction of the whole. We are given orders not knowing what they mean, except that they serve her plan."

"What sort of orders?"

Thalassia was a warm weight on his shoulder, a silken voice in his ear. "Assassination of one target or many. Transport of individuals from one layer to another. Sometimes we'll compel two people to breed together."

"*Compel them to–*"

Demosthenes did not bother to finish. Better simply to move on. Likewise, he would have to be sure to ask Thalassia some other day, among so very many other things, about this term layers. Eden had also used it.

"You mean to say that you kill people, and commit these various other acts upon them, without ever knowing why?"

"Magdalen commands, the Caliate obeys," Thalassia answered. "It is the price for the beings we become, the lives we lead, the wonders we see. But... I have not done many of those things myself. Mostly I transport the ones who do. I am... *was*... a pilot."

Demosthenes could scant imagine the sort of craft in which she and her kind must travel. But lessons in shipcraft were not his foremost objective at present; that was knowledge of those who used them, particularly the one before him.

"Does your kind feel pain?" he asked, thinking of the sword piercing Thalassia's heart, of Eden's head reduced to a mound of pulp and splintered bone.

"I feel as much or as little as I wish," Thalassia said. "If I want, and sometimes I do, I can make it so that the slightest touch"–her finger traced a delicate, meandering line on Demosthenes' linen-clad breast–"sends me to the peak of ecstasy. I can turn intense pain into pleasure. Every bit of my body, inside and out, is in my control." She laughed faintly. "Maybe that adds to your understanding of why we are so willing to follow Magdalen."

It did, Demosthenes thought, even if he did not much like what it said about Magdalen's followers. It also told him nothing about why Thalassia would betray them, assuming Eden had spoken truly.

Thalassia sighed lightly, hot breath tickling the skin of Demosthenes' neck. She was so solid and real, and yet how could she be anything but a wisp, a fantasy?

"I don't need much sleep," she said. "But this hole you put in me will finish healing faster if I do." She added hopefully, "Unless... you've changed your mind?"

"No," Demosthenes said gently. He glanced down at the head on his shoulder and saw that Thalassia's eyes were shut. Since he had lain beside her, Thalassia's tone had grown ever more relaxed. If he was not mistaken, her accent had faded to where she could almost be mistaken for a native Athenian.

A long silence ensued, filled only by Thalassia's soft, slow breathing and the equally rhythmic, echoing crash of waves breaking far below the chamber window on the rugged shore of Pylos harbor. Her heart beat pulsed against Demosthenes' side. She had a heart, then. One which he had cut in half today, yet there it was, still beating...

Just when he thought she was surely asleep, the naked, beautiful monster upon his shoulder asked, "You will take me to Athens?"

"I see little choice," Demosthenes answered. "You are far too dangerous to leave behind to proposition men of other cities... as I presume you did the Spartans on the island." He pondered a moment and concluded, "You warned them of my attack."

Thalassia confessed without shame, "Yes."

"Then your help did them little good... or did it?"

"Styphon made his choice. Things might have been different. But the Spartans are a backward-looking people.

You and yours are different, I hope. I wish only to look forward."

"I would look in all directions," Demosthenes said. "As you say yourself, the past bears heavily on the future, and you must open your past to me, Thalassia. Completely. If I am to work alongside you, I must have greater forthrightness than I yet have witnessed from you."

He looked down and found Thalassia asleep. No matter. If her senses really were so keen as to let her discern truth from lie, then she had heard him. She had heard.

13. Spoil

Sleep was fitful. Demosthenes awoke more than once, and if not for the warmth next to him and the mass of dark hair on his chest, he might have thought himself emerging from a dream. Each time he awoke, realization hit him in the pit of his bruised stomach that his life had been forever changed by this being's entrance into it. In the light of day, he had seen no choice but to accept her, but night was ever the time in which doubts drifted up from the mind's murky depth to bob on the surface. And so, in between rounds of shallow sleep, he began to second-guess himself.

Had it been a mistake not to reject Thalassia utterly? What she suggested was sheer madness, a course of action which had destroyed countless men and toppled empires. Only the worst of fools challenged Fate. The gods ever struck them down with the greatest of wrath.

If Croesus goes to war, a mighty empire will fall, the Pythia once had prophesied. Brimming with pride, Croesus went to war, and an empire did fall. His own.

Two years, Thalassia wanted. Two years to win this war which had burned openly for seven already and simmered for decades prior, flaring now and then when opportunity arose for one side to do the other harm. She claimed that Fate was on Sparta's side, but even if she was right, the question lingered: was it better to stand defiant in Fate's path and risk annihilation... or to surrender to it and be carried on its current to less than pleasant shores? A hundred philosophers would argue the latter, but then, they had never actually had the choice.

At some point, after the blackest depths of night had passed, Demosthenes opened his eyes and found the warm presence beside him gone. He experienced the briefest moment of relief, but the weight came crashing down again when his eyes flicked to the window and found the pretty monster of his dream, or nightmare, filling it. Still unclad, she sat sideways on the window sill with her back against one side and both feet planted against the other, bending her brine-frosted nymph's body into a pleasing, seahorse-like curve.

She turned her head toward him and smiled, but the smile was distracted, as though heavy thoughts weighed upon her mind as she looked out over the black, roiling waters of Pylos harbor.

"Good morning," she said. Her voice, like the smile, was contemplative.

Demosthenes sat up on the bed, returning the greeting with a bare nod. Thalassia swung her legs down and sat facing him framed by the lightening sky.

"I forgot to tell you congratulations yesterday," she said. "For taking the island. I didn't mean to diminish it."

"I thought I might wake to find I had imagined you," Demosthenes observed, shaking off sleep.

"You mean you *hoped*."

As it was impossible to lie to Thalassia, Demosthenes elected not to reply.

Allowing the lapse, she asked, "So where do we stand, you and I?"

Demosthenes could not answer that. Something within him screamed to banish her from his sight. She was a witch, a Siren, a temptress, a creature of the dark. But something would not let him. A sense of responsibility? This monster had to be dealt with in some way, if not by him then by another.

He pressed palms against his face, less to rub away sleep than to push back against the pressure of knowledge that mortal men should never possess.

"I gave much thought last night to the things you said," Demosthenes told her. "I have doubts... questions. I worry that your knowledge of future events will prove of less use than it seems. Once your actions alter one outcome, all that follows is thrown into question, is it not? The very use of your foreknowledge renders it useless. For example, now that you have warned me of my appointed death—for which, if nothing else comes of our acquaintance, you have my sincere gratitude—I promise you that Fate will have a fight on her hands ever to get me to Sicily."

There he stopped, seeing that a crooked smile had appeared on Thalassia's face.

"What is it?" he asked.

"That's... very impressive," she said. "That you would even think of that shows... Well, it's just very impressive. And not wrong. But if I might allay your concerns?"

"Please."

"It's true that every change I... *we* make to the outcome of an event has an effect on what follows. But specific knowledge of outcomes is not the only weapon I can put at your disposal, nor even my most powerful one. As the Spartans' fortunes change, their plans, too, will diverge from what is known. They will adapt, but understanding them, I will be able to *predict*. And more than that..." She gave him a strange, dark look. "Demosthenes, what is a better weapon, a sword of bronze or one of iron?"

"Well, iron, of course."

"Yes. What answer would Achilles give to that question?"

Demosthenes thought briefly. "I suppose he could not properly judge, having known only bronze."

"Yet, today, you use iron. Does some other metal exist

from which still stronger weapons might be made?"

"No..." Demosthenes said. Then, beginning to grasp Thalassia's intended point, he added, "Not at present."

"If I were to ask you," she went on, "what is better, an iron sword or one of steel, what would you answer?"

"I could not know for certain, but I would venture to guess... *steel*."

Thalassia rose from her perch in the window and came to the bed, sat on it and put a hand on Demosthenes' forearm. The night spent in intimate proximity with her evidently had disposed of the feelings of revulsion which her touch had previously inspired. For better or worse, he was getting used to her.

"I think you understand," she said. "There is much I could teach your countrymen, and not only those who make weapons. Farmers, shipbuilders... healers. Had I come before the plague, many who died might have been spared. I can not only make your enemies' lives worse, but also help make the lives of Athenians better and happier, which will in turn make your city even harder to defeat."

Demosthenes sat absorbing this and concluded, "Very well. I grant that you have much to offer, troublesome as it may prove to convince old men to heed the teachings of a foreign female. But I have a further doubt which I fear will not be so easy for you to dispel. There are at least two others like you abroad in our world. What if they were to do for other powers as you propose to do for Athens?"

A shadow fell over Thalassia's flawless face. "Lyka, as you must have heard, has fucked off and buried herself in a mountain. It's far from here, beyond what you call Scythia. She'll be of no concern. As for Eden... I won't bother to bring up again that I might have dealt with her if you could tell the *fucking* difference between a friend and an enemy."

Demosthenes cleared his throat. "I have few friends who have strangled me near to death."

Thalassia shrugged. "Well... you have one now."

"I do *not,*" Demosthenes corrected her sternly. Perhaps with the first glimmer of dawn after a night that was like the fever dream of a mad playwright, he was remembering himself. "You overstep and take too much for granted. You will not *use* me. My world, my city, will not be as tools in the pursuit of your personal vendettas. If I am to partner with you, it will be because I believe such partnership can do more good than harm for the people about whom I care most."

Sitting up in his bed, Demosthenes leaned forward, bringing himself closer to Thalassia, showing he would not be cowed.

"You earlier maligned my view of women in insisting that I treat you as an equal. Well, I demand no less of you. I will play no pliant, backward barbarian to your cultured goddess from on high. If I am to take to you to Athens, it is *my* house in which you will dwell, and you must afford me proper respect both within its walls and without. Not just that, to all except us, you must appear as my *slave,* a spoil of war, for that is the only reasonable excuse I can give for taking you into my home. In truth, I know I cannot be your master, but neither will you be mine. Is that much understood?"

The whole time he had spoken, Thalassia had but stared at him with an expression that was more attentive than usual, as though perhaps she was taking his words to heart. Her lips hung slightly open, but as he finished, they made no move to reply. Instead, Thalassia leaned swiftly and smoothly forward, not stopping until her warm, parted lips grazed his own. Demosthenes leaned back, and when that did not end her advance, he thrust up his palms such that they slid up Thalassia's ribs, all but cupping her bare breasts.

"Will you stop trying to *mate* with me?" he demanded angrily, sliding across the bed. "If you heard invitation in my words, then your knowledge of Greek is less perfect than it seems."

A few feet away, naked Thalassia sighed and tucked a stray lock of dark hair behind her ear. It flopped out, not quite long enough to stay put. In the just-rising light from the window, Demosthenes glimpsed unbroken flesh under her left breast—a spot he had also just touched—confirming the absence of any sign of yesterday's mortal wound. There was not even a scar that he could see. Indeed, there were none to be seen anywhere on her anatomy.

"I heard you," Thalassia said soberly. "I accept it all."

"Good..." Demosthenes said, encouraged by the change in her manner. "Now, as for Eden—"

An insistent thumping sounded on the chamber door, which seconds later flew wide. The bearded man behind it was Agathokles, captain of a force of Messenian exiles from the allied city of Naupaktos. Agathokles had uttered half of Demosthenes' name before the sight in front of him, that of a foreign beauty naked in the Liberator's bed, stilled his tongue.

"Ah... apologies," the Naupaktan said, recovering with a smile. He showed no trace of embarrassment, and gave as much effort to averting his gaze as Thalassia did to covering her nakedness, which was none. "I did not realize you had company."

"I... shall only be a few moments," Demosthenes told him.

"I know well the importance of the part she tends to," Agathokles snickered, "however, other parts of you are much needed outside."

"I'll not be long," Demosthenes said sharply. "If you would, please pass word to the servants that my guest here needs a garment. Anything will do."

The Naupaktan's glance fell upon the torn and stained orange chiton heaped on the floor by the bedside, and his smile spread wider. "Things got rough?"

"Nothing that won't heal," Demosthenes said. "Now, if you please..."

With a final, lingering look at Thalassia, whose return smile he likely failed to notice, Agathokles left.

Even as the door shut, Thalassia picked up where they had left off. "If Eden has not found me within a year," she declared, "I will hunt the bitch down and destroy her. Deal?"

Demosthenes pondered. A year? A being such as Eden—or Thalassia—could do a great deal of damage in a year. Should she not be found and slain sooner? He cursed himself for the fool move of intervening on Eden's behalf yesterday. Yet who could blame him? What he had seen was a very human-looking woman having her skull turned to pulp by a second, crazed woman who had previously assaulted his own person.

Now he wished Eden dead, but for all he knew Eden was in the right in her quarrel with Thalassia. *The traitor. Wormwhore.*

"It will do," Demosthenes decided, for he planned to give Thalassia far less than a year to fully open her own past to him.

She smiled. "So. Are we... partners?"

How many women down the ages had smiled at men in just this way and asked a similar question? Women whose minds were like those of men, only subtler and more dangerous. And how many men had those women consigned to misery and death by luring them into undertakings which, to those looking back, hearing the tale unfold in bard's song or seeing it acted upon a festival stage, are easily seen for abject folly?

Yet... to *be* there, to be that man chosen to walk a privileged path, one set out upon by its share of fools, yes, but walked also by true heroes long before their names became known to all. Not only tragedy but triumph too was immortal.

The risk in what Thalassia proposed was enormous, but so was the potential for reward. Athens might avert a generation of ruinous war followed by defeat and subjugation. It did not make a man guilty of *hubris* to desire that... did it? Fame and glory might result for a man whose name Thalassia claimed was doomed to be eclipsed by those of other men, but fame was incidental. It mattered not who it was who ensured the safety of generations of Athenians yet unborn, only that the job was done.

At least, Demosthenes told himself that, but in truth he knew he had scant choice but to bind himself to Thalassia, for she was determined to wreak changes upon his world with or without him. If he declined, she would only take the same offer to another, or else strike off on her own path. Was it not better, then, for the sake not only of Athenians but of all men and women everywhere, that he stay by her side where he might exert the sort of stabilizing influence it was all too clear she needed?

Still, he hesitated. Why could not he not bring himself to answer plainly, crying out his imminent challenge for the gods and Fates to hear? *Yes!*

Conscious of the business awaiting him, Demosthenes slid from the bed and stood. He had slept in his chiton and so already looked presentable, if barely. He looked down upon Thalassia, on her haunches on the bed, and declared, if none too loudly, "We are partners. With equal say in all decisions, and no secrets held between us. All must stand revealed."

Thalassia shut her eyes in a blissful look, opened them

and said with a grin, "Equals. No secrets." If Demosthenes did not read her wrong, she seemed almost giddy. "I can't wait to get started!"

PART 2

ATHENS

1. Homecoming

Metageitnion in the archonship of Stratokles (August 425 BCE)

That the weather held for the voyage around the Peloponnese and home was doubly fortunate, for every shore passed by the fleet of beaked triremes and round-hulled cargo ships was a hostile one. It thus could not even put to anchor at night to let soldiers and sailors sleep on a beach or in a friendly port, of which there were none. The fleet could only sail on beneath the quiet stars, which was for the best, perhaps, since half of the men aboard had spent a season trapped at Pylos and were scarcely eager to delay their homecoming by even a day.

A swift, unladen ship carried word of their victory ahead, and so a massive crowd was on hand at Pireaus, the port of Athens, in time for their arrival. Priests shouted prayers of thanksgiving and poured libations on the shore, while great masses of men stood in clusters to greet victorious sons and brothers and nephews leaping from the freshly beached prows. Even some citizen women came, under the watchful eyes of their lords, to seedy Piraeus, so auspicious was the occasion and so battered were the ancient social codes of Athens by years of siege and plague.

Demosthenes had no wife, no brother, no mother awaiting him. Plague had spared only his father Alkisthenes, and the old man's health was too fragile to permit him the quarter-day's journey from the country estate where he passed his days, now that the Lakedaemonians weren't slashing and burning it. Thus, while men around him were embraced by weeping kin, Demosthenes was sought out instead by a parade of city officials and various others who hoped he would remember their names when the time came to support their pet projects—a new garden or cult statue for their *deme*, a wider market road, or whatnot. He gave these sycophants short shrift, taking the slightest excuse to ignore them. Boys ran up in search of nothing more than to have their fathers' swords, one day to be theirs, touched by the hand of a hero. Those requests Demosthenes granted gladly, silly as they were. Still others wanted a lock of his sandy hair, but that request he smilingly refused, if only because he would otherwise return home with none left.

Not all could share in the joy. Eighteen Athenians had fallen on Sphakteria, and their loved ones, not yet informed, would find themselves cast into grief this day. Still others present in the crowd would already know they had lost brothers or sons in the first Spartan assault on Pylos earlier in the summer. Shortly after landing, Demosthenes spied the white-bearded father of one such casualty, a tribemate of his, and pushed through the crowd to kneel and kiss the hem of the old man's flowing *himation* and deliver a promise to bring his son's arms and pay personally to his home. Tears welling in his bright eyes, the old man pulled Demosthenes to his feet for an embrace.

At the top of the beach waited another old man: the statesman and general Nikias, with his lined face, square jaw, and gray hair which he kept trimmed back to a near-stubble. His unclouded eyes were fierce, and his limbs had more life in them than most men half his years. Nikias, more than anyone apart from the Spartans, was responsible for the hardship of Pylos. A word of support from him in the Assembly could have ended all debate and dispatched the needed reinforcements months ago, but instead it had taken a long and bitter siege and the posturing of a demagogue—Kleon, who at the moment was consorting with those same sycophants Demosthenes had shunned—to deliver final victory.

But now was not the time to bear grudges. Nikias embraced Demosthenes warmly, showing none of the bitterness which he must surely have felt on seeing a venture he had so strenuously opposed end in a victory that was likely to change the course of the war.

"You'll not lose out for a generalship this year," Nikias told him, and Demosthenes accepted the somewhat backhanded compliment graciously.

Nikias had no compliment, not even a smile, for Kleon, even though decorum dictated he congratulate the man. The ruddy-faced demagogue grinned broadly anyway, as he had throughout the proceedings, shaking every hand and missing no opportunity to remind all comers of the prisoners he had brought back from Pylos in a glorious over-fulfillment of his already ambitious promise to the Assembly of swift victory. More than once, he lifted his hand palm up with fingers curled, as if to demonstrate how the fates of those prisoners rested in his own meaty grasp.

There at the top of the beach, in the presence of most of the Board of Ten, the eponymous archon, who this year was a man named Stratokles, crowned the two triumphant commanders with laurel wreaths, then led them up onto the dusty harbor road where waited two quadrigas bedecked with garlands and pulled by four white horses each. Demosthenes boarded his chariot behind its driver, accepting his effusive welcome and looked back in the direction of the beach, where his trusted men and Kleon's were unloading the spoils and hauling in the empty triremes for drying and maintenance. He had asked Thalassia to follow him some fifty paces behind and she was heeding the request, it seemed, for at about that distance Demosthenes picked her out amidst the thronging crowd of returnees and celebrants. Plying the human sea with ease, she reached the roadside just as the two chariot drivers began whipping their teams forward, and the quadrigas' great wheels, which had flowering vines woven into their spokes, began to turn. She would have to walk alongside the procession, of course, for as far as anyone else in Athens knew, she was but a slave.

At a snail's pace, the procession made its way to Athens between the Long Walls that connected the city to its port. The walls were three times the height of a man and lined with evenly spaced bastions within easy bowshot of one another. By ensuring her access to the sea, the Long Walls had saved Athens from ruin in each of the past seven summers of Spartan siege—a ruinous tradition cut short this year by the successful attack on Pylos. So long as the walls ensured that Athens touched her beloved sea, the city could not fall.

The crowd, traveling on foot and horse and two-wheeled donkey cart to the accompaniment of pipers and drummers and hymn-singers, clogged the wide, arrow-straight port-road for as far behind as Demosthenes could see. Near the center of that seething human mass marched the reason that many of today's spectators had made the trek to Piraeus: the prisoners. The Spartans walked in a formation eight abreast with each rank yoked by neck and arms to a ship's mast laid across their collective shoulders. Clamped on their ankles and hobbling them were irons which had been forged by and for their own freed Helot slaves in Pylos. A constant barrage of stones, mud, rancid vegetables, and anything disposable which came to men's hands assaulted the vanquished Spartiates from all sides, but the prisoners walked on as if the assortment of missiles were no more than a fine, misting rain. Now and then a prisoner would be struck hard in the head or face, but the rigid timbers borne by seven of his comrades ensured that he kept moving, and so the Lakedaemonians' formation remained intact, and with it what remained of their pride.

Whilst engaging in idle chatter with the cluster of hangers-on near his chariot, Demosthenes cast frequent looks back at the prisoners. He understood the rage of the garbage-throwers, certainly, for here before them marched some of the very men responsible for their hot summers of misery, the years of plague and corpse-carts and daily mass pyres when all the folk of Attica had holed up in the teeming city while outside its inviolable walls, their farms were razed and livestock slaughtered by this enemy, perhaps by these very men.

As righteous and justified as the crowd's anger was, disapproval of its behavior nagged at Demosthenes. The articles of their surrender had included a pledge against mistreatment. Vegetables could scarcely harm them, but still. It was like watching a man mistreat a dog, he realized, for that's what these Spartiates were: dogs harshly trained from birth to obey the needlessly complex chain of command bequeathed them by the founder, Lykurgos. Even before their capture, these Spartans had worn every day of their lives an even heavier yoke than the timbers under which they now marched, for what greater curse could one endure than to be a professional soldier, slave to the whims of kings and elders, and never just a free man and master of one's destiny?

He pitied them, and both pity and duty urged action upon him, but was it worthwhile? Could he hope to win a generalship in the coming winter if the citizens present remembered him as the one who had sought to deny them what little revenge it was in their power to take? Would anyone vote for Demosthenes, the Spoiler of Fun?

Some distance to his right, borne by his own chariot, Kleon held aloft as trophies the plumed helm of Epitadas and a punctured, lambda-blazoned hoplon as he addressed the crowd constantly with words Demosthenes was glad he could not make out.

A realization spurred him to act: to think only of *elections* was to think like Kleon.

Demosthenes stepped down from the slow-moving quadriga, turning the head of the startled charioteer, and wove a path through onlookers who cheered the act they did not yet understand. He marched through the crowd to a thick-bearded citizen sitting astride a serviceable brown mare, the reins of which were held by a slave on foot. Demosthenes offered the citizen a silver obol for use of his horse for the remainder of the procession, but the citizen refused payment and surrendered it for free—even if he made a point of mentioning his name, Kallias, three times.

Mounting, Demosthenes rode against the languid current to rejoin the procession some distance back, where, coming up alongside the prisoners, he inserted himself between their third and fourth ranks and wheeled the horse forward. The Spartans' matted long hair was abuzz with insects and their already soiled chitons stained with marks from the same flying debris that now pelted Demosthenes. As they were forced to part to accommodate the horse, the prisoners gazed up at their mounted vanquisher with bitterness in their dark eyes. No doubt they anticipated some new humiliation.

From their laughter, the people of Athens expected the same, but slowly they came to realize their error. The hail of mud and overripe fruit grew gradually thinner, the cheers and jeers died down, and a silent confusion settled over the crowd which Demosthenes did nothing to allay.

Soon he was not the only Athenian in the rank of prisoners. At least eight men who were loyal to him joined in, even daring to go on foot among a humiliated enemy which gave no indication that it appreciated the gesture. Before long, none other than Nikias had fallen back on his white stallion to ride among the prisoners. With him came two more generals of the Board of Ten, the old man's political allies. Those additions served no practical purpose, for the air was by now free of missiles; but here was an opportunity for Nikias and his faction to show the sovereign *demos* which of the two returning 'Heroes of Pylos' had their endorsement. Perhaps Nikias sensed that if and when Demosthenes rejoined the Board of Ten, he might not be warlike Kleon's man after all, but a potential ally of theirs in pursuit of an honorable peace.

The first glimpse of Athens on the ride up the Long Walls was, as ever, her soaring acropolis. Topping it, with its pediment gleaming burgundy and gold beneath the noonday sun, was the mighty temple to the Virgin Athena which Perikles had built. Demosthenes locked eyes on it and, as was the habit he shared with thousands of his countrymen, thanked that goddess aloud for having seen him safely home. The procession ended on the gentle slope of the Pnyx, the ancient hillside theater which was the seat of Athens' Assembly, and there the crowd swelled with those who, for any number of reasons, had not made the trek to Piraeus and back but had waited in the city instead. After the Spartans in their yokes were led away, it was time for speeches to be given in the shadow of the towering acropolis. Nikias, being the senior *strategos*, and this being an occasion of military significance, was invited first to mount the slab of white stone called the speaker's step. The old man spoke for a full ten minutes without ever mentioning the names Kleon or Demosthenes, and when at last he did speak them, the former seemed to stick in his throat.

Even as Demosthenes gave the senior general the courtesy of his attention, he worked his way to the eastern fringes of crowd, the direction in which lay dense pine groves sacred to the nymphs. The nymphs' wood, he hoped, might offer sanctuary to a man wishing to escape unwelcome obligations. He was no bad citizen, of course, and would scarcely dream of shirking his duty to vote in an Assembly (not least because of the fine levied on those caught) but this was no Assembly. This gathering was more an excuse for making speeches to bend the will of the *demos* one way or the other.

By the time the applause went up for Nikias, at least half of it forced, Demosthenes stood by the tree line where only a few pairs of eyes were positioned to observe his departure. He flashed the owners of those eyes a smile and a silencing gesture, and the young men smiled their agreement in return, gratified to be made co-conspirators by one of the day's heroes. When he was safely out of sight, Demosthenes spun on his heel in the grove's floor of dry needles and began walking a line for his home in the *deme* of Tyrmeidai. Behind him, Kleon's voice boomed over the hillside, which meant that in an hour or so, when the demagogue finally finished, the crowd would expect a speech from Demosthenes. It would be disappointed.

He had barely begun the walk home when he heard a sudden crunch of hurried footfalls to his left and looked over in time to see a figure which might have been one of those nymphs to whom the wood was dedicated fall into step beside him on the trail.

How Thalassia had managed to keep track of him in the Pynx, a place where no woman was allowed, remained a mystery. It was one she could keep for now. He had not seen his home in three months and would let nothing slow his return.

2. Libation Bearers

At some point in his flight, the laurel crown which had been set upon Demosthenes' head in Piraeus tumbled off. He left it where it fell as an offering to the whispering goddesses. Thalassia might have been one of those nymphs, a silent shade moving alongside him with no evidence of exertion. They shared no words during the swift passage through the wood, and soon entered onto streets which were mostly deserted on account of the very festivities they had fled. A few turns down residential streets, past houses painted in pale reds and yellows, their neatly kept rooftop terraces and flowering gardens empty but for fleeting glimpses of wives, daughters and slaves, brought them to the well-made wooden gate of Demosthenes' modest residence.

He had scarcely put his hand on the gate's latch to enter its short colonnade of palms when a piercing shriek assaulted his ears. Out of the dwelling's main entrance burst a slight, pale figure with flowing hair of deepest red that tumbled in loose curls from beneath a silvered fillet. Dressed in her finest embroidered long chiton, Eurydike scrambled down the palm-lined path, clutching against her chest the house's ceremonial rhyton, a glossy black horn-shaped vessel painted with a scene of Odysseus skewering five suitors of Penelope. Its contents sloshed in time with the slap of her sandals on the flagstones.

At the small marble cult statue of Zeus that stood just beyond the gate, she skidded to a halt. The two silver pins that fastened her garment over freckled shoulders heaved, and so did the full breasts between which the rhyton was pressed. The lips on Eurydike's likewise freckled face were twisted in barely suppressed laughter.

Demosthenes could scant help but chuckle softly

himself. He had purchased Eurydike two years prior to replace a male housekeeper loaned from his father Alkisthenes. He had gone to the slave markets intending to bring back another male, but red-haired Eurydike, just out of girlhood, had caught his eye. She alone among the poor wretches on offer had a rag clutched between her teeth.

"A beating if she drops it," the slaver explained. "Foul mouth on that one! Since you've got the funds, I can't think why you'd want a Thratta anyway." He laughed. "Those sheep-brains live in mud holes and eat straw, so what can they know about housekeeping, eh? Besides, like I say, this one's got a mouth on it. If she ain't using it to curse or spit at you, she's biting you, the little bugger." He sounded as though he spoke from experience. "Bite your nutsack clean off, she will. No, come over here instead. I've got a fresh-faced little Arkadian for you. Good and docile."

"Let me hear her," Demosthenes requested, for Eurydike's bright green eyes had captured his attention. Those eyes, along with her freckled skin, copper hair, and the bands of black pigment encircling each of her upper arms made her appearance typically tribal Thracian.

Reluctantly, the slaver tugged the rag from Eurydike's mouth.

"Choose me, lord!" she said urgently. "I swear I will be good to you!"

With that, to the slaver's dismay, the deal was done, and Demosthenes walked off with a foul-mouthed barbarian girl in tow, having spent barely half the silver with which he had come prepared to part. Whenever Eurydike angered him, which was often enough, he could recall that day and his anger faded. He had been warned away but taken her anyway, out of spite and perhaps the love of a challenge.

Today, behind the bounding Eurydike on the garden

path leading to his home, making his approach in a more dignified manner, was Phormion, Demosthenes' paternal second cousin and the keeper of his home while he was away. Phormion bore a superficial resemblance to his elder cousin thanks to the sandy curls which crowned his head. His career, too, might have resembled his cousin's but for the fall in his youth which had left him lame in one leg. And so, although he was in his early twenties, Phormion hobbled up to the gate like a man three times that age, leaning on an Egyptian walking stick, a gift from Demosthenes, its ebony head carved in the likeness of a jackal.

Reaching the gate, Phormion opened it while impatient Eurydike bounced on sandaled heels behind him, frothing the wine inside its horn-shaped flask. However eager she was to share fond words and an embrace with her master, etiquette dictated that a slave wait until after any citizens present had said their greetings.

On the threshold, the cousins embraced. "You bring us great pride," Phormion said. He produced in one hand, dangling from a leather thong, the iron key to the *oikos*. Even if the house's gate was rarely locked, its key was the symbol of its mastery. Handing it over, Phormion spoke formulaic words, "I gladly surrender back unto thee that which you charged me to protect."

By now Eurydike threatened to vibrate out of her speckled Thracian skin. Green eyes beaming, she raised the black rhyton in both hands and practically threw it into Demosthenes' arms. Accepting the horn, Demosthenes removed the cover at its tip and splashed wine onto the stone plinth atop which rested the thick-bearded marble bust of *Zeus Herkeios*, Zeus of the Courtyard. As he poured wine onto stone already well-stained purple by libations past, he spoke simple words of gratitude for his safe homecoming. When the rhyton was empty, he stoppered it and set it beside the bust.

No sooner had he put it down than Eurydike lunged, flinging tattooed arms about his chest and burying her cheek in his chiton. Accepting her into his arms, Demosthenes told her, "How I have missed you, bright eyes."

Eurydike turned her face upward and asked excitedly, "Really?"

"How could I not?" He bent his head and kissed her forehead at the center of the triangle formed by the two halves of her center-parted copper hair and the fillet of silver which secured them above her brows. Eurydike despised imprisoning her tumble of curls in fashionable plaits and braids, perhaps because they did not readily lend themselves to taming. A fillet and the occasional ribbon were the most she ever suffered.

"I have a gift for you," Demosthenes said, and the slave beamed still more.

Her gift, hanging at his thigh by a short cord from the belt of his chiton, was the only spoil of Pylos he had carried on his person from the ships. Detaching Eurydike to get at it required more effort than detaching the gift.

"A Spartan's iron dagger," he announced when he had succeeded at both tasks and held the gift out by its plain rawhide scabbard.

Squealing her gratitude, Eurydike took the handle, drew it and admired the blade with mouth agape. The knife was blunt, its edge even curled over in some places, for it had probably been put to every imaginable use by the besieged Lakedaemonians. But that didn't matter one bit to Eurydike. She knew as well as the giver that the item was not truly meant to be useful. It was a token of trust, for an armed slave was one with the power to cut her master's throat in the night.

Tears welled in Eurydike's green eyes by the time

Demosthenes shifted her to his left side, where she nestled under his arm, clutching her gift more tightly than she had the rhyton.

"For you, cousin," Demosthenes said to Phormion, who knew well why he had to come second and betrayed no offense, "a full Spartan panoply. It will be brought to your home. Alas, minus the shield," he added disapprovingly. "Kleon intends to use those to line the Painted Stoa as testament to the victory which even now he claims as his own."

As was customary, Phormion tried twice to refuse the gift, but once the attempts were rebuffed, he accepted with obvious pleasure. Greetings over and gifts given, there was little more to be done to forestall a potentially fraught introduction. Up until now, Thalassia had stood a mute shadow in the street several paces away, drawing occasional flicked glances from Phormion and Eurydike. Now both sets of eyes locked upon her.

Demosthenes waved an arm in her direction. "This is Thalassia. She is..."

Conscience made him hesitate. How could he lie to his blood-kin and the *pallake* he trusted so deeply as to gift her a dagger? Surely, the charade was doomed to crumble. Perhaps this was all a mistake...

"A spoil of the battle, my lord," Thalassia finished for him with head bowed, hands demurely clasped in a pretense of humility that actually was convincing. "Your humble slave."

Demosthenes tightened his arm around Eurydike's shoulders, mostly to reassure the girl, but also to restrain her if need be. Indeed, she tensed. How could she not upon learning that the size of her master's household was to grow by half, and that worse still, the new addition was, by most standards, more desirable than she. Thracian slave girls, *Thrattai,* were commonplace in Athens, while women of Thalassia's more Persian tint were rarer and fetched a higher price.

Eurydike's worries might have been eased then and there by simple reassurance that her master's bedchamber would remain her territory exclusively, but now seemed hardly an appropriate time. Eurydike knew, too, that neither was this a proper time for her to openly express her displeasure, and so she instead gave Thalassia a forced, bloodless smile of the kind in which another woman could not fail to detect stark warning: *I will make your life hell!*

Phormion only said to his cousin with an approving smile, "Well done."

All four, two citizens and two slaves, started down along the palm-lined, stone-paved path to the house. Eurydike walked proudly, and no doubt pointedly, adhering to her master's hip.

"I kept the hearth going the whole time you were gone," she bragged. "Well, almost. And—" She went up on tiptoe, and Demosthenes bent his ear obligingly to her lips so she could whisper to him in her lilting accent of the northern plains, "I was very naughty with Alkibiades again. You will have to *punish* me."

The comment failed to shock Demosthenes, for it was rare to find a concubine in Athens who had *not* been molested by Alkibiades, and Eurydike was one of the playboy's favorites. Not only that, she was ever out to give her master reasons to redden various expanses of her freckled skin as prelude to other activities.

When Demosthenes hushed her, Eurydike obligingly changed the subject. "Why is her name *'sea-thing'?"* Her voice was over-loud and laced with calculated derision.

"Be kind," Demosthenes scolded quietly. "You have nothing to fear from her."

Reassured, or at least feigning it, Eurydike set her cheek against his arm and fell silent.

Demosthenes' home was modest by the standards of his social class. It consisted of two stories with plain, whitewashed walls and a flat roof which served as a terrace from which a quarter of Athens could be seen, not least the soaring, temple-crowned acropolis. They entered into the house's lower floor, which apart from a pantry, storage area, and private bath, consisted entirely of a single room, the megaron, with a round stone hearth at its heart. The room's floor was of hard lime plaster tinted deep red, while the walls and four supporting columns, also plastered, were plain white but for two simple stripes echoing the hue of the floor. Visitors to his home were ever pleading with him to let some artist they favored decorate the blank expanses with frescoes, as had become the fashion of late, but always Demosthenes resisted, joking that the Spartans, thick-skulled as they were, got some things right.

The megaron was furnished with a low ebony dining table flanked by reclining couches. The inherited table was the room's lone extravagance, its edges gilt and legs carved to resemble bear claws. In a rear corner of the megaron, a well-built timber staircase ascended to the private quarters above, while at the room's center, its focal point, the hearth fire burned at a relative flicker. The radiant heat made the air inside the house over-warm and somewhat stifling. It was a typical state, for hearth fires burned even in the depth of summer, not only because it was deemed bad luck to let one die, but also to avoid the necessity of a trek to the nearest shrine of Hestia for a fresh spark. The priestesses charged only a bronze obol, but the little coins quickly added up if one wasn't careful. Eurydike visited Hestia's shrine rather too often, as evidenced by the frequency with which the clay coin-pot on the stone wall of the hearth needed replenishment.

Eurydike went to fetch wine while Thalassia walked to a wall of the megaron, placed an open palm on its surface and walked absently from corner to corner, dragging the hand behind her. Perhaps she was comparing her new home to whatever sort of dwelling it was to which she was accustomed. Demosthenes and his cousin meanwhile retired to the couch. Phormion lowered himself on his ebony cane, and they began to quietly converse.

Phormion explained that since the Spartan invasion force had been recalled to deal with the capture of Pylos, Athens had known its first summer of peace since the war's outset. Harvests were being brought in, flocks multiplied, and men and goods came and went between city and countryside as they pleased. Demosthenes' own family estate in Thria, where his father Alkisthenes dwelt in ill health, had borne its first fruit in many seasons.

Demosthenes in turn spoke of the battle, but Phormion, sensing his cousin's exhaustion, did not remain long. Just before he departed to his own home, discharged from his duties as the keeper of his cousin's, Phormion asked, "Shall I stay for the welcome of your new slave?"

Ordinarily, a new slave would sit before the hearth, swear allegiance to her new master and be showered with sweets and nuts.

"Perhaps tomorrow," Demosthenes said. He was in no hurry to ask Thalassia to submit to such a ceremony.

The door shut, and Demosthenes turned to find both females seated by the hearth. Thalassia watched the dancing flames, and Eurydike watched the other woman with a look of consternation. At Demosthenes' approach, Eurydike shook off that look and leaped to her feet.

"My lord," she said, grabbing Demosthenes' hand. "Come upstairs and see that everything is in order. That one"—she nodded at Thalassia—"can tend to the hearth."

As was frequently the case with Eurydike, her true intentions were transparent, if only because she wished it that way. Demosthenes had learned long ago that Eurydike only played the fool, when in reality she was no such thing. She simply loved life, unkind as it had been to her, and sought to enjoy it.

Demosthenes let her lead him up the timber stair. He went not because he craved sex—though he would not refuse it, not least because it was easier to give in than to defy Eurydike in that regard—but because he hoped to share words with her in private. As soon as they had passed through the home's disused women's quarters and into the master's bedchamber, which was, as promised, in perfect order, Demosthenes said to Eurydike, softly, but gravely enough to penetrate her girlish excitement, "You have no cause for jealousy."

Eurydike's lip curled in an exaggerated sneer. "Me, jealous? Of *her*? You're crazy. Why would I be?"

"Precisely," Demosthenes assured her. "So be kind and try not to work her very hard. Between you and me... I think she is *mad*."

"She would have to be, wouldn't she?"

Demosthenes chuckled nervously. "Why is that?"

Caught in a bluff, the Thracian shrugged. "I don't know, lord, I was just agreeing with you. I'm glad you're back."

Her tongue reappeared, and it came forward to lick the skin of Demosthenes' chest where it was exposed above the drape of his loose chiton. She pressed her warm body into his. During the embrace, an idea crossed Demosthenes' mind which might simultaneously allay Eurydike's fears of displacement and reap practical benefit besides.

Conscious of Thalassia's better-than-human senses, he whispered directly into Eurydike's ear: "I believe she has secrets. Learn what you can from her and bring it to me. Consider it a special mission vital to the safety of Athens."

Eurydike drew back with a sly smile on her lips, delight in her emerald eyes. She put her lips to his ear and nibbled the lobe before whispering back, "She will not have secrets for long, lord. I'll break her!"

When she drew back, Eurydike's best dress was a pile on the plaster floor.

"Enough about her," she said too loudly for Demosthenes' taste, and she kissed him. "You need reminding that there are enough holes in this house to be filled without adding more."

Demosthenes promised, when the other's insistent lips allowed his a moment of freedom, "Her holes hold no interest for me."

Eurydike walked him to his wide, low bed and straddled him on its wool- and feather-stuffed mattress. Surrendering to her, there were two ironies which her master did not bother to address, knowing it futile: one, that although slaves in Athens had more rights than those elsewhere, sexual exclusivity was not among them. And two, Eurydike was not even faithful to her master, as she freely admitted.

Pushing him onto his back, she came down atop him on all fours so that her hanging curls of deep red formed a tunnel between their faces. Pink nipples brushed the chest that one of her freckled hands worked to bare of its linen covering. When the other found his cock, Eurydike frowned.

"Why are you not pleased to see me, lord? You already want her, don't you?" It was mostly performance, but edged with a note of genuine insecurity.

"I was only thinking," Demosthenes admitted in a cautious whisper. "I do not think you ought to try to *break* her, exactly..." He did not dare speak Thalassia's name, knowing that only a floor of plaster-covered beams separated her from the conspiracy above.

"Arrgh!" Eurydike groaned. "Enough about that brown bitch. Leave her to me!"

She descended on him, and quickly made him 'pleased' enough to see to matters at hand in spite of the exhaustion of the voyage. He even managed, he believed, not to let his concubine sense as they fucked how conscious he remained of Thalassia's presence alone in the megaron below.

He was being paranoid, he told himself. If Thalassia was going to dwell here, he needed to try to trust her.

As was the norm, Eurydike climaxed first, some number of times, then deftly spilled her master's seed by hand and mouth so as not to spawn a bastard in her womb. Afterward, they lay in a tau-shape with Eurydike's head resting on his abdomen.

"I'll need some money tomorrow," she said.

"For what?"

"My mission, lord. I'll need to take Sea-thing shopping."

Demosthenes flicked a copper ringlet. "That is a convenient plan." He spoke in normal tones now, abandoning hope of secrecy. "For you."

"I know what I'm doing! Half a *mina* ought to do."

Demosthenes laughed. For a moment, looking into Eurydike's wide, green, honest eyes, he managed to forget about challenges to Fate and hot-tempered otherworldly traitors bent on revenge. "The price I paid for you was scarcely more than that," he lied. "If only I had been told that your upkeep would drain my coffers dry."

He was only teasing her; she knew as well as he that his resistance was but a show.

"I drain other things. And don't start throwing numbers at me. You're hurting my brain!" Eurydike was quick to use her illiteracy as a defense when it suited her. "I only know I can't be lending the bitch my clothes all the time. She needs her own."

"Fine, take it," he said, as was inevitable. "Just promise not to try to 'break' her, all right? And don't call her a bitch."

Eurydike blew a raspberry. "Whatever, lord." The Spartan dagger he had given her appeared from somewhere, and she absently prodded at her own navel with its dull tip. Staring at the blade, she said quietly, "I'm glad you're back."

3. Alkibiades

The next day, Demosthenes rose earlier than he would have liked given the prior day's sea journey, and left his house praying that Eurydike would manage to treat her new housemate well enough to avoid falling victim to the latter's explosive temper. With luck, he hoped, the disaster to which he returned would be less than total. Would that he could have stayed and averted it, or even just helplessly watched it unfold, but there was much business to attend to. There were families of the fallen to visit, pay and spoils to distribute, reports to give to officials of the democracy, and any number of other minor tasks which resulted either from the battle or his long absence from public life. Most importantly, perhaps, the citizen body would just expect its returning hero to be seen, especially after his sudden absence the day prior.

Seen he was, and he made his excuses for having deserted the festivities, while in the meantime even managing to accomplish his business. Towards midday, he was leaving the law-courts, having there made the pretense of his ownership of Thalassia official, when an arm snaked around his shoulders from behind. A familiar, smiling face and sculpted locks the color of chestnuts thrust into sight over his shoulder.

"Demosthenes!" a pretty mouth greeted him.

"Alkibiades," Demosthenes returned, stopping to receive the younger man's embrace.

"Listen," the younger man said urgently, "if Little Red told you I molested her, I swear by Zeus she begged me to do it—three times. You can ask Socrates. He was there, watching and polishing his knob, as usual."

Demosthenes winced and resumed walking while trying his best to forget what he had just heard.

Alkibiades fell into step beside him. "Sorry I couldn't make your homecoming. Had some pressing matters, you know."

"There's no need to tell me what you were pressed up against."

It was obvious enough what Alkibiades had been up to. Events like the return from Pylos drew male citizens out of their homes, leaving wives and daughters guarded by little more than maids who were obliged to turn a blind eye if the mistress ordered it, even if doing so put them at risk of torture and death should the matter come to trial.

"Too right!" Alkibiades laughed. He clapped a hand on Demosthenes' shoulder. "You'll have to tell me all about Pylos, friend, since I'm certain the tale Kleon is spreading like a bad rash bears little resemblance to the truth."

"What tale is that?"

"Have you not heard?" Alkibiades raised a sculpted brow. "According to him, you sat in Pylos sulking and whining all summer long, until your savior Kleon arrived to finish the job."

Demosthenes grunted distaste, but the matter fled his mind quickly enough. Let the demagogue say what he would. Athens was ever harsh with her most outspoken men, even when their reputations were built on deeds and not just words. Solon, Themistokles, Aristides, Demosthenes' own tribemate Kimon—all had been heroes one day, outcasts the next. Had the plague not cut down Perikles, the people doubtless would have done the deed themselves, if in a less deadly fashion.

"Bah!" Alkibiades exclaimed with the dismissive wave of a manicured hand, likely having mistaken his companion's silence for irritation. "I'm far more interested in an interesting rumor I've heard..."

"And that is?" Demosthenes asked without particular enthusiasm.

"It seems there's a new piece of tail in town, and she lives in your house."

"Really? That comes as news to me."

"Hmm," Alkibiades intoned. "Well, as it happens, I was heading to your home right now to investigate. Care to tag along?"

***

They entered the megaron of Demosthenes' home and found Eurydike by the hearth mending a cloak brought back from Pylos worse for wear. There was no sign of Thalassia. Seeing them, Eurydike leaped to her feet, ran across the room and delivered a kiss of affection on each man's cheek, starting with her master.

On receiving his, Alkibiades patted her round backside and asked, "Where's your new sister, Red?"

Eurydike feigned gagging. "She is *not* my sister."

"True," Alkibiades conceded. "One would not want to do with one's sister what I hope that you and she soon will..."

Demosthenes interrupted loudly, "Eurydike, where is Thalassia?"

Relaxing the nose which had been wrinkled in disgust, Eurydike answered, "The cow is on the roof, lord. She has been making drawings, or some such useless crap. She took all the parchment you had in stores. I tried to stop her."

And probably failed deliberately, Demosthenes thought, in the hope of seeing her rival punished.

"Go easy, sweet," he chided. "Remember what I told you."

"I didn't call her a *bitch*. Even though she—"

Eurydike cut herself short when at the top of the timber staircase at the megaron's rear, Thalassia appeared. She wore an ankle-length chiton which Eurydike had been persuaded to lend her, a long, well-pleated one of soft flax linen. Its color was a pale blue-green like frothing sea-foam, a hue that suited Thalassia's golden flesh better than it did the speckled Thracian's, and it made her wintry eyes sparkle like twin crystals. She had washed her skin and too-short dark hair clean of their salt haze, and styled the latter with a borrowed hair clip of silver and bone.

Reaching the floor, she came forward with head bowed demurely, eyes downcast, looking the part she had agreed to play. Smudges of ink showed on hands held folded in front of her.

"Greetings, my lord," she said.

Alkibiades' expression became instantly that of the wolf into whose path a lost ewe has strayed. And not knowing that this ewe was herself at least half wolf, he pounced, stalking a great circle around his prey with predatory gaze locked upon her. Halfway through encirclement, this less-than-helpless quarry raised her eyes and fixed her would-be devourer with a return look of mild curiosity, turning her head to track him.

Completing his inspection circuit, Alkibiades came to stand beside Eurydike, who leaned against a smooth column of the megaron with arms folded petulantly on her chest. Alkibiades asked her, without removing his eyes from the object of discussion, "What do you make of her, Little Red?"

"Not much."

"Try to be impartial," Alkibiades reprimanded. "I want an honest evaluation. Let us start with the most obvious. Her skin."

"Color of dirty bathwater," Eurydike decreed.

"No, no." Alkibiades stepped in closer to Thalassia, appraising her. "Surely it is autumn barley." Thalassia's level stare said she was anything but intimidated. "Or toasted almond." He brushed the length of Thalassia's arm with the backs of his fingers. "And soft, too. Have you felt it, Red?"

"I've petted a bitch before." She shot her master a glance of faux apology. "Sorry, lord, I meant goat."

Demosthenes only sighed and surrendered control of events, taking a seat to watch. There was never any stopping Alkibiades anyway, rarely any harm in letting Eurydike vent, and as for Thalassia, well, this would if nothing else be a trial-by-fire of her forbearance with the inferior denizens of this lesser world in which she had stranded herself.

And if Demosthenes was not mistaken, although Thalassia scarcely let it show, she seemed to be *enjoying* herself.

"Let us move on," Alkibiades continued. "Hair?"

"Where's the rest of it?"

"Short hair on a woman," Alkibiades mused. "It's kinky," he ruled. "I like it. Eyes?"

"Evil eyes," Eurydike said. "And whorish."

"A bit cold, to be sure," Alkibiades agreed. "But that only inspires a man to work harder to warm them. Now we work our way lower. Demosthenes, any chance of asking her to drop the dress?"

"Ask her yourself." Demosthenes half wished Alkibiades would try, just to find out which would wind up on the floor first, the sea-green chiton or Alkibiades. The odds for either seemed about equal.

"We'll make do," Alkibiades conceded, failing for once to live up to his bold reputation. Perhaps he sensed the danger in those cold eyes. "What do you think, Red?"

"Hips too narrow," Eurydike declared after a moment's thought. "Tits..." She snorted. "Boring."

"Be fair, Red!" In his most daring approach yet, Alkibiades placed a cupped hand under Thalassia's left breast, just grazing the linen pleats which hung from it. "She fills a hand well enough, and then some. And gods, those legs, they'd wrap around me twice. But now to aspects of womanhood almost as vital, the tongue and the mind. Thalassia, was it? Odd name. Do you read and write Greek, Thalassia?"

After seeking silent permission from her nominal master, she asked the questioner, "Do you?"

Alkibiades thrust up an eloquent brow. "My, my, she has both looks and wit," he said. "If all barbarians were as you, every home would have one."

"Like bugs," Eurydike inserted.

Alkibiades ignored her. "Music, poetry, rhetoric?" he asked, falling into a close orbit of Thalassia.

She deigned to answer: "Physics, mathematics, medicine, history, engineering, geography... *anatomy*."

Alkibiades' chestnut mane whirled round. "Zeus' left nut, Demosthenes! What have you got here?" He turned back to Thalassia. "I need to let Socrates loose on this one."

Eurydike's face wrinkled. "Blabeddy-blah-blah-blah." She made a farting sound with her mouth.

Heaving a puzzled sigh, Alkibiades returned to the column and asked his fellow judge, "So what do you make to be her final score, Red?"

"One? Two? No, definitely zero."

"Come now," Alkibiades objected. "Much higher than that. She is but a few points shy of you, in fact."

He boxed his favorite Thratta's chin affectionately before putting bright, hungry eyes back on Thalassia. The two gazed steadfastly at one another across the megaron, each waiting for the other to be first to blink. Thalassia emerged victorious, but then bowed her head and became again the good little slave she had proven herself able to resemble when she saw fit.

Retreating to the corner to stand beside his seated host, Alkibiades ran a hand through his mane and blinked rapidly, as though stunned by a blow. He looked thoughtfully at Thalassia, who ignored him.

"Believe me, friend," Alkibiades said, loudly enough for even normal ears to overhear. "I know something about women, and I can tell you this one is something special. A fallen goddess, even, and the path to her sanctuary is warm and slippery. Because I have a sense for such things, I gather you have not yet made the pilgrimage, but I advise you to get started. She is your slave, of course, so I shall give your head a start, but be warned: I am not one to sit idly by while a ripe spoil spoils."

At that, Thalassia looked up at Perikles' ward, and they shared one final, impenetrable look before Alkibiades clapped his host's shoulder, acknowledged Eurydike's feral snarl as though it were a blown kiss, and made his leave.

"He's full of shit, lord," Eurydike remarked the moment he had gone.

"Watch what you say about citizens," Demosthenes chided. "But... yes, he is."

Turning away, Thalassia began to ascend the stairs.

"The garden looks dry," Demosthenes observed to Eurydike. "Would you water it? And then you can apologize to Thalassia by taking her on that shopping trip."

Perceptive Eurydike, who knew when she was being got rid of, muttered something about a cow before dragging her feet to the exit.

When she was gone, Demosthenes caught up to Thalassia, who stopped and faced him.

"Have patience with her," Demosthenes pleaded. "For almost three years now, it has been only the two of us in this house."

"She's no bother," Thalassia said. "She reminds me of someone I knew."

"Not someone you killed, I hope."

Her smile was faint and sad. "A friend," she said. "From when I had them."

A part of him yearned to wedge a question into that opening and use it to pry out more of Thalassia's past. But with Eurydike just outside and no suitable question presenting itself in time, he gave up. Rather, he cleared his throat and changed the topic. "Eurydike said you were drawing."

Thalassia turned to finish ascending the stair. "Yes. Come see."

4. Kiss Me

He followed Thalassia up through his home's unfurnished women's quarters and emerged behind her through the hatch which led out onto the rooftop terrace. In one corner of its floor sat many small sheets of scraped parchment, evidently cut from a larger sheet taken from the house's storeroom. Thalassia stooped to collect a number of them and offered them to Demosthenes.

He examined the sheets. The topmost contained a neatly labeled schematic drawn in a smooth and steady hand depicting what looked like an archer's bow mounted horizontally on the end of a fence-post. The large print above read *Gastraphetes*.

Belly-bow? A nonsense word.

"This is a weapon?" Demosthenes supposed aloud.

Thalassia nodded. She leaned casually on the balustrade looking out over the streets of the *deme* of Tyrmeidai.

The next two sheets showed less portable and less deadly machines. Comprised of complex arrangements of shafts, toothed wheels, and paddle-like blades, they were labeled *Grain-grinder (wind)* and *Grain-grinder (water)*. After them came a page depicting a blacksmith's furnace alongside a set of instructions which were likely only intelligible to a man practiced in using one. That sheet was labeled *Stomoma Athenaion*.

Athenian Steel.

The next was covered with an intricate arrangement of squiggles and dots. The neat letters nestled amongst the fluid lines spelled out familiar names: Athens. Sparta. Thebes. Argos. Elis. Pylos. Delphi.

"This looks like no map I have ever seen," Demosthenes observed.

"That's because it's *accurate*." Thalassia twirled a finger in her hair. "The world's a sphere, by the way," she added in passing. "I'll draw that for you later. Nautical charts, too."

Absorbed in the tiny, snaking rivers, the oddly shaped bays and islands, the flocks of lambdas bearing the familiar names of mountain ranges, Demosthenes set himself to the task of hunting down and reading every last caption. Thalassia interrupted the effort.

"I think we should consider telling Alkibiades."

Demosthenes looked up. "About what? You? Everything?"

"Maybe not everything, but enough to make him an ally."

The first question to spring to Demosthenes' mind was, *Ally or replacement?* But he left that one unspoken. "You told me that history would remember Alkibiades," he asked instead. "What for?"

"Forward thinking," she answered. "Winning battles." She hesitated briefly. "Arguably losing the war for Athens and costing you your life in the process."

Demosthenes' breath caught. With the next, he asked, "How?"

"The plan to send you to Sicily about ten years from now will be his. But, of course, that all takes place in a world that will never exist. Our actions will change his fate as much as they will yours. Alkibiades can be of use to us politically. I think we can trust him. And if I'm wrong... well, he can always have an unfortunate fall from his horse, if you catch my meaning."

"I... do," Demosthenes said uncertainly. "It is disturbing, to say the least, to hear you speak of murdering prominent Athenian citizens. Ones whom I call friend, at that. I must think on whether I dislike Alkibiades enough to–"

"Kiss me," Thalassia said plainly.

Demosthenes' eyes flicked up to meet hers. Just as quickly, they fell away. "Pardon?"

She slid off the balustrade to stand in front of him. The thin stack of parchment hung by his side, imprisoned in an involuntary fist of sweating stone. "The Caliate's headquarters is a place called Spiral. When we are there, we do whatever we wish. Anything that makes us happy. Whatever urges we have, we indulge without shame or regret."

"It's like Corinth, then," Demosthenes muttered.

Thalassia smiled. "I want us to do more than kiss, Demosthenes. Eurydike, too, if you approve. I would like that, the three of us." Her tone gave no indication that she was anything but serious. "But for now, a kiss. And by kiss, what I mean is, you're sixteen and alone in the olive groves with your hot cousin. Not even the gods are watching. No one will ever know. *That* kind of kiss." She took a step closer, coming almost toe-to-toe with him. "Now stop thinking and just do it."

For the space of several dozen loud beats of his quickening heart, Demosthenes said nothing while his mind spun circles in desperate search for a reply. He was hardly one to shy away from a challenge. If he were, he would have neither Thalassia nor Eurydike in his home, nor would he possess any victories to his name as a general, least of all the most recent. No, he would have a pale young citizen girl for a wife and a few properly servile slaves for her to lord it over at home whilst he sought more stimulating companionship elsewhere, as all of Athens deemed proper.

Certainly he could kiss Thalassia, but well enough to satisfy her? It would be a performance, a falsehood, for how could he ever permit himself to lust after such a... a *monster*, however pleasing its appearance?

Yet she was not asking for lust or even sex–yet. Only a

kiss. Perhaps there was no harm in granting her that.

At the end of too long a silence, Demosthenes lifted his hung head, drew a bracing breath and looked Thalassia squarely in pale, opaque eyes which stood almost level with his own. Her face showed no trace of eagerness or anticipation, but as he drew so close that his uneven breath rebounded off the tip of her nose, she gently sucked her lips, moistening them before they parted to receive the imminent contact.

He shut his eyes and paused, breath held, while behind his closed lids he endured the vision of a blood-drenched battle-Fury mutilating the flesh of her foe. He felt the ghost of Thalassia's iron claw constricting his throat, heard Eden shriek at her, *Wormwhore!*

He backed away and opened his eyes to find Thalassia's waiting lips drawn tight in a frown. That melted away, she nodded, and of a sudden it was though nothing had occurred. She touched his shoulder in a friendly gesture and walked around him to cross the tile floor to the hatch that led down into the house.

Distractedly, Demosthenes pretended to study the parchments in front of the precisely no one who was present to witness him. Then he waited until the women of the house had left for the agora on their shopping excursion before descending and returning to the city to resume the day's business.

5. Wet

Demosthenes returned home at dusk to find that Eurydike had filled the recessed bath in the private chamber behind the megaron and warmed it with boiled water from the hearth. The night prior, exhaustion had led him to perform only a cursory de-brining, and so with Thalassia up on the roof reinventing agriculture or some such, Eurydike bathed her master properly, oiling and scraping his skin, washing his hair, and lastly engaging him in some less practical aquatic activities. Afterward, she sat naked and glistening astride Demosthenes' lap in the bath. Her long wet locks of deep red adhered to her cheeks and neck, streaming trails of water over her spotted shoulders.

"Lord," she said in a hushed voice, the sharp tip of her upturned nose grazing his. "Would you have a report on my mission?"

"Tell me," Demosthenes said eagerly.

"Well, first of all, while we were out today I asked Thalassia about her stupid name, and she said it wasn't her real name." Of course, Demosthenes knew this, but he took it as though it were news. "I asked her real name, and she told me it was..." Eurydike's face crinkled. "Dzhenna? I'm not sure exactly. A stupid name that I forget. Then I asked where she was from that they had such weird names and didn't know that *thalassia* was a chunk of wood.

"She pointed to the sky and said she was from the stars. 'Stop fucking with me,' I told her, and she said, 'Actually, a little ball of rock near just one star.' 'You don't really believe that,' I said, but she shrugged and I just said, 'Whatever, *star-girl*.' I didn't want it to seem like I was prying. I did an excellent job of that, I promise. I think you're right: she's just not right in the head."

Star-girl? Demosthenes chuckled. *Astraneanis*. A rather tranquil nickname for a blood-soaked being.

Eurydike's wide eyes and the conspicuous excuse she had just planted seemed almost certain to foreshadow coming failure.

"A little later, I asked if she had any brothers or sisters. She said one sister." Eurydike's grip shifted from Demosthenes' neck to his hands so that they might support her weight as she bent her naked body into an arch and lowered her head back, back, until it was submerged in the bath. Surfacing, she spat a stream of water into the air, fountain-like, before twisting in her master's lap to sit across it. While she finished the maneuver and wiped water from her eyes, Demosthenes waited patiently for what he rather doubted would be useful intelligence.

Eurydike resumed, "I asked where this sister was, and she said, 'Walking next to me in the agora asking questions like her master told her to." Eurydike widened her eyes in an assertion of innocence. "But I swear I was subtle as can be, lord!" Although apologetic, Eurydike did not seem upset by her failure.

"I know you were, bright eyes," Demosthenes reassured her. He kissed the nape of her neck, which tasted faintly of olive oil. "You did well."

Eurydike twisted over her master's shoulder, giving him a face full of wet freckled breast while she reached for the clay cup of wine they were sharing. She poured a trickle onto her lips, which pursed as though the wine were sour, which it was not. "I do have a big problem with Thalassia, though," she said glumly. She put the cup's rim to Demosthenes' lip and made him drink. "Two problems, actually."

"That few? Do tell."

"Well, for one, I know you said not to expect much of

her, but she's fucking *useless*. Sure, she carries water like a horse, but she claims to be able to cook only one thing. It's called *bitchcakes*. She said she made you some already in Pylos, and you don't want to eat them again."

"True..." Demosthenes agreed.

"I'm not stupid," Eurydike said with a look of mild annoyance. "I know there's no such thing as a bitchcake. She's fucking with me, and now so are you. Which is fine, but only because of my second problem."

The slick Thracian's mouth settled into an angry pout, and her eyes cast about the room as if in search of some object at which to direct her spontaneous ire.

"Out with it already!" Demosthenes urged playfully.

Eurydike graced him with a petulant look and sighed just as petulantly. "The second problem, lord, is—" She shook sodden locks. "No, it's too embarrassing. I can't say."

Demosthenes slapped the water, splashing his slave's face and ample breast. "You try my patience, Thratta. Do you want me to set you free?"

It was a common threat he deployed, but never meant. The options for someone like Eurydike upon gaining freedom were, effectively, cheap prostitute and even cheaper prostitute.

The slave giggled, as was her custom when her master chided her. Usually she knew full well she was asking for it, as was the case now. Her warm, near-weightless soft body shifted on his lap until she faced him squarely.

"The problem is that I fucking *like* her!" Eurydike groaned. Her head slumped onto Demosthenes' shoulder in theatrical despair. "I tried to hate her, lord, I did!" she sobbed into his collarbone. "But you know what that useless bitch did? She took my old dresses from me and let me use the money you gave us to buy new ones for *myself!* And you should have seen what we paid because of her! She slithers up and talks with that dumb, fake accent of hers—you notice how it comes and goes—and the shop owners practically hand over whatever she wants. I can't even be jealous of her evil powers because she uses them to do such good!"

After a final, extended groan, Eurydike raised the face she had hidden in mock shame to look at her master. After a moment she put an open palm on one of his freshly shaven cheeks and planted a wet kiss on the other.

"You look frightened, lord," she observed. "What's wrong?"

Demosthenes shuddered, but not from the chill of the rapidly cooling bathwater. "I was just wondering which state of affairs is worse for me," he confessed bleakly, "having you at Thalassia's throat ... or having you on her side."

6. Wormwhore

The following morning, Demosthenes stood on the rooftop terrace alone with Thalassia.

"A clumsy spy you sent," she said. She showed no trace of being annoyed. "You could not have thought that would work. But I suppose the attempt shows that I must be more forthright."

Demosthenes stood beside her on the rail, looking out over the dawn-lit red clay rooftops of Athens. He considered his response and opted for directness. "Foremost, I would know why you are called traitor," he said.

Thalassia fell silent for a long while, just staring over the city. "Your mistakes caused the deaths of many men in Aetolia," she said at length, "including a hundred and twenty Athenian citizens. You felt such shame that you could not bear to show your face in this city afterward. Is the wound not still just as raw as it was on the day it occurred?"

Indeed, her mere mention of the disaster in Aetolia, where more Athenians under his command were slaughtered in one day than should have fallen in any five battles lost, caused a sudden pang in Demosthenes' belly and a knot in his chest. But he drew a cleansing breath and answered with a voice that shook but a little.

"That failure causes me immense shame, which I will take to my grave. But I own the action and make no secret of it, as you seem to wish to do. My life is open to you. The reverse must also be true. I will know of your shame... or have you cast from my house. Whatever the cost."

Thalassia fell silent again, and then, "I *did* betray them. Is that enough? I turned my back on the Caliate, on people who were my friends, and on the leader who had given me so much. I betrayed them for the sake of *him*." She did not speak the name of the Worm, but there was much venom in the referring pronoun. Her wintry blue eyes remained fixed on the rooftops, to which she also seemed to address her quiet confession. "Is that enough?" she repeated, making clear it was her fervent hope that it would be.

"It is not," Demosthenes said. "But... today, it shall suffice. When you are ready, we shall speak again on the matter, although it must be soon. For now, you may tell me of other things. Such as what is a *layer*?"

Thalassia looked over at him, her eyes suddenly brighter, surely in gratitude for the change of topic to one less sensitive.

Then she frowned. "It's complicated... but..." She gestured at the corner of the rooftop which had become her favored workspace. "Do you see that stack of parchments there?"

Demosthenes nodded. The leaves in question were neat squares, each bearing a drawing of some innovation which Thalassia conceived of introducing to Athens.

"Imagine that one of the sheets in the stack is this world," she instructed. "Athens, all of Hellas, is a drop of ink on its surface. Now imagine that likewise every sheet in the pile is a world unto itself, some very much like your own, others wildly different. On the sheet above yours, there is another Demosthenes who never met me, because there is no me there to meet. He marches on in ignorance of the fate he'll meet one day in Sicily. On other sheets, there are still other Demosthenes, some of whom lead lives very different from your own and who will meet different deaths. On others, Demosthenes never existed at all because his parents never met or themselves never existed."

Thalassia paused and looked at him gently, earnestly, as a tutor would at a student, in search of understanding. He was pleasantly surprised by her patience.

"That is what you wish to do to the Worm," Demosthenes observed, hopefully proving that he understood at least a little. "You would cause him never to exist."

Thalassia's answering expression suggested that he had fallen at least somewhat shy of making his tutor proud.

"Yes, but..." she began, and stopped. "I suppose it's as good a time as any to tell you what makes him unlike any other being in the universe, apart from Magdalen. Across all layers, there is only *one* of him. And yours is the layer in which he was, or will be, born, so—"

In the hope of redeeming himself, Demosthenes cut her off: "So if he is erased here, then unlike Demosthenes of Thria, there will be no other Worms left in other layers to carry on the name."

This won him a crooked smile, a cryptic look that said he was right... if perhaps not entirely.

"And then what will happen?" Demosthenes asked. "How will you know when you... when *we* have done enough to erase him?"

Thalassia frowned and returned her gaze to the rooftops. "A good question," she said. "Too good."

"You have no answer?"

"Many answers," she said. "And none. I fucked Alkibiades last night."

Demosthenes stood in silence, caught off-guard by the sudden non-sequitur.

"As my ally, you need to know that," she said. Still she did not look at him, and Demosthenes was glad for it. "I plan to do it again. Regularly, maybe. But you needn't worry that —"

"I am not worried," Demosthenes blurted.

Thalassia threw him a glance and resumed. "I didn't tell

him anything. About myself, about us. But I still think you should consider it. I think we can trust him, and he could be a valuable tool."

Demosthenes dismissed from his mind a vivid image of Thalassia on all fours, Alkibiades thrusting behind her. He snorted laughter.

"What?" Thalassia asked, smile at the ready.

"Nothing..." Demosthenes said. "Only that I know what Alkibiades would say to that. 'My tool is *extremely* valuable.' But—" Demosthenes quickly added, so as to deny Thalassia space in which to comment on Alkibiades' tool, "I will consider it. Especially now that you and he—"

"It's physical, and nothing more."

Demosthenes raised a palm. "No more need be said. You are not my slave—and even if you were, as Eurydike's behavior attests, it would make no difference when it comes to Alkibiades. I would only point out that Eurydike, to her consternation, has grown fond of you. I hope that your new arrangement does nothing to change that."

Thalassia nodded, rather genuinely. "If it bothers her, I'll stop." She paused, threw Demosthenes another glance. "If it bothers you, I could stop, too."

Demosthenes considered his reply carefully, mindful that Thalassia could not be lied to. To be sure, he would rather she did not dally with Alkibiades. It seemed a needless complication, but with or without the complication of Alkibiades sticking his tool in her, it was plain to see that dealing with Thalassia would be complicated. Trying to control her every action was doubtless a losing battle. And, of course, hanging heavily in her offer to stop was an unspoken insistence that he himself be prepared to step in and help her satisfy those urges which had sent her to Alkibiades' bed in the first place.

Rather than saying anything, even unwittingly, that she might sense as an untruth, Demosthenes summoned up the shade of the decrepit rhetoric tutor from his youth and circumlocuted.

"I appreciate your forthrightness," he said. "Yet if I am to exert influence upon your actions, I would just as soon choose ones of greater import."

So as not to extend conversation on a subject with which he felt no right to feel uncomfortable, yet did, Demosthenes excused himself and turned to descend into his home.

"He seduced me," Thalassia said plainly when he was halfway to the hatch.

Demosthenes turned to find her leaning on the rail, facing him, the hem of her sea-foam gown rustling in the warm morning breeze. Dawn's light set Athena's temple aglow at her back.

"Who? Alkib—" he began. Had he taken but an instant to think, and looked first into Thalassia's eyes, he would have known. Not Alkibiades.

The Worm.

"Oh..." he said.

"He made me think he loved me. That I loved him. I... did love him. But he used me against the Caliate. Against Magdalen. When they captured me, Magdalen should have punished me in ways that are unimaginable to you. Instead, she just... forgave me."

Finishing, Thalassia stood looking at him with wide eyes that appeared nothing short of sincere.

Demosthenes showed his gratitude with a faint smile. He was touched by this new willingness of Thalassia to lay herself bare—even while some part of him understood that she surely was better even than Kleon at making lies seem as truth.

He began to resume his exit, but turned again before leaving to address Thalassia once more. He did not want to hurt her... except that he *did* want to.

"You told Eden you were still loyal to Magdalen," he said. "Is it under her orders that you came here, stranding your companions... or have you betrayed Magdalen yet again?"

Thalassia made no spoken reply, but her look and her silence gave the answer.

7. Lamia

The following morning, a team of laborers worked in front of Demosthenes' home to remove from its crowded storerooms and load into an oxcart his personal share of the captured Spartan arms and armor for transport to the family estate in Thria.

When the job was mostly done, the fast slap of sandals resounded down the empty street, and Eurydike appeared, a red-fletched arrow flying down the garden path. Her hair was tamed in a loose braid, and she was dressed for action in a short, boyish chiton cinched at the waist. From its belt hung the Spartan blade, her gift from Pylos, while over her shoulder was slung a sack containing the possessions needed for a stay of several days. Reaching the cart, she vaulted aboard, barely avoiding upsetting its neatly stacked contents.

With the harvest season getting underway, the time had come for Eurydike to begin splitting her time between city and country. Even though hard work was the purpose of her stay in Thria, she always found plenty of time to enjoy the open spaces of the farm, and so she looked forward to the days she spent there. Her excitement this time was somewhat tempered by disappointment that her unlikely best friend Thalassia would not be joining her. She would miss her home, and Demosthenes, too, but still, on balance she was ever eager to go.

Demosthenes mounted his brown mare Maia, freshly brought from the *deme* stables, as up ahead a farmhand on foot goaded the pair of hulking oxen and their burden onto the road. Their destination was the Thriasian plain northwest of Athens, the rural *deme* of Demosthenes' birth and home still to his ailing father Alkisthenes. Since Thria lay along the route to Eleusis, most of their journey made use of the best-maintained road in Attica, the Sacred Way, used each year for the procession of initiates into the Mysteries. Still, burdened by the ponderous pace of the two-wheeled cart, the journey consumed the bulk of the morning. When they arrived, Eurydike enjoyed the farm as she always did, shrieking and running and playing games with the farm workers' children, climbing trees and diving out of them to roll in the dust grappling with some hapless victim of her ambush, chasing rabbits (usually in vain) with her blunt dagger. Here, beyond the civilizing city walls, the barbarian heart in her was free.

To her master, Thria was more like a prison, the miserable warden of which was named Alkisthenes. The old man's first words on this visit, spoken in his coarse rattle of a voice, were not ones of congratulations for his son's success at Pylos. They were, "Xenon three farms over has a granddaughter just turned fifteen and ripe for ploughing. They say she's got fair looks and discipline. You should take her, unless you plan to die without an heir and let your cousins squabble like vultures over the shreds of my estate."

Demosthenes begrudgingly promised to consider the pairing, but Alkisthenes called his bluff by threatening to summon Xenon presently for a meeting.

"Fine!" Alkisthenes spat when the truth came out. "If you won't find yourself a citizen womb and start filling it with babies, you could at least whelp a son on that addle-brained Thratta of yours. Maybe by the time he comes of age, the law will change to let bastards become citizens again."

Thankfully, that was an end to the matter. For a while, anyway. Plenty of Athenian men looked forward to taking an adolescent girl into their homes and did so eagerly. With luck, she would already be well trained in the necessary arts—all but one, of course, the one which would fulfill the union's existential purpose. Having an heir was vital, certainly, to family, tribe, and state, but the responsibilities surrounding it seemed hardly attractive. Not only that, the need to add another female to his household in Athens had hardly seemed urgent before Thalassia's arrival, with Eurydike wearing him out in bed and keeping a decent house to boot. Now that he had sealed a bargain with a rogue immortal to save Athens, marrying appeared an even less wise idea.

Fed up with his father's company, Demosthenes took a walk alone through the olive groves. Half of the trees were close to harvest, while the rest were nothing more than stumps, casualties to Perikles' strategy of retreat behind the city walls whilst the Lakedaemonians ravaged the countryside. Thria had been especially hard hit, being directly in the path of the Spartan advance most years. Perhaps, thanks to victory at Pylos and the two hundred Equals captured there serving as hostages, no more orchards would be razed or fields put to the torch. Perhaps the saplings which this season had been transplanted from safer soil to the east, as had been done every year, usually only to meet the same end a season later, might grow instead to bear fruit.

The walk and the solitude went some way toward relaxing him. For a time, at least, with the gentle breeze that shook the blade-like olive leaves cooling his sun-warmed skin, the war became remote and, perhaps more importantly, the suffocating atmosphere of unreality he had breathed since the taking of Sphakteria began to lift.

He was home.

But it could not last. In the early afternoon, he bid a cold goodbye to his father and a fond one to Eurydike, which included a fuck in the shade of a budding olive tree, then mounted Maia and rode for Athens and unreality.

***

The time alone in the fresh air of the groves had helped

bring him to the decision to invite Alkibiades into his alliance with Thalassia. It had not been a hard decision. With any conspiracy, the fewer who knew, the safer were its secrets, but conversely the burden weighed more heavily upon each conspirator. In this case, Thalassia's secrets were of such weight that Demosthenes worried they might eventually fracture his mortal mind. The temptation of easing that burden by sharing it with a fellow Athenian was simply too great to resist.

Although he was often maddening, Alkibiades might be just the thing to keep him sane. But he did not need to know all; just enough to win him over. He needed not be told of Eden's existence, for example, or that Thalassia's motives had nothing to do with the welfare of Athens.

That evening, in Athens, Demosthenes walked with Thalassia to Alkibiades' deme of Skambonidae.

"Let me do the talking," Demosthenes requested of her along the way, as childish plans hatched in his mind. "We may as well have some fun with him."

She smiled her agreement.

From Alkibiades' door, a male house slave (one of the small, beautiful army of them that inhabited Alkibiades' lavish home, four times the size of Demosthenes' own) escorted them to the back garden where the master awaited. Spotting his guests, Alkibiades rose from one of a pair of benches which flanked the base of a life-sized marble statue of no other subject than Alkibiades himself.

"Demosthenes!" the genuine article greeted with an amiable grin. But he held back several paces while his eyes flicked to the one with whom he had fornicated last night. "I do hope the evening finds you in good spirits."

Demosthenes glared, stone-faced.

Alkibiades chuckled nervously. "I know what this is

about, Demosthenes. She came to *me,* you know. I made no effort to pursue—"

"I know," Demosthenes interrupted calmly. "It was the same for me in Pylos, where I too succumbed. Would that I had possessed the will to resist. You stood no chance."

The unwitting victim laughed again. "What are you talking about?"

Demosthenes conjured up a look of pity. "I belong to her, and now so shall you. She will drink every last drop of our lives' essences until we stand withered husks, longing for the grave. For Thalassia is no mortal woman. She is a *lamia,* my friend, and our skins are the vessels from which flow her favorite drink."

Alkibiades' third laugh lasted for but a single breath. Then he only stared, plucked brows drawn together in puzzlement over aquiline nose. "Come on," the youth said. "Only children and Spartans believe in that stuff." But his bright eyes were laden with doubt. "Besides, you wouldn't let that happen to me... would you?"

"The choice was not mine. She owns me, spirit and flesh." He sighed heavily. "Just as she now does you. And when she has sucked us dry, it will be across the Styx for us both." As he spoke, Demosthenes pointedly avoided glancing at Thalassia, but he hoped that her eyes were full of the otherworldly malevolence which he knew first-hand she could produce.

She opportunely chose this moment to begin advancing on Alkibiades, step by agonizingly slow step with her head declined, eyes narrowed, teeth clenched and lips barely moving as she whispered in a fluid, alien tongue.

In the shadow of his own statue, Alkibiades raised a warding hand and backpedaled. "Whoa," he said. "Thalassia, stop playing."

The shapely shade's back was to Demosthenes, but by the expression of fear painted on her victim's face, her performance was an unqualified success.

"Please, Demosthenes, that's enough. Tell her to stop!"

Thalassia paid no heed, but persisted advancing until her increasingly terrified prey retreated behind one of the two stone benches that flanked the statue.

"There is one way out," Demosthenes said, and Thalassia halted. "If you can defeat her in a test of strength, she is bound to free you. I failed—but then I lack the limbs of a demigod which all of Athens attributes to Alkibiades."

"Yes, yes..." Alkibiades agreed. He rose to his feet behind the stone bench, nodding rapidly at the pale-eyed spawn of Hades. "A contest of strength! I challenge thee."

Ponderously, Thalassia's head swiveled on an exquisite neck bisected by the slave choker which Athenian law required her to wear at all times in public. When she faced Demosthenes, he had to stifle surprise of his own, for the usually pristine skin of Thalassia's right cheek and temple was covered with a marking which had not been there just moments before: an intricate, lace-like design of scrolling lines etched in black. The bright eye at the center of that vortex of flowing lines gave Demosthenes a wink, and then she was a lamia again, raising one arm with an index finger aimed at the stone bench separating her from Alkibiades.

"She bids you lift the bench," Demosthenes translated.

Alkibiades cast eyes wide with disbelief at the stone object which could not have been set into its current place by fewer than three able-bodied men. "But that..." he began despairingly. "It is not possible..."

Still, Alkibiades was never one to yield without a fight. All men who had stood beside him in battle swore he fought like a frenzied god. He had won the prize for valor at the battle of Potidaea, even if some said it should have gone to Socrates.

The youth drew a deep breath, steeled himself, widened his stance, and set his hands on each of the two long sides of the great stone bench. He muttered a prayer to Zeus, another to Athena, drew another deep breath, and he heaved.

The bench rose perhaps a finger's breadth from the ground then fell back into place with a soft thump.

Alkibiades groaned, exhaled a curse and said without casting eyes on his tormentors, "One more try."

For his second attempt, Alkibiades crawled underneath the bench on all fours, braced his back against its underside and endeavored to stand. One half of the bench came up with relative ease, although he strained under its weight; the other half, however, remained rooted in place for long minutes whilst Alkibiades struggled and sweated and cursed. After a long minute had passed, in the space of which his two tormentors risked sharing a smile, the bench came up on all but one corner, at which point it capsized onto the flower bed behind it.

"There!" Alkibiades exclaimed. Breathing heavily, he crawled back onto the paved path and settled on the ground. "I did it! It left the earth, for just a moment!"

Thalassia looked down upon him with a grim expression and, in her own time, stepped over to the fallen bench where she set one slender hand underneath, the other on top. With no sign of strain showing in her supple golden limbs, the bench all but raised itself. Carrying it, she backed up a step and set it back in the spot where it had been rooted for perhaps a generation.

"No..." Alkibiades intoned, in utter disbelief. "No, no, no, that cannot be!" In despair, he threw himself forward onto all fours, crawled to Thalassia's feet and bowed his head. "I will not beg," he declared. "Fair is fair. I concede defeat. But it is a beautiful soul which you claim today, foul creature, and one that was not finished by far doing great deeds!"

Standing over him, her face still bearing the intricate black tattoo, Thalassia threw a look at Demosthenes, asking him silently whether it was time to cut the flopping fish off their line.

It was, and so Demosthenes walked to Alkibiades, knelt beside him and set a hand on his shoulder. The youth's well-groomed mane rose, revealing pretty features ashen with resignation.

"We are almost even now, friend," Demosthenes said. "For your constant molestation of my household."

Confusion spread across Alkibiades' fine features. His lustrous eyes flicked back and forth between his two tormentors. "I... I..." he stammered. "You mean... she is not truly..."

Thalassia smiled warmly at him. In the space of a moment, the strange markings faded from the skin of her face.

"But how did she—" His head sank, and he drew cleansing breaths of relief, after which he fell to laughing.

Demosthenes extended a hand to help the vanquished to rise. Standing, Alkibiades turned the gesture into an embrace, at the conclusion of which he grabbed and kissed Thalassia's fingers. "That was some deception with the bench," he said to either or both of them. "How on earth you achieve it?"

"It was no deception, friend," Demosthenes said. "Thalassia is no evil spirit, but neither is she human."

"Yes, I am," Thalassia corrected, not without offense.

"She is *more* than human, then," Demosthenes amended. "She has come to us from the distant future. From the stars. She cannot be killed by normal means. She is stronger than any mortal man. And she intends, by means of her vast knowledge, to help Athens win this war, a war which, without her aid... we are fated to lose."

8. Council of War

Momentarily overwhelmed, Alkibiades stared blankly at the speaker of such baleful words. After some time, he shifted to direct the same look at Thalassia. Slowly, he grinned.

"I knew you were something special," he said proudly. "So what is it? Sorceress? Nymph? By Zeus' balls, you're not a full-on Olympian are you?"

"She is no goddess," Demosthenes swiftly assured him. He had hoped Alkibiades would keep his head for longer than this, but the youth's imagination was running wild already. "Are you so quick to believe?" he asked. "Do you not still have doubts?"

"Why? She has clearly convinced you, someone whose judgment I trust. Add to that the demonstration of strength just witnessed, the markings on her face, and—"

"Yes," Demosthenes said, "those markings." He tried to keep from his voice the mild annoyance which he had felt on first seeing them and knowing that Thalassia had hidden something from him. "What were they?"

"Magdalen's Mark," she answered. "All in the Veta Caliate bear one. No two are exactly alike. Of course, it can be hidden at will so we can blend in."

Alkibiades fell to one knee before Thalassia, now seated on the bench, and set one hand on her linen draped knee. He gazed up, wide-eyed, as one might at the towering cryselephantine Athena in her temple.

"Golden *astraneanis,*" he said in awe, "I am your willing servant!"

Demosthenes scoffed. *Star-girl.* The name given to Thalassia by Eurydike. Surely she was the least secretive spy in all of Hellas.

"Oh, stand up!" Demosthenes enjoined the youth.

But there was no sign he was listening. Even his mentor, circumspect Socrates, had little influence over the youth when it came to interpreting signs that Alkibiades enjoyed favor in the heavens. The visions likely playing behind his eyes at this moment were ones of his own image set in friezes, battling shoulder to shoulder with the likes of Heracles.

"Listen to me," Demosthenes said sternly. "None but the three of us in this garden knows her secret, and it must stay that way. If you tell another soul, she will rip your cock off and throw it to the crows."

Yet on one knee, Alkibiades rubbed his cheek over the back of Thalassia's hand, seemingly as unbothered by the threat against his manhood as he was by the fact that his goddess thus far had shown no sign of readiness to indulge him in his worship, but only offered forbearance.

Demosthenes took a seat on a second, identical stone bench across the path. "Whenever you are finished," he said testily, "we thought we might lay out our plans. It is after all an accomplice we seek, not a puppy."

On the other bench, Thalassia's right hand went from her lap to Alkibiades' perfect chin. She lifted it with two fingers, gave him an affectionate look, then withdrew the hand and used it to deliver a sharp slap across his cheek.

Face turned by the force of the blow, Alkibiades took reluctant notice of his fellow Athenian. His brows ticked up. "Not the last time I shall feel that particular sting from her, I hope." He rose and brushed dust from his knees and finely embroidered chiton. "So what are we planning? A coup? I would make such a lovely tyrant."

"Nothing like that," Demosthenes admonished. "We shall use our influence to work within the democracy."

"Work to do what?"

"According to Thalassia," Demosthenes explained, "Fate

would see Athens ground down for twenty more years of war, ending in our submission."

Alkibiades laughed. "Twenty years! That's a bit excessive, isn't it?"

Ignoring him, Demosthenes went on. "Thalassia claims we can change that outcome. If you manage to stop drooling on her for a moment, she might tell us how."

Alkibiades' brow furrowed, and he grew intense. Here now was the pupil of Socrates, the co-conspirator they needed, a man who knew when to put lust and levity aside and focus his copious energy. Both men looked to Thalassia, who assumed the mantle of leadership over her secret war council.

"My own preference," she began, "is for a swift, decisive stroke to bring the war to an immediate end. No more lives wasted winning far-off victories that mean nothing. I believe we should attack Sparta itself. But Demosthenes does not believe that the Board of Ten would ever agree to such a thing, and he... *objects* to my ideas on dealing with the Board."

"Ideas which include assassination and the rigging of elections!" Demosthenes interjected. "Ideas which you said you would not raise again. I fight to preserve an Athens which actually deserves to be saved, a place of wisdom and learning and justice, a city which respects the rule of law instead of trampling it when it suits."

"A fine speech, Demosthenes," Alkibiades applauded. "Almost good enough to overcome your opponent's considerable advantage in beauty."

"Let it be clear," Demosthenes said gravely, ignoring the other. "Whatever actions we may take to change the fated outcome of this war must be taken within the bounds of the democracy. Now, Thalassia, would you care to speak on the plan we discussed, or shall I?"

From her bench, Thalassia flicked an opaque glance at Demosthenes. "Apologies," she said, less than penitently. "One other thing which should be clear, in case I implied otherwise, is that the final decision in all matters pertaining to our efforts shall rest with Demosthenes."

"Naturally," Alkibiades agreed, although surely he felt that if anyone was 'naturally' suited for leadership in anything, it was the subject of the sculpture beside which they sat: Alkibiades.

Thalassia resumed: "Next year, the Spartan general Brasidas will march through Thessaly and Macedon gathering up an army of allies. He will bring that army to the gates of the Athenian colony of Amphipolis, which will surrender to him without a fight before help can arrive."

Alkibiades laughed. "So? What will we lose? Some colonists and their sheep."

"And a large portion of Athens' grain supply," Thalassia corrected, "which passes through Amphipolis on its way down the Strymon from Thrace to reach port."

"Not to mention gold and ship timbers," Demosthenes added.

"The loss will be a seeping wound from which the Athenian war effort never recovers." Thalassia said. "Or it would be, if no one stopped Brasidas."

"Which, I take it, falls to us," Alkibiades said with hunger in his eyes.

"If we can convince the Board to send a force there," Demosthenes said.

Alkibiades scoffed. "You'll be back on the Board with the next election. You will reap all the votes you need from the victory at Pylos." He made a sour expression. "Alas, so will Kleon."

"It need not be a large force," Thalassia said, "for it will be equipped with weapons of my design. Men need only be trained in their use."

Alkibiades clapped. "It is settled, then! I love it. But next, to matters just as vital." He set a hand on Thalassia's thigh and leveled an intense look at her. "If you know what Brasidas will do next year, then you know, too, the future of Alkibiades. So... tell me. What is to become of me?"

Demosthenes held his breath momentarily, for he knew the truth, or least as much of it as Thalassia had chosen to tell him. In the world which might have been, and perhaps still could, an older Alkibiades would be behind the disastrous Sicilian expedition which would ruin Athens and cause Demosthenes, a reluctant participant, to be captured and executed. Alkibiades himself, accused by his enemies of blasphemy and recalled to Athens for trial, would turn traitor and gave aid to the Spartans before eventually returning to an Athens desperately in need of an able general, even a treacherous one.

Part of Demosthenes' rewritten destiny, it seemed, was to surround himself with traitors.

In spite of such behavior, as was his fondest wish, that Alkibiades was destined to be admired long after his death. If Fate had her way, he would be better remembered than any general presently serving on the Board of Ten, better than any among the would-be-victorious Spartans.

Far better than Demosthenes.

Thalassia gently cupped the youth's smooth jaw and answered with a pitying smile, "I know only that which men who live after you will choose to record, and it would seem..." She trailed off, her expression becoming one of pity.

Alkibiades grabbed Thalassia's hand by the wrist and ripped it from his face, shooting to his feet. "No! That cannot be true!"

"Alkibiades, do not—" Demosthenes tried to interject.

"Such obvious nonsense throws into question all else she claims to know! What did she tell you of *your* fate, Demosthenes?"

"That I will die on my knees in a ditch and fade into obscurity, my name eclipsed by others such as Nikias, Thucydides... Kleon." *Alkibiades,* he did not add.

"Kleon!" Alkibiades echoed in disbelief. His hand covered a downturned face concealed behind a mane of chestnut curls.

"You have the opportunity to change that," Thalassia said mildly. "Win this war with us, and you will be the savior of Athens."

Alkibiades sighed heavily, tugging at his hair. "I suppose so... It's just quite a blow you have given me. And not the kind I would like from you. To think... all I have done and would do in my life was to be in vain. But..."—he suddenly threw his arms wide and smiled—"I am wholly with you. Let us crush Sparta, starting with Brasidas. But first, we ought to *consummate* this union, the three of us. What say you, Demosthenes? Star-girl?"

Rising, Demosthenes scoffed. "I shall stay out of your bed."

"Out here on the grass, then!" Alkibiades countered. As Thalassia stood, he moved in close beside her, grabbed her hips and examined her form with eyes lit by desire. "We should dress you as a goddess," he concluded. "None of the virgins, though, and Aphrodite doesn't suit you. No, you are an Isis, I think! Your complexion is right, and I have a whole trunk of Egyptian gold."

"Later," Thalassia said unapologetically and brushed past him, following the path which led away from the benches and the statue of Alkibiades.

Demosthenes fell in behind her, and they returned to their host's house, from which, reluctantly, after making one last argument in favor of naked celebration, Alkibiades allowed his guests to depart. Almost unconsciously, Demosthenes chose a back route, away from the crowds of the marketplace and law-courts where men were ever stopping him these days to offer congratulations on his victory.

Was this to be his future? Skulking in shadows?

Suddenly he wished to be alone, or at least away from *her*. Something about Thalassia's very presence seemed as poison to rational thought. It was as though she exuded droplets of madness like sweat through her flawless skin. And he had consigned himself to her keeping, a prisoner of her madness. She would never let him go, he knew. Not ever.

9. Rain

Demosthenes drifted gently from sleep. At first, he was only vaguely aware of the bed underneath him. Then his awareness expanded.

By the quality of light filtering in through the window, it was early morning. The air felt strangely chill for the days which he now recalled should be the tail end of summer. But there was some warmth present in the bed with him, other than that provided by the thin blanket of wool. His policy had always been to bar Eurydike from sleeping in his bed, lest it become a habit too hard to break when the day came that he took a wife. But his enforcement was lax, and sometimes she ended up there instead of in her place by the hearth.

Demosthenes looked toward the heat source, but found no pile of red curls, no freckled tangle of Thracian limbs. There was just Thalassia, with a wavy cascade of long, dark hair half concealing the hand with which she propped up her flawless face, its skin the color of honey. Her pale eyes were wide open and staring at him, and a sweet smile was upon her thin lips. She was naked, of course, and lying on top of the covers rather than under, as though she had been up already and returned to watch him wake.

On seeing her, Demosthenes knew he had spent the night with her doing things which had left his body spent. That did not strike him as strange. (But it should, should it not?)

The star-girl set one hand on his cheek and slithered forward until her lips reached his. She kissed him, and he returned it, at first with innocent affection and then sensually. Raw as it was, his cock stirred.

"Let's stay here all day," Thalassia said when they detached.

"We do that every day," he said (why would he say that?) and swung his legs off the bed.

Thalassia clutched at him and whined, "Don't go!" But he brushed her off and planted bare feet on the cold floor. "There's nothing out there for you," she said dejectedly. "All you need is right here."

He walked to the single window of a bedchamber which was not his, yet at the same time was, and threw back the silken drape. His lover came up behind him, set her cheek and one hand on his shoulder, and together they looked out over Athens, spread far below.

It was not the view from his home in Tyrmeidai.

He could see Tyrmeidai, or what remained of it. The ruins of those buildings which were not flattened utterly swam in a sea of ash. In what once had been the streets, now indistinguishable from what lay around, not a soul stirred, even at this, the market hour. The markets were rubble.

"Come back to bed," Thalassia urged.

"No," Demosthenes answered glumly. "I love you. But I do not love the chains that bind our fates together. One day I shall be free of them. And you."

Thalassia stroked his hair. "Not soon, my *exairetos*. Not soon."

He turned, and Thalassia was gone. When he turned back, the window had gone, too, and with it the bedchamber and the ruins of Athens. In their place was a columned sanctuary on a sunlit mountainside.

Demosthenes' knees buckled. He sank into tall, untended grass and cried out, for only now did his heart explode with the pain and horror of the sight just seen, of Athens laid waste and he its heartless lord, Thalassia his star-born queen.

On knees and forearms, he wept into the weeds until

some other sound, a woman's plaintive moan, began to fill the spaces between his sobs. He picked himself up and moved toward the sound's source, the sanctuary.

He had been to Delphi once before in his life, in his youth. He had walked the winding trek up the base of Parnassos, now behind and below him, but of course he had not been privileged to approach the Pythia within her sacred walls. In his memory, the holy place was packed as far he could see with pilgrims, but now it stood empty. Two of the four columns of the once-great façade had fallen, and all four were festooned with green spirals of clinging ivy. Solemn rituals were meant to precede passage through that portico into the sacred space beyond, but no priests had been here for some time, it appeared, and so no one stopped him following the sad, beckoning moan inside.

The sanctum was shrouded in a thick mist which glowed with a light all its own, and the low moan echoed now off walls invisible beyond the swirling clouds.

"Who is there?" Demosthenes said in a whisper which echoed in his ears far more sharply and with greater clarity than mere stone walls should have produced. Cowed, he said nothing further, but just followed his ears until he found the sound's source.

She was young, perhaps just out of adolescence, and she lay curled naked on the tile floor clutching a blood-soaked cloth between white thighs that trembled. He knew without benefit of evidence that this was the Oracle herself, the Pythia. She should have been ancient and withered, or at least all men said she was.

She moaned on. Demosthenes crouched by her side. "Can I help?" he said, fearful of a harsh echo which never came.

The moaning ceased. The Pythia's head, trailing long

tendrils of oily brown hair twisted in the remnants of what might once have been an elaborate style, rose slowly from the floor. Tears had stained her cheeks with streams of kohl from blue eyes that looked up at Demosthenes first in confusion and then, suddenly, abject hatred.

"You!" she shrieked. More swiftly than he would have thought possible, she launched a hand at him, its thin fingers bent in a claw.

The attack grazed Demosthenes' face, stinging his cheek and throwing him off balance so that he fell back from his haunches. Twisting, he got hands beneath him. His palms slapped on the mist-shrouded tile, and he scuttled backward on the skirt of his chiton.

He soon stopped, for the naked, violated virgin Pythia had collapsed prostrate on the tile, no breath for chase left in her young frame. With obvious effort, she pushed herself up and folded a leg under her thin body. Questing in the thick mist, she found her bloody rag and restored it to its place.

Demosthenes made himself more comfortable but went no closer. "You know me?" he asked.

She leveled an acid stare. "I'm the fucking Oracle! Of course I know who you are, you fucking cunt. Everyone knows the Destroyer of All, the Arch-Coward, the Whore-Slave, the sack of maggot-ridden pig shit called *Demosthenes*." She spat into the fog and lifted her stained cloth, shaking it at him. "This is *your* fault!"

He opened his mouth to protest, but it fell shut. The same way he had known her to be the Pythia, he knew she spoke the truth.

"How could I have known?" he countered feebly.

The young Pythia sneered in disbelief. "How could you have known?" she mocked. "How could you have known that she would rip this world in two and piss down the crack?"

She crawled forward a few inches, maybe meaning to attack again but failing to find the strength.

"Hmm..." she resumed, "I'm a goddamn oracle, so let me see if I can't advise you a bit on telling the future, brainless one. That bitch had the strength of Herakles, the speed of Atalanta, the learning of a thousand philosophers, and if you cut off her limbs she'd grow new ones like a fucking Hydra. There were two others of her kind out there who hated her, just like everyone who's ever known her does. The being she wished to destroy, and the leader she betrayed—*twice!*—are presumably even more powerful than she is. Yet you foresaw no danger in forming a pact with her? Need I go on, *idiot?*"

Demosthenes declined to answer, only swallowed hard.

"Kronos' ass, but you are dumb!" the Pythia raged. "She even helped your enemy at Pylos before she helped you. She told you she didn't give a shit about your city or your war! She only cares about her vengeance, and knowing even a fraction of her history, you thought she would suddenly start playing nice because—why? She likes you? Gods, you kept your groin in check, so if you weren't thinking with that, what exactly were you thinking with? What's your excuse for not seeing her for the lying, chaos-craving, world-devouring Wormwhore that she is? Can you not see, you sucker of diseased cock, that this enemy of hers that she aims to wipe from existence is not the Worm? It is not one man at all. Her enemy is humanity!"

The Pythia stared at him with deep hatred written in her sneer. Demosthenes whispered blankly, "What must I do to save us?"

"Moron!" Apollo's prophet roared in frustration. "How thick does Athens make men? Kill her!"

"But how? I cannot plot against her, for she will know—"

"Find a way, goat-scrotum, or watch Athens burn!" the

Pythia hissed. Sending him a final look of utter contempt, the raped virgin oracle laid back down in her fetal ball and resumed her soaring, eternal moan just in time for the mists to reclaim her.

A warm wind blew. The mist faded, and Demosthenes stood alone on a silent, corpse-strewn battlefield. No, not merely that, for not even in the days of Xerxes' invasion could a field of corpses ever have stretched from horizon to horizon in all directions. Worse still, among the bronze-clad warriors and their broken shields were women of all ages, their rent garments of linen and silk clinging to crimson, shredded hips and breasts. There were slaughtered children, too, some dressed in armor and with swords in their small, lifeless hands. The sky above was uniformly gray and heavy with clouds, whilst underfoot the space between corpses, what little of it there was, ran so deep with standing gore that it sloshed cold between sandal and sole. A shock of coppery curls bobbed in that vile sea: Eurydike, her green eyes unseeing. Not far from her was the mangled form of lame Phormion. Elsewhere lay Kleon, Nikias, Alkibiades.

Demosthenes did not mourn them, for he knew he had no right. Looking down he saw that he wore a blood spattered breastplate of bronze embossed with the image of a twisting snake. No... a worm. A short sword hung at his waist, its handle gummed with blood, and where the blade protruded from the scabbard, there was visible the start of some inscription.

He slowly drew the bloody blade out, wiping it as he went, and revealed the letters one by one. Μ-Α-Γ-Δ-Α-Λ-

He dropped it back into place and looked up. He was not alone. In the middle distance, a figure walked toward him. It bore a spear and wore a hoplite's helmet of the Corinthian style which covered all but the eyes and a sliver of mouth drowned in shadows. Below the face was a breastplate so coated with blood that its emblem, if it had one, was lost. The warrior's shins and forearms were covered by greaves. The only flesh left uncovered on the body of this metal beast was that of its upper arms and the legs between knee and the breastplate's leather skirts. The limbs were slender and caked in black blood.

Spear-butt thunking and splashing, the hoplite approached him, sandaled feet churning gore. It stopped. Released, the spear toppled sideward, and two bloodied hands went to the helm, gripped the cheek pieces and raised it. A thick, black braid spilled out over the hoplite's left shoulder. The helmet crested a cocked head and tumbled off into the human morass, and Thalassia stood unmasked.

Thunder crashed. The pregnant gray sky let loose a gentle, misting rain. Droplets tapped the bronze on both of their bodies and sent tiny red rivulets coursing down Thalassia's shell of gore, which could not be so easily washed away. She put out a hand palm-up as if to playfully catch a few drops, then she smiled and slowly laughed. It was a laugh of triumph where no triumph had been expected, and far from making Demosthenes the laughter's target, her pale, warm eyes invited him to join her.

He did not laugh, but he did take a step toward her. He wanted to draw his sword on her but only got as far as flexing the fingers of his right hand. Thalassia moved closer too, stepping on the tattooed arm of slaughtered Eurydike. She laid a hand on his neck and pulled him toward her. He wished to resist, but could not. Instead, he brought both hands up and planted them one on either side of her encrusted armor to draw her body against his. Bronze first met bronze, then flesh met flesh in a tender kiss of affection.

"I love you," he said. He said it sadly, and the helplessly

watching soul within him screamed in revulsion.

"I know," the star-born Wormwhore said sweetly to her slave, and she kissed him again.

10. *Aichmolotos*

Every night for twelve nights after the war council in Alkibiades' garden, Demosthenes awoke in tears, and more often than not fully erect, from gore-soaked nightmares of Thalassia. He was glad on those mornings when he could not remember his visions, for the ones that he did recall went on to haunt his days as well as his nights.

He tried his best not to let his demeanor towards Thalassia change, but that grew ever more difficult the longer the dreams continued unabated. Even were she just a mortal woman with mortal senses, Thalassia could not but have noticed. But evidently she knew mercy: apart from a look now and then, and the increase in frequency and duration of her stays with Alkibiades (which came rather as a relief) she did not force the issue. Eurydike meanwhile came and went between Athens and Thria. Demosthenes was pleased to have her back when she came, for her presence in the house acted as a buffer and a distraction. When he was alone, his mind turned over and over in endless cycles reviewing his few options. Should he put his reservations aside, hope that the baleful visions relented and simply continue to trust Thalassia? Or should he cast her out of his home and hope he survived the wrath which was all but certain to follow?

He even once let himself ponder the unthinkable: taking her by surprise with a sword or heavy ax, doing to her what she had done to Eden, only finishing the job. If there was some way to kill her kind, she had not shared it with him, and he could scarcely ask... but burning her mangled remains seemed a good start. Surely that would be the end of her? If not, of course, the consequences would be terrible. And practically speaking, murdering a slave was not without its legal consequences if the act were to be discovered. This was not Sparta, where slaves lived at their masters' whims.

No. Both practically and morally, killing her was out of the question. He barred his mind permanently from travel along that course.

Once or twice he saw Eden, too, in his dreams. However little he understood of Thalassia, he knew less of the other. Who was to say Eden was not in the right and Thalassia the villain? In fact, on nothing more than the evidence at hand, that seemed more likely than not to be the case. Thalassia was the outcast, the traitor, the self-obsessed fugitive, and if, as his visions warned, she truly was more monster than woman, then Eden might one day prove a valuable ally against her. A counterbalance, at least. As such, he resolved not to remind Thalassia of her pledge to hunt down and eliminate Eden in the coming year.

At some point during those twelve vision-plagued days, it occurred to Demosthenes that there was yet one other Greek in Athens besides himself and Alkibiades who was aware of Thalassia's otherworldly nature. And so on the thirteenth morning, Demosthenes rose to an empty house (Eurydike being in the country, Thalassia with her playmate) and set off to gain audience with him.

The sprawling jailhouse of Athens was not a single structure but actually a complex of six buildings, each added by a new generation to accommodate the growing legions of the accused and convicted. The wall which enclosed it all was likewise a patchwork project that had changed its course a number of times over the years, but it had only one gate, with a stout guardhouse beside it, and that was where Demosthenes went. He had made no prior arrangements, but rather counted on his face to win him the access he desired, and the plan worked. The jailer, half-asleep at his post, shook himself to alertness, then appeared gratified to have as a visitor the very man who had helped to fill his cells to bursting with prisoners of war. He summoned a guard to bring out the requested prisoner, and scant minutes later Demosthenes sat in a cupboard-sized room staring across a tabletop of knotted planks at the Spartan Equal whose unprecedented surrender he had accepted at Sphakteria.

Styphon sat rigid in his chair. Gone was his armor, of course, for that had been among the spoils. In its place he wore a plain chiton of undyed wool, on the front of which had been painted, in deliberate mockery of Lakedaemon's crimson lambda, a red alpha, which stood for *aichmolotos*, prisoner. Shackles of black iron were bolted about his wrists and ankles and connected to one another by heavy chains which gently clinked. His long black hair was combed and tied back, and he had been allowed to shape and trim his unruly facial growth. The only similarity this man bore to the ash-encrusted warrior of Sphakteria was the pair of gleaming, flinty eyes that bespoke a lifetime of discipline and which were, in fact, considerably more alert than those of his jailers.

Demosthenes spoke first, not bothering with the pleasantries and prefaces for which he knew Spartans had no use.

"Tell me all you know of Thalassia," he demanded.

At first, Styphon's heavy, clenched jaw did not budge as he engaged his interrogator in a round of staring. But at length his thick scowl twisted, and grated words emerged: "Why should I?"

"I have influence in this city," Demosthenes said. "More now than ever. I could hasten your release, or stand in its way." It was an empty promise, of course, for nothing said here would bear on his votes in the Assembly.

The Equal snorted. "You think I will scramble to save our lives? If our city sees fit to let us rot here, or to be executed, then so be it. Whatever our fate, we will suffer it gladly."

"Did Thalassia speak to you of your fate?" Demosthenes asked.

Again there was a long delay. Finally Styphon said, "You took her offer."

"Offer?" Demosthenes echoed.

The twitch that moved Styphon's lips was the closest Demosthenes had ever seen to a Spartan smile. "You know of what I speak," Styphon said confidently. "She told you the outcome of this war and made you believe you could change it."

He paused, and Demosthenes waited in silence, trying his best not to let on that the Spartan was right.

"She tried to change things on the island," Styphon finally resumed. His smugness had faded. "She failed, and here I sit, in chains"—he rattled them—"as she told me was my fate. But I am a man and an Equal. I know my place, and I accept it." A sudden sneer turned his lip. "That sea-bitch meddles in affairs that rightfully belong to men and should be settled by men. If you let her, she will be the ruin of both our cities. And more besides. That she would fight for whichever side would have her shows her to be no more than a *mercenary*."

This last word was a curse in the Doric tongue, for Spartans held in great contempt all who would take up arms for so base a cause as personal gain.

"Be rid of her," Styphon urged. "Carve her up and throw the pieces back into the sea, as we should have done. Maybe she has already changed our cities' fates, but maybe not. Either way, let us not see our war decided by some woman and outsider. Let us fight it out as men and as Greeks."

"If she is so vile a creature," Demosthenes reasoned,

"why did you try to win her passage to Sparta?"

The question did not throw the Equal, who scoffed. "She is a weapon, *Athenian*." This last word was almost a curse in Doric, too. "If she cannot be sheathed or unmade, at least she can be kept out of enemy hands." His broad shoulders jerked in a chain-clattering shrug. "I need not tell you she has charms." He leaned forward intensely over the table. "I bet she has you stuffed right up inside her woman parts, seeing what she wishes you to see, thinking what she wishes you to think." He leaned back again, shook his head and stared with his flint-hard eyes at his vanquisher. "But you came to me," he said, "and that is a good sign. You have doubts. Your instincts are yet your own. Trust them, Athenian, before they vanish. Before she comes down upon you, and everything you hold dear, like the hammer of the gods."

With that the chained beast arose from his chair, signaling the end of the interview. Demosthenes knew it should be he who had the last word, but none came to him. Even if they did, his lips were painfully dry and jaw so tightly clenched that it seemed his head would crumble if he opened it. And so he rapped on the wall behind him to summon a guard, who took the Spartiate away.

It was a rare day when a Spartan's words lingered past his leaving, but so they did today.

11. Soft Things

Boedromion in the archonship of Stratokles (September 425 BCE)

For many days after Demosthenes' visit to Styphon, he hid his suspicions from Thalassia, trying to behave around her as though nothing had changed. He knew he was failing. She could not be lied to. Yet, for reasons apparently her own, she went along with the charade as they began building the cover which would help them introduce her changes to Athens.

Demosthenes financed jointly with Alkibiades a trading vessel assigned with bringing to Athens, along with the more typical trade goods, whatever it could in the way of scrolls, wax tablets and papyrii in any language. The sailors would not know or care what was written on them in various foreign tongues, if they were even literate—and it did not matter, since upon translation they would become whatever Thalassia wished them to be: 'long lost' secrets of agriculture, weaponcraft, metallurgy, medicine, and more, which then might be 'reintroduced' to Athens.

Thalassia herself split her time between the homes of her two co-conspirators, as Eurydike did between city and country. She furnished Demosthenes' empty women's quarters perhaps more lavishly than he would have himself. Demosthenes bore the expense without complaint, largely out of a desire to avoid any confrontation which might give her cause to raise other matters between them. But this strategy of avoidance could only last so long.

At last, a month after his victory at Pylos, Demosthenes returned home one afternoon to find Thalassia lying in wait for him. She stood alone in the megaron, dressed in the long chiton the color of sea-foam which was her favorite, her hair bisected by a straight part, on either side of which hung a tightly braided pigtail. The hairstyle gave her an absurdly childlike appearance quite at odds with the jewel-like hardness of her wintry eyes as she pushed the door shut behind him and set her back against it—her trap sprung.

"I've waited patiently for whatever is bothering you to go away. Clearly it won't," she said. "So out with it."

Demosthenes laughed feebly. "Nothing... nothing is wrong."

Thalassia declined even to respond, just stood against the door freezing Demosthenes' feet to the floor tiles with a gaze that he managed to meet for a short while before deflating.

He felt relief, in a way, to have the charade at an end. He walked slowly to the low dining table of ebony and stood by its edge. Thalassia followed and faced him across its polished, gilt-edged surface, which cast up a mirror image of the stargirl's hard look and those wildly inappropriate twin braids which framed it. It was this dark reflection at which he stared, rather than the real thing, while he searched for words.

He found them rather easily. What took slightly longer was digging up the courage to speak them. "I have changed my mind."

"About what?" Thalassia's stony expression, devoid of sympathy, did not change.

He spoke still to the image in ebony, in a voice just above a whisper. "Everything."

The lower half of the reflection's face tightened. "Continue."

"Fate should not be tampered with," he said. "I was wrong to start."

"Hmm," she said. The sound was heavy with judgment. "So your new plan is to watch Amphipolis fall, let your supplies be choked off and watch Athens wither until it's time for you to fuck off and die in Sicily." Abruptly, she commanded, "Look at me."

Demosthenes did so. Her pale eyes bored through him.

"Is that what you want?" she insisted on knowing.

"I have no other plan," he admitted, and let his gaze fall again.

Thalassia forced his chin up with the tip of a finger. "I said look at me." He complied, and channeled into his eyes a rising anger at being spoken to like some errant youth. "If you were having doubts, you should have come to me about them," she said sharply. "Tell me now."

Far from cowing him, her belligerence and lecturing tone only helped him find his voice. "You care nothing for this city or anyone in it," he said. "And I would sooner go down in defeat alongside men who love Athens than win victory by means of some ... *mercenary*." He barely remembered to pronounce the word in Attic, rather than mimicking Styphon's Doric dialect.

"Go on."

Thalassia's calm made him wonder: was she manipulating him even now? Had her intention in trapping him thus been to push him into open rage?

So what if it was? He could not turn back. The temptation of release after a month spent pretending was simply was too great. His nightmare visions, his visit with Styphon, the fears and doubts festering in his thoughts, all of these had caused him to... if not *hate* Thalassia, then something closely resembling it.

"You care for none but yourself," he said. "You respect the laws of neither gods nor men. Every one of us is but a marker in some great, cosmic game you play with unseen opponents. And if that weren't bad enough—"

His next words he knew to be foolish even as he spoke

them, but such momentum had he built that he could scarcely stop them spilling out.

"—you put your cunt to work like a shameless street whore, manipulating men into becoming your playthings. I will be no plaything."

Having, for the moment, run out of harsh words with which to follow these, he stopped speaking. Anger seethed behind Thalassia's calm features, and he tensed, half-expecting another sudden attack like the one she had launched on him in Pylos.

"It hurts that you would go to Styphon instead of talking to me," she said, relieving him somewhat... or perhaps giving him fresh cause for concern, since it meant she knew of his prison visit. He had even fewer secrets from her than he had thought.

She smiled frostily and raised the fingers of one hand to the delicate choker of braided silver around her neck.

"What is this, Demosthenes?" she asked. When he did not immediately give reply to a question he took to be rhetorical, she prompted more forcefully, "What is it?"

"A slave collar," he said quietly.

"Yes, a slave collar. You do recall that I am one of the three most powerful beings on this fucking planet, right?" Her calm broke for the space of the expletive, then returned. "If I had wanted to, I could have been a goddess. I could have had the *kaloi kagathoi* of Athens scraping at my feet, doing all they could to please me so I wouldn't end their little lives. Do you think I *need* you to change this world? I could slaughter the Board of Ten. I could walk into Sparta and kill Brasidas and every one of their leaders. I still could, if I changed my mind. Yet instead, I walk behind you in public and call you*master*. Why is that?" she asked. "I hope you can tell me, Demosthenes, because I'm starting to forget." Her calm broke again, and she grated: *"Why is that?"*

Her rage set back Demosthenes' own efforts to keep his own rising anger in check. "You are a curse upon my world," he snapped. "You have the power of a god and the mind of a *child*. My home, my city, my world, were better off without—"

Demosthenes did not hesitate before speaking his next word, but even as it poured out, he knew he should have held it back. Once spoken, it could not be taken back, just as once a wall of spears was charged, no matter how great the fear that gripped a man, there remained only one path—forward.

"—the *Wormwhore!*"

In the several silent seconds which followed, Thalassia showed no visible reaction. She ended them by looking down at the table, though hardly in concession. She stepped around its corner to draw closer to him, looked at him with her jewel-hard eyes and commanded, "Say. That. Again."

"I will not." In front of a charging Demosthenes, the bristling wall of gleaming spear-blades neared. "You heard me."

Deep within, he knew that it was likely his life depended on an apology. But he could not bring himself to give it. There was but the one path, whatever lay at its end.

"Say it."

"I will not."

She screamed, "Say it!"

As if punctuating her command, Demosthenes' hand rose, almost of its own accord, and delivered a hard slap across Thalassia's cheek.

A part of him knew that his life was ended anyhow at this point, and so he did as she wished and spoke again the forbidden word, filling it with venom: *"Wormwhore."*

Like a golden javelin, Thalassia's hand shot up, grabbed a handful of his hair and pulled, slamming Demosthenes' forehead into the ebony table with skull-rattling force. Without releasing her grip, she used his hair to drag him to his feet.

"You fucking asked for this," she said. She strode toward the timber staircase at the megaron's rear, pulling him behind her. Demosthenes grabbed hold of her iron wrist, but knowing the futility of trying to pry that hand loose, he limited his aim to creating some slack to ease the pain in his scalp as he walked in an awkward bow behind her. Seeing her foot mount the first step, he knew what would happen next but was powerless to stop it.

Shifting her grip seamlessly from his scalp to his wrist, she wrenched Demosthenes' arm with such force that his feet flew from under him. He landed hard on his knees and was lucky to slap one hand down on the bottom step's edge before it collided with his skull. Thalassia ascended the stairs two at a time. Each step sent Demosthenes' body rebounding off the wood, battering his arm and knees when he was lucky, his head and shoulders when he was not.

They reached the second floor women's quarters, but the punishing ascent showed no sign of ending. The smooth plaster floor across which Thalassia next dragged him was a welcome respite before what was inevitably to follow. The ladder. Pain lanced through Demosthenes' right arm as she used it to hoist him up it, whilst his legs flailed in vain for purchase on the rungs.

She yanked him bodily through the hatch and deposited him on his back on the tiled floor of the rooftop terrace, finally releasing her grip on his burning arm.

A cloud-strewn afternoon sky spread above him. At its far edge hovered Athena's high temple. A fitting enough last sight to carry with him into gray Hades, he thought. Then the view was blocked by Thalassia, who came to stand astride him, a pigtailed colossus, with one expensive sandal planted on either side of his ribcage. Crouching, she grasped a handful of his chiton and used the material to drag his head up from the plaster and bring his face within inches of hers. The brush-like ends of her twin braids tickled his cheekbones.

"Look at me!" she demanded.

Demosthenes looked up into wide, wild eyes that were all but devoid of reason.

Thalassia hissed into his face, each word battering its way past clenched teeth: "You have not earned the fucking right to touch me without an invitation. I gave you more than one, and you *refused* them."

Aching body limp, Demosthenes looked up at the stargirl's face, framed by clouds. It was the beautiful, savage face of a predator—probably his murderer—and, of a sudden... he felt a strange pity for her.

He forced words from lungs short on breath: "He... must have hurt you... so deeply."

Effortlessly, Thalassia hoisted him from the sun-warmed tile, her lips let loose a blood-chilling roar of the kind heard on a battlefield just before the clash of spears, and like a child abusing her toy, she drew her helpless victim back against one shoulder—and threw him.

Demosthenes' stomach pitched as he sailed backward through space. Fortunately, by chance or design, he struck the balustrade full-on, and the wood held fast against the impact, keeping him from dashing his brains on the paving stones of the garden two stories below. Still, the back of his head ricocheted before bouncing back and coming to rest in the void between two posts.

On opening the eyes he had shut against the pain, he expected to see Thalassia advancing on him to inflict further harm. Instead, he found no threat, at least not an imminent one. Rather than stalking after him, Thalassia had gone to the rail opposite and collapsed, head on her knees and body folded into a ball. Suddenly, her arm flew out and struck a wooden post of the railing. The force caused it to splinter and fall loose.

Aching with even the slightest move, Demosthenes could only sit drawing labored breaths and waiting to learn whether or not his already battered bones would be the next to splinter thus. When Thalassia failed to move again for nearly a minute, he dared to begin pondering the possibility that his life might extend beyond the next few moments.

As if sensing that thought, Thalassia picked her head up and looked over with pale, indignant eyes. She unfolded her limbs as if to move, and Demosthenes began composing words of apology which might stave off death, if only his pride would yield and let them be spoken.

But what came next was no attack. On all fours, sea-green dress dragging behind her, Thalassia crawled across the tile. She advanced slowly toward him, knee to palm, knee to palm, until her hand brushed Demosthenes' outstretched leg. There she settled back onto her haunches facing him, staring silently with a tight-lipped look he failed to decipher.

"I told you I can choose whether to feel pain or pleasure," she said. Her voice had lost its hard edge. "That's not only true of my flesh. It's also true of the things we feel within. The things that make us human. *Soft things.* Some in the Caliate are barely more than machines. The temptation sometimes for me to become that way is..."

She blinked, and from each of her cold, perfect eyes a heavy tear slid free. One fell on Demosthenes' bruised knee, but his attention remained on the face in which, for perhaps the first time, he saw an expression which did not seem to be at least partly an affectation.

"The truth is I'm damaged, Demosthenes," she said. "I was before I ever met him. He saw that, and that's why he could..." She paused and let that thought die. At length she whispered, "I'm not a monster. I'm not."

And the starborn killer wept.

12. Spartlet

Demosthenes lifted his good arm, the left, and touched Thalassia's wet cheek as if to prove to himself the tears upon it were real. She shrank from the contact and lowered her head into his lap, facing away from him. Her soft, strong body, wrapped in pleats of sea-foam green, curled up by his side.

"Are you badly hurt?" she asked.

The slightest movement of Demosthenes' neck sent waves of pain down his body. "I feel... as though someone dragged me up two stories and pitched me across a roof."

Thalassia chuckled softly. "I didn't intend to hurt you. Really. You deserve to live, Demosthenes, and to be happy. I understand if my promises mean nothing, but I swear that I will never lay a hand on you in anger again. You shouldn't fear for your life from me. You don't have to."

Looking down–carefully, without moving his neck–Demosthenes laid a hand on Thalassia's bare shoulder. "I wish to believe you," he said. "But that you did not intend to hurt me tonight gives me *more* reason to fear you, not less. You are... impulsive. To say the least."

After a brief silence, Thalassia observed, "You called me a child. You know, you've never asked me my age. I'm older than I look. Much older."

Demosthenes had guessed that Thalassia could not be the mere twenty or so years that she appeared, no more than deathless Aphrodite was a blushing youth. But no, he had not asked and was not certain that he wished to know the true answer. But having raised the subject, she clearly now wished to tell him, and he surely was not about to encourage her to keep secrets.

"How... how old?" he asked.

"Two hundred and thirty eight of your years," Thalassia

answered. "And of them all, the best six were the ones I spent with him." She paused and drew a long, unsteady breath. "I hate him so much."

How very human she seemed... or quite possibly, how human she *could* seem, when it served her.

She hesitated, and Demosthenes waited patiently. He stared at her thickly braided pigtails. *Handles,* the errant thought slipped into his mind. *For what?* It was not a hard question to answer.

"He can't be killed by normal means," she resumed. "And not just like I'm hard to kill. He always survives. Always. That's why I'm here trying to unmake him instead. If it's even possible. Succeed or fail, this will be the last thing I do. The last world I ever see. That's why..."

She trailed off briefly, and Demosthenes noticed he was stroking her arm. He quickly stopped.

"That's why I wear this collar, and try to make friends, and spend your money on pretty, shiny things in the agora." She laughed, faintly. "I'm glad I wound up in Athens. They don't have pretty, shiny things in Sparta, do they? I wouldn't have lasted there."

Setting palms to tile, Thalassia raised herself, causing Demosthenes' thigh to rue the absence of her warm cheek. She settled into an awkward seated posture, the fabric of her long chiton stretched taut between widely parted knees. Her head came level with his.

"Please," she said, and the cool eyes of the crestfallen goddess, still moist with tears, begged. "Don't give up on me. At least give me until Amphipolis is held. After that, if it's what you want, I'll leave Greece altogether. I'll never trouble you or your descendants again. That's a promise, and in spite of what you may think, I do keep them."

Demosthenes met her stare, ignoring the pain in his flesh

and bone, pain of which she was the cause, and he measured her such as he, or any mere human, was able.

"I..." he began, uncertain of what should come next. "I believe you, I think. But I still fear you. I suspect I always shall."

Thalassia's lips twisted in a melancholy smile. It faded, and she said softly, " I hope not." She reached out and touched his head, which throbbed. "Let's get you downstairs."

Leaning in close, she slipped her left arm under his right, while her other snaked around him from behind. The move put her cheek against his. Instead of quickly hoisting him to his feet, she paused and let the touch linger for longer than could be accidental. She nuzzled him, just a little, and she exhaled, her warm breath tickling his cheek. And then he was lifted, with great ease and set on his feet such that he needed not bear his full weight. From at least a half-dozen places, Demosthenes' body screamed for attention or better still, the bliss of unconsciousness. He had come through hour-long battles feeling less bruised than he felt now.

"So... partners still?" Thalassia asked on the way to the hatch.

"Until Amphipolis," Demosthenes agreed, with rather less certainty than he would have liked.

Somehow Thalassia managed to lower him gracefully through the hatch, and thence onto his bed. "Wait here," she instructed. "I'll bring you something for the pain."

For a short while, he lay looking up at the ceiling, making peace in advance with any gods that would listen for the sins which were doubtless to follow on this path he had chosen in defiance of Fate and all good sense. Down below, the hearth rattled with the sounds of whatever remedy Thalassia was preparing. Momentarily she returned and sat on the edge of his bed with a cup filled with a steaming, milky liquid.

"Drink this." She set the rim to his lip, and Demosthenes, trusting in her as a physic, if not in all things, emptied the contents.

Smiling, she set the cup aside. "You'll sleep soon," she said. "In the morning, there is something I must tell you. It's why I had to put to rest tonight these unspoken things between us."

Warmth radiated from Demosthenes' chest, down his limbs, pushing them down into the bedding and making movement implausible. The sharp pains and dull aches of Thalassia's maltreatment began to fade, and with them his clarity of mind. Thoughts began to slip like silvery fish through his mental grasp.

"Tell... me... what?"

"Tomorrow," Thalassia said soothingly. He could see, but not feel, that her hand was on his arm.

Demosthenes laughed. With effort, he lifted the hand nearest Thalassia and flicked one of her braids before letting it fall. "You have handles..." he said sleepily.

She smiled. "Yes. Do you like them?"

"The better to ride you with." Demosthenes laughed at his own feeble joke. "But... no, I... they could grow on me." He laughed again. "They... grow on *you*, actually. On that thing... your... *head*."

He let his heavy lids fall shut. He dragged them open again and slurred, "What... you... want... tell..." He got no further before sleep claimed him.

***

Demosthenes awoke with a start and with words upon his lips: "...tell me!"

Morning light streamed in through his window. As he tried to sit upright, he found that his right arm, which aside from his neck was presently the source of the most pain on his body, was tightly bound against his chest with linens.

"Thalassia!" he cried out.

"Morning," she said gently, appearing quickly in the open doorway. She came to his bedside with a cup of water. Realizing his mouth was parched, Demosthenes took the cup in his good hand and emptied it in a few gulps before speaking.

"What is it you wished to tell me?" he asked urgently, anxiously, knowing that it could scarcely be anything he wished to hear.

The look she gave fed such a conclusion. Since last night she had changed her sea-foam chiton for a pink one, and her hair was different. The 'handles' (gods, had he really said that to her?) were gone, and in their place were loose waves still kinked from their prior confinement.

"Dress and eat breakfast first," she said. "Then I will show you."

"Show me? No, you will tell me. Now."

He swung his legs off of the bed's edge, and the wool blanket slid from his body, leaving him naked by the time his bare feet touched plaster. Standing, he wobbled on unsteady legs. Like lightning, a strong hand caught and held him.

"Alkibiades is expecting us at his home," Thalassia said, helpfully inserting her face into his line of sight and saving him the painful necessity of turning his head. "I'll explain there."

"Fine. Then we shall go now."

Thalassia brought him a fresh white chiton with red embroidered hem, the donning of which required assistance from the same nominal slave who had caused his injuries, aid which he found himself resenting as she knelt and laced his sandals. When he was dressed, they walked the streets slowly, a slave appearing to hang on her master's arm when in fact she was helping keep him upright.

"Tell me," Demosthenes insisted many times along the way. Each time he failed to get an answer, his trepidation grew.

"I told you that I keep promises," she conceded at last. "I made one at Pylos, and with help from Alkibiades, I have kept it. I want you to know that I went to him not because I trust him more, or like him more. Neither is true."

Demosthenes knew well why she might go to him for help in some secret venture: being vastly more susceptible to her charms, Alkibiades was easier for her to manipulate.

"What did you do?" he demanded, readying himself for some terrible blow the shape of which he could not yet imagine.

"It's better to show you."

Seething silently, Demosthenes allowed the answer to stand. Better anyhow that he show his anger in the privacy of Alkibiades' home than out here in the streets, in front of all.

In silence, in what seemed to Demosthenes an age, they reached their destination. Alkibiades greeted them in his private garden with a grin that was too wide by half. His bright, guilty eyes flicked to Thalassia briefly, but mostly his nervous attention stayed on Demosthenes.

"Did you know that people describe you as the most cool-tempered and circumspect man in Athens?" Alkibiades asked, eying his visitor as though expecting attack. "Did you know that?"

"No."

"Well, they do!"

There was subtle hesitation in Alkibiades' steps as he crossed the few stone pavers separating them and opened his arms for an embrace. A chlamys of blue wool concealed

Demosthenes' bound right arm, but now, as the youth's arms encircled him, there was no hiding the sling. After a half-hearted half-embrace, Alkibiades stepped back and used a set of well-manicured fingers to draw the cloak aside and reveal the injured limb.

Oddly, there was no surprise in his look, only sympathy. Demosthenes felt a fresh surge of anger, and with it humiliation. Had Thalassia told him what she had done?

"Such a shame," Alkibiades lamented. "Please don't tell me you'll get rid of her just because she threw you one time."

Demosthenes' tongue declined to move, while embarrassment warmed the flesh around it.

"Of course," Alkibiades went on, "if you insist on parting with her, I might make you an offer. I have room in my stables."

Demosthenes opened his mouth, but got no further than that, for all his thoughts were occupied with furious bewilderment.

It was Thalassia, the object of his fury, who came to his rescue.

"He would not sell Maia for any price," she said. "He knows that when a good horse throws a man, the fault lies always with the rider."

Alkibiades nodded. "It happens to the best of us," he commiserated. "Did you break her yourself?"

"I... did not. She came to me quite broken, I assure you. But *not* tamed."

The answer won Demosthenes a questioning look from his fellow cavalryman and a sidewise smirk from Thalassia.

"But we are not here to talk of my past injuries," Demosthenes moved swiftly on. "We are here, I gather, to add a fresh one."

Talk of the betrayal which evidently was to be revealed

this morning prompted a shared look between the two accomplices in some as-yet-unknown deed. Alkibiades' look was nervous; Thalassia's gave reassurance. With a resigned sigh, the former turned and retreated down his garden path, passing by a bust of himself on a pedestal half-enveloped by honeysuckle. He vanished around a bend and was gone for thirty silent seconds.

When he reappeared, he was no longer alone. Marching mechanically in front of him was a little girl, not yet at the age of curves, with long, straight, dark hair contrasting starkly with the white of her plain short chiton. Wearing a blank expression, the girl was about as animated as one of the many sculptures that dotted Alkibiades' estate.

Thalassia stepped forward and set a gentle hand at the back of the girl's neck, turning so they both faced Demosthenes. Alkibiades hung behind, chewing his lip and eyeing the stones at his feet.

"Who is she?" Demosthenes demanded.

Looking only fractionally less guilty than her partner, Thalassia reluctantly accepted the task of answering. "Her name is Andrea. She is nine years old, and she is the daughter of Styphon."

Demosthenes shut his eyes in the hope that this was another of his nightmare visions, but when he opened them the girl yet stood there. Armed with her identity, Demosthenes could pick out traces of the girl's parentage in her keen, pitch-black eyes and flat nose, not to mention her aura of fearlessness. A version of her might have stood among Equals in a shield wall. Indeed, one had.

The necessary next question was obvious. "Why is she here?"

Neither of the two who knew its answer leaped to give one. Alkibiades declined even to look at his questioner, leaving Thalassia once more to explain.

"I made a promise," she said, inadequately.

Demosthenes asked through clenched teeth, "Of what sort?"

Thalassia removed her hand from the Spartlet's neck, said to the girl, "Thank you, Andrea. Please excuse us now."

With no change in her flat expression, the obedient daughter of an Equal departed in a measured pace along the garden path. But as if to prove she was a child, as she rounded the bust of Alkibiades, her little arm shot up and smacked its nose.

When only adults were present, Thalassia spoke. "In Sparta, she would have lived her life reviled as the offspring of a coward. I convinced Alkibiades to arrange her transport here."

"*Transport?*" Demosthenes scoffed. "You mean *kidnapping*." He looked at skulking Alkibiades. "I know you did not go to Sparta in person. Who did the deed?"

The younger man's eyes roved the garden, settling anywhere but on the one whose trust he had broken. "Messenian exiles," he confessed.

"You paid them?"

A nod.

"Can it be traced to either of you?"

Now Alkibiades found confidence. "Not a chance."

Of course he would say that.

Demosthenes' simmering anger bubbled over. "Did either of you consider the consequences of sending raiders to a city with which we are at war and stealing her citizens? What if they did the same to us? This is treason! And one of you shares my roof, which implicates me."

"No one will know," Alkibiades insisted.

"Shut up! You and I could be exiled for this, and she

could be executed." He caught his error. "Well, they could *try*. No! This... *Spartlet* has to go back."

There was no quick objection to this suggestion, a strange thing considering the lengths to which the two must have gone to achieve the deed.

Their silence, it turned out, represented something other than concession.

"Andrea lived with her widowed aunt," Thalassia announced bleakly. "The Messenians took it on themselves to kill her the night they took Andrea."

Taking a moment to absorb this tiny detail which greatly enhanced the severity of the crime, Demosthenes concluded, "Still, she must return."

"No." Thalassia spoke softly, but an iron look said she would brook no argument.

Alkibiades came forward with open palms out in a gesture for calm. "Demosthenes," he started reasonably, "as it stands, a Spartan child that no one much cares about has disappeared. But if we send her back, she can tell the Elders what happened and name us all."

"Shit." It was the only reply Demosthenes could conjure, and it properly summed up the situation. Alkibiades was right: this deed could not be safely undone. "I will not have her in my house," Demosthenes declared, already resigning himself. "I do not even want to know what your plans are for her."

Heedless of the prohibition, Alkibiades said excitedly, "That's the beautiful thing. We are going to educate her, Thalassia, Socrates, and I. We'll give her the best of all worlds–body and mind, Athens and Sparta, male and female. She'll be like nothing that has ever come before!"

"I said I did not want to know!" Demosthenes tried to interrupt.

But Alkibiades persisted: "If Andrea is a success, I shall found a school–in secret of course–and fill it with orphan girls. I don't have a name for it yet..."

"That's enough!"

Demosthenes turned his back and would have walked away but for the golden hand that appeared on his shoulder.

"Would you give us a moment alone?" its owner asked of Alkibiades.

"Of course." Before excusing himself, Alkibiades added in somber tones, "I am sorry, Demosthenes. But I think you know that I am not my reputation. I do not just follow my cock. I would never have agreed to this if I thought it put you at risk, or if it were not worth doing."

Demosthenes let the other leave without giving him the favor of a reply, even if his words did ring true and go some way toward easing his ire–toward he who had spoken them, at any rate.

As for the other irresponsible party, when they had privacy, she said in placating tones, "You have a right to be upset. I knew you would be. But–"

"But nothing," Demosthenes cut her off. "I will hear no more. Since entering my life, you have caused me to feel nothing but fear, anger, and physical pain. I have an interest in what you can accomplish for Athens, and for that reason I will uphold our pact for the defense of Amphipolis. However..." He turned away from her and looked instead upon the flowering garden. "I would prefer it if in the meantime you made your primary residence here. Alkibiades' home has a great deal more space than mine, and I know he will be glad of your company."

Thalassia clicked her honeyed tongue, nudged him gently. "Come on," she said softly. "It's not that bad. I made a promise. I kept it. Doesn't that count for something?"

"You are not well, Thalassia. Or... Dzhenna, or whatever your true name is. You are a madwoman. I can work with you for the good of my city, but that is all. We are not friends, nor do I suspect we ever can be. So, please–"

She chuckled. "Jenna," she intoned. "Eurydike told you. That's the name I was born with. Jenna Ismail Cordeiro. Geneva is my Caliate name. I'm from a nothing little colony planet... sort of an *Amphipolis* of the the stars. What I did there... well, I suppose it wouldn't help you to trust me. I was a smuggler. I got things, dangerous things, to people who shouldn't have them." She laughed again, and the laughter seemed anxious, much like her chatter. "I told you I was damaged even before..."

She sighed sharply, stepped closer and set a hand on Demosthenes' bandaged arm.

"Please don't throw me out. I promise, no more–"

"Enough promises!" Demosthenes shook off her touch. "Tell me one thing, truthfully and in great detail, and I will consider changing my mind."

"Name it," Thalassia said too quickly.

"How do I kill you?"

She fell to silence, her expression dismal. Her gaze sank to the paving stones, and Demosthenes left her thus to return alone to the home from which Thalassia was banished.

13. One Year

Months passed by. Summer turned to frosty winter, doing so, according to Thalassia, on account of the spherical Earth's journey around the sun. The Assembly met, and Demosthenes and Alkibiades did their duty as citizens, casting their votes and saying little, lest they accidentally nudge Fate off her intended track too soon, spoiling their planned ambush of Her at Amphipolis.

Not that they introduced no changes to Athens. The trading vessels which they financed returned to port with writings from far-flung lands which were distilled, through the tip of a new, self-inking stylus, into treatises on surgery and disease, hygiene, metallurgy, engineering, and a half-dozen other subjects. The knowledge thus revealed was made to fall beneath the proper eyes while garnering just enough fame, but not too much, for those responsible for 'importing' it.

Coin began to roll into the oikos of Demosthenes, a little faster than he would have liked, partly from the conventional goods brought by the trading ships and partly from the sale of two of Thalassia's inventions: a sweetly scented, olive-oil-based alternative to the traditional soap recipe of goat fat and ashes; and a cheaper alternative to papyrus made from the pressed pulp of mulberry wood. The family estate in Thria was equipped, and its laborers trained, for the production of both goods. Alkisthenes, resistant as ever to innovation, met the changes with reluctant approval, until the profit came and helped cure his reluctance.

In early winter, four skilled Athenian blacksmiths, having sworn oaths of secrecy in the Hephaestion, were paid from public funds to set aside their regular work in favor of perfecting a new process said to have originated in India. The metal thus produced in their four modified ovens was hard enough to hold a killing edge in the face of gross mistreatment, yet resilient enough to bend rather than break. Swords and spear blades could not be forged of the so-called 'Athenian steel' quickly enough to keep pace with demand among those wealthy enough to afford it.

Not long after, Thalassia presented schematics for new seagoing vessels with two masts instead of one, triangular sails, and other strange features.

"Where are the oars?" Demosthenes asked.

"They have none," she replied.

"For the future, perhaps," Demosthenes humored her. "You could sooner teach an eagle top build nests of bricks instead of twigs than convince an Athenian shipwright that the best fleet in the world requires improvement." He handed the sheets of pulped mulberry back to her. "Anyway, Nikias is admiral, and he would never agree. There are few in Athens more adherent to tradition than he."

Thalassia met the verdict with indifference, and her ship designs went otherwise unseen.

The winter solstice came and went, and so did Athens' plethora of festivals large and small. At one of them, the Lenaea, the poet Aristophanes entered into competition a comedy which skewered Kleon while portraying in a rather flattering light a character by the name of Demosthenes. The poet himself played the demagogue, the powerful and popular object of his ridicule, and thus well earned, if for that brave act alone, the first prize which the jury awarded him.

In the month of Elaphabolion the sun was eclipsed, and soon after an earthquake struck the coast, causing the sea to rise and swallow the land bridge connecting Euboea to the mainland, making of it an island. Thalassia had forewarned her two partners of both events, rather needlessly, since neither entertained any doubts when it came to her knowledge of future events. Apart from such occasional oracles as these, and the semi-regular meetings of the three conspirators in Alkibiades' garden, Thalassia might well have been no more than the domestic slave she seemed to outsiders, and even seemed to Eurydike, who was kept in the dark about her friend's true nature.

Given the deception, it seemed only logical that Thalassia avoid bringing public attention upon herself. Demosthenes, at least, saw the logic in this, and so was less than pleased on learning that Alkibiades, having scoured Athens for an artist willing to sculpt an unclad female form in life-size, had commissioned a man by the name of Kallimachus to produce a statue for his garden of Thalassia as a nude Pandora, with box in hand. Upon its completion and proud display in front of Alkibiades home, the city was divided on the work, with many thinking it distasteful, just as many more a masterpiece. In either case, fame came quickly to Kallimachus, who found himself deluged with commissions, and to Pandora herself, whose body became sought after by scores of young men who lined up at Alkibiades' gate, clutching their chisels.

Some were actually sculptors.

"Should Eden come to Athens, or if she is already here, you are making it rather easy for her to find you," Demosthenes warned, and his words went ignored.

None who viewed the marble Pandora suspected that the woman who was its model possessed also a mind and abilities far exceeding her beauty. With Alkibiades as her tutor on horsemanship, Thalassia became as skillful a rider as any member of the citizen cavalry. Or perhaps she only humored her playmate by pretending to let him teach her. Hardly a month after learning to ride, she became the instructor, training her two partners in the use of improved riding tack which, once one grew accustomed to it, offered all the advantages she promised. Here was a being of more wiles and travels than Odysseus, Demosthenes thought, a woman whom he had no doubt could, if she so desired, single-handedly bring cities to their knees, just as she claimed. Instead, she designed ships and saddles, shopped and laughed with Eurydike, posed for statues, and tutored a kidnapped Spartan girl. Demosthenes did not understand her, not because she was *not* human... but the opposite.

The plan to track down and eliminate Eden dissipated like smoke, leaving no trace of its passing. Alkibiades had no inkling of her existence, of course, and for his part, Demosthenes almost wished that Eden would appear and that the two enemies would destroy each other. Thalassia never raised the subject herself. Demosthenes suspected she was afraid, for Eden was after all one of two beings in the world capable of killing her–or worse, bringing her back to face Magdalen, the leader who had already given her wayward servant one second chance too many.

They did not speak of Magdalen, either, but Demosthenes conceived of her as some dark goddess of serpents from the world below, like those deities whose altars ran black with the dried blood of captives in tribal lands like Thessaly. He shuddered to imagine what power Magdalen must have to set her above one such as Thalassia, who walked this world of mortals as a demigoddess.

With the snows came elections to the office of strategoi, the only office of Athens not chosen by random lot in order that those who led the city's armies be those deemed to be most proficient at it. It was likewise the only annual office to be filled before the summer solstice ushered in the new year, since the city had learned in the early years of her democracy the folly of replacing generals in the middle of the campaigning season simply because that was when other offices changed hands.

Among the newly elected Board of Ten were many of the usual faces: Nikias and his staunch old ally Laches; the glowering plague survivor Thucydides, whose destiny was shortly to be rewritten in his favor (no longer would he face exile for failing to save Amphipolis); the pauper Lamachos. But it also included, by a wide margin, both of the Heroes of Pylos: Demosthenes and Kleon.

The frosty ground thawed, fields were ploughed and sown again, and when the summer solstice came, the annual eponymous archonship of Athens passed from Stratokles to a sailmaker called Isarchos, whom Thalassia had named well in advance of his randomly drawing the winning lot.

"Stop showing off," Demosthenes told her, only half-joking. "We believe you."

***

Though Pylos yet seemed like yesterday, suddenly Demosthenes looked back and found that a year had passed.

It was a year lacking in the customary invasion of Attica by a Peloponnesian army. Instead, the Spartans sent an army of envoys looking to reach some accord by which the hostages taken on Sphakteria might be returned to them. The effort smelt of desperation, and the odor was pleasing to Kleon, whose public following swelled and swelled as his increasingly warlike rhetoric in the Assembly ensured that the Spartan heralds were always sent packing back to Sparta empty-handed.

Thanks in part to Kleon's empty words, the fickle democracy grew certain that victory was at hand. But their hopes slammed hard into reality, for Fate yet had setbacks in store for Athens. Her ordained instrument was the Spartan general Brasidas, already a bright star rising among his people. The prior summer, Brasidas had been a trierarch in the naval assault on the beaches of Pylos, the first to run his ship aground in the failed attempt to establish a foothold. Brasidas had been thrown back, bleeding, long black hair and lambda-blazoned shield left bobbing in the surf. In the thick of that battle, Demosthenes had not known the man's identity, of course, but armed with it thereafter by an all-knowing star-born oracle, he recalled the scene.

Every year of the war thus far, Athens had invaded the territory of its western neighbor and perpetual enemy, the Spartan ally Megara, and this year was to be no exception. But this year, as Fate would have it, Brasidas happened to be passing by Megara on his way north with a small army, and lent assistance to the city. Demosthenes was fated to participate in the battle, and he did so in ignorance, since Thalassia steadfastly refused to tell him the outcome. And she was right to do so, it seemed in the end, for had he gone to war with foreknowledge of failure, he surely could not have made as good a showing for himself as he did, being among the first to infiltrate the city and then later smashing a band of Theban cavalry against its walls and killing its leader.

A defeat was a defeat, but at least the fault could not be laid at his feet.

It was not to be Athens' only defeat of the year. The next one left a bitter taste. Rather than let him march blindly into this next failure, as she had at Megara, Thalassia came to him with counsel.

"Hippokrates might suggest that you join him in an invasion of Boeotia," she said. "Do not become involved."

"He *might?*" Demosthenes asked. "Why the uncertainty?"

Her blunt answer was as much a surprise as anything she had said in the year of their acquaintance. "Because if he does not, then it may well have been your idea instead of his, if not for my having occupied you with other plans."

He did not like to speak of his 'other self,' the Demosthenes who would have lived a different life had Thalassia not fallen into it.

Seeing his discomfort, she shrugged her dismissal. "It doesn't matter now."

"No, tell me. What was to have occurred?

Sighing, she offered up knowledge forbidden to mortal men. She explained how that other, blissfully ignorant Demosthenes, after gathering allies from among his friends in the northwest, would have landed at Siphae, on the west coast of Boeotia, only to discover that one of those friends had betrayed him. His intended diversionary attack beaten back by the forewarned defenders, he would be forced to sail home, leaving his fellow general Hippokrates to face the might of an enemy ready and waiting for him at Delion to the east. Hippokrates and a thousand Athenians would lose their lives, thanks in part to his failure.

After a few moments of stunned silence, the more fortunate Demosthenes whispered, "We must stop it..."

"If you can, then do," Thalassia said, too casually. "So long as you do not participate directly and get yourself killed, I doubt it will affect our purpose."

Demosthenes knew he had little right to be appalled by such talk, but he was. Too frequently, after her exile from his home, he had found himself vocally at odds with Thalassia, mostly on occasions when he knew full well the wiser choice would be to walk away.

Foolishly, he ranted, "How can you say it does not affect us? A thousand men! You pledged to aid Athens."

Her pristine features flashed annoyance, as they always did when he snapped at her. "Don't confuse a city with its people."

"A city *is* its people!"

She dismissed him with a wave and a sneer. "Have this debate with with Socrates sometime, up in the fucking clouds. Meanwhile, down here, I can't protect every man, woman and child of Athens. These are men who would have died anyway if I had never come." Two fingers stabbed Demosthenes' chest, hard enough to force him back. "And who knows, maybe without you there fucking up, they won't die after all."

Demosthenes let her verbal attack land uncontested, and thereafter managed more often to avoid argument with her, if not avoid her altogether.

Weeks later, at a meeting of the Board of Ten, over a table built from the planks of a decommissioned trireme, Demosthenes first laid out the vital importance of Amphipolis to Athens: its timber supplies, access to gold mines and control of the lone bridge over the river Strymon. He noted that Brasidas had spent the summer marching north with seven hundred hoplites who were reported to be Helots serving in exchange for their freedom, and even though the purported purpose of Brasidas's march was to aid the Macedonian king Perdikkas against his enemies, the Lynkesti, it begged the question: what could lead Sparta to send one of her stars on such an errand except the expectation of fair return? Surely Perdikkas, in gratitude, planned to provide Brasidas with troops; and once in the region with such a force assembled, what greater prize could Brasidas seek than Amphipolis?

"And what would stop him from taking it?" Demosthenes posed of his fellow strategoi.

"Thucydides is at Thasos and can sail to the town's relief if needed," Lamachos grumbled.

And fail, and be sent into exile! Demosthenes did not reply.

"It will not be enough!" he said instead, and made what argument he could without insulting the absent Thucydides. "If I am wrong," he finished, "and Brasidas does not come, then I shall be well placed to punish the Macedonian king for betraying us–twice now, by my count."

"Premature, premature," Kleon declared of the plan with a ponderous shaking of his red cheeks. The demagogue's assignment to the post of City Defender in this, his first year of generalship, was ideally suited to his undoubted aim of leveraging the office into more power to sway the very masses to whom he shamelessly catered.

Nikias concurred with his arch-rival; Laches followed, and the answer was sealed.

"It is just as well," Hippokrates said next. "For I was hoping you might aid me, Demosthenes, in a venture I have conceived. You have friends among our allies in the northwest, do you not?"

The venture was as the star-born oracle had ordained: a two-pronged invasion of Boeotia by land and sea, and Demosthenes rebuffed it with a prepared list of reasons why the actually quite reasonable-sounding idea was flawed. In the end, he succeeded to a degree: Boeotia was to be a target of attack this season, but using some other strategy to be determined at the Board's next gathering.

On the way out, Demosthenes caught gray-haired Nikias by the arm.

"I did not wish to say so in front of the rest," he lied to the old man in a conspiratorial whisper, "but the slave I took at Pylos is a servant of Isis and a keen reader of omens. She predicted the eclipse of the sun last year, and the earthquake which caused the sea to rise, and knew that Isarchos would be archon. I do not want it to get out, lest she be labeled a witch or an oracle and my house be swarmed with suppliants, but if she says that Amphipolis is threatened, I cannot stand idle, do you understand?"

The deep creases around superstitious Nikias' lined mouth grew deeper still as he scowled, more in consternation than disbelief, it appeared.

"Hagnon, your son, is there," Demosthenes said, pressing a second line of attack without waiting to see if the first had met with success. "Ask yourself: if Brasidas appeared outside the walls of Amphipolis, absent defenders within, what would Hagnon do to save the town he built with his own blood and sweat?"

Suggesting to any man that his son would yield to the enemy without a fight was a move that risked offense, but he trusted in Nikias' reputation for fair-minded analysis to bring him to the proper conclusion.

Nikias gave no quick answer, but there were signs of deep thought underway behind his sharp eyes. Demosthenes affectionately clasped his shoulder.

"Think on it, friend," he said. "I ask only for two hundred of the citizen cavalry and a hundred volunteers who can shoot a bow. I will raise the infantry myself in Thrace. It seems to me there is little to lose by sending me, and much to gain."

Whether it was fear of omens or knowledge of his son's character which changed his mind, at the next convocation of the Board, Nikias proposed that Demosthenes, son of Alkisthenes of the deme of Thria, be dispatched, along with the meager force he requested, to Amphipolis. Nikias' allies concurred, the nominated general accepted, and the motion was carried. And so, at the time when men and women with tall rakes combed the branches of olive trees so that the fruit fell into the sailcloths spread on the ground below, marking Athens' first fully successful olive harvest in eight summers of siege, one of her generals set sail in defiance of Fate.

PART 3

AMPHIPOLIS

1. A Few Shots

Pyanepsion in the archonship of Isarchos (October 424 BCE)

He missed Athens less than usual, enjoying his time alone in the tiny but lively town on the Thracian side of the serpentine Strymon. Athenians, even Greeks, were a minority in Amphipolis; its population was mostly local, which perhaps explained why this colony yet existed on the same spot where all attempts before it had been quickly laid waste by one Thracian tribe or another.

There were no signs of such tension here. Green-eyed vendors barked a mix of Greek and Thracian from their stalls, women hoisted laden baskets on tattooed arms, and children both black-haired and red darted in and out of alleys waging mock battles. The war between Amphipolis' mother city Athens and her perpetual foe Sparta, burning hotly to the south and west, had not since its earliest days sent a spark sailing in this direction.

For that reason it was unsurprising that the residents would be less than thrilled to have an Athenian general suddenly appear, build a barracks at the foot of their quaint acropolis with its single stone sanctuary of Apollo, and commence raising an army from among nearby Greek allies and the Thracian tribes to the north. Even Nikias' son Hagnon, the colony's founder and still its 'first among equals,' radiated an aura of indifference to the struggle into which his town had been dragged, even if he gave proper lip service where was concerned his allegiance to his home city.

Having now met Hagnon, Demosthenes knew that he would indeed throw the gates open to Brasidas to spare his people from slaughter. Amphipolis would agree with the choice, and rightly thank him for it. The men and women who walked the streets around Demosthenes this chilly afternoon, shopping and hawking and fetching water from the spring, did not much care whether the men who ran the day-to-day affairs of their town gave nominal allegiance to Athens or Sparta.

Their indifference caused Demosthenes no annoyance. He envied them, in fact, and spent as much time as he could just walking aimlessly among them, trying to absorb some of whatever made them happy, sometimes halfway succeeding.

At present, his walk was not aimless. It took him beyond the city walls and down the wide, straight, unpaved path down to the town's little port on the Strymon. He arrived early and sat on the sandy slope above the jetties, looking down on the black water sliding lazily toward the sea, for about an hour until the ships appeared. This morning a messenger had ridden north from Eion, on the coast, bearing word of the three sleek triremes' appearance at the river's estuary. There the ships had furled their sails, stowed masts and dropped oars to push upriver. Now they were here, churning the Strymon's dark, placid surface in difficult maneuvers which the Athenian crews made look easy, pointing their curved prows toward the shallows. Demosthenes stood and watched them come, searching among the standing figures on the decks.

It was but seconds before his eyes found the one he sought: Alkibiades waved madly at the sandy-haired, blue-cloaked figure waiting for him on shore. Demosthenes raised his hand in return. As he did, his gaze fell to the youth's left, where a second familiar figure stood, hooded and cloaked in a gray chlamys for which she had no earthly need, since the limbs it concealed suffered not even from extremes of cold. Thalassia looked back at him, her expression indiscernible at this distance. Why had she come? He searched for sign of Eurydike, too, but found none.

The ships' drafts scraped gravel, stone anchors were thrown, Amphipolitan portsmen caught thick, tarred ropes and secured them to deep-driven mooring posts, and gangplanks were dropped. Alkibiades was among the first to set foot on shore, carrying an unwieldy wooden cross half his own height. Demosthenes went to meet him, and they embraced, while nimble, cloaked Thalassia descended the gangplank as though her soles never touched it. In similar fashion she glided over the pebbles and came to stand at her playmate's shoulder. Demosthenes met her pale eyes and returned the nod and the paler smile that she offered. Hers was not an unwelcome presence in Amphipolis, but neither was it one he felt compelled to receive warmly. They had fallen to hardly speaking in the last year, and to be sure, he had not missed Thalassia. He felt that way not on account of her personality, which apart from a tendency to fly into anger without warning was not all that unpleasant a thing. Well, there was her arrogance, but that was common enough in the circles he traveled. No, Thalassia was unwelcome for what she represented: the encroachment of dark, barely comprehensible forces upon what until now had been his remote, pastoral Thracian sanctuary.

He had spent a month in the clear, fresh air of reality, away from the intoxicating vapor of her madness, and here it was again, caught up with him in a fragrant, beautiful cloud.

Alkibiades raised the gastraphetes he had set down to offer greeting and stood the device in the sand on its tau-shaped, leather covered butt-end. Its wide, curved arms jutted out an arm's length to either side.

"Fifty belly-bows," Alkibiades said with a grin, announcing the ships' cargo. "Plus thirty more men to train at using them and eight hundred skewers ready to taste Spartan meat."

"Well done." Demosthenes spoke dully, but the sentiment was genuine. This shipment brought the total number of belly-bows with which they would meet Brasidas to one hundred. The number of volunteers to train in the weapons' use, men from both Athens and Thrace who had proven their ability with bow or javelin, was even greater.

Looking down at the fencepost-like weapon with its metal rails and catches and currently unstrung crosswise bowstave, Alkibiades lamented, "I've not yet had the chance to play with one. What say we let off a few shots?"

"Let me gather the new volunteers and see to the unloading first. Then we will go to the range."

"No need," Alkibiades returned. He hefted the unloaded weapon and leveled it at Thalassia. "Star-girl, care to act as target?"

"Try it and see," she answered coldly.

"Bah!" Alkibiades lowered the bow. "You are so lucky you got to run her through, Demosthenes. I'd love to have seen that!" He added quickly to Thalassia, "No offense."

She answered with a facial tick that left ambiguous whether offense had been taken. To one who could read her, as well as one so alien could be read, it was apparent: she was in a mood. Demosthenes wondered if he was the cause, but only wondered for a moment before accepting it for a certainty.

When he had rounded up the thirty men and given instructions to the sailors on the unloading and removal of the cargo, he joined his two fellow conspirators for the walk to Amphipolis.

"What news is there?" he asked either of them, but really Alkibiades; he had not yet fully reconciled himself to the other's presence. Though he declined to specify, there was really only one bit of news from home in which he was interested.

Knowing that or not, Alkibiades addressed it: "Defeat and six hundred dead at Delion."

The blow landed softly. Some restless nights of worry had prepared Demosthenes for worse. "And Hippokrates?"

"Among the living. But Thucydides may yet face exile for his part in the failure."

That news provided more of a chill, evidence that perhaps a determined Fate could fight back after all.

In silence but for some idle chatter from Alkibiades, the trio walked at the head of the band of eager, laughing recruits to the barracks complex at the town's eastern edge, just inside its limestone wall. There, in the shadow of the steepest face of the acropolis, a space had been designated for gastraphetes practice. A dozen of the wielders were taking aim and letting loose iron-tipped, javelin-like bolts—launched two at a time, side-by-side—at man-sized targets built from old planks and bailed hay. To one side of the targets sat a heap of debris which prominently included old hoploi, each round shield so full of holes as to be rendered unrecognizable. After a first round of experiments, the users had abandoned using real armor, even retired pieces, for there was no further need for such waste. They knew what they needed to know: the bolts of the belly-bow could punch through both shield and bronze breastplate at up to three hundred yards. It could also do considerable damage to flesh even at its maximum range, which well surpassed that of any hand-drawn bow.

They were met at the range by the captain of the belly-bowmen, an Athenian hunter by the name of Straton. Demosthenes handed the fresh recruits over to Straton and informed him of Alkibiades' desire to 'play' with one of his weapons. All too happy to oblige, Straton had a gastraphetes fetched and told a lieutenant to instruct Alkibiades in its use before leaving to shepherd his recruits through the start of their training regimen.

While the lieutenant demonstrated for Alkibiades how to draw the bowstring by setting his stomach against the propped weapon's butt-end and throwing his weight onto it, Demosthenes suddenly found himself alone beside the silent shadow which had crossed a sea to haunt his life anew.

She was not long silent.

"I don't rate an embrace?" she asked.

Bitterness was imperfectly concealed in her voice. Almost surely the lapse was by design, a silent observation which inspired a moment of rage which Demosthenes contained.

He scarcely knew how to answer, and so just silently watched Alkibiades take his lesson, as did Thalassia. Alkibiades knelt and held the gastraphetes level with his shoulder, took aim at the straw man downfield and, shrugging away the close guidance of his trainer, squeezed the trigger mechanism. With the brief but harsh sound of iron scraping iron, twin bolts let fly.

Both missed the target by wide margins, but the shooter turned to share a wide-mouthed laugh with his two observers, who smiled faintly back.

"Another go," Alkibiades said to his patient trainer. "I want that thing dead!"

As Alkibiades reloaded, Demosthenes found words with which to break the heavy silence.

"Why did Eurydike not come? Did she not wish to see her homeland?"

"No," Thalassia answered coldly. "I'll tell you why later, if you' have a moment and are interested."

"Of course I am interested," Demosthenes snapped. Still he stared at Alkibiades, who seemed to have all but forgotten his observers as he fired bolt after bolt at the target, finally grazing it once.

"Why did you come?"

Thalassia scoffed. "You really expected me to stay in Athens? I did half the work that brought us here. More," she added quietly. "Much more."

Demosthenes, exercising discretion and the muscles of his jaw, gave no reply but stared out over the training ground.

"You should kill Brasidas if you can," Thalassia observed at length. She might have been remarking on the chill in the air.

Now it was Demosthenes' turn to scoff. He had been on his own for a month now, captain of two thousand men and not used to feeling second-in-command. He returned acidly, "Is there any particular spot where you would like his fucking corpse to fall?"

Thalassia's harsh sigh was the very voice of frustration. She took her pale eyes off of the practice field to frown at her rebellious pawn.

"I know you want to be your own man," she said. "That's a good thing. You are. But I am on your side, idiot, and Brasidas is dangerous. That's all. He's smart and clever, and to be honest, if I had gone to Sparta, I probably would have picked him. So just kill him if you can, all right?"

She turned her attention back in time to see Alkibiades, a grown child with a new toy, finally score a hit and raise the heavy gastraphetes skyward in triumph.

"I am so tired of you," Thalassia whispered. Her eyes were on Alkibiades, but it wasn't him she addressed.

2. To the Wolves

She fucked Alkibiades that night in a room above the megaron of the modest, vacant home Demosthenes had rented from its owner for the duration of his stay in Amphipolis. He doubted that the sounds of slapping and groaning and laughter that drifted down through the thin floor of oak planks—Amphipolitan houses were built almost entirely of timber, on account of its abundance—just as he returned from meeting with a band of Thracian recruits represented any deliberate effort by Thalassia to spite him. But neither did he put it past her.

Rather than sitting under the squeaking floorboards, or worse, going up and interrupting, he walked outside in the twilight. His aimless steps took him to the base of the acropolis and thence to a rocky outcropping above the barracks which still smelled of freshly cut pine. From this height one could look over the city wall of Amphipolis and see the mountains to the north looming over blue-tinted grassland that was alive in the night's gentle breeze.

There he sat and tried to clear his thoughts. His head would need to be clear. According to accounts provided by sympathizers in Macedon, Brasidas was on the march, and his army was growing. The day of his arrival at Amphipolis, if indeed he chose to come here at all, knowing, as he must, that it was now defended, could not be known precisely. But it would be soon.

Demosthenes had taken measures to ensure that Brasidas would at least try to claim the city. With Amphipolitan accomplices, he had planted bait. If Brasidas took it, he would come believing that the sole bridge over the Strymon, which lay within sight of Amphipolis, was to be turned over to him by pro-Spartan traitors in the town, allowing him to cross easily and lay siege.

The traitors did exist. But so did the loyal men who were spying on those traitors, planting ideas in their heads and helping to compose their 'secret' dispatches to Brasidas.

Yes, Brasidas would come. And he was clever and dangerous. Why had Thalassia felt the need to tell him that? As if he did not know, and as if he needed more weight on his shoulders than he already bore in knowing of Athens' fated defeat.

Bitch.

Athene would bring her favored city a victory, Demosthenes told himself. But he had trouble believing it. Not believing that victory would come, although that could scarcely be certain, but of who would bring it.

Not the virgin goddess, but a whore and her slave.

Thalassia's hubris, her easy dismissal of the gods, was infectious, and that was another reason he had come to resent her, he realized. Over the past year, he had slowly lost his gods, for was there any room for Olympians in Thalassia's universe of lines and layers? Praying had become a struggle for him, and when he did pray, it was so plainly insincere that it seemed impossible that Pallas, if she existed, could answer with anything but a sneer.

If she existed. Damn, what had star-girl done to him?

"Am I interrupting?"

It was *her* voice, as if summoned by his thoughts. The sound of it tensed his limbs and sent pebbles tumbling off the outcropping from under his sandal as he shot upright. He looked up and saw her. Between her breasts Thalassia clutched a thin shift of Amorgos silk that wrapped her deceptively soft flesh. The garment was all but translucent in the starlight, and each gentle wind that gusted up the slope endeavored to steal it. Her feet were bare on the cold, rough rocks, but of course she would scarcely notice that.

"Sorry if I scared you." She smiled, took a long stride that exposed her hairless cleft, and sat gracefully beside him.

For a while they stared out over moonlit Thrace together.

"I'm sorry about earlier," Thalassia finally said.

"You are good at that," Demosthenes said.

"At what?"

"At saying and doing things and then apologizing for them later."

In Thalassia's silence, Demosthenes sensed swallowed anger.

Likely not the first thing she had swallowed that night, he thought, and was surprised by his own pettiness.

But when Thalassia spoke, it was softly. "I think the words you were looking for were 'I accept.' Or if you actually give a shit, maybe 'I'm sorry, too.'"

Demosthenes exhaled, and his breath turned to mist in the night air. Plains winters could be harsh. There might well be snow by the time battle came.

"Alkibiades will be missing you by now," he said. "Do not let me keep you from him."

"Just stop being an asshole for five minutes. I had hoped..." Thalassia bowed her head to look down either at the rocks or at her feet drawn up in front of her barely clad body. "Never mind. Let me tell you a story about those mountains in front of you."

Indeed, Demosthenes' eyes were on the distant dark peaks, even if his mind was not.

Without waiting for his approval, Thalassia began, "Of course you know of Sitalkes."

He did. Some five summers ago, all Greece had shuddered in terror at the thought that the great horde raised by the Thracian king Sitalkes to ravage neighboring Macedon might next turn its attention south, to Greece. When instead the great army dissolved by internal intrigue, all Greece had heaved a sigh of relief.

"His army was really a collection of tribal war bands," she said, once more stating the obvious. "The leaders of those bands did whatever was in their own interest, including using the forces they had raised for Sitalkes to settle old scores. One such band was on its way west to join the horde when its path took it through the territory of a rival tribe, where it paused long enough to raze villages and slaughter its enemy near to extinction.

"Some lived, of course. One survivor was a girl of fifteen, a month away from her wedding. She was enslaved along with her younger sister. The two were taken west, through those mountains there." Thalassia's pale gaze was on them now, too. "The girls' captors beat and raped them every night."

The tale's dark turn chilled Demosthenes' blood, but Thalassia pressed on.

"The younger one was beaten to the edge of death. Since she could no longer walk, rather than carry her, her captors threw her off a cliff. Her sister tried to follow her, but she was pulled back from the edge and bound. She made it through the march alive and was sold to a Thessalian slaver, who sold her to another, who eventually brought her to the slave markets of Athens."

Well before Thalassia had finished, a weight had settled on Demosthenes' chest and steadily increased, stealing his breath.

Thalassia, as if in spite, added another stone to the pile: "The slaver gave the girl a new, Greek name," she said, "to replace the Thracian one he knew his buyers wouldn't like."

Mercifully, she didn't speak the false name. Demosthenes knew it, and she knew he knew. *Eurydike.*

Overcome, he shut his eyes and used a long breath to drag himself back from the brink of tears. "What name was she born with?" he asked feebly.

"It doesn't matter," Thalassia said. "She never wants to hear it again." She nodded at the distant peaks. "Just as she would prefer not to look again on the mountains where her sister's corpse was food for wolves."

As the speaker surely intended, the image sprang up of its own accord in Demosthenes' mind's eye of a half-dead Thracian girl plunging to her misery's end, while from above her sister watched, helpless screams resounding off the mountainside.

The corners of his eyes stung anew.

"She told you this?" Demosthenes asked.

"Yes," Thalassia said. "I think she would have told you, too. If you had ever asked."

Demosthenes gave her a hard glare. Though she was right, the shortcoming was his own, and Thalassia was only the messenger, she was present, and made a satisfying target besides, this woman who had stolen his gods and ate his manhood for breakfast.

"You burden me with this now," he said angrily, "so soon before the most important battle of my life? Why? Because I didn't greet you warmly enough? Is that all you know how to do—cut down anyone who slights you?" He raised his hand in a wave of dismissal. "Go back to your man-whore and suck what pleasure you can from him before he looks at you wrong and you have to cut his throat."

He finished with a growl that in fact masked fear. Why did he knowingly provoke her? Did some part of him wish to die?

He did not dare look over at Thalassia, but he heard her wet her lips as though to speak. Ultimately she said nothing, just sat there in silence for long, agonizing moments in which Demosthenes could only stare with bated breath at the horizon and wonder whether his mad, almost suicidal assault had breached her walls to expose the molten fury he knew dwelt within.

At long last he heard Thalassia stir. She rose, clutching her silk about her. Without sparing him a glance, and with nimble, soundless steps, she retreated from the outcropping. Demosthenes did not watch her go.

For four days he did not see her. No one did. She vanished, and with her a horse from the cavalry stables.

Four days passed, and Brasidas came.

3. Arrhidaeus

"I fear treachery, my prince."

This warning came from Beres, captain of Arrhidaeus's personal bodyguard, sworn to him in all things and trusted above all others by the young prince, who was nephew to Perdikkas, long reigning king of Macedon. The two rode side-by-side on the tree-lined western shore of Lake Koroneia, just north and east of Therme, the Macedonian port city where Arrhidaeus had spent the season.

"You always do, Beres," the prince observed with a smile.

"At least a quarter of the time, I am right," the older man replied. "It's why you're alive."

"True, Beres. Very true. But our purpose in coming here today is to thwart treachery, is it not?"

"One should never fully trust an unsigned note, my prince."

Arrhidaeus waved a ring-laden hand. "Ah, but when said note offers to give up names in a plot against me, can you not see how the sender might be wise not to sign it? Should it be discovered, it would mean his death."

Scarred, silver-haired Beres emitted a low growl. "Still, my prince..." His keen eyes never stopped scanning the wood and mirror-smooth surface of the lake.

"We are solidly within Macedonian territory," Arrhidaeus reassured the man who had been his protector for all of the prince's twenty years. "Surely there could be no force at large this close to Therme that your men cannot handle. And all twelve of them are at present scouting the shores of the lake for the messenger we have been instructed to meet, which furthermore is to be a lone female. Hardly any threat, if that's what they find. And should they discover otherwise, I fully trust in you to deliver me safely back to town." The prince chuckled. "No, I feel no fear today, Beres. There is but opportunity afoot."

"I suppose, my prince."

A quarter-hour later, three riders of the Arridhaeus's personal guard galloped down from a rocky, pine-covered promontory overlooking the lake and halted before the prince and Beres. One of the three had seated on his horse in front of him a dark-haired, foreign-looking female passenger in a gray hooded cloak.

That man reported to Beres, "She was alone, Captain, and unarmed."

Arrhidaeus grinned. "You see, Beres. It is not always a trap!"

The guardsman on whose horse the woman sat helped her to the ground, where she knelt.

"Prince Arrhidaeus?" she asked.

She used the Greek to give his title. Greek had only lately been adopted by the Macedonian court, but Arrhidaeus's Ionian tutor had served him well, and so he answered her fluently in that tongue. "You have found me, sweetling. I take it you have something for me? Better still if you *are* the something." He laughed, and so too did the guardsmen, even though they knew not a word of Greek between them.

Beres, who did know Greek, laughed not at all. He rarely did. He only stared with narrowed eyes at the messenger, who momentarily stood.

"Would you answer me a question, lord?" she asked in suitably respectful tones.

"If I can and must," Arrhidaeus said. "But I hope it is only one."

"It is, lord, and a simple one," she said. "Do you have any

sons?"

Arrhidaeus laughed. "Sons? No. And as yet no wife to plant one in. Is that all? Strange question."

"Enough chatter," Beres interjected. "Give us the names."

The woman whirled and in a flash had drawn the sword of the nearest mounted guard.

"Kill h—" Beres began to shout, but before he finished, his neck was spouting blood from the deep gash carved into it with precision by the stolen blade. Hot droplets of it peppered Arrhidaeus's arm, which like his other limbs was frozen in place by disbelief.

Two more guards were slain by the time Beres's silent corpse had finished sliding from the saddle to settle upon the earth in a heap. The third guardsman was raising his blade for an attack which had no hope of landing when Arrhidaeus at last found the presence of mind to wheel his mount and kick its flanks in desperate flight.

A final groan rose behind the prince, and not a second later some force yanked him backward from his saddle. He landed hard on his back, the breath knocked from his body, and into view above him stepped the cloaked woman, the messenger, wielding the guardsman's sword, its blade smeared with blood.

"Please..." Arrhidaeus whispered. "I will make you wealthy beyond imagining. You may have whatever you wish, only spare me."

To Arrhidaeus's despair, she gave no answer. The expression on her youthful face was impassive, but the eyes... her two eyes were like shards of pale ice, and their gleam told Arrhidaeus something of his killer: this woman was no hapless, disposable wretch who had been bribed, coerced, or otherwise cynically manipulated, as many assassins were, into embarking on a virtually suicidal undertaking. No, here was an assassin who had slain many men before today, and the light in her eyes bespoke not pleasure—for a good assassin was no bloodthirsty cretin—but a certain calm satisfaction.

"O sweet Koure, embr—," Arrhidaeus next intoned.

His prayer to the Maiden went unfinished, for the sword borne by a supple, unlikely hand plunged swiftly down, piercing his breast from front to back, straight through the heart, and making of his royal blood an offering to that dark, venerable goddess.

4. Bridge of Death

The quiet roar of two thousand soldiers lying in wait filled the broad space just inside Amphipolis's southwestern gate. Armor clattered, men's shields grated against those of their neighbors, and the butt-spikes of spears narrowly missed skewering feet, prompting muttered curses. Soldiers could be kept largely silent with threat of the lash, but horses could not, and there were two hundred of those drawn up with their riders behind Demosthenes this night, whinnying and snorting with little regard for stealth. But fortunately, an army lying in ambush needed only to be quieter than the army whose arrival it awaited, which was of necessity on the march and louder by far.

For unknown but likely self-evident reasons, the closed gate behind which they waited was called the Horseman's Gate. Tonight it would live up to the name. When two pegs in Amphipolis's stone walls were yanked free, releasing massive counterweights and throwing open the gate's heavy double doors of iron-girt firs, the frost-hardened Thracian soil would shudder with the passage of a column of Athenian citizen cavalry five wide and forty deep.

Demosthenes sat at the head of this waiting column, not astride Maia, who was not bred for war, but on a charger named Balios who perpetually tossed his black head back and forth in anticipation of the charge. The beast's neck and sides were armored with hanging sheets of stiff leather onto which were sewn thin plates of iron, and Balios' head was protected by a faceplate of contoured bronze. The horse's harness was equipped with reins, but they would see infrequent use, for war-horses were trained to respond to a rider's legs, leaving arms free for the business of dealing death.

A season ago, when Demosthenes had charged the

Boeotian cavalry at Megara, then as now atop Balios, reins and a felt saddle had been the extent of his riding gear, but Thalassia had changed that. On the beast's back was now a seat of stiff, padded leather and from its either side hung loops into which the rider placed his feet. They gave better leverage and control, Thalassia claimed, and from having trained with them Demosthenes knew she was right–when he could remember to keep his feet in them. A number of the other riders today would use the new equipment, but most had scoffed. Doubtless even more would laugh when and if they heard Thalassia's suggestion of giving their mounts iron shoes.

Under his right arm Demosthenes cradled his lance, like a hoplite's spear but thinner and lighter and with a conical iron tip less likely than a flat blade to become lodged in its victim. Yet the lance inevitably would be lost or broken anyway, and that was when he would draw the long, slashing cavalryman's sword of virgin Athenian steel hanging in its hide scabbard beneath the armor of Balios's left flank. While most of the citizen cavalry wore the same bronze breastplates they wore when fighting on foot as hoplites, Demosthenes wore a corselet of overlapping iron scales, like the armor of his mount, which left his arms bare and stopped just above the thigh. His legs below the knee were wrapped tightly with strips of plain leather; few Athenian cavalrymen wore boots into war, for boots to them were signifiers of their membership in the *hippeis* class, too ornate and expensive to risk seeing slashed open or soiled with gore. His helmet was a shell of bronze which left the ears uncovered and flanked his bare face with scrolling, downturned cheek pieces, and from its crest flowed a mane of white horsehair, the sign of his rank.

So arrayed, Demosthenes waited atop eager Balios for word on the progress of the enemy army. Brasidas had marched his force through the night over rugged terrain from the pro-Spartan city of Stagiros on the belief that the key bridge over the Strymon would be turned over to him by traitors in Amphipolis. In this, one might say he was half-right: roughly *half* of his army would be allowed across the river before the trap was sprung.

Where Brasidas expected the sun to rise on an Amphipolis besieged, daybreak would find instead a battle already well under way.

Sparse, tiny flakes of snow began to swirl gently in the pre-dawn darkness, vanishing as they touched the cold ground or the skin of a horse. After a seeming eternity, the Thracian youth serving as runner at last appeared at the top of the city wall, rappelled down on a waiting rope and raced over to Demosthenes to deliver a message in heavily accented Greek.

"Five minutes and they'll be in range!"

Were secrecy not a requirement, Demosthenes would have used those five minutes to wheel his horse to face his men and exhort them to battle, telling them, rightly, that a victory today would deliver a crushing blow not just to one Spartan army but to Sparta herself. He might remind them that Brasidas's host had just completed a forced nighttime march and was not expecting a fight straightaway, whereas the Athenians and their allies were well rested and looking forward to battle. But this was an ambush, and so he said nothing, but just stared straight ahead at the starlit Horseman's Gate and counted down in silence.

When but a few seconds remained, he whispered a quick prayer to a goddess whose existence he doubted and raised his left hand skyward. The hand then descended to point at the trumpeter standing not far off, who in response raised his horn and blew a low, clear note which soared into the night sky and settled there for a moment, alone, before falling into a sea of blood-curdling war cries. The pegs were pulled, the sandbags descended, the Horseman's Gate flew wide, and two hundred Athenian chargers bearing two hundred riders wrapped in bronze and leather thundered out five-by-five onto the plain south of Amphipolis in search of an enemy to kill.

They galloped into a land of shades, of deep blues and flitting black shadows, of swirling snowflakes and glints of silver moonlight on the distant enemy's spear blades and helmets. As expected, Brasidas had marched his heavy troops, his hoplites, over the bridge first. Once there, they began forming up into a phalanx six deep facing the city on the possibility of just such a sally as that which Amphipolis's defenders were mounting.

The enemy hoplites furthest east, those who had crossed over first and assumed the place of honor on the army's right wing, were Demosthenes' targets of choice. The blazons on their round shields were not visible yet through the inky darkness, but there was little doubt of what the light would show. According to informers on the route of Brasidas's march, the core of Brasdidas's three thousand spearmen and lighter troops was a band of seven hundred Helots offered their freedom in exchange for service on the battlefield. Maybe they were not true Spartan Equals, but here on this plain, to the men obliged to face down their gleaming spear blades, they were Spartans all the same.

An enemy trumpeter sounded a note of alarm, and Brasidas's troops raised a shout of their own that drowned out the cries of the far fewer horsemen charging them. The defending hoplites locked their round shields, dug spear-butts into the cold earth and lowered the points to receive the charge.

Were this how the battle were to unfold, with cavalry charging formed-up hoplites on open ground, the horsemen would have been doomed, for when faced with ranks of bristling spears, horses would ever turn aside at the last moment, even throwing their riders in their refusal to consign themselves to certain death. But that would not happen. Death remained a possibility today, as on any day of battle, but Demosthenes had no intention of throwing away the life of Balios or those of the two hundred citizens, among the wealthiest in Athens, following in formation behind him.

The thing which was to avert doom this day passed noiselessly overhead in the night sky, insubstantial black wisps which became real only when they hammered the enemy line, sending men's shades screaming into the kingdom of the eldest god. The one hundred wielders of the gastraphetes had released their first volley before even the Horseman's Gate had swung open, and now they fired a second over the heads of the charging Athenian cavalry. To give the bowmen time for at least a third round and perhaps a fourth, Demosthenes led his column not straight at Brasidas's line but in an undulating arc which had the secondary effect of making the enemy wonder where the blow eventually would land. An arrow slashed harmlessly to the earth just inside Demosthenes' vision, showing that Brasidas, despite his people's hatred of arrows, had not turned down a contribution of archers from some ally or another. But the hail of missiles was sparse compared even to the sprinkling snow, and it accomplished about as much.

The same could not be said of the mighty black bolts which plunged two-by-two into Brasidas's line. The shooters atop the walls of Amphipolis, all archers skilled with normal bows before their half-season of training with the new weapon, concentrated their fire on the enemy right, where the play of winter moonlight at last illuminated a solid wall of lambdas.

Even more than most fighters, a Spartan trusted none but a countryman to stand at his right and share his shield, but today the massive arrows of the gastraphetes refused to treat the shield of a Lakedaemonian differently than any other. Great holes were punched in the crimson lambdas and in the leather curiasses behind them. The spears of dying men scythed groundward, forcing the living to break ranks to avoid the loss of life or limb. In the darkness it was impossible to know how many fell, but four volleys of two hundred arrows each meant that by the time the clash of arms began, nearly a thousand merciless iron-tipped bolts had already ripped into a segment of the enemy line where stood just a few hundred men.

It was just after that fourth volley struck that Demosthenes drove the Athenian cavalry into the very same spot. It had been a great risk to rely on an unproven weapon to buckle a wall of shields held by the most fearsome fighters in all of Greece, if not the world, but the risk had paid off. Thanks to the belly-bows, instead of plunging headlong into certain death, the citizen cavalry of Athens ploughed the field of Lakedaemonians, whose ash spear shafts parted as stalks of wheat before the hippeis going to work with their lances. They jabbed down into necks and collarbones while their hoplite victims struggled to bring shields and unwieldy spears into position in time to give something back. Some threw down their spears and drew short swords, which made up for their lack of reach with swiftness of stroke, and from behind shields riven with fist-sized holes they stabbed upward at horses' necks and riders' thighs.

Their efforts were in vain. So weakened by missiles was the Spartan line that the Athenian charge lost almost no momentum in colliding with it. Each rider raced through the widening gap in the broken Spartan ranks and remained within the phalanx only long enough to thrust lances into one picked target each, skewering men like goats for roasting. By the time the Athenian cavalrymen had swords in hand to replace lost lances, they had ridden through the body of enemy troops entirely and burst out through the rear.

Demosthenes led the column far enough that all the ranks behind him could pass clean through the body of enemy troops without slowing. Then he brought Balios around and doubled back in time to see, over the helmets of the Spartan ranks, a thousand more shadowy defenders of Amphipolis pouring out from the Horseman's Gate to form up opposite Brasidas's army, which now suffered a wide gap in its right. No sooner had the defenders drawn up than they advanced at a run against a reeling and confused enemy.

Strewn with the corpses on the ground in his path, Demosthenes made out the dark, still hulks of three horses. The loss of their citizen riders was plenty of cause for mourning, but in the cold calculus of war it was as nothing, for no fewer than two hundred enemy now lay dead or dying. The Spartan contingent of Brasidas's army, its heart, had been effectively cut out. Brasidas himself, perhaps, was dead, for his helmet crest, assuming he wore one, was nowhere visible. Absent, too, were any long Spartan locks beneath the toppled pilos-style helmets of the Spartan corpses, lending credence to the reports that they were Helots.

Now, with the Spartan contingent broken, would be a proper time to pause and offer terms to the allies who had marched with Sparta, but Brasidas's army should be not just stopped here, but smashed–or so spoke a certain star-born prophetess whose current whereabouts were unknown. Instead of losing Amphipolis without a fight, Athens would keep the rich gold deposits of Mount Pangaion and vast forests of shipworthy Thracian timber. Best of all, a half-dozen other subject cities of the Athenian Empire would not be prompted out of fear to throw open their gates to Brasidas.

Thalassia had given him reason enough not to halt the battle and offer terms, but he had another reason. The battle delirium had taken root in him, much as he tried to stave it off. Madness was not useful in battle except to those barbarians who fought with no cohesion or order but relied instead on the feats of frenzied individuals bent on winning personal glory, but who were likelier by far to win themselves a grave. But today a civilized Athenian yielded himself, at least a little, to possession by the war god and ordered no pause. Instead he raised his long sword high and kicked his horse to a gallop. Seeing the bright white horsehair plume of their hipparch's helmet streaming through the dark in the direction of the enemy rear, the rest of the citizen cavalry followed.

Brasidas' force was now beset on two sides, front and back, and many of its rearmost ranks turned to face the returning Athenian horse, setting their spears.

Many of them turned–but not all–for in the darkness, confusion reigned. Demosthenes aimed his charge at those who seemed the least prepared, and the column of heavy horse thundered with little resistance through the ranks of the center-left, Chalkideans by the appearance of their arms, scattering most of those who were not cut down by slashing Athenian steel. But this time, instead of leading the column straight through, he caused it to linger within the mass of enemy spearmen, deadly though they could be to man or mount, to inflict as much havoc as their long blades could wreak in the short time that remained before the two armies collided.

When that time did come, Demosthenes withdrew, along with his comrades, behind the enemy's shattered right wing to watch and wait. The two armies met, filling the brightening sky with a sound like the clap of a Titan. The *othismos*, the pushing match, was joined. Bellowing war cries faded into groans of exertion and, for the unlucky, into screams of pain as the two masses of men packed themselves flesh upon flesh, bronze upon bronze with life-saving shields interlocked, dug their feet into the snow-covered plain of Thrace and pushed with all the strength in their hearts and limbs. Such contests could and often did last for hours. This one did not. Having been cut in two and deployed in a makeshift fashion to begin with, Brasidas' force was almost immediately enveloped on both wings. First the Chalkideans on the left, and next the center, began to break and run south. Some men, the last to have crossed the bridge just before the attack, even shed their armor and cast themselves into the Strymon to be carried by the freezing current to what they hoped would be safety downstream.

Heart soaring, Demosthenes rejoined the battle. He could not know how many men's blood he spilled that day with long, sweeping strokes of his sword from the back of Balios. No fewer than ten, certainly, but he did not keep count. He had kept his feet the whole time in Thalassia's dangling saddle-loops, and they likely saved him more than once from being thrown. They lengthened his sword stroke, too, and increased the force behind each blow. Well before the battle had ended, that portion of his mind which remained rational had concluded that all of Athens' cavalry must be so equipped, regardless of its natural resistance to change.

By the time pink fingers stretched across the sky, the battle east of the Strymon had turned to a rout. Demosthenes worked his way toward the river's bank, cutting down a group of fleeing Argileans on the way. At first opportunity, he looked across the river in search of some sign of how the fighting had gone in the western hills, where Alkibiades had waited overnight in a wooded depression with a thousand light infantry. Half of those under his command were Thracian swordsmen who had come down from Rhodope for nothing more than glory and the opportunity to strip the arms of those they killed; Demosthenes caught sight of a band of those men now, unmistakable with the fox-tail tassels of their soft caps flapping in time with their steps. They were running hard in pursuit of some enemy infantry who had slung their shields on their backs and fled north, toward where plains gave way to marshland. Perhaps the routed enemy did not know that they soon would find themselves trudging through knee-deep water and suctioning mud, or perhaps they did, and wrongly hoped the fox-tailed Thracians, who knew the land well, would be discouraged from following.

***

By full sunrise, the Athenian victory on both banks was complete. Five or six hundred of Brasidas's light troops were on the run through the northern marshes ahead of their tireless Thracian pursuers, but nearer and more pressingly, a band of about two hundred enemy hoplites had managed to withdraw to the bridge and hold it against sustained infantry assault from the eastern bank. Demosthenes had not ordered such an assault. No one had–it had simply developed in the frenzy of battle, as was often the case–but when he arrived on the scene and saw the Athenian corpses piling up, he called its halt.

As the Athenians withdrew, he saw who led the band of holdouts on the bridge. He had met him once before, briefly, having stood almost face to face with him during the failed Spartan naval assault on the beaches of Pylos, where the Equal had been the first trierarch to run his ship aground. The honor it had won him had helped make him a general.

Brasidas.

5. Brasidas

He stood unhelmed, flowing dark Spartiate locks clinging to his high forehead and angular, bloodied cheekbones. His right hand rested defiantly on the hilt of his sheathed sword, and on his left arm hung a battered lambda-blazoned hoplon.

That Brasidas was not among the dead would disappoint Thalassia—wherever she was. (Why did he sense she was somewhere near, watching the battle with her overkeen eyes?) Let her call his survival a failure if she would. By any reasonable human measure, a great victory had been won this day.

And the day was not yet over. There was still time yet for Brasidas to join the ranks of the dead.

The bridge was packed from bank to bank, rail to rail with soldiers. They spilled onto the land, too, forming walls of shields facing east and west. Half the Spartans and allies were bloody and battered while the rest were fresh, as though they had been caught between the two battles on the east bank and west, participating in neither. All of the holdouts were hoplites, and the gentle, chaotic motion of their tall, closely packed spears made the bridge seem almost a living thing.

At the head of the pack, on the side facing Amphipolis, Brasidas stood. Around him and comprising the front two ranks were perhaps thirty more survivors of his army's core of freed Helots. At the Spartans' feet stood a tangled heap of corpses of Athenians and Amphipolitans, a makeshift palisade of flesh bound to interfere with any further attempt to dislodge them.

Of course, the standoff had an obvious solution, and it did not escape Demosthenes. After the end of the battle's first phase, Straton had brought his troop of gastraphetes-wielders down from the walls of Amphipolis; but consulting with the huntsman now, Demosthenes learned that the belly-bows could not be put to further use until a stock of used bolts could be harvested from the frosty earth and from the bowels of enemies already slain.

There was nothing to lose by talking, then, and something to gain, if not the holdouts' surrender: time for ammunition to be collected.

"You men!" Demosthenes called down over the bridge from his lines a safe distance away. "Spartans and their allies! You have nothing to be ashamed of this day! There is no dishonor in suffering an honest defeat, and so I offer you the chance to leave this place with your honor intact. Surrender only your arms and your general, and you may keep your lives and your freedom!"

Brasidas, long hair matted with blood and cheek bearing a deep gash, did not give his men time to consider deserting him. He shouted back, "That is ever the way with you Athenians, is it? Willing to fight so long as the going is easy, but when the real work begins you start throwing about something even cheaper than your arrows: *words!* Come finish us if you've got the balls, *hippopornoi!*"

The term was new to Demosthenes. *Horse-whores.* Perhaps Brasidas had invented it, or perhaps it was a part of the vocabulary of the Spartans, who so despised horsemen—ranking them second only to archers in cowardice—that the unit Sparta called its 'cavalry' marched and fought on foot.

Whatever the insult meant, Demosthenes brushed it off along with the fat snowflakes which had settled on his cloak, and replied, "I think my offer is a magnanimous one. Refuse it and find yourselves spitted like sheep by arrows that treat bronze like the silks your wives wear now while they seduce your slaves. The archers are on their way, and you make good targets packed shoulder-to-shoulder on that bridge. Those of you who would use reason and think for yourselves, be not afraid of one man, this general who has led you to defeat! Be afraid of the skewer that bears your name, for we have plenty to go around!"

By the time Demosthenes finished, he was forced to shout over a war-chant, some words of blood and honor by Tyrtaios or other martial poet of Lakonia. Brasidas was the first to raise his voice, but soon was joined by the whole of the thirty-strong Spartan contingent. These uplifted Helots, it seemed, were as willing as any Equal to die at the word of their highborn commander.

After one verse, Brasidas withdrew his voice from the soaring elegy, drew his sword and clashed its blade against the edge of his battered shield, once, twice, three times. On the first clash, the chanting ceased. On the second, the Spartan contingent around him locked shields and set their spears, those who had them, while the rest of the seething mass on the bridge turned its backs to the hundreds of watchers arrayed on the Strymon's western bank.

On the third clash, they charged.

The tide of men surged east, toward Alkibiades and the men he led, freshly emerging from the hills. Alkibiades' force consisted almost entirely of javelin-armed Imbrian light infantry, whose crescent-shaped shields of hide-covered wicker had no chance of withstanding a crushing metal tide such as that which they faced. Had the Thracians stayed with the main body instead of breaking ranks to chase their enemy into the marsh, it might have been different. Then, at least, Alkibiades might have made up in numbers what his force lacked in quality. As it was, the scant one hundred Athenian hoplites under Alkibiades' command stood only two ranks deep between hastily formed wings of light infantry.

To their credit, they all stood their ground, the Athenians at the center setting their spears and locking shields to receive the charge. Alkibiades himself was among them, in front, easily picked out by his shield rimmed with gold and inlaid in fragile ivory with a figure of winged Eros wielding a thunderbolt.

To prevent Demosthenes' men on the east bank intervening, Brasidas had left a rear-guard, and a fearsome one at that: about half of the total surviving Spartan contingent kept their hard eyes and lambda-blazoned shields facing the rising sun while their fellows streamed away. Those left behind were the most grievously wounded of the bunch, men whose faces were masks of gore, whose breastplates bore round holes from which blood issued; men who could hardly stand without the aid of their spears. But their wounds made them hardly less formidable, for as the bridge emptied they had slowly fallen back to its mouth where they formed up seven across and two ranks deep to form a spear-studded wall of flesh and bronze that filled the space between the bridge's rails. They were doomed, these men, and they knew it, but they knew also that their sacrifice was not in vain. Though fourteen men could not hope to defeat an Athenian army, given the strength of their position they could hardly fail to delay it long enough that by the time any relief crossed over, the fighting on the west bank would be over.

Before joining the westward tide, Brasidas clapped several of the doomed men on their armored shoulders and spoke words inaudible over the war cries of the three hundred or more men getting underway behind him. He could hardly have told them much more than, "Die well."

The order for a frontal assault on the bridge hovered on Demosthenes' lips, but it never landed. No, there was simply too much to lose. Any force that managed to cross that bridge would do so over a heap of its own dead.

The lone alternative was a trail leading north through the marshes, which led to a ford. Cavalry could reach the ford and cross it in eight minutes, give or take, and then to reach the battlefield would take them the same again, by which time the fight was all but certain to be over.

Still, something had to be done.

Digging his heels into Balios' flanks Demosthenes drove forward into the Strymon's chill, swift waters. When the charger sensed no end in sight to the rising water, Demosthenes laid a hand alongside the beast's twisting neck to calm him as the current lapped his sweating haunches. By the time they reached the river's midpoint, Balios' back was fully submerged and the cupped iron plates of Demosthenes' armor clinked and flapped as foaming water swirled under and around them. The horse was scarcely visible but for his snout, but still he obeyed the labored, submarine kicks from his determined rider until at last, fighting the current that labored to shove him into the sea, Balios emerged from the broad Strymon trailing water in streams like some steed of Nereus bursting from a white-capped wave. The horse's forehooves planted at last on solid earth, he resumed his gallop and must have shared his rider's sense of triumph as together they set their sights on the backs of fleeing Spartans. The deep crossing had been new to Balios, but this, the riding down of a fleeing enemy, was an endeavor he understood.

Behind, encouraged by their hipparch's success, others of the citizen cavalry were attempting the ford, some with better luck than others. Of the eight who set out and at whom Demosthenes gave an occasional backward glance, five made it, the other three being washed downstream where men and beasts were sure eventually to find some way to shore, with or without the aid of the comrades who scrambled to offer aid.

Ahead, to the west, two masses of men, one screaming and running full tilt, the other grim and still, collided. The great clash of hundreds of overlapped shields rang out over the Strymon, and dying groans soared skyward whilst shades fled into the earth as men on both sides inevitably were cut down. Brasidas had aimed his charge directly at the Athenian hoplite center rather than at the weaker flanks which almost certainly would have given way. It was a risky strategy which required the Athenian phalanx to collapse immediately, for if they held for even a few minutes then Brasidas's force risked envelopment by the light-armed wings, who could then cast javelins at will into his unshielded flanks.

But if the center broke, the Spartans' way to freedom would be clear. Demosthenes knew he would have made the same choice in Brasidas's position, or he wished to think so.

He rode hard toward this freshly developed Battle of the Strymon Bridge, where the shoving match was on. Defeated men pushed with all the strength left in their tired limbs to steal freedom back from the maw of defeat, while their foes dug in heels to complete a victory already won. The latter had heart, but the former had cause to fight harder, and they had the momentum, too.

The prayer that Demosthenes sent into the bleak Thracian sky on Alkibiades' behalf was a somewhat empty one, but even had the words been heartfelt, not even a god could have staved off the inevitable. After holding fast for less than a minute, the Athenian line shattered.

Maybe the gods did send one small blessing: knowing that he was beaten, Brasidas gave no pause for slaughter. The instant the way was clear, his men broke into a run, making a line straight for the woodland cover which not an hour ago had been used to deadly effect against them.

But whether they knew it yet or not, their freedom was

far from certain. Pursuit was hard on their heels. Demosthenes' eyes hunted down Brasidas in the mass of troops, and found him quickly enough near the rear of the fleeing mass. Having stood on the eastern edge of the bridge, he had been among the last to leave it.

Demosthenes craned his neck to shout back at those comrades who had succeeded in fording the river with him, a number which was growing as more made the attempt for a second and third time.

"Brasidas!" he cried. "Kill Brasidas!"

He kicked his heels in the stirrups and urged Balios on, though the beast could hardly move any faster. The frosted plain shook beneath pounding hooves, chunky snowflakes flew past in a blur, and all Demosthenes saw was Brasidas, hair flying around the rim of the bouncing hoplon slung on his back.

But the enemy general must have felt those hooves and known what they meant for his chances of escape, for after shouting orders left and right he stopped short and whirled to stand his ground, and so did all the fifteen remaining Spartans, whose shields flew from their backs to form a hasty wall. Those who had lugged their heavy spears from the bridge were glad now to have kept them; they dug in the butt-spikes and lowered the shafts to welcome the oncoming pursuit. Brasidas had only his sword, which he drew and held ready.

The sight sent a fresh surge of battle delirium through Demosthenes' veins, but not enough to turn him into a blind fool. Squeezing Balios' flanks, he veered right, away from the shield wall, denying Brasidas the engagement he desired, and raised a hand in the signal for encirclement. The five or so Athenians immediately behind him obeyed, splitting left and right and riding a ring around their trapped quarry.

Even now, Brasidas was not one to give up. He shouted another command, and the wall of fourteen brave freed Helots disintegrated. Its members, shrieking war cries, charged their mounted pursuers with weapons held high like so many sheep-raiding Illyrian hordesmen.

Three of their number—along with Brasidas himself—came after Demosthenes, easily singled out by his helmet's white plume. He wheeled Balios away, but the four assailants spread out with the aim of converging on him from different directions. As quickly as that, hunters had become prey.

Demosthenes kept what distance he could from his attackers. An eastward glance told him another handful of citizens had made the river crossing, while closer still Alkibiades' hoplites had regrouped and begun to race to help. If he could stall and avoid Brasidas long enough, he would have numbers on his side.

But no. A day might be won by stalling and avoidance, but not a war. Certainly not a war against Fate herself. Ignoring all else, he set his doe eyes on Brasidas, grit his teeth and surrendered to the battle delirium. A few pounding hoofbeats, and his long cavalryman's sword, already held poised, swooped in a flat arc aimed at Brasidas' neck.

The Spartiate's blood-streaked, hawklike face vanished behind his hoplon and the sword's edge bit not flesh and bone but bronze-shod wood. Demosthenes wheeled round and attacked again and again, forced to fend off attacks from the Helots as he went–he stabbed the face of one who tried to drag him down–but always he fought toward Brasidas. Only with the general's blood soaking the frozen earth of Amphipolis would today's victory be complete.

Help came to his side in the form of a pair of citizens driving off the Helots, and the way to Brasidas was clear. Demosthenes charged. Brasidas dropped down onto one knee and set his sword and battered hoplon to meet it. As he galloped past, Demosthenes' blade sheared a corner off of the Spartan's shield. Balios screamed, and soon enough Demosthenes saw why: black blood streamed from Brasidas's sword. Horse blood.

Stricken Balios' forelegs buckled, sending Demosthenes tumbling to the ground. Thankfully, his scale armor bore the brunt of the landing, but the wind was knocked out of him and he knew he had scant seconds to catch it if he hoped to live long enough to fight for his life.

He had hardly sucked one shuddering breath before the gore-caked, soiled figure of his Spartan counterpart filled the empty expanse of clouds between the cheek pieces of his helmet. His hands were empty, he realized, his sword nowhere to be found. At least not quickly enough to matter. Yet if he made no move, he would be dead and the laurels due him in Athens would crown his corpse here in distant Thrace instead.

Forgoing a frantic search for his weapon, Demosthenes set his hands and feet instead to getting upright, but he barely made it into an unsteady crouch before Brasidas was on him. Pain lanced through his midsection on the left just below his ribs, where any hoplite worth the price of his panoply, not least a Spartiate killing machine, was trained to aim the death blow. The back of Demosthenes' head struck the cold ground, bounced and struck again. The earth rose up to swallow him, and a winter sky the color of a goddess' eyes faded from view. Laughing at himself for having had the gall to challenge Fate, the chains of which bound even the gods, Demosthenes surrendered himself to the grip of death.

6. Prisoner

The chill, uneven surface rumbled under his back. His own breath rasped in his ears, overwhelming the din of frantic shouting from somewhere outside the bronze shell encasing his head.

He opened his eyes, looked up on an expanse of winter sky, and he remembered.

At once, all the muscles of his body sprang to life. He scrambled upright, or tried to. In a clatter of iron and bronze, he lost his balance and tumbled onto one knee before rising and whipping his head around in search of Brasidas.

His eyes found instead the hulking forms of horses and their riders swirling around him. One of several unmounted cavalrymen he discovered standing closer to him cried out, "Demosthenes lives!"

Yes, so it seemed. But how? He remembered the killing stroke, still felt its spider-like ghost on his torso just under the ribs. And where was his killer? He cast urgent looks about, still half expecting attack, but Brasidas was nowhere to be found, only fellow Athenians. Accepting that the danger was past, Demosthenes struggled to remove his heavy helmet. As he did, a supporting hand appeared under his arm.

"If you're looking for Brasidas," the arm's Athenian owner said with a smile, "he is on his way to Amphipolis via the ford to the north, slung over Leokrates' saddle and roped like a goat!"

"Captured?" Demosthenes asked, perhaps stupidly. "How?"

"Leokrates struck and wounded him just after you fell, only minutes ago. A few other Spartans were captured, too, but we thought it best to get our prize safely behind the walls as quickly as possible."

Demosthenes nodded instant approval, even if privately he would as soon have left Amphipolis without such a 'prize.' Once captured, an enemy general could not safely be killed, lest the same treatment befall the next Athenian of high value who fell into enemy hands.

Brasidas had his life, but so did Demosthenes, and he was determined that it had not only been saved so he could do Thalassia's will. Who cared if her plans were better served by Brasidas's death? She had run off to who knew where, perhaps forever.

Good riddance was surely too harsh a thought, but *So be it* seemed apt. Athens had a chance to rise now because of her, and it would be mortal men who squandered that chance or made good on it. That was as it should be.

"I'll see Leokrates gets the prize for valor," Demosthenes said of the comrade who had saved his life, then asked, "What of the bridge?"

"Still held by half-dead slaves. Perhaps once they hear of Brasidas's fate, they'll yield."

Thanking his comrades as he broke from them, Demosthenes went first to the crumpled corpse of black Balios, whom someone had had the decency to put out of his misery. He knelt beside the fallen beast, touched his mane and thanked him for his part in bringing victory. Then he started for the Strymon, learning along the way that the Athenian casualties of the breakout had been light. Only eleven men, and Alkibiades not among them.

He had not forgotten, of course, that Athens that day should have counted Demosthenes among its dead. So why did she not? He surely had not imagined the blow. As he walked, his hand kept going to the spot where there should have been a wound. Instead there was only a dull throbbing which flared to mild pain with every breath. He searched among the iron scales of his armor in search of the spot where the sword had entered and at length found a split in the leather and worked a finger through it.

No matter how it turned and twisted and pushed, the finger never met bare flesh. And neither, he realized, had Brasidas's blade. Smooth and pliable, the layer of fabric between leather and skin stretched and conformed to any attempt at penetration, then snapped back.

Spun bronze, he had called the small scrap of her clothing which Thalassia had brought with her to Pylos, and she, without his knowledge it seemed, had affixed it inside the leather lining of his armor at precisely the spot he was most likely to be run through.

Already his city owed her, as did he personally for naming the time and place of his appointment with death so that he might avoid it. Now, in an even more meaningful sense, he owed her his life.

Shit.

He came at last to the bridge where the grim, blood-streaked faces and demonic eyes of fourteen steadfast martyrs were as hard as the blades of their set spears. Alkibiades' men had begun to gather on the western bank, forcing the bridge's defenders to split in half to face either side. Those facing west could hardly have missed the defeat of their comrades, but if so, the sight seemed to have made them no less determined to die.

A voice called to Demosthenes from the opposite bank: "Strategos, we have more than enough bolts to kill them! Shall we?"

It was Straton, and after a moment's thought Demosthenes signaled him the negative and descended the bank to take up a spot hardly two spear lengths from the west-facing line of Brasidas's rear guard, the fourteen men who were all that yet stood of the force which was to have taken Amphipolis.

"You men are Helots, no?" Demosthenes said to them. "The leader who brought you to this place will be my prisoner, if he survives his wounds. Those of you who wish may leave here as free men. We will even do our best to treat your wounds. Any who choose to stand fast and die, we shall oblige, but I fear you will have to settle for death by spindles. I would be glad to starve you, but unfortunately we need to use this bridge. You have as long as it takes me to step out of harm's way and give the command to fire."

With that Demosthenes turned his back on them and began withdrawing to the Athenian line at a leisurely pace, confident that at least some of the slave-born fighters behind him would question their loyalty to their distant masters, even as they wondered whether word of the decision they made here could somehow reach home and affect the fates of their families.

A cheer suddenly erupted among the Athenians, and Demosthenes turned to see a bowl shaped shield rocking on the planks of the bridge. The owner who had cast it down ran for shore with one stiff, bloodied leg dragging behind him. His example made it easier for the others to choose life, which they proceeded to do almost to a man. Within the space of a minute, only four men remained on the bridge, one of them standing in such a pool of blood that it streamed off the planks and into the Strymon. Another likely remained upright only thanks to his spear shaft. The four were given one final opportunity to stand aside, which they refused, before Demosthenes signaled gravely to Straton on the opposite bank.

The unwieldy belly-bows, already strung, were raised and aimed, and enough iron-tipped skewers flew to kill those four men and ten more besides. The Helot's shields and battered bodies were pierced, and they crumpled without a sound to the bridge, surrendering their shades to Hades for a city which had enslaved their forefathers.

Demosthenes was first to cross the reclaimed bridge on his path back to town. A thin layer of snow had settled over the war-churned grass in the shadow of the city walls, the earth there sown with silent corpses and groaning wounded. The battle fully at an end now, exhaustion overtook him, making each step a struggle. He had cheated Fate and a Spartan general this day in saving Amphipolis, and those two in turn had conspired to cheat him back by stealing his life.

That they had failed was due in large part to starborn witchery.

But the witch was gone. Or was she? Whether or not Thalassia returned, she would claim no share of the victory's accolades. But somehow the mortal beneficiary of her aid could not help but feel, as he returned to town, that he would see her again.

Soon, and to his regret.

7. Not a Goddess

Under a cloak of clouds which hid the winter stars and a cloak of wine which clouded his mind, Demosthenes walked the streets of sleeping Amphipolis. With war gear bundled under his arm and slung on his back, he hunted for his rented dwelling. Soon he would abandon that house to return to his own and face the tiresome adulation of the crowds in Athens, men who could never know, never comprehend exactly what he had achieved for their city this day and so would remain forever ungrateful.

The idea rattled in his muddled mind that maybe he could make his home here and never return to Athens.

Where was that house? Every few steps, he forgot exactly where he was and how he had got there, then stopped and took a moment to get back on track. Damn Alkibiades, and damn all the citizen cavalry, who had dragged him into the barracks, where excellent Macedonian wine had flowed in torrents all evening from two jugs, each as tall as a man, that had appeared as if from nowhere. Whores had appeared, too, along with Amphipolitan civilians by the dozen, drawn by the music and raucous cheers and word of mouth. However indifferent they were to what distant city wound up ruling them, a party was a party.

The last Demosthenes had seen of Alkibiades, just before leaving on his last legs, the youth had been sandwiched between a pair of Thracian twins, his chest stained purple with wine. Now Demosthenes clambered alone through the unlocked door of the home he realized he had passed by at least twice already and shuffled into its megaron, where the hearth crackled in its slow, overnight burn.

The orange glow barely illuminated a human shape. No, the shape of a nymph. But Thalassia was not a nymph. She stared at him in the firelight with those damned awful eyes of hers, and he stared back. He dropped his war gear. When its resounding clatter faded, his breath was loud and harsh and filled the room.

His eyes adjusted, bringing the star-girl into sharper focus. She wore a dark chlamys thrown over a simple chiton of some light color, belted at the waist, the hem falling just above the knee. It was a man's garment, though none with sight could ever mistake the wearer for a man, or even a boy. Her hair hung in loose tresses over bare shoulders the flesh of which, like that of the exposed upper part of her chest, arms and lower legs, glowed dull gold in the hearth's light.

"You're back," he said in a breathy grunt. "If you came looking for your fucktoy, he's out fucking other toys."

"I came to say congratulations," she said. "And goodb–"

"Congratulations?" Demosthenes sneered. "I failed, didn't I? Brasidas lives!"

"You wounded him," she said. It came as no surprise that she knew. "Men can die from their wounds." There was perhaps more than just hope in the suggestion.

Scoffing, Demosthenes dismissed her with a wave that nearly cost him his balance. He recalled what she had said to him on the day of her arrival in Amphipolis. They had stuck with him these past five days. "You're tired of *me?*" Finally, he had his chance to reply. "I'm tired of *you!* You're not a goddess!"

"I know that."

"Shut up! You took my gods away from me, and left me what? *You?*" He stabbed a finger at her through the flickering darkness. "There's just you and me and walking corpses in this world now. You're no goddess..." He advanced on her with lurching steps across the floor of hard-packed dirt. "You might be from the stars, but you are still just a woman, full of... woman parts, and tears, and lies and-and–" He staggered to within arm's reach of her. Thalassia stood fast, a statue, even as he put a hand out, picked a lock of hair from her collarbone and finished, "and pretty hair, and those... fucking evil eyes."

He pulled on the lock of her hair. Thalassia twisted her neck, bowing her head to accommodate, her expression showing no sign of pain or even annoyance. Demosthenes eased the pressure and she righted her head, but rather than release the dark locks he buried his fingers deeper in them and yanked again. She yielded a small step toward him, drawn closer, again without evidence of pain. She made no sound. There was only the hollow rasp of his own breath and the faint crackle of the hearth.

He walked, pulling her by the hair, in the direction of the narrow staircase set against the megaron's rear wall. She followed, unresisting, body bent awkwardly, and they ascended into the bedchamber above. It had no fire and was lit only by cloud-filtered moonglow streaming in through a pair of windows. He went to the rough bed that he had not shared with any companion during his stay in Amphipolis, stopped at its edge and turned Thalassia to face him.

She yet wore the same tranquil, if dark, expression as she had below. Somehow that fact angered him, and Demosthenes raised his other hand to cover her face, fingers spread out wide over her cheek and lips and chin. He shoved her head back, keeping his grip in her hair. It was a pointless, childish move with no aim but to express displeasure with the face's owner.

"I could have won without you," he said. The words came with difficulty on account of his heavy tongue, but he deemed them understandable. He uncovered her face, but kept his grip on the controlling reins of her hair. "You're no goddess," he went on, still to no reply and no resistance. "Just a woman ..."

By her hair and a hand on her back, he dragged her face down onto the low bed, or half on it, rather, her knees striking the plank floor. "You're just a woman," he slurred again, uncertain of whether he had said it once already or not. He knelt behind her, nudged her knee outward with one of his. "I could have done it without you!"

Exchanging the clump of her hair in his grasp for another at the back of her skull, close in to the roots, he pressed her head down while using the other hand to throw aside her cloak and lift the skirt of her chiton. When the way was clear, he used the same hand to part her smooth cleft and thrust his cock inside her. It had been ready since the stairs.

He took her violently, alternately burying her face in the wool blanket and yanking her head back by the hair. She made no sound, offered no resistance, made no move to eject him from the warm, wet, soft place into which he intruded on an invitation long expired.

"You're just a woman..." he said, an accusation. Sure enough, she felt like one.

The planks creaked under his weight as he braced one foot and one knee against them for extra leverage, even while jerking the recipient harder onto him. He grunted with each relentless thrust, ignoring the pain in his bruised ribs until, rage and arousal spent, he lowered his weight fully onto her back and drifted into sleep.

Some time later, perhaps it was minutes, perhaps hours, he regained a shard of consciousness. Finding himself ready, and the warm body still present and in position under him, he entered her again. This time, he went not by the garden path, but thief-like through her back channel. She accepted it soundlessly, a lump of supple, golden clay bent before him.

"Just a woman..." he breathed on her neck, and collapsed on her again.

8. Appointment

Awareness returned. Demosthenes lay on his back with timber beams above him. But something was missing, something warm and soft. Something which should have been pleasant but was not.

Memories came. One by one, he dismissed them as irrelevant until only one remained. It sent heart into throat and dragged him upright in spite of the satchel of rocks someone appeared to have emptied into his skull. He opened his eyes on blinding daylight and shut them again, let out a moan and learned that the night had turned his mouth to sand and ears to linen.

No, not that. He could not have done that. It was a dream, a nightmare. Gods knew he had had enough of those about her. But denial was futile. The vision fit the facts. Here he lay at the very scene of the act, dressed as he had been in the same wine-stained chiton. And there was no mistaking the sensation of cooled and dried fluids on certain areas of sensitive, now-shriveled skin.

He sank back into the bed and wished for sleep to envelop him again, so that when next he opened his eyes this nightmare world might be vanquished and reality restored. If that did not happen, he would return home to public glory and private shame. According to the courts, Thalassia was his slave. To them, he had done no wrong. But the heart in his breast told him otherwise. For the last year, he had not particularly wanted to look into Thalassia's eyes, but now... *could* he, if he tried?

At length he managed to drag his eyelids open, but the nightmare persisted. Morning light streamed in through the rustling, gauzelike curtain in the window of his plain Amphipolitan bedchamber. How long he could hide here in bed?

Not long at all, for fresh memories surfaced and caused alarm. Thalassia–proud, vindictive Thalassia–had wanted Brasidas dead. If she got it in her mind to make that happen, a lock on a cell door and a few guards were scarcely enough to stop her. But if she carried out an execution, Sparta would surely retaliate by doing likewise to the any Athenian strategoi who might be captured in future battles.

Driven by a fresh sense of urgency, Demosthenes stood upright, in defiance of the lurching floor, his battle injury and the wild throbbing of his temples. He descended the stairs, hugging the roughly plastered wall, and crossed the megaron, passing the cold hearth to reach the door. Exiting into bright light, he shielded his eyes and made his way, half-blind at first, to the nearby barracks complex, where the enemy general was held. Fellow Athenians sought to speak to him as he passed, some addressing him as strategos, others just offering cordial greeting. He ignored them all and pressed on to his destination.

Brasidas's prison was a long, narrow shed of rough-cut timber; the other prisoners were kept in a stockade outside the city walls. On sighting the structure, Demosthenes called urgently to the Athenian guard by its door, "Is the prisoner safe?"

The guard comprised six men, all of whom, reassuringly, were accounted for and looked unalarmed. "Yes, general," one answered, though not without raising a brow in a show of puzzlement, if not mild offense.

"Let me see him."

Demosthenes held his breath, which only exacerbated the ache in his head, and noticed as the guard turned to comply that the thick wooden post meant to bar the door from without sat uselessly on the ground.

"Why is the door unb–" he began angrily, but before he could finish, before even the guard could set hand on the door, it opened on its own from within.

Thalassia emerged. She saw Demosthenes, and her eyes locked on him, but her face was blank. Her plain white chiton was smeared all over with blood.

Demosthenes managed to speak through his shock, but not to that vision in red.

"What is she doing in there?" he asked the guard, who appeared not to share his general's surprise.

"Treating the prisoner," he said casually. "She's been tending our wounded all morning. As she did yesterday. On your orders, I thought."

Thalassia stepped out of the open door, the guard closed it behind her, and she came forward, a red-smeared hide satchel slung on her shoulder, wintry eyes giving nothing away about what might lie behind them.

"Bar that door," he instructed the guard unnecessarily. Then, abruptly, he turned and stalked away, from the guard, from the shed, but mostly from her. Not out of anger or fear but impotence, a loss for words and inability to meet her stare.

He had taken a few long strides when her voice sailed after him: "Really?"

Guilt slowed then halted his hasty retreat.

"Are you really going to walk away from me?"

She drew up behind him, circled around, and they stood face to face, though not eye to eye. His were on the muddy grass under his sandaled feet.

"Will he live?" he asked.

"He'll be fine. You thought I would kill him? I could have killed him ten times before he even reached Amphipolis."

This exchange exhausted the catalog of words

Demosthenes had on hand to share with her. Fortunately, Thalassia was better prepared, even if she seemed no more enthused about the encounter than he was.

"I want to take you somewhere," she said.

Demosthenes gave it a moment's thought and nodded agreement, partly out of guilt but mostly to avoid lengthening the conversation. "Where?" he managed.

"Outside the city. No place in particular."

He agreed, in spite of the very obvious potential danger of going into the wilderness alongside a living weapon with of the strength of several men and an ax to grind. Thalassia's manner gave no particular cause for alarm, but then she was a consummate deceiver.

"Meet me by the north gate an hour past midday," she said.

Still unable to squarely meet her eye, he gave another nod. It was not conventional for a general of Athens to vanish into the hills the day after a major victory when there was yet work to be done, but then neither had it been convention to drown himself in a vat of wine the night prior. He would manage to slip away.

Doubtless she knew all the reasons for his current discomfort. She chose to address one.

"I promised never to hurt you," she said, "and I won't. We will only talk."

The reassurance did put his mind at ease, even if that same dark part of himself which last night had acted unforgivably urged him to press thumbs to the hollow of her throat and demand that she just say whatever she wished to say now and be done with it.

But once again, he only nodded silently, impotently.

"Good," she said. Her features showed no sign of either pleasure or gratitude.

Without further word, she departed his presence, leaving Demosthenes to wonder, while attending to the building of a trophy, deciding the fates of prisoners, dividing spoils, composing a dispatch to the Board, and doing the dozen other things that needed doing, what her intentions were.

He did not finish wondering, or completing the tasks at hand, before the appointed time arrived. Outside Amphipolis' northern gate he found Thalassia waiting with one horse which they were to share. He mounted it, moving delicately on account of the bruise under his ribs, after which Thalassia hoisted herself into the saddle in front of him. They struck off on the wide, well-worn trail, less than a road, deeply rutted by the wheels of carts which seemed to be absent this day, heading northeast toward the low, gold-bearing mountains on the horizon.

"It would help to know the destination," Demosthenes suggested blandly.

"Just follow the trail. I'll tell you when to leave it."

He did as she bid him, trying to keep his hands on the reins from brushing the hips of body in front of him, the warmth and undeniable allure of which penetrated her cloak. But there was no preventing that contact which, but for a few layers of linen and wool, was almost as close as that they had had last night. There was plenty of friction, too, as their bodies jostled.

The silence grew quickly awkward, and after some minutes spent penning up the desire to say something, anything, the pressure in his chest became too great and a question burst forth.

"Where did you go?"

He could not see Thalassia's expression, only waves of dark hair, the hair that he had...

By the quickness of her answer, he gathered that she welcomed the breaking of silence.

"Macedon," she said, surprisingly. "Do you know of Arrhidaeus?"

Demosthenes had heard the name. "Some prince or other."

"King Perdikkas' nephew," Thalassia clarified. "His line was removed from succession when Perdikkas took the throne."

Her words thus far had not seemed ominous, but the pause which followed was.

"What about him?" Demosthenes prompted innocently.

"I lured him to his death."

"What? Why?"

"In that world where Amphipolis falls and you die in Sicily, Arrhidaeus's grandson Philip would have conquered Greece. And Philip's son Alexander would have conquered everything from the Nile to India, spreading Greek culture and the worship of your gods. And himself."

"Conquered...." Demosthenes echoed, incredulously. "Spreading Greek culture? But Macedonians are... *barbarians*."

"They style themselves Greek. Or they will. Or would have," Thalassia said dismissively. "In one day, with one act, I have done vastly more to change this world than I have in the last year helping you alter the outcome of your little war."

Demosthenes pursed his lips, sealing them against those words which belittled his city's struggle–indeed, all men's struggles.

"Then why have you bothered with our war?" he asked through grit teeth.

She said nothing for a short while. Then, "Turn off the trail here."

9. Thracian Idyll

They rode in silence for a while, the Thracian countryside rolling past them at a leisurely canter. Skeletons of trees stood naked in pools of their shed leaves beneath the shadows of pines, while in the distance low hills rose and fell like the backs of mating serpents. When at last they crested one of these hills, the mirror-smooth surface of a lake came into view, reflecting sunlight into the vault of winter sky above.

Near its edge, Thalassia slid from the saddle, landing in the grass as though her weight were barely enough to bend a blade. Demosthenes followed with somewhat less grace and stood with reins in hand, ready to walk the horse to the lakeside where he would hobble her forelegs and let her drink. Before embarking on that task, he paused to let Thalassia remove a linen-wrapped bundle from the saddlebags. It clanked slightly as it moved. Her instruments of torture, perhaps?

No, this torturer needed no instruments but her mind and tongue.

Thalassia took the bundle to a spot on the grass, where Demosthenes joined her after leaving the horse to drink. She spread out a blanket and laid out on it the bundle's contents: bread and relish, meat pies, a clay jug of water and two cups. Throwing off the cloak she had no need for against the chill, she seated herself on the grass beside the square of white linen with legs crossed under the skirts of her sea-foam chiton. Demosthenes lowered himself to the grass beside her, facing, as did she, the tranquil lake.

Thalassia continued the surreal, oddly domestic display by pouring water for them both. She handed him his cup, and he drank. Thalassia drank, too, something which she did far more frequently than she consumed the Athenian food she neither required nor particularly liked; she ate only often enough to keep Eurydike convinced that she needed to. Over her cup's rim she stared out at the lake's still, reflective surface. Though he tried, Demosthenes could not read what thoughts might inhabit those pale eyes. At one time he had thought himself able, but no longer.

She drained her cup and set it down while he sipped at his, neither speaking until at last Demosthenes could bear the silence no longer. He thought perhaps he should ask her if she had made the food herself, thank her or compliment her if need be, but he could not bear the thought of engaging in small talk while words relating to other, more important matters clawed at his throat, begging for release.

There was one matter, however, on which he did not wish to speak. And so he did not.

"You plan to leave," he said. Through the haze of last night's drunkenness, Demosthenes recalled her having begun to bid him farewell. Before he had interrupted her and...

She looked over at him, and their eyes met, perhaps not for the first time that day, but it was the first time the contact lasted more than an instant. While it endured, Demosthenes' heart began to fill with regrets, as though someone had poured them from above, searing hot, into the open cavity of his chest. Last night Thalassia had been a malign force in the darkness, a body deprived of the face and name she had spent more than a year earning alongside him and Alkibiades and Eurydike in Athens. The face he had known had been too easily erased by hardly a month of separation, and written over the blank space where it had been were his own fear and hatred. The face of a monster.

What he looked upon now was no monster.

"I am sorry," he said in a whisper, even before she had

answered his prior question.

Thalassia turned her head and gazed out over the little lake and the forests of Thrace on its far edge. "I know," she said. Then, "You should eat."

He did not, could not. But he did swallow his emotions, a meal of guilt and pity, lest he be driven by such hot forces where cold reason must rule. He asked, "Where will you go?'

She sighed and spoke idly. "There is a city in Italy called Roma. Right now it is probably no greater in significance than Athens, but in a few generations it will carve an empire to make Alexander's look small."

Ignoring the insult to city and people, to which he had by now become almost accustomed, Demosthenes asked, "What will you do there?"

"Destroy it," she said. "Kill them all. A few generations from now, this world will be unrecognizable compared to what it would have been."

"And your task will be complete," Demosthenes ventured. "The Worm will never exist."

"I suppose," she said indifferently. "It doesn't matter much. I have spent a year here. I will spend a few there. And then maybe somewhere else. Maybe he will blink out of existence, or maybe he won't. Maybe the Caliate will cease to exist without a Worm to oppose it." She spoke the name smoothly, without falter or hesitation. "Maybe this whole layer, and others, will crumble to dust. Maybe the whole universe will collapse into a single point." She scoffed. "I don't know. Maybe Magdalen knows. Maybe she knew that I would come here, and it's all part of her plan. I don't care anymore."

Demosthenes listened with mouth agape. *Her enemy is humanity!* the Nightmare Sibyl had screamed. He swallowed hard, opted not to address those matters of layers and universes, which he could scarcely comprehend.

"Is your aim to get me to beg you to stay?" he asked.

Thalassia looked over at him blankly, resignedly. "I wish you wouldn't say things like that." She shifted to draw her legs up in front of her, a finger absently picking the braided leather cord at the top of one well-wrought but well-worn sandal. "You think I am always trying to manipulate you." Anger rose in her voice. "Of course, I fucking want you to ask me to stay, idiot." As quickly as it had come, the fury faded, but bitterness remained. "Decide for yourself. I'm done trying to ingratiate myself all over again every time you change your mind about me." She shrugged. "I've enjoyed Athens. I love Eurydike. I... care for you all. In my own way. You amuse me." She frowned, corrected herself, "No, not amuse. More than that. Much more. I told you a year ago what were the best years of my life... but maybe..." She shook her head thoughtfully and bit her lower lip, declining to finish.

So human...

She laid her head atop the folded arms that bridged her knees and looked sidewise at Demosthenes. Her pale eyes seemed as though they might at any moment begin to well with more of the tears he had witnessed once before. But her gaze eventually drifted groundward, and she waited, presumably for some reply.

She deserved a clear answer, but what? Wish her well in destroying Roma, or ask her to remain? With Amphipolis in Athenian hands, Fate had already been beaten once. The plans set in motion a year prior in Alkibiades' garden had been achieved. And perhaps it was enough. Perhaps the long war would end more quickly now, with Athens the victor and Sparta finally yielding, while Thalassia went far away, to where whatever destruction she wrought would have scant effect on distant Athens during a mortal's lifetime.

There was much to recommend letting her go. Had he

not wished time and again to be rid of her? She was a powerful weapon, yes, but also a curse to the wielder, on whose back she laid the responsibility of battling Fate to avert tragedy and ensure a bright future for all those he loved.

What was the alternative? Bring her back to Athens, continue to exploit her as a weapon on the city's behalf, holding her to her promises of an Athenian victory, while trying his best behind closed doors to coexist with her? Why was that so impossible? Thalassia possessed flaws, but did not everyone in his life, not least those closest to him? Alkibiades, Eurydike, his father Alkisthenes... One might fairly say of each of them that their negative qualities outweighed the positive. Deny it as some might–as Alkibiades did–every man and woman who walked this earth was deeply flawed. Just because she had fallen into it from the heavens, was Thalassia to be held to some higher standard of perfection?

Last night, his drunken self had insisted she was no goddess, and that was true. She had never claimed to be. Yet some part of him insisted that she be just that, or at least more than mortal, for she had upturned all he previously held as ironclad fact and unquestioned law, stripped him of his ability to believe in words spoken by anyone but her. Yet she was as flawed as anyone. More. His faith, his gods were gone, and in their place was a treacherous, manipulative, vain, vindictive, volatile, broken being of neither this realm nor the next. An in-betweener, an exile, a paradox, an enemy of democracy, a slayer of men, a friendless nomad of space and time upon whose altar, his dreams yet screamed at him now and then in terror, the bleating lamb of his own Fate was bound by chains every bit as thick and oppressive as those freshly broken on the plain of Amphipolis.

This being seated beside him on the lakeshore was lonely, unique, so strong yet so fragile, repugnant yet beautiful. She was Madness. She was the Wormwhore. She was Geneva. Jenna. Thalassia. Star-girl.

"Do not go," he pleaded, before even he knew he was saying it, before tongue could gain mind's approval for what foolish heart had chosen.

Thalassia lifted her gaze from the blanket laid out with untouched food. When they found him, he saw in her face first disbelief, then a quick return to melancholy, as one who has just woken from a dream that a dead love yet lives: the joy extends a heartbeat into reality, and then in a flash it is gone.

A breeze off of the lake alerted Demosthenes to wetness on his cheek. Under her gaze, he wiped the tear away.

"Why did you let me do it?" he demanded, more petulantly than intended. There was no need to name the deed; she would know of what he spoke.

"For spite," she answered plainly. "To hurt you. To scar your memory of me."

The pettiness of that answer momentarily stunned Demosthenes. But Thalassia was human, he reminded himself, and humans were petty creatures who hurt one another for no profound reason. Of that, he was surely as guilty as she.

She surprised him by adding, in softer tones, "You owe me a kiss." It was a plain observation, delivered with cheek still laid on drawn-up knees.

"What?"

"Anyone who fucks me like an animal should kiss me first, if I want it. So you owe me one. Soon we might need another's permission."

At a loss for understanding, Demosthenes stared at her. He found a faint glimmer of mercy in her eyes, if not anywhere else. He had no wish to kiss her, nor speak on the possibility.

Neither did he want to speak on his misdeed, but he knew he must.

"I was not myself," he said lamely. "I do not know what possessed me."

"The same thing that drives any man to rape." Thalassia's soft voice competed with the soaring cries of the lake birds. "The desire to tame. To reduce me to something you need not fear."

The naked proclamation of his crime summoned forth fresh tears that he worked to stifle. Anger came, too, not at himself but at his victim, for no better reason than that she was right. He had meant to diminish her, to master his fear. Something in him remained desirous of those things even now.

"You try so hard to hurt me," she observed. She might have plucked the thought from his own mind.

"And have I?" Was that hope in his voice?

"Trying is success," Thalassia returned, and thereby avoided voicing the simple, true answer.

The confirmation gave him no satisfaction, only guilt, and in an instant that part of him which had desired to do her harm shrank back into the primordial darkness, where it slept. Freed of its influence, Demosthenes collected his thoughts in the hope that reason and not emotion, negative or otherwise, might rule him.

"Some have said the antidote to fear is knowledge," he said. He was sure he had heard some sophist or other say something like that. "Perhaps if I knew you better than I do."

"You threw me out of your house and barely spoke to me for a year."

"That... can be remedied. It shall be."

Demosthenes looked out over the lake and its grassy shore, the blanket laid out with untouched food, a plain, pastoral scene made surreal by the company.

Thalassia sighed, rolled onto her side, reclining on the blanket with head propped on one bent arm which became lost in a sea of dark hair. Abruptly, she pushed one of the near-forgotten plates of food in Demosthenes' direction. "Will you eat something already? Someone went to some amount of trouble to provide this meal."

For the first time, Demosthenes gave his attention to the food. "'Someone'? Not you?" he asked in mock surprise.

In spite of Eurydike's efforts to improve it, Thalassia's cooking was horrendous. Given how she excelled at anything else she put her hand to, he wondered if the failure was not by design, so that she might be spared the chore.

"I will eat only if you will," Demosthenes said.

The condition won him a sneer, but Thalassia yielded and took a morsel of bread, piled it with pickled vegetables and popped it between the lips she preferred to use for other pleasures than food. With a show of reluctance, she chewed and swallowed, then opened her mouth wide to prove the deed was done by displaying a wet tongue peppered with moist, clinging fragments.

"Satisfied?" she asked with a fresh sneer. But almost instantly, her features warmed. She shrugged and reached for another bite. "It's not awful," she conceded. "Just flavorless."

Having taken one mouthful himself by then, Demosthenes could not agree. It was near perfection. He dug in, at last giving his morning-after self the remedy it had craved for some hours now, or would have craved had the pangs of guilt and shame and fear not overshadowed those of hunger.

"So, this Italian town, this *Roma,*" Demosthenes asked as he ate. "It will one day subjugate all the cities of Greece?"

"And much more."

"Then..." Demosthenes mused, "perhaps... one day, when my own 'little war' is over, for the good of my city and country... I might go to Roma and help you to destroy it. Perhaps," he quickly emphasized, lest it be given the weight of a promise. "It seems that doing so might serve both our purposes. If, that is, you have not abandoned yours."

Thalassia stared into the tree-line by the lake's edge and said with a decided lack of fire, "I will finish what I started. But first..." She looked back at him with a wan smile. "There is Sparta to finish, if you'll have me. And so many pretty, shiny things in the agora."

"Aye," Demosthenes said, laughing although he knew he should not, for his next words were no cause for lightness. "It seems you are a gift that I am powerless to reject."

For a while, Thalassia nibbled and he ate voraciously.

"There is one last thing I must tell you," she said when the meal was nearly done.

Demosthenes stopped eating mid-bite, as all thought of eating fled his mind. "Those words frighten me to no end," he said. "It is a fear born of experience. I cannot help it."

Thalassia smiled; he did not. Rather worryingly, she looked away, up at the hazy winter sky which her eyes so reflected and resembled.

"What?" he demanded, growing ever more alarmed. "Tell me!"

At last she spared him a look which was neither foreboding nor playful, the two looks she gave best, but rather lay somewhere between.

"You know that you'll need to marry soon," she said, sounding unusually philosophical. "For the sake of your reputation, career, estate, and–" Her gaze returned to the clouds. "Honestly, I think it will be good for you."

Blood rushed in Demosthenes' ears, the sound of alarm.

"What are you saying? Out with it."

Star-born, pale-eyed Madness leveled another look at him, apologetic but at the same time unyielding as stone. "Eurydike and I have found you a prospective bride," she said. "A widow. We meet her at the spring nearly every day. The war took her husband, the plague her children, and now her brother is her keeper. She lives in his home in misery, but remains quick to laugh. She is accommodating but not docile, willful but not impulsive. She is affectionate, intelligent, generous, patient, and frankly, very fuckable. But she doesn't have a tin pisspot for a dowry, so no man will touch her," Thalassia finished earnestly. "Her name is Laonome."*

---

* Lay-ON-ah-mee.

PART 4

ARKADIA

1. Dog

Maimakterion in the archonship of Isarchos (November 424 BCE)

Leuke's square sail billowed overhead in a too-strong wind (the season for smooth sailing was well past) and white waves swirled in her wake as she cut a path for Athens, one of ten triremes returning home with angry-eyed prows draped in ivy garlands that were sure to be blown to the sea god well before port. No one much liked having a woman aboard, but inevitably they had to be transported, and anyway, this was the general's woman. As was customary, extra prayers had been said, extra sacrifices made, and the voyage then was surrendered into the hands of Fate.

Broken, vanquished, disgraced Fate. It only remained to be seen whether she would stay down or staunch her wound and rise to right the wrong done her.

Demosthenes stood near the prow alongside his ship's bad luck charm. Thalassia had unbound her hair and let it fly in the winter wind as though flaunting her womanhood to the sailors who eyed her with suspicion. Demosthenes did not let the indiscretion bother him. His spirits were always high in the early hours of a sea voyage, before the boredom of the flat, unchanging seascape set in.

"Let me see if I have everything straight," he said idly to her. "We currently exist in one of some very large number of 'layers,' in a subset you call the Severed Layers because of the difficulty in reaching or leaving them. Which is good for you, because if your cult of Magdalen, this army of kidnappers and exterminators that you have betrayed... twice... learned what you were doing and got their hands on you, they would subject you to a fate worse than death."

Thalassia's pale eyes stayed on the horizon, face into the

headwind. Her lips formed a distant half-smile. "Mmh," she said. *Go on.*

"One more of your kind is asleep under a mountain in Scythia and another is somewhere nearer, probably, licking her wounds and biding her time before she pays you back for stranding her, not to mention caving in her skull and cutting off an arm."

Thalassia cocked her head as if in a silent, dark laugh, but she did not interrupt.

"If you change the course of our war drastically enough," Demosthenes continued, "maybe raze an Italian city, then the one who wronged you will be wiped from existence, and maybe so will Magdalen and her army, and–well, things past that are fuzzy for both of us, it seems, so we shall leave it there for now. Thanks to your help, Athens has held a town it should have lost and captured one of the enemy's best commanders. That accomplished, for some unknowable reason, you want to choose my wife for me. How did I do?"

Her distant smirk turned to a chuckle. "Not bad."

"Did I get something wrong?"

"Well, yes," she said, momentarily knocking Demosthenes' pride. "Eden will be healed by now. Long since. I'm not sure what's keeping her. And... the way you tell it, I sound a little crazy. A compliment or two would not have been out of place."

"Hmm," Demosthenes said neutrally, stalling while he angled his head into the whipping wind to study her face and determine, perhaps, whether he might be in physical danger if he failed to stroke her ego.

He could not tell and so just took a chance with his life. With only a rail and ten feet or so separating him from the rushing waters, he declined to flatter a being capable of tearing him in two. "I will be sure to fix that the next time I tell it," he said.

Thalassia's eyes, vibrant in this space between sea and sky, flicked toward him, and her easy smile confirmed he had chosen his words well.

With her help, for better or worse, he was learning not to fear her.

His half-laugh, half-sigh was lost on the wind. "I have an interesting life," he observed.

"It's good that you can laugh about it," Thalassia said. "Very good."

***

Spartan command structure was a complex beast with bones of pitted iron. Where most cities knew but two ranks of officer, *lochagos* and *strategos*, Sparta counted ten, and that time-tested structure did not simply dissolve in an enemy prison. Thus, for the year-plus of his imprisonment, Styphon had retained nominal command over the men captured with him on Sphakteria, even if most singled him out for resentment as the direct cause of their disgrace. If not for him, they might have died warrior's deaths instead of languishing in chains.

Now something had changed. Brasidas had come, made prisoner in Thrace by the very same general who had seized Pylos and filled the walls of this Athenian prison to bursting. Since taking part in the naval assault on Pylos, Brasidas had risen to become one of Sparta's five polemarchs, and from the minute of his arrival in Athens there could be no question who ruled the cell blocks and yards of the jail complex. Upon the minute of the polemarch's arrival, it had become more likely than not that, whether on direct orders from Brasidas or just with his tacit approval, some violence, possibly death, would befall the phylarch, the trembler, accursed Styphon who had led all present to their miserable end.

Having arrived wounded, Brasidas was kept for three days in a cell by himself, three days in which Styphon's countrymen grew bolder in showing their contempt. But thanks to the forty or so who remained loyal to their present commander and ready (at least for now) to defend him, the displays rarely went further than an icy glare or muttered insult.

Strangely, on the day that Brasidas entered into the general population, nothing changed.

On the next, Styphon was summoned. Duty-bound, he answered the call and went unafraid, for his life and his fortunes meant far less now, in disgrace, than they had in times past.

Twelve Equals formed a curtain of thick, tanned limbs in front of Brasidas in the cell block's small exercise yard. These were the general's freshly picked honor guard, and among their number were several of those men who had long made no secret of their desire to see Styphon deposed as leader, if not worse. Some now wore triumphant smirks, others glowering looks with which they tried, and failed, to intimidate the summoned. Some moved aside only when Styphon shoved them, and then only forewent retaliation for lack of permission from Brasidas.

Piercing the curtain of flesh, Styphon stood face to face with the general.

"Leave us," Brasidas told his guard.

With more than a few choice insults thrown at Styphon through clenched jaws, the gang reluctantly moved off, giving the pair about as much privacy as one could achieve in this crowded place.

Taller than most men, with angular features anchored by a beakish nose, Brasidas was seated on a stone slab with his back against the prison's inner wall of brick and timber. Like his fellow prisoners, he wore an undyed smock bearing a crimson alpha for *aichmolotos*, 'prisoner.' His injured left shoulder was wrapped tightly in linen, and a fresh black scar ran parallel to his hairline.

"I'll end any doubts you may have," he said brusquely. "The ephors haven't branded you a trembler yet, but they will the moment you set foot again in Lakonia. If ever you do." Face a hard mask, Brasidas glared with utter contempt. "What were you thinking?"

Styphon answered humbly, meeting his superior's withering gaze. "I did what I thought was best for Sparta, not for my reputation."

"The two are one and the same," Brasidas lectured. "But I have not brought you here to debate whether or not you are a coward. You are. I want to talk about a woman."

There was no need to explain, no doubt in Styphon's mind what woman he meant.

Brasidas removed his eyes from Styphon as if to suggest he was nothing worth looking at. Instead he kept them on the far wall of the courtyard, which was not particularly far.

"I've heard remarkable things about her from the men here," Brasidas explained. "They also say that you must know more than they do. Tell me."

Even while awaiting reply, the general denied Styphon his gaze. For his part, Styphon was not quick to answer, for he sensed that much depended on his words. At the same time, it was never wise to keep a general waiting.

"She came from the sea a corpse, as sure as you're sitting on that bench, and then, after a day had passed, she returned to life," Styphon offered plainly. "I gave her the name Thalassia to replace the barbarian one she gave, which I scarcely recall."

Obediently, Styphon went on to recount to the man in

whose hands his fate rested the truths of Thalassia's accurate foretelling of the Athenian attack, of her unearthly strength, of her assurance that Sparta was destined to win the war in spite of defeat and disgrace at Pylos, and of his own choice to surrender in order that the pre-ordained ultimate victory might come to pass. He told Brasidas how Thalassia had caused the warning beacon on Sphakteria's heights to be lit, and of the slaying of Epitadas by a single arrow while his sword hovered at Thalassia's throat, even if Brasidas surely had heard this last tale already from other prisoners. And he told of his attempt to secure Thalassia's passage to Sparta by ransom, so as to keep her out of Athenian hands.

Left out of his account was his promise of some future favor to Thalassia in return for her pledge to rescue Andrea from the miserable existence due her as the offspring of a trembler.

Lean Brasidas flashed a self-congratulatory smile at the far wall. If he was pleased with Styphon's explanation of the events of a year ago, he gave no sign.

"I think you must understand the tenuousness of your current position," Brasidas said instead. "Not only here, where any number of men would gladly cut your throat if I neglected to tell them not to, but also back home. As it stands, the life to which you'll return will be less worthwhile than the one you have here in prison. On the other hand, if a polemarch, even one who had just suffered an honest defeat, were to appeal to the Elders on your behalf, they might be persuaded to let you keep your property and a shred of honor. It may not be in their power to prevent other Equals from spitting on you, but they can do their best. I might be willing to do you such a favor, if you were willing to work for it. Rather hard." Brasidas finally spared his disgraced subordinate a single, contemptuous glance. "What do you say to that?"

"I say that you are a general and I am not," Styphon answered swiftly. "I am bound to do whatever you say, with or without any promise of reward."

"A good answer," Brasidas said. He seemed to mean it. "But I fear you may not understand completely. What I am looking for is a *dog*. Will you be my dog, Styphon?" He snorted. "I imagine there were many dogs born in Lakonia this year whose owners called them Styphon."

Styphon hesitated. What he had said already was true: he was bound to follow Brasidas's orders no matter what, but that was out of loyalty to his office and to the State, not his person. Helot slaves were called dogs often enough by their masters, and were treated as such, but slaves, too, served the Spartan state rather than any one man.

Was that what Brasidas wanted: an Equal reduced to Helot?

"Well?"

"Yes." Styphon forced the word out. This was likely the best and only opportunity he would ever get to salvage his name.

"Good," Brasidas said. "Now, dog, kneel at my feet."

Lowering himself to the hard-packed dirt of the courtyard floor, an act which prompted a chorus of jeers from Brasidas' honor guard, watching from a distance, Styphon sat on his haunches before the polemarch's bench.

"Good dog," Brasidas said. "Now let us talk more of this witch. She was not ransomed."

"No, sir," Styphon offered when Brasidas, purely by the length of his pause, granted him leave to speak. "She was brought to Athens by their general Demosthenes. I saw her myself at Piraeus, where she wore a slave's collar, but walked freely. Later, Demosthenes came to me here asking questions about her."

"*Demosthenes!*" Brasidas said, then purged the name's taste from his tongue by gathering and spitting a ball of phlegm into the dirt. "What did you tell him?"

"I said he should fear her. That she was a whore and a liar and a curse who would lead him and his city to ruin."

"Not bad," Brasidas conceded grudgingly. "I'd bet my balls the witch is helping him. I dealt the coward a killing blow at Amphipolis, and my blade stopped cold." His intelligent eyes burned, his bloodless lips were tight. "Like magic. The giant spindle-throwers that skewer men right through their shields are witch's work, too, I guarantee it."

Not wishing to draw any share of the general's obvious bitterness at the defeat onto himself, Styphon remained silent. At length, Brasidas's calculating side reasserted control and he gazed down at his kneeling dog.

"Now it is my turn to tell a story," he said. "Being privy to the goings-on in the Gerousia," Brasidas began, looking down his beak at Styphon, "I had occasion to hear of a certain message sent to our Elders last winter by the leaders of an Arkadian village near Bassai. I recall it because of the strangeness of its contents, which I laughed at then, but no longer. The letter, carried urgently by horse, pleaded that a detachment of Spartan troops be sent to purge their woods of a deadly presence.

"The presence was that of a female, the letter claimed, who had shown up in their town a day earlier with severe wounds. They described her as white-armed–the one arm she possessed, at any rate–with hair as snow. Somehow or other, an... altercation developed involving this female, ending in the deaths of six men. A force of locals gave chase, attempting to kill or subdue her.

"All but one man was slain, and he who escaped did not

long survive his wounds. Before dying, he described an encounter in which the already injured fugitive pressed her attack even while absorbing fresh wounds that rightly should have finished her. As you say of the sea-bitch, he described this woman as possessing the strength of Herakles. That is when the village leaders sent urgently to Sparta for aid."

Brasidas snorted. "Now, understand that hardly a month passes in which the Gerousia does not receive a request for help in dealing with a centaur, a satyr, a serpent, a minotaur, gorgons–even Kerberos, once. If the village-folk of our peninsula were to be believed, we live in an age of monsters. Even were there not a war to fight, such requests as this one from the Arkadians would go ignored. It only springs to mind now for my having come to this wretched city and heard tell of your sea-bitch from Sphakteria. Arkadian sheep-lickers as witnesses are one thing, thirty Equals another entirely." He raised a scarred brow. "Or just one Equal, even if he is a *dog*.

"I cannot say how the tale from Arkadia ends. Perhaps this woman evaded them and fled. The village still exists, for I rather think we would have heard of its destruction, and so it would seem that whatever occurred next, there was no further slaughter."

Brasidas gave his kneeling dog a look of impatience, unwarranted since the copious words were flowing down, not up. "So if you fail to grasp it, dog," he concluded, leaning forward to set chin on hand, scarred elbow resting on bruised knee just inches from Styphon's face, "what we have are two accounts of extraordinary females, both occurring within the space of a month. One goes to Athens where she helps a coward win battles, the other vanishes in the woods of Arkadia."

Brasidas raised his right hand, its little finger twisted from some long-ago injury, to tap Styphon's forehead.

"So let me ask you this," he said in time with the taps. "Did your sea-bitch mention having any friends?"

"No," Styphon answered. "Not that I can recall, at least."

Brasidas's reaction to his dog's memory lapse was surprisingly gentle, just a slight increase in the depth of disgust in his sneer. He sighed, settling back on his bench. "Nevertheless. There is enough evidence, in my mind, that in this one case, at least, the sheep-lickers might not be wrong, and Hellas may be stricken with a plague of witches. Since you're the only one among us to have shared words with one, in addition to being my dog, you can be my..." He snickered and finished, "witch expert!"

In the polemarch's eyes shone the excited gleam of a deposed king dreaming up his return to the throne.

"The minute we are free of this place, which will be *soon*," he declared defiantly, "you and I will go to Bassai. If we can find her, and if this snow-haired woman-thing is capable of reason... we will convince her to fight for Sparta."

2. Widow-Maker

In Athens, after Demosthenes endured the usual pomp of a general returning in triumph, there was Eurydike to deal with. He could not forget, nor did he want to, what he now knew of her and how she had come to Athens from her homeland. His heart fell and appetite fled for hours every time his mind conjured up, usually of its own accord, visions of the Thracian's young self, green eyes wild with anguish as her raped and ravaged sibling's half-dead body was ripped from tattooed arms and tossed into a gorge, worthless, a used-up, discarded item, food for beasts.

How had she carried on after that? His frequent term of endearment for Eurydike was *bright eyes*, but how was there any brightness left in them?

He did not even know her real name.

Eurydike raced out to meet him, and he greeted her with the usual warmth, or perhaps more. They went inside, and before long (once Thalassia knowingly excused herself) fell to fucking by the hearth. In the days which followed, his new perception of Eurydike was ever-present at the back of his thoughts, but since it was always easier to say nothing than to say something, he chose nothing.

He continued thus until the morning of the fourth day after his return, the day on which he was slated to pay a visit to the wife-candidate which the two women of his household would see added to their number. Even then, he said nothing directly.

Usually the mood in the bath chamber behind the megaron was light, but today when Eurydike had slipped pale and naked into the water beside him, he spoke to her earnestly. "I would have expected you to be upset at the idea I might marry," he said. "Yet you do not seem bothered."

Her freckled features twisted in consternation. "You think I only think of myself?"

"Hardly. But you must admit, in the past you have been less than eager to see me wed. And no one could blame you."

Eurydike took up a square of Thalassia's olive oil soap and began lathering his skin. "That's your own fault. You let me think a wife had to be one of those pasty, hollow-eyed little ghost girls you see in the agora, who can barely balance the babies in their bellies. Laonome's different. I liked her long before Thalassia ever brought up that you could marry her."

"So you approve?"

Eurydike's green eyes glazed like the tiny soap bubbles into which she stared. "Laonome says she wouldn't make you get rid of me, and I believe her."

Suddenly, almost angrily, Demosthenes grabbed her arm, surprising her enough that her instinct was to jerk away. But she fell still, and her emerald eyes were expectant.

"I will never get rid of you for anyone," he said. His lips hugged close around every word, and he meant them. He was, in effect, chastising her.

Then he softened, determining in that moment that this would be the day, the time, when he revealed what he knew of her past.

But not yet. There was a secret of his own that he could reveal first.

Seated, with water lapping at the purple bruise under his ribs, he pulled Eurydike's naked body against him. "Maybe you guessed this," he said, "but I never told you. Seasons ago I put you in my will. If anything should happen to me, you will have enough to live out your days, assuming you are wiser with money than you pretend to be. No wife, no heir will change that. You are not a piece of property to be disposed of. Even while you wear that collar, you are... free here. Do you understand?"

She melted into the embrace, her skin warmer even than the water surrounding them. She sighed, "Thank you."

He put a palm alongside her face, compressing dry red curls that were yet to submerged. She sat quietly in his embrace, business of the bath forgotten, but not with the usual distractions. He sensed disquiet in Eurydike. He raised her chin to look upon her face and perhaps kiss her lips and silence the scream that echoed from her past, heard by his ears alone. But when she raised her eyes, that bright place where true sadness was so rarely seen, they were liquid with checked tears.

One slid free, and it might has well have been her blunted Spartan dagger sliding into her master's breast. Before he had recovered from the wound, Eurydike said in an apologetic whisper, "I know she told you."

He affirmed it, with nothing more than a look, and pulled her head close under his chin.

She did not resist. "I'm glad," she said. Her breath licked the skin of his throat. "But I don't want to talk about it. About her. It hurts." Her voice was choked as she finished, "She would understand."

She. The nameless sister now dust and bones in a valley of Thrace.

What is your true name? he longed to ask, but held back. If she was happier in silence, and in being Eurydike, then let her be silent Eurydike. She was hardly the only one in this oikos to have left a name and a life behind her.

"Pfft!" Eurydike said suddenly. She sank from his embrace, submerging her whole body. An island of floating coppery curls was last to slip under, and then she rose up, a slick, speckled fish with head thrown back and straight, sopping hair trailing behind.

She cleared her face and brow of water and accused with acrimony that was wholly feigned, "You fuckwit! You made me cry!" Her tears, rare as Thalassia's, rare as his own, were gone now and would drain with the bathwater.

With a look of disdain as false as her own display, Demosthenes growled back, "I see the mistake in letting you be taught to read and write by someone with such a foul mouth."

Retrieving the cloth and cake of soap, Eurydike shrugged. "First, mine's fouler. And second, it doesn't matter 'cause I'm a shitty student anyway."

"At least you can count to two."

She swatted him.

***

When he was clean and shaved, he dressed in the finest himation he owned, one of brilliant white linen with geometric trim that was in fact nondescript by the standards of an Alkibiades or a Kleon. The day prior he had had his hair, grown rather wild in Thrace, trimmed back a bit, though it remained, on advice of both his women, rather longer than he had worn it previously. In the megaron, Thalassia stood facing him, making final adjustments to his appearance. Her fingers traced tingling lines on his scalp.

"Perfection," she declared. Her hands fell away, but she did not withdraw.

He had come to know when Thalassia was holding something back; or, at least, he knew when she wanted him to know when she was holding back.

"Out with it," he said, in no mood for games.

"There's one thing," she admitted, as no doubt she'd planned to all along. "It really isn't that important, but you ought to know so that it won't be a surprise should it come up in conversation today."

Demosthenes told her with a dark look that he did not much care for her prologue.

"Laonome's husband died in the Aetolian disaster," Thalassia revealed, "under your command."

He gaped. "Not important? How is that not important? I made her a widow! You tell me this *now?*"

"If you'd known, would you have agreed to meet her?"

"We will never know that now! But I would have had good enough reason not to. I killed her fucking husband!"

"If it's any consolation," Thalassia said, smoothing his chiton, utterly unperturbed, "he treated her like garbage."

3. Laonome

Rattled but undeterred, Demosthenes called on his prospective bride at the house of her brother and *kyrios*, Autokles, in the deme of Koele. Autokles greeted his illustrious guest wearing what was doubtless his own finest himation, and he fawned so much that he threatened to soak both his own and his guest's garments in drool.

"What an honor it is to welcome the hero of Amphipolis into my humble home," Autokles droned, bowing low in the doorway. "Not to forget Pylos, of course! To think we might become kin! But I get ahead of myself. Here, come in, come in. This is my wife, Chrysis. That's a special pomegranate cheese she is bringing you. It comes from her father's farm. She sells it in the agora, or tries her best to, but thus far it appeals only to customers with truly discerning palates. A shame we have to resort to such measures to make ends meet, but–well, let us not dwell on that. I suppose you would like to meet Laonome!"

"Aye." It was Demosthenes' first contribution to the conversation, such as it was, and he made it whilst seated on a worn couch and holding a morsel of vile pink cheese. Thankfully Autokles wasted no time dispatching his giddy wife upstairs to send down the sister-in-law who had dwelt with them since her husband's death.

Moments later, Laonome descended the stairs. She was pale skinned, notwithstanding a pink cast to her cheeks which was likely temporary, and her long, straight hair of light brown had been pleated into a multitude of small braids fastened in loops around her head in a mock garland that was peppered with small, white blossoms. At the nape of her bare neck nestled the only piece of jewelry she wore, a silver brooch turned into a necklace by the addition of a silken ribbon. Her chiton was of pale pink, with an embroidered hem that dragged just slightly behind her heels. Its bodice had been gathered and pinned at the front to mimic the pleating of a more expensive gown.

Thalassia had not lied. Laonome was eminently fu–

Inviting.

The widow reached the floor of the megaron, halted and stood before her suitor with hands clasped and brown eyes dutifully downcast. Autokles, seated beside his guest on the couch, beamed at his sister's entrance and set to nudging Demosthenes with an elbow in the hope his own enthusiasm would prove contagious.

"Sit, sit, my beloved sister!" Autokles urged.

Laonome glided in her long chiton to a chair set far enough from the men to preclude her participation in the conversation, but close enough that she could easily serve as its object. When she was seated, Autokles produced a scroll which he opened and presented to her suitor.

"I could go on and on about how well she cooks and how you will get no trouble from her," her keeper said, "but no doubt you will think me biased. So let me show you this instead. As you can see, it is a sworn statement by her deceased husband's father to the effect that his son found Laonome's personality unobjectionable and her household skills more than satisfactory. Here, read for yourself!"

"High praise indeed," Demosthenes remarked after pretending to scan the document. He glanced briefly at Laonome to see if she might be receptive to a smile at her brother's expense, but she demurely averted her eyes.

Autokles tucked the affidavit back into his chiton for future use, should today's efforts come to naught. Abruptly, he threw an urgent look over his shoulder in the direction of a street-facing window. He leaped to his feet and ran over, peering outside.

"You must excuse me for a few moments," he said. "There is a man outside who borrowed twenty drachmae from me and then vanished without trace. What terrible timing it is for him to reappear now, but I really had better chase him down!"

Autokles raced out his front door, but not before drawing the curtains on the window and flicking a curious glance at his sister.

Demosthenes had never been a suitor before, but he knew, as anyone did, that a guardian never left a man alone with his potential bride. Even if she was not a virgin. And so for several awkward minutes, Demosthenes waited for Chrysis to descend and replace her husband as chaperon, but she never came.

Laonome sat rigid in her chair with hands folded, head bowed. At the risk of being caught staring, Demosthenes studied her face. It was fine and feminine, its highlight a pair of full pink lips the upper of which was marred by a tiny, bloodless scar which was prominent enough to be noticeable, but which failed to detract. Besides finding her face a pleasant sight, he detected on it the trace of some inner struggle. Did it have something to do with that cruel twist of fate which Thalassia had convinced him did not matter, that he had been the one to lead her husband to his death in Aetolia? Thalassia had told him the dead man's name, but no face matched it in his memory.

When the long silence lurched from awkward to intolerable, Demosthenes smiled and tried and failed to gain eye contact with Laonome. He said anyway, "I suppose it cannot be pleasant to be talked about like a sow at the butcher's."

If possible, Laonome's posture grew even stiffer. The

brooch at her neck pivoted briefly as a lump passed underneath it.

"Apologies," Demosthenes said. "I did not mean to call you a sow. It was meant as a joke. You have met Thalassia and Eurydike, so you know I need a sense of humor to suffer keeping them in my home." To offset the inadvertent self-compliment with praise for her, he added, "They speak very highly of you."

Laonome's reaction was a series of rapid eye blinks while she stared down at her folded hands. Whatever conflict had been written on her features seemed to come now to a head. She looked up and gave a thin, tentative smile, at last meeting her suitor's gaze.

"My brother did not leave by chance," she said, voice just above a whisper. "He expects me to flirt with you. More than that. Because I have no dowry, he says the only reason anyone would ever marry me is to save money by getting a wife and a whore for one price. He told me to... show you my tits." She had the courage to use unladylike vulgarity, but not without blushing. "But I will not. I hope you are not disappointed."

"Quite the opposite," Demosthenes returned, relieved to have the tension broken. "I think that if you had followed that advice, I would be on my way home now."

Laonome coyly broke off her gaze. "Not that I don't have a nice body," she added. "I do, I think, for having borne two sons."

Demosthenes had no chance to reply before Autokles returned to carry on his charade.

"The thief swears he will have it for me next month!" the master of the house lied. He cast what he thought was a subtle look at Laonome, who in answer turned a pink cheek on him. Autokles sat and said eagerly to Demosthenes, "Did I mention that sons run in our family? Both of Laonome's children were strapping lads right up until the plague took them, poor souls."

Just as Autokles' backside hit the couch, Demosthenes rose from it abruptly. With panic plain on his face, Autokles followed suit.

"Do not leave so soon!" he sputtered. "We have not discussed–"

"Autokles of Koele," Demosthenes addressed the man, "I formally request the hand of your sister Laonome in marriage."

He had made the decision only in that instant. He could not quite say why. He knew that he liked Laonome, and not only out of pity for her unenviable situation, and neither for guilt over his part in causing it. Maybe in truth what he had decided was to trust in the instincts of those who knew him best. Sure, it was a risk adding to his oikos a third female who was such a natural ally to the two willful ones already inhabiting it. But he was unlikely, instinct said, to find a more suitable match than Laonome without scouring the city, a task which he had no intention of undertaking.

The wind flew out of Autokles in a single, hot gust. As quickly as he had risen, the distasteful man fell to his knees and scrambled to clasp Demosthenes' right hand. There came from upstairs a loud clatter followed by the fast scrape of sandals on the stairs, the result of which was the timely arrival of a surely eavesdropping Chrysis.

But Demosthenes' attention was not on them. He watched his betrothed. Laonome's lower lip gently trembled beneath the upper with its white scar, which he already found endearing. Her lashes fluttered and tears slid down her cheeks. Whether they came from sadness or joy, it was impossible to tell, and she covered them quickly. They were tears of change, perhaps, but Autokles and his wife took no notice of them. Euphoric, they embraced then praised the gods and danced in delight before their prestigious soon-to-be brother-in-law.

"The wedding should be modest," Demosthenes declared, "and as soon as possible."

"Of course!" Autokles veritably sang. "My new brother!"

Claiming he had pressing business, which he did not, Demosthenes made a hasty exit.

4. Princess and Fool

Poseideon in the archonship of Isarchos (December 424 BCE)

They were hostages in an enemy land, technically at the mercy of the mob-rule which Athenians labeled democracy, but inside the jailhouse walls, as far as any Spartiate was concerned, Brasidas ruled. He treated the men just as he would have if they had been here in Attica as invaders: assigning duties, organizing drills, leading calisthenics and enforcing an iron discipline to which, owing to the authority bestowed on Brasidas by the ephors and a reputation untarnished even by his capture, the prisoners happily submitted.

The crookedest of the Athenian guards greeted the new discipline and unity with disappointment, since it robbed them of the chance to administer beatings and ended the intra-Spartan violence which had until then broken out periodically, and which the jailers sometimes wagered on, intervening only when necessary to prevent the loss of a valuable hostage. But they were in the minority; most guards were happy to see their jobs made easier. In exchange for making their lives easier, the Athenians treated Brasidas well and gave him considerable leeway in managing the lives of his prisoners. In time, it hardly seemed as if the Equals were imprisoned at all, so closely did existence within the jail house walls mimic barracks life in Sparta.

Of course, it was all a facade.

The routine, the compliance, the discipline ushered in by the arrival of Brasidas were only a cover for the digging of an escape tunnel. Two tunnels, in fact, on account of the large number of prisoners. Due for completion by winter's end, the tunnels were to terminate not just outside the wall of the prison compound but further off, in places chosen in stolen glances through and over the wall, where the escapees might emerge into the cover of densely packed homes.

Styphon was discreetly emptying a load of loose earth from the pocket created by the fold of his prison smock over its rope belt when an Athenian guard emerged into the prison yard and made a line for him. Keeping his nerve, Styphon let the last of the dirt fall whilst slowly turning to face the oncoming guard.

"Come with me," the guard said. His hand rested casually on the club slung at his hip. The jailers wisely did not carry edged weapons, lest one be taken and used by the prisoners who greatly outnumbered them.

Under the suspicious gazes of his fellow prisoners, Styphon followed the guard into the building which housed the bulk of the jailhouse offices. When the door was closed and latched behind them, another Athenian came up and bolted irons connected by rattling chains onto Styphon's wrists and ankles.

"You have a visitor," the second Athenian said.

The announcement set Styphon's mind at ease: his summons did not concern the tunnels.

The guards brought him to the same small interview room in which, until his replacement by Brasidas, he had sat in one day each month to confer with a Spartan envoy allowed in by the Athenians. Once, some sixteen months ago, he had shared the room with the general who had put him here, Demosthenes.

The visitor who waited across the table now was neither of those. In the eyes of any Spartan, the man now present was the prototypical Athenian: meticulously clean-shaven with fluffy waves of womanly brown hair, an intricately decorated chiton that would be the envy of any Persian princess and porcelain fingers that looked as if they might break off were he to wrap them around a spear. The nails he intermittently tapped on the table were devoid of the tiniest speck of dirt.

Styphon sat. The door was shut behind him.

"I know how much you Equals hate idle chatter," the visitor said, "so to be sure you listen to me instead of humming battle paeans in your head, I shall not bother with any. I am Alkibiades. You may have heard of me."

Styphon had not. Even if he had, he would have given the same reaction, which was none. The effeminate fool paused, as if playing role in one of the dramas his people adored so much.

"We share an acquaintance," the Athenian resumed. "You named her, I am told. Actually I am rather more acquainted with her than you are, I think, unless–well, I digress. I come to tell you that she kept the promise she made to you on the island. Your daughter Andrea is here in Athens, and has been for a year."

However much Styphon had reviled this arrogant ladyboy from the moment he laid eyes on him, he now could not help but take an interest in his words. Not that he would let that show, if he could help it.

The blowhard proceeded: "I am caring for the girl as if she were my own. Her tutors are Thalassia and the wisest man in Athens, Socrates. Maybe you have heard of him? No?"

Alkibiades shrugged, oblivious to the boiling of Styphon's blood at the thought that his offspring might be raised by this worthless preener.

"No matter. I have not forgotten that she is Spartan, and neither will she. I was suckled on Lakonian tit, not that I would insult you by saying that makes me even half-equal to an Equal. But I do know and respect your ways. I know you let your females shed their clothes and compete in games," he put a manicured hand over his heart, "a practice of which I wholeheartedly approve.

"Maybe you already knew that Andrea is quite the little runner. And her mind is no less fleet. It is as though she is a grown woman and a child in the same skin. One minute a quiet intelligence lurks behind her eyes; the next she is up to mischief." He laughed sharply. "And gods help any child who insults her. Or insults Sparta!"

Some revelation creased Alkibiades' smooth brow. "Shit," he remarked to the tabletop, "she is just like a miniature–"

The end of that comparison went unspoken. He looked back and nodded earnestly.

"I just thought that a father should know such things."

The Athenian's expression was open, sincere, and Styphon had to admit to himself that his opinion of the fool had risen since the start of the interview. As for Andrea, Styphon had spared thoughts for her from time to time while rotting in his cell. While she certainly could have a better keeper than this princess seated before him, she could surely do worse. Her current situation sounded better for her than what she would face in Sparta, at any rate. Cruelty toward cowards and their kin was enshrined in Lykurgan law, and Sparta's children could be crueler even than her grown men and women.

However, gratitude to this preener did not preclude attempting to pry information from him. After a long, stony silence which should seem nothing strange to anyone claiming familiarity with Spartan ways, Styphon summoned up an ability he rarely exercised, that to deceive.

"I appreciate your coming to tell me of these things," he said. It was not quite a lie. Hyperbole, perhaps. Almost certainly it was what the princess, an ego-stroker for certain, had arrived hoping to hear. "I have worried for Andrea, and it lifts my spirit to learn she is in good hands. I very much hope that the gods will let me out of this place one day to see her again."

Alkibiades was quick to insert, "Would that I could bring her here, but as you may imagine, there is a need for discretion."

"On both our parts."

This was the truth, undiluted. It would not do for Brasidas to learn of Andrea's 'defection' or how it had come about.

Styphon resumed, less honestly, "I know we are enemies, Athenian. But on our shared love for the girl, perhaps you might tell me: is there any talk of what is to be our fate?"

The visitor appraised Styphon with a pensive frown before apparently deeming there to be no harm in answering.

"I would not worry too much," he said. "You are too useful as hostages to kill. The problem is–for you, anyway, not us, and least of all me–the problem is that given our recent victories, few voters have interest signing a treaty, which is your only path home. The exception is..."

He trailed off, as if catching his loose tongue. But he had caught it too late; there could be only one 'exception' in these cells.

Styphon leaned forward, chains dragging on the floor. "If it is Brasidas you mean," he said conspiratorially, "he may be my superior and my countryman, but he is no friend. I ran this place until he came. Now his word is the only thing separating me from death, and I fear the barrier may fall any day."

Another, briefer appraisal, and Alkibiades smiled. "There is talk of executing him," he divulged. "It would be madness, of course. He is too valuable, and not to mention it would doom the next Athenian strategos to find himself in

Spartan hands. But then, Kleon has a talent for making madness sound as reason." He chuckled. "I am a little jealous of it, actually. I shall surely vote for it. Reason is overrated." His light expression grew grave as he urged, "Keep yourself alive another month, Styphon. You may yet find yourself a tyrant again." He grinned, teeth agleam. "Tyrant of Shitopolis, sure. But better that than its fool, right?"

The real fool present, the Athenian, rose from his chair.

"It was a pleasant chat," he said. "I hope the next time we have the pleasure, Andrea can be present with us. Somehow, somewhere. I have learned of late something that I only suspected before: that nothing is impossible."

The princess punctuated those final, hopeful words with a knock on the doorframe. An invisible iron bolt slid back, the door was opened from without, and Alkibiades' presence in the tiny room was replaced by that of the guard. While returning to the yard, Styphon pondered carefully his next move. Plenty of men had seen him taken into the prison office. Likely someone had already reported the summons to Brasidas. That left no option but to go straight to the general himself and make a report, lest it seem he was hiding something.

All eyes were on him as he returned. Meeting some of the hardest of those eyes with his own dark gaze, he marched straight to Brasidas. The general shared a cell meant for twenty in the overcrowded jail with just the twelve members of his honor guard. Six were present. The most senior put a hand on Styphon's chest, barring his way.

"You know the drill, dog," the guard warned. Behind him, Brasidas looked down his sharp nose with neither approval nor disapproval, but no intention of interfering.

Swallowing his pride, a task which had become easier by the day since Sphakteria, Styphon lowered himself to his hands and knees in the open cell door. To howls from the honor guard and not a few kicks in the rear, he crawled forward, the ends of his long, matted hair gathering pebbles and dust from the floor of packed dirt.

"Leave us," Brasidas said to his guard, silencing them, more or less. When they were alone, Brasidas commanded, "Sit up and speak, dog."

Styphon fell back onto his haunches before his pitiless master and related tonelessly, "An Athenian by the name of Alkibiades visited me."

"Perikles' ward." Suspicion lit Brasidas' keen eyes. "Why should he come to you and not me?"

"I have no idea, sir," Styphon lied, and swiftly moved on. Though the prospect of seeing Brasidas dragged off to face the garrotte before a cheering Athenian mob was not without its allure, the sense of obedience drilled into him from birth forced the truth from him: "He says that their Assembly will soon consider your execution."

Brasidas failed to appear shocked by the pronouncement. He directed a blank stare over Styphon's head and mused, "Execute me, hmm? Do you gather that this Alkibiades is a traitor?"

"He gave a few reasons for sharing the information with me," Styphon improvised. "Spartan sympathies, the belief that you are too valuable to kill, distaste for the politician behind the proposal."

All true, of course, but none the truth itself: that the information had been coaxed from Alkibiades by means of a bond best kept secret.

Pursing his lips, the polemarch sank into thought while absently twisting strands of long, straight hair between thumb and forefinger. Momentarily his focus returned, and he said to his kneeling dog, "I rather suspect you are hiding something.

But never mind that. Our escape needs a new timeline. I think we might just make do with one tunnel instead of two, don't you?"

5. Wedding

Gamelion, the winter month which drew its name from the fact that most Athenians considered it ideal for a wedding, was fast approaching, but no one involved in this particular union, not least the groom, saw fit to delay the ceremony until then. And so, only a few short weeks after their betrothal, declarations were made and witnessed in the law courts that both parties were the legitimate offspring of two citizen parents, and Laonome's keeper Autokles gave her willingly into the guardianship of her new lord, Demosthenes of Thria.

The *gamete,* the wedding feast thrown by Autokles, was as small an affair as could be managed when one of the principals was a person of some renown. At its conclusion, Laonome was borne in a garlanded wagon trailed by a small entourage of singing and dancing women to her new home in Tyrmeidai. By the time it had completed its passage through the interlying demes, the procession had swelled with enough clingers-on to clog the streets for blocks. In Athens, few men (and fewer women, where weddings were concerned) were willing to pass up the chance to join in a celebration of any kind.

Having gone on ahead from the banquet, Demosthenes awaited the arrival of his bride at his home alongside his two slaves, both of whom were dressed in their finest. As slaves, of course, they could not participate in feast or procession. Eurydike seemed genuinely excited, while Thalassia's expression, if he read it right, which was hardly certain, held a glimmer of pride at having made it happen.

When the sound of flutes and singers came to ear, Eurydike raced to the window hoping to catch first glimpse of the procession.

"It's here!" she cried, and ran back to take her place at her adoptive sister's side, a step behind her master.

The wagon drew up and halted in front of Demosthenes' garden, its followers choking the street. The bride's chief attendant, the *nympheutria*, Chrysis, descended from the wagon and extended an arm to help Laonome down in her flowing, borrowed gown of gold-trimmed yellow. Her hair was molded into elaborate ringlets piled high on her head, and draped over it, partly obscuring her face, was a veil of translucent Amorgos silk. She walked the garden path under gently swaying palm fronds to reach the open doorway in which her husband waited.

At the threshold, with Chrysis gathering up the gown behind her, Laonome lowered herself and raised a braceleted forearm above her head. Demosthenes responded by clasping the proffered wrist, drawing the bride to her feet and walking her through the doorway and to the hearth of her new home. In Sparta it was said they clung even more closely to the ancient practice of bridal abduction, but today, in Athens, this was the civilized remnant of a barbaric past.

Returning hand-in-hand to the door with his new wife, Demosthenes was heartened to find not tears in Laonome's eyes but only a mix of exhaustion and relief as she stood waving and blowing kisses at the cheering crowd of friends, relatives, and strangers until at last, long minutes later, the door was shut. Eurydike came forward, knelt before Laonome and planted a kiss on her hand. Thalassia did the same, if less girlishly, and then the three women exchanged hugs more in the manner of friends than mistress and slaves.

When that was finished, Laonome pressed close to her new husband, resting her cheek on his chest. "Are you as glad as I am that is over?"

"More," Demosthenes replied truthfully.

That night they went to bed early, or rather they retired

early to their bedchamber, where they made love in several sessions punctuated by light sleep in one another's arms. Laonome was a skilled lover, neither too timid nor too aggressive, with a body full of pleasing curves. Demosthenes' lone complaint was that being unused to sharing a bed for the purpose of sleep, he found it hard to do so with a leg draped over him and the weight of a head pinning his shoulder to the mattress. But in sleep Laonome looked so serene he did not dare disturb her. He would get used to it soon enough, he assumed.

Their second night began much as the first, but when Demosthenes ran out of strength and seed, they talked. He ran a finger over the scar on her upper lip, asking how it had come to be there. When Laonome just self-consciously pushed his hand aside and covered it, he kissed her gently and let the matter drop. An hour later she raised the subject herself, tentatively and unprompted. Years ago, she told him, her late husband, returning home drunk as he often did, had shoved her, and in falling she had struck her face on the edge of a table. She showed another scar on her inner forearm where her husband, drunk again, had carelessly cut her while threatening her with a sword.

They did not speak at all of how the perpetrator of such abuse had met his death in Aetolia, yet neither did that potentially sensitive matter hang over them.

On their third night of marriage, Laonome said she was sore and invited Eurydike to join them. Laonome lay on her side and watched with interest, occasionally stroking her husband's arm or Eurydike's naked thigh. Just before culmination of the act, she interrupted and took the slave's place so as not to waste any chance to conceive. Showing no sign of dissatisfaction with the new arrangement, Eurydike gathered her crumpled chiton from the floor and left the room as giddy as she had arrived.

"Did you enjoy that?" Laonome asked when they were alone.

Rather than speaking, Demosthenes grunted a positive-sounding note, all he had strength for.

"My first husband whored behind my back for many years. Eventually he took a concubine. Most nights I went to sleep on linens damp with her juices. I do not want that humiliation again. I know that Eurydike is your *pallake,* and I want you to keep her. Do whatever pleases you, but give me the dignity of knowing."

Demosthenes held his new wife tight, kissed the tip of her nose. "You are what pleases me," he said. "But Eurydike is..."

"Thracian?" Laonome finished for him.

He laughed. "I was going to say complicated. But Thracian works well."

"And Thalassia?"

He heard the name often enough, but for some reason now it made the muscles of his body tense. "We did the deed once," he confessed. He hoped he kept shame out of his voice. "But not deliberately. I was drunk." Recalling Laonome's tales of her drunken husband, he hastened to add, "It was the first time I have been drunk in ten years, mind you. Neither are mistakes I shall repeat."

"Why was it a mistake to fuck her? Have you seen the way men stare at her in town? What flaw is it you see that they do not?"

Uncomfortably considering his response, Demosthenes wondered if the object of their conversation, with her predator's ears, was eavesdropping now through the walls.

"She is... unstable," he lied. Or was it a lie? He almost hoped Thalassia listened. She likely would laugh that thin-lipped, breathy, inward laugh of hers which made the giver proud to have earned it.

Laonome's own laugh, also a sweet sound, turned his thoughts back to her, their more rightful object. She fingered the tiny hairs of his chest underneath the heavy woolen blankets, outside of which the winter chill froze the plaster and tile surfaces of the bedchamber.

"We women are all unstable, are we not?" Laonome reflected. The question was rhetorical, something with which any Athenian, male or female, with few exceptions, would agree. "We are ruled by our bodies. I would think one like hers would have certain needs."

"It does. She satisfies them with Alkibiades."

"Him? You allow it?"

"I see no reason not to."

He was not about to explain right now, and maybe not ever, that it was not for him to allow or disallow Thalassia anything, or that one of his slaves was not really a slave at all but in fact his partner in a conspiracy against Fate.

He knew that if that battered deity were present with them in the marriage bed, she might well have hissed in his bride's ear, *Your new husband consorts with a star-whore and invites a doom far worse than that your last one met!*

But Fate, cowed for now by defeat, remained silent.

Laonome stretched her neck up to peck her husband's cheek, then laid her head down on his chest and shut her eyes.

"A strange name, Thalassia," she remarked lazily. "'Sea-thing.' Isn't that the wood that washes up on the beach, that men whittle into animals and sell in the agora?"

"It is," Demosthenes confirmed, and squeezed his wife's body tight against his bare flesh.

The next morning, Laonome bought Thalassia a gift: a driftwood carving of a dolphin.

6. Jailbreak

Morning filled Demosthenes' second-story bedchamber with rays of cold winter sunlight, the scent of baking bread, and the sounds of bustling activity. For the first time in its current occupancy, that bedchamber was shared by husband and wife. Both lazed naked under covers of wool and fur, and as had been the case on each of the five mornings which had passed since their wedding day, they were in no hurry to rise.

Thus Demosthenes was still half asleep when the muted sounds of life in the deme of Tyrmeidai were drowned out, then silenced, by the distant shrill wail of a trumpet, a long, sustained blast. When the note ended, another soared with barely the space of a breath between.

An alarm. He sat upright. Laonome did the same, clinging to his side with deep worry overtaking sleep in her almond-shaped eyes. *What is happening?* the look asked, and Demosthenes answered with a comforting hand on her wool-draped thigh. Since he knew no more than she, it was the best answer he could give.

"Stay near to Thalassia," he told his bride, and hoped his tone struck the right balance between urgency and calm. "Do whatever she tells you, without question. Understand?"

Laonome's look betrayed confusion at this strange command to obey a slave, but she only nodded. As Demosthenes made to leave the bed she clasped his wrist, pulled him back and kissed his lips hard with the force of passion.

"I love you," she said for the fifth time in as many days. He was blessed. These were words that most men never in their adult lives heard spoken truthfully. "Do not make me a widow again."

He tucked a lock of uncombed hair behind Laonome's

ear, reassured her with a smile. "Rise, dress, take breakfast, go about your day. I shall be back very shortly."

He tried to rise but found Laonome's hand still firmly clamped on his arm. "Promise me," she pleaded. "Promise you will put me first. Before honor, before glory, before elections. Before Athens. Just for a year. Then give yourself back to the city if you must."

Demosthenes let the beginning of a chuckle slip before he saw the fear and hope in his new wife's eyes, saw the jaw clenched so tightly that it trembled, knuckles that were white on his wrist as though her life depended on the grasp. Seeing the intensity and sincerity with which she implored him, he lost any thought of laughter and answered in a heartbeat, "I swear it."

He dressed quickly in a himation suitable for the winter chill, took up his short sword in its scabbard and, with a final kiss gentler than their last, he left Laonome.

In the women's quarters, now a miniature Persepolis to their former Sparta, he found his two slaves standing in wait with his scale armor corselet. While they buckled it on him Demosthenes shared a secret look with Thalassia, conveying without need for words what was expected of her: *Protect them.*

Her pale eyes calmly accepted the burden. He slung his shield on his back, did the same with the canvas sack containing his helmet and the rest of his war gear, and he descended the stairs to emerge into a street where confusion reigned.

"What has happened?" he asked his neighbors. Some, like him, wore armor and carried weapons, while others yet hoped the raising of the general alarm was some mistake. Their answers proved them just as clueless as he.

Suddenly at the street's north end there appeared dozens

of men, women and children all moving south with purpose in their strides. Demosthenes met the odd stream of refugees at a run, shouting questions at whomever would listen. When no one replied, he grabbed a fleeing male slave by the arm.

"The Spartan prisoners," the slave blurted in a panic, trying to wrench his arm away. "They are loose!"

Demosthenes let the man go and hastened north, against the human current, in the direction of the jailhouse and the sound of the still-blaring trumpet. Several minutes spent at a run, sweating under the weight of his panoply, brought him to the law courts. There he grabbed a stunned Scythian policeman who, recognizing him, guided him not to the jail but to the edge of a winding, densely built street in the nearby deme of Melite.

A cluster of soldiers and police captains and generals stood there, Nikias and Kleon among them. Neither was geared for war; likely they had been in the agora or civic offices just next door when the alarm had sounded. It was where any strategos would be at this time, if he was not using the excuse of his recent wedding to laze about the house.

Nikias was issuing urgent orders to police and armed citizens, while the City Protector, Kleon, loudly punctuated each of the old man's commands with, "Yes, yes, as he says!"

Demosthenes pushed his way through to them, and Nikias filled him in.

"The prisoners dug a tunnel," the elder general said. "We have them cordoned in this neighborhood, but they have hostages and whatever weapons they have obtained from the houses."

Demosthenes felt a surge of mingled anger and relief: anger at the grievous lapse of security, relief that his own household was in no immediate danger. There was little to do but wait. Nikias seemed to have matters well in hand, even if

Kleon–whose official responsibility on the Board was homeland defense–wished to believe the hand was his own.

The wait was short. In the narrow street overlooked by the small plaza in which the generals stood, the figure of a man appeared: a tall, long-haired Spartan in his prison chiton bearing the mocking sign of the crimson alpha.

Demosthenes knew the man by sight, having fallen to him in single combat.

Brasidas stood unarmed, holding aloft horizontally over his head a makeshift herald's wand, a stick garlanded with an anemic laurel vine doubtless cut from some citizen's garden. Nikias's balled fist went into the air in a hold command directed at the bowmen who stood on nearby rooftops with arrows nocked and aimed. Brasidas was allowed to draw up to a point just beyond the barricade of carts and tables and couches which the Spartans had hastily thrown up at the head of the evacuated street.

"Athenians!" Brasidas called out. "We hold thirty citizen women and seventy children. They are untouched for now, and we have no wish to harm them. All you need do to secure their return is accede to our demands, which are simple. We want our shields back and a guarantee of safe passage to Megara." He paused briefly and scanned his rapt audience. "Is Demosthenes among you?"

"I am here." Demosthenes stepped forward, even as his thoughts went to his home and Laonome and their warm twin comforts of a soft bed and her softer body.

Brasidas laughed, a cold sound. "Do your countrymen know that it is a woman who gives them victory?"

Demosthenes' heart plunged, for the space of one beat, into icy water. So Brasidas knew of Thalassia; Styphon had told him of meeting Thalassia on the island, naturally. The rest he must somehow have deduced on his own.

"Let the innocents go," Demosthenes said flatly, more to change the subject than in real hope of achieving that result. Brasidas was hardly about to relinquish his sole advantage.

Addressing the whole crowd, Brasidas shouted, "I will free twelve wives and all their children if Demosthenes, who should be dead already, takes their place! If he is brave enough! You have our demands. If our shield arms remain empty a half hour from now, this street begins filling with corpses!"

With that Brasidas spun on his heel and receded down the captured street. His improvised herald's wand clattered on the paving stones where he threw it. The time for talk was over.

The generals present, which comprised most of the Board, closed in a tight circle. Even though Kleon had jurisdiction, all looked to Nikias for the first word.

Demosthenes forcefully preempted both: "Bring them their shields."

Red-faced Kleon scoffed. "Not a chance!"

The captured shields, still on display in the Stoa Pointile, were his treasure.

"Half an hour is ample time to ready an assault," Kleon went on. "We shall take them alive and save as many women and children as we can. To which end, dearest Demosthenes, you must take him up on his offer. I have no doubt that any one of us would do the same in your place. But since it is *you* he has asked for..."

In the air above Melite, a infant's droning cry arose, and then abruptly, by some means or another, was silenced.

"Give them their shields!" Demosthenes repeated through gritted teeth. "And their safe passage. It makes no difference if Sparta gets them back. We will win this war all the same. You must trust me. Holding onto them is not worth one Athenian's life!"

"Of course it is!" Kleon came back testily. "How many Athenian lives have I saved already by bringing them here? And how many more might continue to be saved so long as they–"

"Shut your fat fucking mouth," Demosthenes said, and he looked impatiently to Nikias for a decision.

But Nikias remained silent, and the demagogue was not done.

"I am City Protector and the final word is *mine* to give!" Kleon raged. "No shields! No passage!*Nothing!* We will recapture them, and if in the process they kill the helpless, the blood-guilt will stain *their* souls, not–"

Kleon did not finish. Instead he fell reeling to the ground, sent there with blood streaming from his ruddy face by the clenched fist of Demosthenes.

Rubbing his knuckles while his victim twisted and crawled, barely conscious, on the cold earth, Demosthenes said, "Seeing as the chief of homeland defense is incapacitated, do any object to my assuming his duties?"

No one did. The hard, gray eyes of Nikias showed neither approval nor remonstration. He could hardly have felt much grief on seeing Kleon, the constant thorn in his side, laid low.

Demosthenes' eyes sought a trustworthy face in the gathered crowd and found one in Leokrates, the man who had subdued Brasidas at Amphipolis, and won for it the prize for valor. He told Leokrates, "Round up as many able men as you need, collect the shields from the Painted Stoa and bring them here."

With a proud nod Leokrates raced off to comply, tapping a dozen men to accompany him.

"I need a priest and a clerk of the law-court!"

Demosthenes called out over the crowd. "Tell both to bring their seals."

He wasted no breath declining the trade that Brasidas proposed, mostly so as not to call attention to the fact that he had given no thought to accepting it. The lives of the families trapped in Melite were precious, but he had sworn a pledge to his own new family that morning, and it was one he would keep. He would not trade Laonome's happiness for that of others, for he knew with near certainty that his walk down that street would end not in captivity but sacrifice.

Well before Brasidas's deadline had passed, stacks of battered lambda-blazoned shields began arriving on handcarts pushed by slaves and citizens alike. In with the first cartload of shields to be sent down the captured street went a sworn document signed by six generals, four priests and the *archon basileus* promising the escapees safe passage to Megara. Minutes after the guarantee went in, women and children began streaming out. Some walked, looking as shades escaped from Hades, but most, especially the young, raced up the street into freedom and into the arms of waiting relations. The reunions were both joyous and tearful, but as the last cart laden with shields went in and the trickle of freed hostages dried up, there remained a dozen frantic men in the plaza yet to greet their missing loved ones.

A citizen woman who was among the last to emerge told why.

"They will take twelve wives with them to the border," she said. "Unless Demosthenes takes their place."

Her fearful eyes found the man she named. The gazes of the other strategoi swiftly followed, insistent on a response.

"He has his freedom and his guarantee," Demosthenes said, stifling shame. "Send word that his revenge for Amphipolis will have to wait. Tell him that every able man in

Athens will shadow them to the border in full arms, and the first woman's death scream will be their call to charge."

Nikias swiftly departed with his aides to see to the promised escort, which he would have no trouble raising. The remaining Board members present were doubtless all disappointed to some degree, either simply at what they saw as a display of cowardice or else the lost opportunity to be rid of a political rival, but (perhaps mindful of Kleon's bloodied face) they kept their feelings to themselves.

There was little chance Brasidas would kill the hostages. To avenge his humiliation, he might dare to cut the throat of one general on the Megarian frontier, but he was not bloodthirsty enough to begin slaughtering women, not with such an unprecedented success in sight. He would return home to even greater glory as the rescuer of his countrymen than he would have won as the conqueror of tiny, remote Amphipolis. The loss of so many of their best men at Pylos had frustrated the Spartans for long seasons and now, thanks to Brasidas, they would get their men back bloodlessly, with nothing given up in exchange.

While others attended to the Spartans' departure from Athens, Demosthenes remained in the rapidly emptying plaza. Thalassia had foreseen nothing like this occurrence. But she had labeled Brasidas as clever and dangerous and pressed for his death. Now it became clear why. Demosthenes did not look forward to informing her of the day's events. Thalassia was not likely to reprimand him, but then she did not have to; the lesson was well taken that no warning of the star-girl was to be dismissed, lightly or otherwise.

There was another lesson, too: Fate would not consent to stay down after one blow. She was in a fighting mood.

Still, not even the prospect of delivering bad news to Thalassia was enough to make him dread returning home, for

Laonome was there, and solace.

The Spartans were filing triumphantly into the street to form up in orderly rows for the march to the Dipylon Gate, and their freedom, when Kleon, earlier carted away insensate by a gaggle of his devoted followers, returned.

"You will regret this, Demosthenes!" the demagogue fumed, pointing a meaty finger. His lips and chin still were crimson with smeared blood. "I will have your generalship and every obol of your patrimony for this!"

There was a fair chance he was right.

7. Slaughtergoddess

Gamelion in the archonship of Isarchos (January 423 BCE)

Dressed in his war gear and a shabby winter cloak, Styphon stood on the frost-hardened road in the shadow of the Temple of Apollo, waiting. He waited for Brasidas and for news, news of whether or not the Gerousia of Sparta had branded Styphon, son of Pharax, as a trembler.

Already he had been denied the homecoming granted his fellow prisoners. Instead, Brasidas had sent his dog to Bassai, in the thickly wooded hills of western Arkadia, to gather what information he could on the supposed witch who had reportedly slain men by the dozen more than a year ago.

Most men here, he had learned, did not call the woman a witch. They called her Eris, the slaughter-loving sister of Ares, She Whose Wrath is Relentless

Three days Styphon had spent in Bassai, and now the day had come on which Brasidas was due to arrive with a detachment from Sparta. Styphon awaited them in the appointed place in front of the modest sandstone facade of Bassai's temple to Apollo. Hours passed and the sun sank, taking with it what little warmth it shed, before the shadows on the road to the south finally coalesced into a band of crimson cloaked Equals on the march. They came traveling light, their lambda-blazoned shields and ash spears and helot servants left behind.

Styphon went out to meet them on the road, finding his master at the band's head.

"What news, dog?" Brasidas asked. "Have you learned the ending to our tale of the White Witch of Bassai?"

"I have, polemarch," Styphon reported. "And I know where she is located, although I have not yet been to the place."

"You have found her already!" Brasidas's scarred face veritably glowed. "Quite the hound you are. Where is she?"

"A half-day's march into the woods," Styphon answered, conscious of the hateful stares directed at him from the band of ten Equals at Brasidas's back. A few had come from the prison, while others were fresh from Sparta; all seemed to despise Styphon with equal intensity.

"We shall camp and embark at dawn," Brasidas said, resuming his stride. The band of Equals followed, some grumbling obscenities at Styphon as they shoved past with unnecessary roughness. Ignoring them, Styphon joined the general's retinue, and to the cadence of crickets they walked past Bassai's timber houses, drawing anxious stares from their occupants. Men here had no love for Sparta. Their grandfathers' fathers had been conquered by her, and their own fathers had risen in rebellion. Now the place was more loyal to Sparta, but still fiercely proud of its Arkadian heritage.

"Sir," Styphon dared to address his master.

"Yes, dog?" Brasidas taunted. "You wish to ask something of me?"

"No, sir," Styphon lied. He would not show weakness by asking to know the elders' decision on him. "I thought you might wish to know what else I have discovered concerning the witch."

"You may tell me after camp is made."

Said camp, in the wood on the edge of Bassai, consisted of little more than a crackling fire, which the Equals would have done without were it any earlier or later than midwinter. As purple dusk turned to night, a party of Arkadians appeared–the Spartan-appointed governor, some city officials and a troop of servants carrying food. Unchecked by any order from their general, Brasidas's men had fun at the

Arkadians' expense, threatening and insulting them, stealing their torches and shoving a few to the ground before taking by force the food that had been brought as a gift and chasing the givers off into the night. The band dined on roast lamb that night, all but Styphon who made do with barley cake and boiled onions rather than even try to take the portion of meat his tormentors would have derived great entertainment from denying him.

Brasidas, seated on a log, face stained with the dripping blood and grease of his portion, summoned Styphon over and bid him speak of the witch.

"First, the name by which men call her here is Eris," Styphon began.

The polemarch scoffed, shreds of meat flying from lips. "Yes, just as the poets describe her: One-Armed Eris, Slayer of Sheep-Lickers!" Some other Equals nearby took to laughing. "However," Brasidas went on, "lacking any better name for her, that one will do. Go on."

"It was in a village to the west of here that this... Eris first appeared, killing several men. After those who gave her chase were likewise slaughtered, the villagers appealed to Sparta, but they also sent a rider on to Bassai, which lay in the direction she was last seen traveling. The leaders of Bassai were convinced to raise their infantry as if an invasion force had suddenly appeared.

"The next morning, they sighted her in the woods and engaged. Of the nearly four hundred men who opposed her, fifty-six were slain and thirty wounded before Eris fell. Her corpse was further mutilated, but left on the spot where it had fallen. A tomb was dug and lined with cut stones. They pushed the remains in and spent three days carting in every heavy stone they could find to pile atop it. The locals now count the place as cursed and are loath to go near it."

"Hmm," Brasidas intoned. "The prospect of recruiting her seems... less than promising. Still, if your sea-bitch managed to cheat death, this one may yet live. Tomorrow we shall visit this cursed place and learn what we can."

Tearing off one last chunk of meat with his teeth and grinning as he chewed, Brasidas held the almost-stripped bone toward Styphon. "A bone for the dog."

Having no choice, Styphon took it from him. "Thank you, polemarch." But he did not, would not, eat from it. When Brasidas waved him away, Styphon rose and walked away, casting the bone into the fire.

"Dog!" Brasidas called out. Styphon turned. "The elders have delayed their decision on you until next year, pending my report on your behavior. So if you've a brain in that thick skull, you will serve your master well until then."

Styphon nodded and resumed walking. It was good news, considering. It meant at least another year of humiliation and servitude, but at least there was hope that at its end Brasidas might deliver on his promises. The elders of Sparta gave a polemarch's word great weight.

***

Before first light, Styphon was awakened by a kick in the ribs, and as dawn broke, the band of Equals struck off into the woods. Along the way, an Arkadian youth was compelled to act as guide. Though frightened of the cursed place, their boy knew well enough to fear Spartans more, and so he led the party without complaint or misstep.

They hiked all morning, until the winter sun reached its zenith. Then the youth halted abruptly and pointed ahead, to where a gray mass was visible through the thin, bare trees. Brasidas clapped the boy on the shoulder and passed him a few coins of the currency that Equals were by Lykurgan law forbidden to possess, and the boy sped off back the way they had come.

Brasidas waved the band forward. They filtered through the trees until they reached a clearing in which rose a man-made hill of limestone, sandstone, marble, and granite: boulders and plinths, broken pieces of fallen columns and statuary, millstones, lintels–anything heavy which the barely victorious Arkadians could find to heap upon the resting place of their deadly foe. Surrounding the burial mound, hanging from wooden stakes in the earth, were charms and wards of every variety, most comprised of the skulls and bones of birds and other small animals.

Placed prominently at the base of the small mountain was a stone slab bearing a scrawled inscription: *Here lies hateful ERIS, Destroyer of Men. Let he who removes a single stone be dragged below to where she dwells, his line forever mired in misery and suffering.*

"Begin removing stones!" Brasidas called out loudly, in a clear voice.

No Equal budged. Brasidas turned both ways, surveying the band behind him. He spat. "I had no inkling that my judgment was so poor! It seems I have brought with me a bunch of cunts."

He strode forward to the base of the mound, wrapped his thick arms around a chunk of limestone the size of his chest, and heaved it aside. As that piece rolled and settled, Styphon made his own choice, becoming the first among Brasidas's band to join him in the surely foolhardy endeavor. Would that his current circumstances allowed him the freedom to make wiser choices; but they did not, and he could not. And so he hastened forth to help his polemarch, his keeper, potentially unleash a destructive force which dozens of men had given their lives to contain.

Likely not wishing to be outdone by a coward and dog

in the eyes of their commander, the other ten Equals were right on Styphon's heels, and the band set in silence to the work of flattening a small mountain of rubble. The labor was rough, and still incomplete when the better part of an hour had passed. Styphon rolled a roundish boulder clear of the mound and paused, leaning on it for but a moment to rest and wipe sweat from a forehead cold with winter's chill.

"Tired already, dog?" Brasidas cackled at him from behind, tossing a block of marble close enough to Styphon's feet that he was forced to dodge.

"No, polemarch," Styphon said, straightening and making to return to the mound.

That was when he witnessed, along with Brasidas at his side, the sight of one, then another, heavy chunks of debris fall aside by themselves, as if possessed of their own motive force.

Only for seconds did the cause of their movement remain a mystery, for out from the gap thus created rose a slender, filthy arm, and then a head crowned with hair which glinted gold in those few spots where it was not caked with all manner of filth and dried gore.

"Equals, form up on me!" Brasidas bellowed.

There was a bare moment's confusion among the band on hearing this order in the midst of hard labor, but a moment was all it took for them to remember that theirs was not to question the voice of command. They threw down whatever was in their arms and clambered over and around the constituent parts of the much-diminished mound to reach Brasidas's position. As the dropped stones tumbled, the blood- and soil-blackened apparition, rag-clad, completed its emergence, freeing first one sandaled foot and then the other, which was bare.

Just as Eris drew upright, an Equal named Menes became the last of the band to pass by her. Her sea-blue eyes, bright behind the crust of filth, caught and followed him, and in that instant Styphon saw that Menes was doomed.

Eris lunged, and her arm flew out to grasp the passing Equal's trailing cloak. She jerked it, and Menes fell in a clatter of stones, and she fell into a crouch upon him, sliding his sword from its scabbard. Although Menes fought her, with one arm braced on her chest, the other trying to prevent the theft of his weapon, his struggles were as nothing. Breaking his grip, she plunged the blade straight down through Menes' chest, piercing his armor of stiffened leather as though it were the sackcloth of a slave.

"We seek only words with you!" Brasidas called out over Menes' soft death groan. The rest of the band, as one, drew their bronze swords–and surely every man, as Styphon did, wished for the greater reach offered by his broad-bladed spear.

The eyes of Eris flitted to the speaker, but her lips, faintly pink behind the filth, failed to part in answer.

"We have no quarrel with you," Brasidas continued, and even this most feared of Equals could not hide a tremor in his iron voice of authority. "We came here to free you. We can find common–"

The black apparition sprang from her perch. Eleven men tensed in surprise and followed her path with their blades–a path which led over their heads in an impossible leap. She landed nearest to a man named Galatias and batted his blade aside with her own before poking a hole in his throat with the point of her sword. Antigonos was the next, her blade cleaving his skull as he made an ineffectual swipe. Two more fell challenging her before Brasidas cried out, "Scatter!" and the band of Equals, its renowned courage in the face of certain death sorely tested by this army of one, gladly obliged.

Only two did not budge: Brasidas, for reasons his own,

and Styphon, who, having chosen to put his fate entirely in the polemarch's hands, opted to ignore his own instinct and do as Brasidas did.

Now Eris leaped again, and down she came on the back of fleeing Menandros, whose face met the earth moments before his back was pierced by bronze and his life met an end. Menandros had spoken last night of the girl he was due to wed, Melissa.

She would have to find a new man now.

The twins Kallikrates and Dion went next to the slaughter. They had shared the hour of their birth and now they died each within seconds of the other, blood spilling from twin wounds in their necks.

Apart from the general and his dog, only three Spartans then remained of the twelve who had ventured into the woods, and their six feet pounded the earth in a frantic dash for the deep forest, as if it might bring them safety. But this enemy was unrelenting, and as a lioness chases down her prey, she bounded after them.

The Equal named Timon, one of those who had been on Sphakteria and tormented Styphon in prison, lost his footing and tumbled hard down a rocky slope. Eris swept her sword across his flailing form, sending an arc of blood into the air, delaying by not an instant her pursuit of the remaining two.

Long before those two reached the imagined safety of the woods, she caught up with them. One fell with a piercing shriek as her sword blade cut his legs from beneath him, then his shriek was silenced with a earthward stab. The tenth Spartan to die that day in the orgy of slaughter which had lasted hardly more than sixty seconds, was felled by a hurled hand-ax, taken from the belt of another fallen Equal. It caught him in the base of his skull, and he collapsed against the trunk of a tree, hugging it as if to keep himself upright. But he was dead already, even if his desperate limbs were the last to know.

Ten Equals lay dead, and Eris turned to face the last two remaining, who out of courage or stupidity had failed to flee. The terrifying goddess did not run at them but rather walked, bearing now two stolen swords, one in either hand.

"Convince her or kill her," Brasidas said breathlessly. "I do not care which, and you'll be an Equal again. I swear it."

Styphon could not help it: he laughed the dry laughter of the doomed.

She was upon them now, a sinister smile adorning her crusted lips. Her sword came up, and by the light in her bluest of eyes, Styphon knew she was taking pleasure in the slaughter. This was vengeance, perhaps, for her imprisonment–it being apparently lost on her, or of no consequence, the difference between Spartan and Arkadian.

The dealer of death was but two paces shy of reaching them in her unhurried advance when a single word came unbidden to Styphon's mind. He had forgotten its syllables, but they returned now as if by the intervention of some benevolent god at this moment when his very life depended on them.

Ten men today had tested the strength of their arms or the swiftness of their feet against this enemy; all had failed and died. Styphon put his faith instead in the tongue which he managed to pry loose from tightly clenched jaw.

The word forced its way out without preamble or explanation: "*Geneva.*"

The beautiful, terrible bringer of death froze in her soundless tracks. Sensing salvation, Brasidas echoed the foreign syllables just spoken by his dog.

Eyes like the depths of Ocean flitted between the two speakers. Without lowering her bronze or relaxing her guard, bloodstained Eris posed them a question in calm, heavily accented Attic.

"What do you know of that worthless fucking cunt?"

8. Witch-Tamer

Being a practiced master of the Athenian legal system, Kleon managed to carry forward with a public rather than private lawsuit against the man whom no fewer than thirty witnesses identified as the assailant who had done him harm. The charges included assault, of course, but also obstructing the duties of a public official and, worst of all, cowardice in the face of the enemy. This last was the fourth most serious charge (after murder, treason, and impiety) which could be leveled against any public defendant.

The accused, Demosthenes of Thria, reported to the law courts as ordered and entered his plea: guilty of all but the final count. A day later, he went before the jury of a thousand-and-one citizens and waited patiently while red-faced Kleon exhausted the three hours allotted for his prosecution.

Then Demosthenes stood under the gray winter clouds and spoke calmly in his defense. His argument was simple. Eight days ago, he asserted, three hundred of the most feared killers in all the world, implacable enemies of Athens, had taken civilians prisoner in a quiet corner of Melite. Hours later, the escapees had left the city and marched to the border where they released the last of their hostages and went on their way.

"My prosecutor today should be thanking me rather than accusing me," he said in the conclusion to his abnormally short defense. "Had I not stepped in to relieve him of the job for which he was eminently unqualified, the gutters of Melite would have run red with children's blood, and Kleon would stand in my place today, the target of half a hundred suits brought by the husbands and fathers of wives and heirs put in the earth before their time.

"Instead, no one lies dead. And Kleon calls me a coward

for not having taken the place of twelve of those women whose lives my actions saved. Nine of their husbands you heard speak today as witnesses on my behalf. I am a husband, too, do not forget, and I swore to my bride that very morning that I would return to our bed unharmed. Only by declining to deliver myself into the hands of the enemy whom I humiliated at Amphipolis did I keep that pledge.

"What I am guilty of, I freely admit: silencing a voice of incompetence on my city's behalf. Punish me accordingly for that if you must. Still, I would do the same again, and laugh at the idea that I am a coward, if not for the sobering knowledge of what might have happened had Kleon had his way."

With those words, composed a night prior, Demosthenes put his fate in the hands of the jury, which proceeded immediately to a vote. Muttering amongst themselves, a thousand-and-one men shuffled over to two urns, one of copper, one of wood, that were set at the rear of the open Heliaia. Each man carried two nearly identical disc-shaped bronze ballots. One ballot was marked for the prosecution, the other for the defense. When his turn came, each juror deposited both of his discs into the containers, one into each. Ballots dropped into the bronze bin would count toward the verdict, while those in the wood would be discarded. In the end, each urn would contain a thousand and one ballots, and every individual vote was a secret, if the caster wanted it to be so. Some jurors cared nothing for secrecy, of course, and would walk up to one party or the other to wish him luck or assure him that victory was his. It seemed to Demosthenes that he received more of these well-wishes than Kleon, but such observations were worthless, since men's mouths were under no legal obligation to vote in the same direction as their hands.

In a private chamber of the court building, in the

presence of both prosecutor and defendant and any male citizens chosen by each to serve as witnesses, the bronze urn was overturned and counting began under the supervision of the hegemon. Well before the process was complete, Alkibiades, a witness for the defense, clapped his friend on the neck and gave him a celebratory shake, for the verdict was clear: acquittal. A sputtering Kleon departed early, without bothering to discover whether he had achieved the one-fifth of votes needed to avoid being struck with a fine.

He did, it turned out, if barely. But this verdict was only on the charge of cowardice. Other charges existed against which Demosthenes had put up no defense, and the jury yet needed to decide upon his penalty. When the sentencing hearing convened, Kleon returned and argued for a massive fine and jail-time. Then the defendant made his counter-proposal. Precedent clearly showed that it was rarely wise for a guilty defendant to ask for no punishment at all, since the jurors were only able to choose between one proposal or the other, and so Demosthenes made no such argument this day.

As morning turned to afternoon, the redistributed ballots were cast and a sentence was determined.

***

Alone, Demosthenes came to the gate of his home and walked down the palm-lined garden path, seeing three women waiting for him in the open doorway ahead. On the right, squatting on her haunches with ink-banded arms folded in front of her, was Eurydike. On the left was Laonome, brow furrowed with the fear that she would lose her new husband to prison or exile. And in the center, behind the other two, stood Thalassia, quietly confident, exuding certainty that whatever news may come would prove no obstacle to her plans.

Demosthenes did not smile as he walked the path, a

cruel oversight, perhaps, and it caused two bleak expressions to grow bleaker still. As he took the final steps, Laonome surged forward and laid hands gently on his chest as her wide eyes silently begged knowledge of the day's verdict.

Though unintended, Demosthenes' sharp intake of breath preparatory to making the announcement almost certainly sounded ominous; both Eurydike and Laonome tensed as if to receive a blow.

"Four months," he declared evenly. "To begin at nightfall."

On hearing the sentence, Laonome gasped. Eurydike loosed a whimper.

Now he really was toying with them, knowingly, although it had not been his intention–some of Thalassia's bad habits evidently had rubbed off on him. But he had not the heart to let the cruel trick go on more than an instant. He slipped his arm around his bride and pulled her close.

"House arrest!" he said brightly. "You will be sick of me soon."

When his words had sunk in, Eurydike sprang to her feet and joined the embrace, while Thalassia looked down from the threshold with a smirk. She begrudged a laugh, shook her head and retreated into the megaron.

Demosthenes did not spend his last few hours of freedom in his home, but in public carrying out a small amount of business but mostly just receiving praise and congratulation on the verdict. Word of it had spread quickly, and the common wisdom was that between the fame Amphipolis had won him and his humble acceptance of guilt, his own influence would shortly eclipse that of Kleon.

Good news for the future of Athens, perhaps, but a mixed blessing for the recipient of the public's esteem. The *demos* was nothing if not fickle, and as likely as not to dispose of its most notable public figures the moment their stars stopped shining.

His sentence presented a more immediate problem with regard to his political career. Elections to the Board of Ten were to be held two months from now, and a candidate under arrest was ineligible. The reason was simple and logical: no matter how many votes he received, he would be legally unable to go abroad on campaign.

"What now?" he asked of Thalassia later that evening, when they had a chance to be alone. They stood against the balustrade of the rooftop terrace, under smooth clouds white with moonglow.

"I am glad for you," she said reflectively. "And Laonome."

"Brasidas knows about you. And with the hostages gone, Sparta will invade this summer for certain."

"You chose the sentence. You might have asked for half the time spent in jail instead."

"I might have," Demosthenes agreed, and let the matter drop. "What of Brasidas?"

Thalassia shrugged. She seemed strangely subdued. "What can he do? The invasion will come, and we will be ready. Much liquid stone has been prepared. It will let us build fortifications quickly and cheaply. And you will be free by then."

"I will not be a strategos."

"You weren't at Pylos, either. The Board will not let you go to waste."

"Fortifications..." Demosthenes observed. "A year ago, you spoke of killing strokes. Now we prepare again to defend against theirs."

Thalassia smiled, but distantly. "That almost sounds like an insult. And here on this roof, no less. Very bold."

Demosthenes might have laughed–at this, a reference to his own maiming a year prior–had he not become certain by now that Thalassia was holding something back. As was always the case when she behaved thus, he was not certain he wished to know what the something was.

She waved a hand. "It's not me who lacks the will for a killing stroke. Convince your democracy, and I'll be ready. You'll have four months to write speeches."

Demosthenes set a hand over hers on the balustrade. How long and difficult a road he had traveled to be able to make such a simple gesture as that.

"Tell me," he said.

"Nothing..." she answered at first. Then, "I think I should leave."

Demosthenes stomach lurched and he was glad for the support of his arms on the rail. "Leave Athens?"

Thalassia quickly faced him and smiled reassuringly. "No, idiot." The insult was an affectionate one. "Your house. But I appreciate the severe reaction."

"Why?" he demanded, ignoring the rest.

Thalassia hung her head, face vanishing in lustrous waves of unbound hair. "Your sentence. Soon enough, these walls will close in on you. I don't want us to fight. Our fights are dangerous."

"We are past that," Demosthenes countered.

"And other reasons," she continued. "The more time we spend together, the harder it will be to keep our secret from the others."

"We have done well thus far. What else? Now the true reason."

Looking out over Athens, at the jagged, serene, moonlit acropolis, Thalassia said reluctantly, "You should have something in your life that's just for you, something that I don't infect with..."

Madness, Demosthenes finished silently.

"–madness," she simultaneously spoke aloud, as if reading his thoughts. "Being married is hard enough as it is. Or so I'm told."

Demosthenes stared at her profile and wondered. She was right, of course. For all those reasons, it would be better if she moved out. But should he insist anyway that she stay, as he would with any mortal guest?

No, no games. She was no mortal, and no guest either. This was her home.

"I could free you, file the papers to make you a resident alien," he said.

Thalassia flashed a half smile. He had not used the legal term in jest, but he certainly saw the irony–or, rather, the literal truth–in it.

"It's not much concern of mine whether I wear a necklace or not." She flicked the thin silver choker on her neck, rattling the small amber pendants which hung from it in the soft shadow of her collarbone. "I'll stay with Alkibiades," she confirmed needlessly.

Demosthenes nodded. "Only while I am confined. Then you will return."

Thalassia looked over with her pale eyes which could see through all men, and spoke in the blunt way she often did. And as she often did, she replied to the meanings of words rather than their form.

"He is still a tool," she reassured.

She left her own true meaning up to the hearer to interpret, and Demosthenes did: *He shall not replace you.*

Such reassurance implied a belief that Demosthenes was jealous. And again, as usual... she was right. There was no other way to describe what he felt, and no denying that he felt it. Others could have Thalassia's body, but her madness, her violent, destructive madness, had to be his alone.

He must be mad, too, to want such a thing.

The rooftop fell into silence, and against the backdrop of the Grove of Nymphs, where shrill insects droned, Demosthenes studied his raven-haired witch from the stars. There was no question but that her seasons in this world had changed her. She was more circumspect, less volatile. In Amphipolis, he had given her the perfect excuse to feed him his own severed cock and instead there had been only... a picnic. Something had tamed her. Maybe it was him. Maybe it was the loneliness of being so separated from anyone that was capable of understanding her. Then again, maybe it was the opposite of loneliness. She had come to see the pawns in her scheme for revenge as more than pawns, while revenge required a single-mindedness that left little room for affection.

What dwelt in the mind and heart of one so alien as she, a mortal could only guess.

Sensing sorrow brewing in her, Demosthenes took a stab at alleviating it.

"I have reached a decision," he said. "If we win this war, assuming I live through it, and if you will have me... then I shall help you burn that Italian city to the ground once or twice. I will bring an army with me, if I can."

Staring into the night, Thalassia remained expressionless, a serene beauty. In this light, her flesh was nearly the same pale blue as were her eyes in the day. Eventually she directed those eyes at him, smiled with her dark, thin lips and answered, "I would like that. But you will have children by then. If they change your mind, I won't hold it against you."

There was a coldness in her voice as she spoke of children. He conjured an image of Thalassia with one infant on her angular hip and another growing in her flawless belly, and the absurdity of it almost twisted his lips in a smile. Never had he witnessed a glimmer of the maternal in her soul, in spite of the fondness with which she treated her pupil, the Spartlet Andrea.

Thalassia would not be tamed in that way, not ever.

He could be, though, or so her words implied.

"Time will tell," he conceded.

Before another silence could descend and make things awkward, and before he could talk himself out of it, he proceeded to do something with vastly greater potential for awkwardness than any mere silence. Mindful of the greeting he had failed to give her on the bank of the Strymon, he set a hand on her shoulder, atop the thin, sharp pleats of her dress, he pulled her into a parting embrace.

"I shall miss you," he said softly, genuinely.

Slowly, woodenly, Thalassia's arms came up. Halfheartedly, as though from obligation, she reciprocated. His cheek near to hers but not touching it, Demosthenes waited for her to melt against him, as Eurydike and Laonome always did.

He waited in vain. Just as he gave up and lowered his arms in defeat, the hard body in his arms softened. Thalassia bowed her head and let their temples touch. Demosthenes restored his arms to the small of Thalassia's back and left them there for all of the heartbeat that its recipient allowed the embrace to endure. Long hair scented with *iasme,* jasmine, brushed his neck, warm, linen-covered breasts withdrew from his chest, and they were separate again. Her face angled downward, Thalassia looked up at him past her perfect brows.

"Idiot..." she said. She made it sound almost as a term of endearment. "You won't have time to miss me. We'll still see too fucking much of each other."

9. Late

The remainder of the winter put the lie to Thalassia's prediction. Within half a month, she had moved with Alkibiades to a village of Attica in the mountains north of the city. Like Amphipolis, Dekelea was an undefended place with a size and appearance that were all out of proportion to its vital role in Athens' might-have-been history. A collection of wooden structures with more passers-through than residents, Dekelea sat in the mountain pass through which poured vast quantities of the imported grain on which Athens depended. And just like Amphipolis, it was a town which Fate would have seen, and may yet see, captured by the enemy. Once seized, Thalassia said, Dekelea would be fortified by the Spartans and used a base from which to strike all over Attica, not to mention helping to starve the city by interrupting its grain supplies.

But Fate would be foiled in that design, or so it seemed. Demosthenes, by means of intermediaries, had managed to convince the Board of Ten to fortify the place in recognition of its importance. In that other world which, thanks to Thalassia, could never be, the Spartans would have taken the idea of seizing Dekelea from a certain Athenian turncoat by the name of Alkibiades. Now that very man, blissfully unaware of his own capacity for treason, instead oversaw the fortification of Dekelea for his own people.

Perhaps more than the Board was interested in protecting a remote village, it aimed to test Thalassia's 'liquid stone,' which they believed to have been brought from India or beyond by traders who had sold it on to the crew of Demosthenes' ship. It was a powder, comprised mostly of limestone, which when mixed with water became a viscous, mud-like substance. Poured into wooden molds and left to dry, it grew as hard as stone, or nearly so. Athenian state engineers and architects were only just discovering its many uses, and since the best way to learn was by doing, the construction of an encircling wall at Dekelea served all well as a test.

From Sparta, there was silence. They sent no more heralds with proposals for a truce, since their main goal in seeking peace, the return of the hostages, had already been achieved by Brasidas. Snows and the elections came, and the name Demosthenes was not listed among the ten winners of a generalship. Kleon's was, and so were those of Nikias and eight others who were mostly holdovers who had failed to disgrace themselves enough in the prior year to warrant being deprived of another opportunity to fail.

Demosthenes took the news well, less because it was expected than because he was happy. He awoke every morning beside his chosen bride, or the bride well-chosen for him, and every morning his love for her burned as brightly as it had the night before. The walls did not close in on him, his prison felt like no prison, and he saw no sign of marriage becoming the ordeal it was taken for by Thalassia and so many others.

He was fortunate, and knew it.

Eurydike felt the absence of the friend and sister she had found in Thalassia, and missed Alkibiades, too, who had not given up his Little Red as a playmate on account of taking on Thalassia (how intimately connected were the two female legs of that tripod, Demosthenes did not quite know, and let it be their concern), but she mitigated the loss with regular visits to the pair at Dekelea. While at home, Eurydike got along well with her new mistress, partly owing to their acquaintance prior to the union, but even more because Laonome, having been on the bottom in her former oikos, was not one to lord it over a slave. She was regularly on the bottom in her new oikos, too, but in a more enjoyable way, by all accounts, in sessions which often enough found Eurydike joining them.

It might have been in one of those sessions that seed finally found purchase in her womb.

Laonome whispered in Demosthenes' ear one night while seated in his lap on their bed, nothing separating their two skins but a sheen of sweat: "I should have bled by now."

The declaration took him by surprise.

He asked, "How late is it?"

"Very," she answered, laughing. Demosthenes laughed, too, crushed her in an embrace and rolled playfully on top of her. Her shriek summoned Eurydike, who knew already, of course, for this was the kind of news women eternally shared with one another first. She joined the pile and screamed with them as spiritedly if the child to come were her own. She was all the more enthusiastic, perhaps, for not having to bear the burden in her own hard, flat belly.

He was to have an heir! Possibly. Or a daughter. The former would be more practical, of course, but either was an equal blessing, but for one consideration. If the gods, whom he now doubted, saw fit to give him a girl, the influences most certain come to bear in shaping her seemed as likely as not to be ones which would turn her into an outright menace: an oversexed, foul-mouthed, strong-willed, probably lethal, fucking beautiful menace to Athens and the world.

But she would be his menace, and born of love, and loved.

10. Engines of Destruction

Mounichion in the archonship of Isarchos (April 423 BCE)

The four cold winter months of his sentence passed in what seemed as many heartbeats. He spent it not only lazing and laughing and fucking, of course, though there was plenty of all that. Demosthenes sent letters to influence the Board and other key citizens seeking support for the war plans laid during Thalassia's businesslike visits to Athens. He would lead a force of Athenians, Argives, and Messenians–this last group eager to repay the Liberator of Pylos–into wooded Arkadia. All would be light infantry and archers, and their ostensible purpose would be to disrupt and distract the enemy by destroying supplies, burning crops, slaughtering herds and horses, making roads impassible, inspiring Sparta's slaves and allies to rebellion, ambushing their detachments. Damage done, they would melt back into the woods whilst avoiding ever going shield-to-shield with the enemy in pitched battles they could not win.

The force's arms would include two hundred of a new weapon, a lighter version of the gastraphetes which men had come to call a *khiasmon*–loosely, "cross-bow,"–sure to prove more useful in close combat than any traditional bow.

They would be raiders, marauders, saboteurs, pirates of land. Demosthenes had led some fighting of this sort in Aetolia. It had ended badly there, to say the least, but until disaster had befallen, such tactics had worked extremely well in allowing a small, light force to challenge a much stronger foe.

The Spartans did possess such fighters of their own: the feared and elite Skiritai, Arkadian mountain men who, when summoned to Sparta's defense, would have the added advantage of operating in their homeland. So highly regarded were they by their Spartan masters that to the Skiritai alone went the privilege of scouting ahead of the King.

Thalassia would see to them. Going ahead of Demosthenes' main force, she would assassinate as many Skiritai as she could before Sparta even knew a threat existed. Thereafter, she would remain in the Arkadian wood, shadowing Demosthenes' force and acting on her own to spread terror and havoc, employing her skills to making it appear as though Sparta faced an army of shades capable of striking at will in ten places at once.

The effect, Demosthenes had told the Board, would be to put Sparta so off balance that they would not feel secure in mounting any assault on Athens, but would instead keep their forces in Arkadia dealing with this threat so close to home. In the best case, a general uprising of the helots–an everpresent Spartan fear–might be achieved. In truth, he and Thalassia intended even more. If all went well, then by harvest time, Sparta itself, a city which lacked walls, might find itself at the mercy of a few hundred lightly-armed troops–and one fighter not of this world.

Demosthenes' son or daughter would be born in a city at peace.

Would have been. Might have.

Now, those plans were as dust.

On this, his first day of freedom, Demosthenes had attended the Straegion expecting to be granted the special dispensation from the Board of Ten which would allow a private citizen to lead an armed force, as he had done at Pylos. That was not to be. There was fresh news, and it was of a kind which must be delivered immediately to Thalassia's ears, by him alone. And so he left the city by the Acharnian Gate and rode Maia north for Dekelea at a gallop, halfway wishing that he could slow and savor the air and the open sky and the plains. He savored instead speed, something else which had been denied him during his term of house arrest. In short order, he traversed the arrow-straight road across the plains, dodging rattling ox-carts both coming and going, and the ground ahead began to rise up into the peaks of the Parnes range in which Dekelea sat nestled. Now he was forced to slow Maia, letting her rest and choose her footing on the rockier, more sinuous path.

On the final approach, he found his way blocked by a lone Spartan. This Spartan bore no shield or spear, wore no armor and stood a good three heads shorter than shortest Equal ever to take the field. Still, the hard glare of two coal black eyes left Demosthenes with no choice but to rein in Maia and take notice.

"Good morning, Andrea," he said.

The eleven-year-old glared. Her brown hair was braided back, and the bare legs showing below the hem of her short chiton were caked with dried mud.

"Why didn't you bring Eurydike?" the girl demanded. Andrea had developed something of a bond with Eurydike during the latter's regular visits to Dekelea.

"Laonome needs her help these days," Demosthenes answered. "Now, if you'll pardon me, I"

The Spartlet tossed her head in rejection of the excuse and put herself once more in the way when Demosthenes made to guide Maia around her.

"If Alkibiades agrees," he offered in the hope of winning passage, "then I shall take you to visit Eurydike on my return to the city. Now, I"

"The city is boring," Andrea scoffed. "Tutors had taken the edge off of her coarse native Doric, but her origins were plain enough when those tutors were not around.

"Ride with me the rest of the way to Dekelea,"

Demosthenes offered.

"I'm used to riding on my own."

"Then you give *me* a ride," Demosthenes proposed, "and after you drop me off, you can take Maia out."

With a petulant sigh, wiry Andrea stretched up an arm to be pulled into Maia's saddle. Demosthenes set her in front of him, gave the girl the reins, kicked Maia's flanks, and together they rode the short distance to Dekelea's stout walls. The walls were freshly built from giant blocks of Thalassia's liquid stone, poured on site, and so were uniformly dull gray but for embedded gravel of irregular shapes and hues. This last was a concession to the engineers of Athens, who felt that the unadorned liquid stone was simply too ugly. The resulting effect was similar to what a tile mosaic might look like if no subject were depicted, just swirling chaos.

Dekelea's gates had not yet been hung, so they entered the village by passing between two empty pylons. Silently, Andrea guided Maia to a bastion on the northern side, where the walls were incomplete.

Reining the horse, she cried out, "Uncle!"

Alkibiades appeared up at the tower's edge, leaning over its low wall. He looked down and beamed. "Demosthenes! Welcome back to the world!"

Demosthenes dismounted, leaving Andrea in the saddle. No sooner was there soil beneath his sandals than the Spartlet wheeled Maia and sped off.

"Feed and groom her!" Alkibiades yelled after his charge. Then, to Demosthenes, "Freedom at last! How does it feel?"

"Would that I could enjoy it. I bring grave news freshly gained from"

A faint tinkling sound, then motion, drew Demosthenes' eye to the base of the sixteen-foot bastion on which Alkibiades stood. There, in an open, timber-framed portal stood a familiar figure, unfamiliarly clad.

Thalassia was a vision in black. At the top, her black gown left exposed an expansive patch of skin above her breasts, where hung an elaborate necklace of dangling silver pendants, matched by bracelets on her smooth forearms, all barbarian creations, as the dress itself must have been. The garment's pleated skirts flared out below a waist marked by a belt of interlocking silver rings, many segments of which hung down, tinkling like tiny bells with each movement of the pleats. The skirt ended abruptly at mid-calf, leaving it a mystery how much farther up the wearer's shapely legs climbed the vine-like laces of sandals as black as the cloth. Her long hair was unbound and tumbled over her shoulders in chaotic spirals, the twisting edges of which screamed a playful violet, like unmixed wine, where they were struck by rays of midmorning sun. The sun caught silver, too, in her hair, threads of it binding a multitude of tiny braids anchored in the depths of that dark, roiling sea.

Most startling of all were Thalassia's eyes: bounded all around and artificially elongated with a thick application of kohl which managed, impossibly, to render the already striking pale irises more arresting still.

Mind and breath momentarily stolen, Demosthenes stared in stunned silence for a time while she hung there, suspended in the door. Then she lifted both arms, bracelets sliding in a clatter, and casually set the palms of ring-adorned hands on the timber frame to either side, filling the portal with her dark, foreign presence.

A name flew to mind. She surely had not set out deliberately to emulate that most famous and deadly of witches, but the sight of Thalassia emerging from the base of that tower could not have more fully resembled what the ancients must have seen when sharp-hearted Medea stepped ashore from *Argo*. Perhaps Jason's first reaction on seeing his future bride, and the slayer of his sons, had been such a chill burst of fear of the unknown as Demosthenes felt now. But, likewise, that storied hero must have quickly acknowledged the primal allure of such a creature as this, a stirring of something deep within which certainly included, but was not limited to, a flowing of blood to the groin.

The ghost of a smile played on the witch's lips. She saw what magic she had wrought.

"You... look..." Demosthenes sputtered after some time, but he failed to finish.

"For fuck's sake!" the voice of Alkibiades sailed down from above. "A compliment costs you nothing. Doesn't obligate you to fuck her, either!"

"Thank you! You are a credit to Socrates!" Demosthenes yelled back sharply, dragging his eyes from those of the sorceress.

Upon this exchange between ground and tower, Thalassia stepped out from the doorway, and said with a smile, proving herself a merciful witch, "Grave news?"

"Aye," Demosthenes said, his sober mood instantly returning. He bid Alkibiades descend so that he might not be forced to shout information to which the public was not yet privy. While he waited, Demosthenes stared at Thalassia, holding her kohl-rimmed eyes as much as he could, but also looking her all over with a feeling that he hardly knew her. She had never looked thus on her visits to Athens. How many aspects of her existed? She was assassin, lover, tutor, sister, sorceress, immortal, oracle, physician, engineer, betrayer, matchmaker, artist, vengeance-seeker. She seemed to shed and adopt guises with abandon, settling not quite on any, or else on all. How could any man hope to keep up?

"How is Laonome?" she asked when Demosthenes

persisted in but staring and thinking.

"A faint breeze and she vomits," he answered. "The herbs you gave her help."

Behind the seamless gray wall of liquid stone, echoing footfalls scraped a timber stair. Alkibiades leaped down the final few steps and set a hand on the bodice of Thalassia's barbarian gown, a gesture which the recipient subtly appeared to forbear more than relish.

"Out with it," Alkibiades said eagerly.

Demosthenes obliged: "Sparta's invasion force has already marched. It is not led by King Agis this year, but by Brasidas. Since his escape and return with the other prisoners, the ephors reportedly grant him leave to do almost as he pleases. His army travels with some number of extremely large, wagon-borne burdens of which nothing is known by our sources except for a name: *mechanamai*."

He let the word hang ominously. It might refer to a literal device of some sort, a machine, but more idiomatically, it could mean any complex contrivance, or a trick, such as those used by Odysseus.

"Perhaps they bring us gifts of hollow horses," Alkibiades suggested, unhelpfully. More helpfully, he asked, "Any ideas, star-girl?"

"They will be siege engines," Thalassia declared. "Unlike others you have seen. Likely they will be capable of hurling very large stones over the Long Walls, causing destruction within, or into the Walls, creating a breach."

Demosthenes met her pronouncement, the accuracy of which he did not doubt, with grim silence. It was Alkibiades who posed the question to which only he, of those present, did not know the answer.

"How could they have built such machines?" He scoffed. "Much less thought of them. One might almost think they had starborn aid of their own!"

"Nikias withdrew his support for our Arkadian campaign," Demosthenes said quickly, by way of changing the subject. "His allies followed suit. He believes it is too late for it to have an effect. He may be right. I pressed the Board instead for an ambush on Skiron's Road, where Brasidas's army will be at its most vulnerable before it enters Attica. That, too, met with refusal. Nikias and his party are too cautious, and Kleon and his allies are... well, let us say their personal feelings prevent them from agreeing with me."

"You must go anyway," Thalassia urged. "With or without an official appointment, you will find no shortage of volunteers. Those machines must not be allowed within range of Athens. If they are, and if the Board takes its past strategy of retreating behind the Long Walls for a siege, then Athens is doomed. The Walls will not stand."

"My understanding is that they will try to stop the invasion at the frontier, near Eleusis," Demosthenes said, "even though the fortifications there will not yet be complete. No one is ready for a return to the years of starvation and plague."

"Thank Virgin Athena's tits for that!" Alkibiades blasphemed. "We could have had this place finished by now, and the frontier besides, if the engineers would just listen to *her*." He nudged Thalassia. "But instead it's 'let's try this, let's try that!'" He sighed. "But they get there in the end, Dog bless 'em."

Demosthenes threw a glance at black-clad, silver-adorned Thalassia and remarked, "Some of us take longer than others to adjust to change. Now, Alkibiades, if it pleases you, I would share a few words with my... *spoil* in private."

Alkibiades laughed. "Of course, my friend." His hand, which had been on Thalassia's back, slid down her in a sort of parting caress, and he sped off shouting at some laborers stirring a vat of liquid stone.

"Shall we walk?" Demosthenes asked.

They started away from Dekelea's wall, heading deeper into the small mountain village which was presently being circumvallated. Thalassia, a black presence who left in her wake the scent of jasmine and an ethereal music of tinkling bells, drew lingering stares from the villagers they passed, and not a few warding signs against evil spirits.

"It must be her," Demosthenes said in a hushed tone, as if the mere mention of Eden might summon her into their presence. "Unless you have another explanation?"

"I know only what you have told me, and reached the same conclusion. We must assume the worst."

"Why should she aid Sparta? Has she guessed your aim and begun working to thwart it?"

"No." Of this Thalassia seemed certain, but the explanation which followed emerged with some hesitation: "By compounding any changes I have introduced, Eden's helping Sparta... is more likely to aid my purpose than hinder it. My *original* purpose. My present goal is only the safety of Athens. I hope you believe that."

"I do," Demosthenes said. Then, mindful that he could not lie to her, "Mostly. You were ready to fight and kill with us in Arkadia."

"More than ready," she interjected. "Looking forward."

"Will you take the field with us instead, and stand against the invaders?"

"I would consider no other course."

"Your secret will be out," Demosthenes reminded. "Your existence in Athens will be forever changed."

Thalassia considered this for no more than a beat, the would-be silence filled with the tinkling of tiny silver chains as she walked. She concluded, "I like change."

"So I see," Demosthenes agreed.

Their path through the village delivered them to the stables, in front of which they found Andrea grooming and watering Maia. Demosthenes thanked the girl, who declined his offer to take her with him to "boring" Athens, although Thalassia granted permission, and he mounted for his return ride. Sharing a last, long look with Thalassia, whom he knew he was not likely to see again before leaving to battle, but speaking no further words, he wheeled Maia and kicked her to a gallop, departing through the unhung gates beneath the kohl-blackened stare of Dekelea's witch.

11. On Skiron's Road

In the black of night they set out in four fishing boats from Eleusis, twenty volunteers cloaked in black or gray and wearing no conventional arms or armor apart from a short sword, strapped to each man's back, and these they hoped not to use. At their head was a two-time general who had twice had lost the post and who tonight, as at Pylos two years prior, acted as a private citizen. This time, unlike then, he had no special dispensation from the Board of Ten strategoi, but acted in defiance of the democracy. It was a crime for which there might well be a price to be paid even in victory.

The twenty beached their craft on the western side of the Bay of Eleusis, where the black land rose up sharply from the pebble-strewn shore into rugged mountains which blotted out clouds awash with starglow. The moment their feet were planted on solid earth, they began unloading their boats' cargo: twenty stoppered, liquid-filled amphorae each as big around as a man's waist and to which had been affixed rawhide straps so they might be worn on the back, slung from the shoulders. From the stopper of each jug dangled a length of thin, tarred cord.

Bearing these, along with heavy coils of climbing rope, the Athenians left their boats on the beach and struck up the slope to begin the treacherous climb. The ascent up the sheer rocks took the better part of the night, but by dawn they were in place overlooking the coastal road which ran from Megara to Athens. It was the route that Spartan armies had taken into Attica six times during the current war, and if the Board of Ten's informants in Megara were correct, then today it was the route by which yet another Spartan army would come. In ancient times, the bandit lord Skiron had plagued these mountain passes; this day, twenty Athenians would play the role of Skiron's bandits lying in wait, and Brasidas, with luck, would play the hapless trader and be deprived of the deadly goods he aimed to bring to Athens.

The sky began to brighten. Atop the sheer ridge, the volunteers spread out in groups of two and three so that they were spread over a half mile or more of road, and they anchored three heavy ropes along the span to ease their descent when the time came. Each group had a blacked-out oil lamp, and as the sun painted the clouds purple, they lit them, looked down on the road from their hiding places, and they waited.

Since Megara was a Spartan ally, traffic on the road into Attica was light. Parties on foot and donkey and mule passed by oblivious to the waiting ambush, but Brasidas's scouts, when they came by mid-morning, were easy enough to spot. Spartan Equals were taught to ride, but their ingrained contempt for cavalry led them to depend on allies to serve in that role. And so, unsurprisingly, the six light horse which passed below the rocks on which the Athenians perched were not Spartans but men from elsewhere in the Peloponnese. Perhaps if the scouts had been Equals or Skiritai, they might have been more watchful, might have noticed that the high, jagged rocks on the seaward side provided the ideal place for an ambush. Perhaps Equals would have doubled back to fetch climbers to scale the heights and ensure the way was clear. But these scouts were incautious allies, and they talked and joked with one another as they rode by, their voices and laughter echoing up the canyon walls.

Within minutes of their passage, a dust cloud became visible in the west. Minutes after that came the distant, rising thunder of an army on the march. A band of Equals came at the army's head, red-cloaked in the summer sun with lambda-blazoned shields on their backs and helmets slung, spear blades cutting the air back and forth as the butts struck the hard earth with each step. The road here was wide enough for twenty or so men to march abreast, and that is how they went, but even Spartan discipline could not keep them in even ranks all the way from Megara to Athens, and so they looked more like a mob. After them came a dozen covered supply carts pulled by donkeys and oxen. The Spartans always traveled light on their invasions of Attica, intending to strip their sustenance from their enemy's farms before razing them.

Next came the Peloponnesian light infantry of peltasts and skirmishers, then a second, larger troop of Equals. It was this latter body which guarded the targets of today's ambush, the first of which Demosthenes and his volunteers watched in awe as it passed. The lumbering hulk was pulled by a massive team of oxen, six rows of beasts walking four abreast. Their burden, shrouded in sailcloth and bound with rope, was four times the length and height of a typical oxcart, and its eight wheels were thick and solid rather than spoked, like the wheels on the platforms on which Cyclopean blocks were transported from quarry to city. Taller than a house, it lumbered along, filling every ear in the seaside canyon with creaks and pops and the crunch of stones being ground to dust under iron-shod wood. A second behemoth rumbled by, and then a third, and each giant wagon and its train of beasts swam in a sea of red-cloaked Equals.

These could be nothing else but the *mechanimai*, Brasidas's siege engines.

A fourth came into sight, and then it was time. Demosthenes pushed the cord of his giant amphora into the flame of the blacked out lamp and held it there until the pitch-soaked fuse was well alight. The two Athenians beside him did likewise and signaled down the line of ambushers that the rest should make their payloads ready. Demosthenes heaved the heavy jug onto his shoulder, took careful aim down the steep, jagged slope at the foremost of the lumbering engines, and he heaved. The amphora, lit cord spinning, sailed out into space.

For a moment, time ceased. Then came a pop, barely audible over the din of the giant wagons' wheels. The amphora smashed into a thousand shards, and its viscous contents, the witch of Dekelea's recipe, formed an irregular black blot centered on the front right wheel of the second-to-last engine.

Spartans cried out in alarm, and Demosthenes' racing heart ceased beating. The black blot burst into flame. White hot, sizzling, intense, the fire engulfed the front of the engine and shot up the sailcloth covering it, just as two more amphorae flew down. One struck higher up than the first and doubled the blaze, the second landed just short, setting red cloaks alight and sending up screams of pain and terror.

All down the line, the scene was repeated. A second engine caught fire, along with the ground beneath it and a number of its escorts. Further back, a yoked pair of blazing oxen ran amok through a swarm of panicked soldiers. That put all the other snorting, braying beasts of burden were to fright, and they began pulling in every direction. The burning shroud fell away from the most immolated of the engines, revealing a complex wooden frame, toothed wheels, and a long, stout timber arm. It was a throwing arm, if Thalassia was correct, as she doubtless was, capable of heaving wall-smashing missiles over great distances.

In half a minute or less, all the Athenians on the heights had sent their deadly pots into the valley, and in as much time, the orderly advance of an army was transformed into fiery chaos. Six of Brasidas's great stone throwers, *katapeltai*, had been set alight to varying degrees. Perhaps more followed further back, but twenty men had done all they could today, and now all that remained was to retreat. The volunteers raced along the ridge to whichever of the three escape ropes was nearest them, and once there, each clipped on an iron ring that fastened his belt to the rope. Then, with as much haste as due caution allowed, he shoved off backward into the void.

Demosthenes, like the others, had practiced this means of quick descent on cliffs nearer Athens, and now, when it mattered, it came as second nature. Suspending the altogether natural fear of throwing oneself off a cliff, he plunged at stomach-churning speed from jagged rock to jagged rock, lighting for less than a heartbeat on each before shoving off again. He controlled his speed, barely, by means of rawhide straps covering his palms. Beside him, above and below, the band of volunteers likewise fell. At least one undisciplined soul let loose a triumphant wail which echoed over the bay, but declarations of triumph were premature in Demosthenes' mind, even if there was no sign yet of Spartan pursuit on the rocks above. There would not be, since even were enemy climbers to have sprung to action at the moment the ambush began, they would arrive at the top to find nothing but a few discarded oil lamps.

The ascent had been measured in hours; the return took but minutes. By the time Demosthenes' feet struck earth with bone-jarring force, others were already dragging the waiting boats down to the waterline and setting oars to oarlocks. In no time, and with no instruction needed, all four craft pushed out into the surf and rose and fell on the gently rolling waves on a return path for Eleusis.

While men around him congratulated one another and roared in exhilaration, Demosthenes' eyes continually checked the heights from which they had just come. They were empty still, and he hoped they would stay that way. A mortal man would hard-pressed to scale the height in time to achieve any result, but as he alone among the Athenians present knew, Brasidas' army did not consist entirely of mortal men.

Just as the four escaping craft reached cruising speed on the bay, the heart inside him sank. A lone, crouching figure stood up and was outlined against the bright sky, sunlight glinting off what at first appeared to be a polished helm until a gust of wind off the bay showed it for what it was: a crown of flowing, golden hair.

12. She Whose Wrath Is Relentless

Eden raised a short, curved stick at the end of an outstretched arm. Before Demosthenes even recognized the thing for a small, strangely double-curved bow, a groan sounded in the boat rowing alongside his, and a man by the name of Enytos fell back with an arrow in his eye. He was dead before he hit the boards, and his oar flew wild. A quick-thinking benchmate grabbed it, only to be struck down next by a shaft to the center of his chest. The boat of the two dead men veered right, one oar lost to sea, as the living in that craft, and in the remaining three boats, hunkered down to utter prayers or curses.

A third short, red-fletched arrow fell, and another rower in the same craft fell dead. No, not dead. Just wounded, but not for long–the fourth shaft did not fail to steal his life.

Even a troop of bowmen should have been capable of nothing more than harassment at this range, killing a man or two out of every fifty arrows, if luck was with them. But Demosthenes knew that this shooter's eye and arm were of the stars, built to kill, and she needed no luck.

The two men who yet lived in the boat of corpses, seeing that nothing awaited them but death, leaped overboard and began to swim. The closest shore was the one they had just left, but to go back there was certain doom. There was no way they could reach Eleusis either, and so they split the difference and headed for a point ahead of the invading army, in the hope they might beat its advance into Attica. If they reached land, perhaps they would live.

On the heights, Eden lowered her bow and vanished among the rocks. Demosthenes lost sight of her momentarily, then found her golden halo again atop the cliffs at the place where the drop to the sea was sheerest. She made some strange swift movements which he identified, with a feeling of dread, as the shedding of her outer clothes. Once those sat in a pile, she stepped to the cliff's edge and without a second's hesitation, dove off. Her form cut a smooth, straight line, a pale dart against the dark brown of the rock behind, and she slipped into the foaming sea with scarcely a splash.

"Steady on," Demosthenes told the four men in the craft with him, for lack of anything better. "Be ready for anything."

He sensed, if not knew, that the warning was useless.

The three remaining craft rowed on in silence but for some hushed pleas to the gods for deliverance and on behalf the shades of the dead. After several minutes of hard rowing, the oarsmen of each boat eased back, either from weariness or the belief they were out of bowshot. Whichever was the case, Demosthenes ordered fresh rowers to take the oars, taking one himself, and he urged no let-up. Even if they believed the danger was over and pursuit was impossible, they were stunned by the sudden loss of their comrades and so obeyed without question.

There were the sounds of a hollow thump and then screams, and Demosthenes' eyes flew to the source: the prow of the rearmost boat had dug into the waves, sending the aft flying upward, as might happen in a violent storm. All five men within tumbled screaming into the sea, where they treaded water and scrambled to reoccupy the empty hull.

One man slipped abruptly under the waves, as if tugged from below; then another. Moments later, both bobbed to the surface, dead, their dark cloaks billowing. Then a third was pulled down, thrashing and screaming, and when he surfaced, too, life had fled his limbs.

The two men left in the sea reached their boat and clambered aboard, while near them a smooth and flowing white shape, dolphin-like, grazed the green surface of the bay.

"Swords!" Demosthenes cried. Most of the surviving volunteers already had drawn the weapons strapped to their backs, but the rest did so now, all except those manning the oars, which included Demosthenes.

Three strokes of those oars was all their hidden enemy allowed. Then another boat lost an oar, yanked from below out of the rower's grip. The men around him brought their blades to bear and hacked blindly into the waves on the spot where it had vanished. While they were thus occupied on the port side, the boat's starboard lifted, dumping all three in a storm of flailing limbs. One by one they slipped into the deep and became prey to a sleek white shape flitting just below the surface, and then their corpses were set adrift on the gentle waves. The two rowers of that emptied craft gave up their oars, clasped hands and raised voices in prayer, and Demosthenes watched helplessly as a pair of white arms rose from the bay to clap hands on the boat's topstrake, and Eden emerged from the deep.

First revealed was a slick sheet of flaxen hair; below that, a slim torso and rounded backside clad in nothing but white linen rendered translucent by the sea. Then came bare legs which flew, first one and then the other, into the hull, and finally the killer stood fully revealed. Standing at the prow, she gazed upon the victims who cowered at the boat's far end hurling useless prayers at Olympus.

Rowing on in spite of the near certitude that there could be no escape, Demosthenes watched Eden run the two men through with a sword she stooped to pick up from the boards. They had accepted death, it seemed, and chosen to go this way rather than beneath the waves. This way, they could hope for eventual burial, that their shades might not drift eternally.

The white daimon of the bay turned in the empty hull to

face the final craft, Demosthenes' boat, which had never stopped moving and which now plied the waves some twenty yards from her. With scarcely a pause, she cast her sword aside and dove into the water. The four men around Demosthenes wailed in despair, knowing they were next.

Demosthenes stopped rowing, dropped his oar and drew the sword on his back. He had seen Eden heavily mutilated, seen her lose an arm, even if she showed no trace of missing it now. Granted, another of her kind had inflicted those wounds, but the fact remained, she could be hurt.

"I say we kill the bitch," he said, rising from the bench and adopting a low, stable crouch in the rocking vessel. "If we fail, at least we can die well."

The response was not what it might have been. The other rower shipped his oar, and one by one, eyeing the ominously quiet surface of the bay, the four muttered reluctant assent. They carefully stood and arranged themselves in a tight ring at the craft's center, all eyes facing out. Every man's sword rose; every set of shoulders tensed. The man to Demosthenes' left drew a shuddering breath and resumed a rambling prayer.

Something slapped the hull. It was no wave, no bit of flotsam: eight white fingers appeared on the prow. The boat rocked, and in one swift motion the daimon came aboard. Golden hair longer than a Spartiate's streamed water onto the benches and along the contours of a body clad so thinly that every detail was visible. The ring of Athenians broke, and its members turned swords shaking in unsteady hands to oppose her.

She had the face of Leda, this glistening goddess of death, and it showed first interest and then amusement. She smiled wickedly, and without warning she lunged, forming raised hands into claws while hissing loudly through teeth bared in a snarl.

The move was a feint, but four screams split the air, four swords clattered onto the boards, and four of Athens' bravest men, men who had volunteered to ambush a Spartan army of thousands, jumped into the Bay of Eleusis and swam for their lives.

Their commander stood alone, pointing a feeble short sword at a being he knew could, with the barest of effort, rend him in two.

The eyes of Eden were a richer, deeper blue than Thalassia's and harder by far, and the stare they leveled across the rocking boat at him was a measuring one. She came forward and sat facing Demosthenes on the forward bench with her legs parted, putting all she had on display without any thought for modesty.

She had this in common with Thalassia then.

"Like what you see, Athenian?" she taunted. She overenunciated as Thalassia once had, and her words were a mix of Attic and Doric. "Or do you prefer darker meat, like Geneva's? Or Seaweed, or whatever it is you're calling her."

Demosthenes stood frozen. His sword's point was still aimed at her, for what little it was worth.

The deadly nymph scoffed. "I know you, Demosthenes. I remember you from Pylos. I will not go so far as to say that I owe you my life, but..." She smiled. "Your intervention was timely. A shame that the decision to put a sword in Geneva was the last good one you made. You have become her pet, no? Are you a good dog, Athenian? Do you bend over when she tells you, and yelp when she–"

"Enough," Demosthenes said, lowering his blade. "I care nothing of your feud with Geneva. My one concern is the safety of my city." In the long seconds which Eden had spent taunting him, Demosthenes' mind had not been idle, nor was it now. His words had purpose. "A mere human cannot deceive your kind, so you must know I speak truly. Perhaps I am possessed of other truths which might be of interest to you?"

"You think you can play games with me, Athenian?" Eden asked with a malevolent smile. Then, "Very well... until it grows dull. Tell me a truth."

"I know Geneva's purpose, the one which has stranded you here in a... I believe you would call it a Severed Layer?"

"Go on," Eden said. Interest was apparent in her sharp, pale features.

"According to her, this layer, this world, are those which shall give birth to the being you call the Worm. I can guess from your face that this comes as news to you. Geneva knows not the precise time or place, but she hopes that if the course of history is thrown far enough from the path which leads to him, the Worm might be... uncreated."

Demosthenes paused, and Eden glared, tight of lip and narrow of eye. "No," she concluded at length. "If that is possible, why did Magdalen not order it so? Unless Geneva acts under Her command?"

"She does not," Demosthenes was pleased to inform her. "As to your other point, I can hardly say. Geneva was the Worm's lover. Perhaps that gave her insight which your Magdalen lacks. I only know that Geneva came here by her own design with the aim of uncreating the Worm–an aim which," Demosthenes added calculatedly, "she believes that you, in lending your knowledge and assistance to Sparta, are presently helping her to achieve."

He watched Eden absorb this in silence, betraying no outward reaction for some seconds. When she did react, it was to smile. Demosthenes had come to hate that thin, cold smile. He still had not forgotten it from Pylos.

"Astonishing," Eden remarked. "The Wormwhore's mouth is good for but two things. Lying is one of them. Yet I believe in the truth of what she has told you. Just as I see why you wish for me to know it." Her smile became a sneer. "You hope it will save your city. It will not. No more than will the damage you have done today to a few machines. More of them follow... and they are not our only surprises."

Star-born, nearly naked Eden stood, a graceful movement that interrupted the rhythm of the hull's gentle rolling not one iota.

"You have given me much to think on, Athenian," she said. "For the future. For now, our little contest must have resolution. There is pride at stake. Which will triumph, her city... or mine?

"Go back to your mistress now, pet," she commanded. "Tell the Wormwhore I will see her on the day of battle. Hope for the sake of Athens that she chooses to stand and fight. Should she run, I will have little choice but to see my *frustration* taken out on your people." A sick gleam tainted Eden's eye. " In exchange for your having helped me once, I grant you your life today, along with those others I spared. Make them last, if you can, and use them well."

Sleek Eden turned to face the cliffs. Setting one bare foot on the boat's topstrake, she dove and slipped beneath the waves, leaving cold corpses bobbing in her wake.

PART 5

ELEUSIS

1. A River of Flesh and Bronze

Beaching their two boats at Eleusis, Demosthenes and the eight survivors of Eden's attack loaded onto a cart the five bodies they had managed to fish from the bay and by twilight completed the grim overland return to Athens. A rider carried word ahead of their return, delivering it straight to Nikias that he might meet them alone at the Sacred Gate. Though Nikias had withheld his support for the ambush on Skiron's Road, Demosthenes had informed him of his intention to undertake it. Such defiance had not displeased Nikias, who was content to wait and see the raid's outcome before deciding whether to bestow his approval retroactively and perhaps claim a share of the credit with no risk of blame.

As the slain volunteers were carted away, the survivors swore to make no mention to anyone of Eden, the she-daimon whose name they still did not know. Eden would remain a state secret, as were the siege engines which had been the raid's target. Better that the populace not be thrown into a senseless panic. Rumor eventually would take to her wings and flit over the city sowing seeds of fear, but for now, only those Athenians who had just escaped Eden's wrath, and Nikas, would know of her existence.

Nikias's weathered skin turned the color of bone when he heard that as many as eleven men (three were last seen living, but remained unaccounted for) had died this day at the hands of a lone female.

"Some god has finally seen fit to join our war directly," old Nikias reflected, his gray eyes misting. He was never one to take lightly the gods' favor; in years past, he had spared no public expense in attempting to gain it for his city. "Will another come down on our side, I wonder?"

Demosthenes laid a hand on the pious old man's

shoulder. "She is no goddess," he assured. "Trust me to deal with her." Not a fraction of the confidence that he projected was genuine.

As survivors eager to return to their families dispersed around them, Nikias's gaze fell upon a spot in the middle distance behind Demosthenes. Turning, Demosthenes saw what the old man did. Thalassia stood with her back against an expanse of city wall between the ornate, closed Sacred Gate, opened only for processions to Eleusis, and the larger, plainer Dipylon Gate which stood open. Dressed in sea-foam green (the black witch of Dekelea evidently having declined to make an appearance in Athens) she stood watching intently, gravely. She was out of human earshot, which meant little where she was concerned.

"Your slave," Nikias reflected. "You told me that she was an oracle. Or was it a sorceress?"

Surprise and fatigue kept Demosthenes from producing any reply, much less the whole truth.

"The belly-bows, the fire-pots, the riding gear," Nikias listed. "And all the rest that you have supposedly acquired through trade. They came from her?"

Demosthenes' silence amounted to an admission.

Nikias continued, "I would hide it, too, if I had something so valuable under my roof."

Demosthenes finally set his tired mind to work on a denial, but it was too late. Nothing said now would be plausible. Perhaps it was for the best; the senior general was receptive and might prove useful.

"Can I count on your discretion?" Demosthenes asked.

"Indeed. Particularly if she has one or two more tricks that might be of use." The strategos sighed, a melancholy look descending upon his lined features. "Witches are always bringers of evil. In time of peace, I might be inclined to burn one. But in such a storm as now looms," he nodded toward the west, "help from any quarter is welcome." He frowned in thought. "You have done well burning Brasidas's wall-breakers, even if it is true what the she-daimon told you, that others are yet on the way. As of today, please consider yourself the first holder of a new title. Since I have just devised it now, it may have to remain unofficial. *Chief of Special Weapons.* Its mandate is simple: deploy ours and destroy theirs."

Nikias's gray eyes returned to Thalassia, who yet waited, less than patiently, near the wall, eavesdropping. Looking at her, Nikias sighed, and there was weariness and nostalgia in the sound, as though he longed for simpler times. He said to Demosthenes, "While we are at it, you may as well be Archon of Witches, too."

Leaving Nikias perhaps to ponder new ways in which one or another of the gods might be persuaded to act on his city's behalf, Demosthenes passed through the Dipylon Gate into Athens. Thalassia came silently up and walked beside him.

"I should have come with you," she said penitently.

"I would not have had you. And I would have been right. Eden might have hurt or killed you, and now Athens would stand at her mercy. Nikias did not need to know this, but you should: she said that if you do not face her, there will be consequences for Athens."

"You say that as if you fear I might do otherwise."

Demosthenes avoided answering. "You beat her once," he said. "Can you again?"

Thalassia permitted the evasion. Knowing truth from lies might at times be a curse. Perhaps she did not wish to know the truth, which was that he did harbor some doubt, however small, that she would not now–as she had at at least two vital junctures in her past–choose to serve herself.

"In strength and speed and by all other physical measures, we are equal," Thalassia said, somewhat bleakly. "I could win, or she might."

"Even though you are only a pilot and she... something else?"

"Hey." Thalassia grabbed his arm, halting him and prompting him to face her. "Athenians are *only* fishermen and bakers and carpenters, but you hold your own against Spartiates who do almost nothing year-round but train for war. I beat her once, I can again."

Demosthenes touched the hand that was gripping his arm rather too tightly, and he smiled for as long as the weight of the horror looming over Athens allowed, which was not long.

"I was rather hoping to hear 'I'll fucking destroy her,'" he said, "but your answer will suffice."

Thalassia released his arm with a quiet laugh. "I fucking will," she said.

Demosthenes needed no truth-sense to tell him she was confident of no such thing.

He took her just-lowered hand in his and said, holding her pale-eyed gaze, "I do not understand what death means to you. But it is not lost on me that you are willing to risk it, not to bring us victory or alter the course of Fate... but only to keep my city safe."

Thalassia regarded him silently, strangely, for a moment. Then her lips twisted in a good-natured sneer. "Idiot," she said softly. "It's my city now, too."

She patted Demosthenes' shoulder in mock condescension and turned to resume the walk into town.

"I'm not needed at Dekelea," she called back. "Is there somewhere else I might spend the night?"

Demosthenes caught her up and took to walking side-by-side in the streets of Athens with his spoil of war. "Always," he answered, and managed to add in jest on this day of doom, "even were it not required of me by law."

***

Two dawns passed from the burning of the *katapeltai*, and a third saw the Spartan invasion force of thousands massing on the western frontier, while the defenders of Athens, as many or more in number, arrayed themselves on the plain of Eleusis to meet the threat. The defenders might have enjoyed some advantage had the proposed defenses of liquid stone not been delayed by squabbling in the Assembly over what to build and where. With the fortifications incomplete, the rival cities would meet on more even terms, army against army, shield against shield... machine against machine, star-born witch against star-born witch.

Today was surely the day of battle. Laonome's eyes were dry now, but her cheek was still cold to the touch where the night's tears had cooled and dried. In his megaron, Demosthenes held her close, forehead to forehead, nose to nose, palm cupping her jaw and thumb rubbing the tiny white scar on her upper lip.

"For luck," he said, and kissed the scar, prompting the mouth which bore it to form a sad smile.

He embraced Laonome again and again, wishing that a layer of iron-scale armor did not separate their bodies so he might carry her off up the stairs and curl unclothed with her in the marriage bed as they had done each morning for the four months of his arrest. But such days belonged to the past for now, and, he dared hope, to the future. And so he contented himself to lay a hand on the belly that had begun to swell with his seed and kiss the smooth expanse of white skin between Laonome's silver fillet and hairline.

"I shall return, my love," he promised, as they separated.

His wife's eyes slammed shut to bar fresh tears. Eurydike, more used to such partings, laid a tattooed arm about her mistress and drew her in until their temples touched. Demosthenes parted a curtain of fiery curls to touch the cheek of his slave, who said nothing, only smiled. He smiled back. They had done this enough times that words were not needed, not even a late reminder that in the event that no one was left to defend them, she was not to employ the blunt Spartan dagger, his gift to her, which hung at her waist, but instead throw herself and Laonome on the questionable mercy of Athens' conquerors.

The sound of the door opening made Demosthenes look that way. As he did, a figure stepped into his megaron out of forgotten verse.

The mansion of Alkibiades contained many odd things. Among them was a corselet of stiff leather, studded with discs of highly polished bronze and trimmed in gold brocade, which was, according to its owner, the armor of Penthesilea, the last great Amazon, beloved of Achilles, he who had slain her with tears of regret on the plains of Troy. While Alkibiades claimed to have stripped the armor from a woman warrior in Scythia (where he surely had never traveled), it was far likelier that he had bought it, along with the story, from some less-than-honest dealer in antiquities.

Whatever the truth of the armor's origin, it was worn now by Thalassia, who stepped into the megaron geared for war like a man-killing Amazon. Two short swords hung down her bare thighs, the bronze tips of their scabbards scraping the rims of ivory-inlaid leg-greaves. Her forearms were wrapped in leather, her lustrous black hair woven into a thick braid that began at the center of her forehead and followed her hairline to the right, falling over her right shoulder, one of the more pragmatic of the styles she favored. She lacked shield and helm; either they were outside with the horses she had brought or she saw no use for them.

The three other members of the oikos to which she belonged spent some seconds staring in awestruck silence. Demosthenes was first to recover, and he looked over to find his wife and Eurydike agape. Both had been told a day ago, by necessity, what perhaps they already suspected: that Thalassia once had been a warrior among her people. Indeed, neither had quite been surprised, yet neither could have been prepared for a sight such as this.

Slowly Eurydike cracked a smile, a reluctant shadow of which Thalassia returned.

"You look better in it than I did," Eurydike said.

Blinking out of her own stupor, Laonome flicked her gaze to her husband and declared softly, confidently, "A goddess fights with you."

In the smile he returned, Demosthenes gave neither confirmation nor denial. He certainly would not burden her with the knowledge that the enemy possessed a goddess of its own.

Giving his wife what he hoped would not be their last kiss before Hades, he preceded Thalassia out the door and, exerting an effort not to look back, walked the corridor of palms that bisected the garden. He secured his helmet and hoplon to the saddle of Balios's successor, a war-horse named Akmos, then set sandal in stirrup and threw himself astride the beast. Behind him, Thalassia mounted soundlessly on a mare called Phaedra which, like her armor, was borrowed from Alkibiades, under whose tutelage she had learned to ride at least as well as any plainsman.

Turning, Demosthenes saw the women of his house standing in the open doorway, Laonome's face buried in a curtain of Thracian curls. He raised his hand in a final farewell which only Eurydike returned, and he kicked his mount's flanks and set off for war.

"You were cold to them," Demosthenes observed to Thalassia as they rode the empty street.

"Was I?"

"There is a balance to be struck when leaving a loved one, for their sake more than yours. If you are either too emotional or too distant, they will know you are preparing for death." He added deliberately, "You might bear that in mind for next time."

Whatever Thalassia's thoughts were on that matter, they remained private, and the focus of her pale eyes was distant as they cantered side-by-side. As they progressed north toward the city gate, the streets grew less empty. Not unexpectedly, Thalassia drew stares from all they passed. By mutual agreement they had determined that this day would mark the end of all efforts to conceal Thalassia's true nature from the public. What counted now was the city's safety, and anyway Eden was unlikely to exercise discretion. From now on, whatever the public of Athens saw, it saw.

What it saw right now was an Amazon riding to war on behalf of the city which in a time long past, but hardly forgotten, had suffered invasion by her people. Not far from this very spot sat the graven stone which marked the point where tradition said the Amazon invasion had been thrown back under the leadership of Herakles and Theseus. By trick of time, those two saviors of Hellas, one-time allies, were the patron heroes of the opposing cities set to clash today.

The stares grew thicker when they reached the broad thoroughfare called the Dromos, on which traveled a heavy stream of armed and armored men on foot. The banks of that stream were lined with women, children, and grandfathers showering their sons and brothers and husbands with well-wishes, prayers and cut blossoms. When Akmos and Phaedra turned onto the street and joined the stream, a hush fell over the onlookers. Even the eyes of the fighting men turned to see what had caused it. Thalassia paid the scrutiny no mind, and Demosthenes, beside her, acted as if nothing were amiss, merely guiding Akmos at the slow collective pace of the procession. The crowd's curiosity proved impermanent; few devoted any more than a handful of heartbeats to gawking at Thalassia.

When they were halfway to the Dipylon Gate, via which the river of flesh and bronze and towering canvas-wrapped spear blades was to exit the city, a young girl pushed through the crowd to come up alongside Akmos and walk in pace with him. She was brown-skinned, the child of a slave or resident alien, and her small, outstretched hand held aloft a purple flower, an iris, which she waved by the stem. Demosthenes smiled at the girl, reached down and tried to pluck it from her hand, but before he could, the offering was withdrawn. The girl shook her head and pointed past him. Nodding understanding, Demosthenes anchored himself tightly to his mount, leaned down and hoisted the girl from the ground, setting her carefully on Akmos' neck. Thalassia looked over and, briefly letting a smile pierce her gloom, she leaned her head closer to let the girl insert the bloom's stem into her braid. That done, Demosthenes returned the flower-giver to the earth.

For the better part of the next hour, they made their way slowly to the Dipylon Gate and passed through it into the countryside of Attica. There, unconstrained by streets, the human current spread thinner, and the mood among the fighters grew decidedly more somber as all began to set their minds to what lay ahead. Thalassia's mood was already grim, and that did not change. Demosthenes rode alongside her in silence, through the tall grass which flanked the Sacred Way, making no attempt to dispel whatever cloud it was that hung over her.

Their plans were already made and required no further discussion. They were to separate. Thalassia was to ride with Alkibiades and a host of citizen cavalry on an attack across the frontier meant to destroy any remaining Spartan siege engines. Demosthenes, meanwhile, would report to the Athenian forces' left wing, nearest Eleusis, where Nikias, in overall command, would be stationed. It was also where Brasidas, doubtless leading the enemy right, the place of honor, would be, and where the 'special weapons,' as Nikias had called them, were to be deployed: belly-bows ready to skewer Equals, assuming Eden hadn't equipped them with some countermeasure, and firepots to be hurled into the rear ranks and burn men alive with clinging, unquenchable flame.

How much more horrific could war become? Demosthenes scarcely had time to wonder. Thalassia knew the answer, no doubt, but he felt no desire to ask her, even if he got the chance.

When the city had receded behind a hill at their backs and the land became more thickly wooded, Thalassia steered Phaedra into a copse of trees and there halted. Demosthenes followed and waited impatiently for Thalassia to make clear the purpose of her diversion.

"It's time for you to know my last secret," she said.

2. Her Last Secret

Scenting war ahead, Akmos whinnied angrily at the delay. Thalassia slid from Phaedra's saddle in the stand of small trees and came toward the eager beast, whose rider swung down to meet her. Reaching him, Thalassia raised in her fingertips a small object which caught the sunlight. Demosthenes studied it: a sphere roughly the size of an olive, composed of a dark, highly polished metal. Barely visible on its surface were short inscriptions in some foreign alphabet.

"What is it?" her silence forced him to ask.

"A Seed," was her answer. She stared at it, rather than him. "Just as a temple begins its existence as stone in a quarry and the plans of an architect, so this Seed contains plans and a small amount of material."

Demosthenes stared into the metallic sphere, brows furrowing in puzzlement. "Plans for what?"

Her pale gaze rose from the object and fell upon his face, and she smiled as she made her simple reply. "Me."

Demosthenes stared at her, then back at the so-called Seed, and shook his head.

"Whenever we leave Spiral, we carry six of them inside our bodies," Thalassia explained. "If just one survives, then we can live again. Four of my six lie at the bottom of the sea. One is near my heart." With her free hand, she tapped Penthesilea's breastplate. "And this last I removed..." The same hand raised the stiffened leather and linen of her skirts to display a pink scar on her upper thigh as she finished, "to give to you."

Now she took Demosthenes' hand and pressed the Seed into its palm, closing the fingers around it, and she clasped it there, her hands enveloping his. The sphere within seemed to radiate a warmth of its own.

Thalassia lowered her face for her next words: "Know

that in no world, in no layer, is there another hand in which I would sooner place this."

Demosthenes scoffed, gently. "You have poor judgment. I have not treated you well."

"Nor I you," she said quickly, still avoiding his gaze. "But we are past that. I don't know what it is that exists between us. Right now, it is small. But I believe that if it were allowed to grow, it could become something... terrible. And beautiful. And destructive. I have told you what is my life's greatest regret. It is what brought me here. But I think that..."

Demosthenes sensed that she had composed these words in advance of this moment and so did not search for words but only the ability to speak them.

Finding it, she finished, "If this were to be our final meeting, then I would end my existence with an even greater regret." She laughed, and finally met his eyes, and they were bright but sad. "You should hope the opposite," she said, "that we never do meet again. It would be better for you, and your world. But... I would very much like for us to go to Roma together one day." Her gaze sank again, and she released his hand. "We could do a lot of damage, you and I."

"Of that, I have little doubt," Demosthenes quietly concurred. "I hope it will be the case today. But..." He exposed the Seed in his open palm, marveling at the possibility that another Thalassia might spring forth from this shell fully formed, as Athena from the skull of Zeus. "What am I to do with this?"

"If I felt the need to tell you that, then I would not be giving it to you. You do with it as you see fit. The Seed by itself will take the better part of a year to recreate me. Should you possess my body, or part of it, reunite it with the Seed. That will significantly speed the process. Lacking that, surrounding it with any meat, human or animal, will help, too. If ever you wish to destroy it–"

"I will not–"

"Let me finish. You need to know, to dispose of Eden, if for no other reason," she said. "Seeds are difficult to damage, but roughly the weight of a temple column will be a start. Then just keep adding weight until it's crushed. You could drop it in the sea, with my others. That would not destroy it, but it's easier. With Eden's, though, I recommend you take the more thorough approach."

Sighing with what sounded disturbingly like resignation, armor-clad Thalassia started back toward Phaedra, whose tail whipped violently. Demosthenes took a last look at her gift to him, this share of her very existence, and dropped the polished sphere into the rawhide pouch under the skirt of his scale armor, where it warmed his death-token, the silver drachma which was to be placed in the mouth of his corpse for passage into Hades, should he fall.

"Wait," he said, succeeding in halting her. "I... owe you something."

Lips that pursed momentarily in mild derision said she understood what was owed. She scoffed. "Forget it."

"It invites misfortune to let debts be erased," he said. "They should be paid."

"Fucking hell," she cursed, then conceded, "All right. In that case, I owe you something, too."

Demosthenes tried and failed to recall what this debt might be, but she preempted his asking by insisting, "You first."

She clearly had no intention of making herself an easy recipient. Legs planted in the tall grass, she stood unmoving, forcing Demosthenes to approach her to give the thing owed. He was not entirely certain he wished to give it, but at least a part of him did. It was that same part which knew that the unique being now facing him, his ally, his... *friend*...was as likely as not to end this day as lifeless, mutilated meat. For that matter, so was he.

He summoned up his will to act, or rather suppressed the will not to, and he moved. He stepped in close, set his hand behind Thalassia's neck, under her braid, and kissed her, paying back the debt accrued by his abuse of her in Amphipolis. He kissed her softly, but with neither passion nor tenderness. It was a simple kiss, one of affection, and Thalassia reacted to it not at all. Her lips were not quite iron, but something like it. Spun bronze, perhaps, but less pliant.

He lingered on her mouth a second longer than he might have, hoping she would give in, but each heartbeat only increased the extent of potential embarrassment when they broke, and so before long, he withdrew in defeat.

Thalassia's pale eyes regarded him distantly. Her mouth remained a thin line. She said nothing, and so it was up to him to move them past the awkward aftermath of his miscalculation.

Trying not to show the dent in his pride, he asked, "What is it that you owe me?"

Finally her stony mask cracked for a tick of her sublime features, less than a smile. "I just gave it."

Demosthenes puzzled over this, and presently the memory surfaced. It had been almost two years prior, on his rooftop terrace, that her soft lips had been insistent, his the ones unwilling. Now she had repaid him back in kind, with rejection.

He laughed at himself, easily, feeling neither discomfort nor embarrassment. "I suppose that settles accounts between us."

"For a few hours, maybe," she said. "If I save Athens today,"–she held her hand out, palm up, and waggled its fingers–"I expect you to go broke making it rain fucking jewels on me."

The sight before him, of Thalassia geared for war, her lips freshly parted from his, one hand extended to catch rain, sent a new memory coursing through his mind, and it weakened his limbs like a physical blow. This memory was of a long-ago nightmare, in which he had stood alone with blood-soaked Thalassia upon a field of endless slaughter.

"Hmm," hyper-perceptive Thalassia intoned, with a vaguely dejected look. "I don't know exactly why you're looking at me like that. I would ask, but..." She glanced at the road to Eleusis fifty yards off, where the ongoing current of man, animal, bronze, and steel was barely visible between the trunks of trees. "We should go."

When she turned her face back to him, it had changed: she wore her mark of Magdalen.

"Warpaint," she offered in explanation.

Demosthenes stared into the flowing, complex network of lines he had seen only once before. In turn, the bright eye at the web's center regarded him back with a distant glimmer of amusement. She made a surreal sight, this wintry eyed witch, a star-born Pandora in her Amazon's garb, with twin swords of Athenian steel on her hips, elegant and savage masque covering a quarter of her face, and lastly the forlorn purple flower, bizarre accompaniment to her panoply of war, helplessly adrift in a jasmine-scented wave of raven hair.

Clearly the world had gone mad, or he had, or both, for this was the champion of Athens. And if dreams were windows on a future immutable, then to him Thalassia was more than just that. She was his lover and queen and his partner in visiting untold devastation upon all he loved. He might pray that those visions were only phantoms–except how could he even pray when she had stripped him of gods and left in their place only this figure before him?

"We can't stand here all fucking day," said that terrible, beautiful figure. She spun to complete her earlier, aborted walk back to Phaedra.

"Thalassia," Demosthenes called after her.

She paused with her hand on Phaedra's mane.

"Fucking kill her."

The demigoddess' head whipped round, just far enough to reveal a faint, reluctant smile of approval. Mounting, without a final goodbye, she galloped off north to meet up with Alkibiades and undertake their appointed mission behind the Spartan lines, to seek out and destroy Brasidas's machines.

Left alone in the grove, Athens' first Archon of Witches mounted, too, and went to meet his own half of their shared destiny.

3. The Arrows of Eris

The defenders of Attica, their ranks numbering in the thousands and swelling still, arrayed themselves on high ground in time to watch the army of Brasidas emerge from the shallow valleys of the Megarid. It spread across the green plains north of Eleusis like a great black blot spreading across the page from an overturned inkwell.

"We should attack now, before they can form up," Demosthenes urged, but he did not hold command here. He was not even a general. The man beside him, Nikias, was the one charged with Attica's defense, and Nikias was a man both praised and derided for his excess of caution. The trait had served him well at times, been his downfall at others, but either way, his word was supreme this day.

"Our forces are not ready," Nikias declared.

He was right in that men were still streaming north from Athens to be dispatched to left, right or center based on need and on what weaponry they owned. But Brasidas' army numbered, by most accounts, no more than six thousand, while the Athenian forces stretching in both directions in an undulant line extending as far as the eye could see in either direction might already have numbered twice that. Not only every able-bodied citizen, but every foreigner, too, who called Athens home was coming out.

"Much longer and we'll be fighting with the sun in our faces."

This argument came from Nikostratos, friend and political ally of Nikias, his colleague on the Board of Ten and second-in-command this day. He was twenty years Nikias's junior and marginally less inclined to circumspection.

But Nikias held fast: "We wait."

And so Demosthenes watched from a grassy hilltop as

the army of Brasidas formed up in orderly ranks. He watched the mass in particular for the sight of a crown of long blond hair, but he could no more pick that out over such a great distance than he could the red horsehair plume of Brasidas himself.

Late in the morning a rider arrived, a scout of the *prodromoi,* the light cavalry, bearing dire news. A Theban army thousands strong was on the march south into Attica in support of Brasidas. Even if its full mass of footsoldiers did not arrive in time for the start of battle, their much-feared cavalry surely would.

Nikias received the news stoically before instructing his junior strategos and band of gathered aides to send more of the fresh arrivals north to strengthen the right wing, where the Thebans were liable to strike. Then he said to Demosthenes, "Take the cavalry north and guard against the Theban horse. If Alkibiades and your witch have not launched their attack yet on the siege engines, cancel it and take them with you."

"But that is–" Demosthenes cut short his protest. It was not his place to second-guess. And anyway, Nikias was right: the Thebans rolling up the Athenian right wing constituted a far more immediate danger than the lumbering siege engines. And so he conceded, "Aye."

It was not long after news of the Thebans arrived that the *mechanamai* made their appearance on the western horizon. There were three of them pulled by teams of oxen, and their canvas shrouds had been removed, surely not because their use was imminent but rather because the Spartans had learned the hard lesson that the shrouds were flammable. The *katapeltai* each comprised a simple frame from which extended a tall, stripped tree trunk, tapered and topped with a sling. Only a handful of Athenians present knew that a massive projectile could be placed in the sling and hurled over great distances. The behemoth's certain target was the walls of Athens, and they could breach them with one well-placed blow.

There next appeared at the head of Brasidas's horde a small cluster of spearless hoplites bearing the lambda blazon on their shields. They broke off from the assembling force and made their way slowly toward the Athenian lines. When they drew near enough and came to a halt, the identity of the man at the body's head became clear.

Brasidas wore no crimson plume but rather just a simple pilos-style helmet like any of his men. He raised overhead a leafy herald's wand and cried out, "I would address Demosthenes!"

Nikias looked nonplussed. It was Nikostratos who stepped to the front of the hilltop and called back, "It is Nikias who commands this army!"

A wind blowing in from the nearby coast kept the Spartiate's flowing mane of black hair in constant motion. The same wind bore up the hill his bark of laughter.

"I doubt that old man commands his bowels!" When his fellow Spartans had finished an uncharacteristic chuckle, Brasidas resumed, "You Athenians love to talk before you fight, do you not? Well, here is a Spartan willing to do the same, but only with Demosthenes!"

Immediately, tens of pairs of puzzled, wary Athenian eyes turned to Demosthenes. He had avoided a face-to-face encounter with this man who so despised him once, after the jailbreak, but today there would be no avoiding it. Not even if it was a trap, which seemed as likely as not to be the case.

Demosthenes stepped to the fore and tugged off and discarded his helmet of plain bronze, revealing himself. The summer breeze cooled a scalp matted with sweat-soaked, sand-colored locks. He was already unarmed, for his long cavalry sword was sheathed on the flank of Akmos, who snorted and churned the soil with his hooves some yards back, behind the crest of the hill which hosted the Athenian commanders. At an even pace, Demosthenes traversed the wide space between the Athenian line and Brasidas's Spartiates. Such a maelstrom of thoughts swirled in his head that he could scarcely even spare one to wonder if his deceptively confident march downhill was to end in his death.

He came to stand three spear lengths from Brasidas, who stepped out from among his comrades, wielding his herald's wand like it was the club of some thug out spreading fear in the streets. The staff rose and fell, striking the palm of his other, empty hand.

"Much as I would prefer to just get on with honest slaughter," he said, "there is another conflict which must be fought out first. Where is the bitch who wins your battles for you, coward?"

"Where is yours?" Demosthenes came back. It was a feeble response, perhaps worse than none at all, but it was out of his mouth before he could stop it.

Brasidas ignored him. "If she fails to show in a quarter-hour, Eris will turn her attention instead to that sad, motley wall of shields behind you. You know there can only be one result. If she is denied her fair fight, then when Athens is ours, it will be put to fire and sword, no woman or child spared from slavery."

"This woman is no goddess, Brasidas!" Demosthenes cried back. "Not Eris! Her name is Eden, and all she wants is–"

"–the Wormwhore's head. Yes, I know. I am giving it to her, and if Eris in turn wishes to help Sparta set Hellas free from the yoke of Athenian tyranny a generation early, I shall not refuse." He shrugged. "I hope she shows. We Equals always prefer a fair fight to one-sided butchery."

With that pronouncement, Brasidas whirled and rejoined his comrades, who likewise turned and headed back down the slope with him toward the dark mass of Spartans and their Peloponnesian allies. Demosthenes returned to his lines, too, in no hurry in spite of the short deadline just set. There was little he could do but hope that wherever she was now in these hills, Thalassia with her superhuman ears had heard the challenge and would hasten back in time to meet it.

He walked up the hill and rejoined Nikias and the others.

"What did he want?" Nikias demanded. His justifiable bitterness at having his authority usurped was well disguised, but not absent.

"Matters of witchery," Demosthenes reported, and left it there. What was the point of explaining to him at length the details of an arrangement entirely outside of his understanding and control?

A scowling Nikias grudgingly accepted the answer and resumed discussion with his war council. Watching the distant enemy host assemble, Demosthenes paid them little heed.

A lone horseman caught his eye. Typically, the Spartans brought little cavalry to war (the Thebans, it had turned out, were providing it today) so any rider would have stood out among them; but this one was even more conspicuous for being on its own, far from any mounted formation. It was moving, too, at full gallop, on a straight line oblique to the two armies, in the direction of the Athenian force.

His eyes tracked the rider for half a minute or so before they caught the glint of a golden mane. Eden's left arm was outstretched, and in its hand was the same double-curved bow she had put to deadly use on the cliffs near Skiron's road.

Demosthenes drew a breath with which to shout warning, but the words were stillborn, drowned out by other men's cries of shock and alarm. He turned and saw the generals' entourage in chaos, bright red blood covering someone's hands.

His eye found Nikias. Eden's arrow had struck the old man's throat and bored right on through to emerge under the rear rim of his bronze helmet. The customary dignity and composure with which Nikias always held himself fled him now, and his limbs flailed wildly. Dumbstruck colleagues scrambled to restrain him and keep him upright, but his fate was clear. By the time he had slipped from Nikostratos' arms to bend over double, head striking the earth, the general in charge of Attica's defense was dead, his long life cut short by the woman the Spartans wrongly called Eris, Slayer of the Brave.

Even as Nikias fell from his friend's grasp and his shade slipped the bounds of his body, Demosthenes was running for Nikostratos. He collided with the junior general bodily in a clash of bronze and iron and dragged him to the ground so close to the fresh corpse that the fletched end of the stubby arrow jutting from Nikias's throat scraped Demosthenes' arm as they landed.

Just in time–a second arrow cut the air above their heads and descended past them to clip the heads off blades of tall grass and light harmlessly in the soil behind the hill.

With tens of witnesses, half of them already crying out the news of Nikias's death, there was no way to stop word spreading up and down the lines: the gods were with Sparta today.

4. Breach

Like most Spartiates, and anyone the gods had blessed with an obol's worth of sense, Styphon had no love for the sea. Yet here he was, not only sailing it but sailing it in a vessel which lacked oars and had been designed by a witch who slew men for sport.

The trireme had had its bronze ram removed, and its two sails were triangular, each shaped like a half-delta. The sails' complicated rigging was a mystery to Styphon, but luckily the ships' crew of mothakes—the bastard sons of Equals not entitled to full citizenship—had been training on them in secrecy in the Lakonian Gulf since spring. Somehow, by a method the sailors presumably understood, the delta-sails allowed the vessel to turn and travel in any direction, even into the wind. What happened when there was no wind at all, and no oars to pull, Styphon did not want to find out. The sailors' skills were adequate, it seemed, as were those of the shipwrights, for the new-style ships had been at sea two days without incident on this, their maiden voyage.

Styphon's ship was named *Potnia*, Venerable, and her twelve sister ships dotted the waves around him, cutting the wind and water at greater speed than any that had sailed before them. Each hull, relieved of its need for a hundred and seventy rowers, now could carry eighty hoplites and all their gear, three times the usual capacity. Currently each held a conservative sixty, which translated to plenty of elbow room for the men, greater speed for the fleet, and fewer lives at risk should one or more of the experimental ships wind up on the sea floor.

The destination of the fleet and its force of eight hundred came into sight past the looming, dark bulk of the isle of Aegina: Piraeus, the port of Athens. But between the fleet and landfall lay an obstacle: triremes of the Athenian harbor patrol, their square sails twisting this way and that in the effort to change course and intercept, as from their decks came the shouts of crewmen driven to near-panic by the sudden appearance of a fleet unlike any they had seen. Their efforts would be for naught, though, just as had been the case already for the lone Athenian sentry ship already left in the Spartan fleet's wake. That ship's crew, on learning they could not possibly hope to outrun or outmaneuver this new threat, had pulled down their sails and thrown masts overboard to give chase under oar. Athenian rowers were supreme in all the seafaring world, but soon enough the piper's shrill rhythm had faded and the pursuing ship had shrunk into a black dot on the southern horizon.

The five Athenian patrol vessels ahead had no more luck, though they did their level best to put themselves in the path of the oncoming fleet. One ship even hurriedly furled its sail, dropped its oars and tried in vain to reach ramming speed with masts still in place. But the Athenian trierarchs, one and all, were unready for the speed and agility of which their stripped-down cousins were capable. The thirteen ships with lambda pennants fluttering on their prows ran the gauntlet with ease, and the defenders were left behind, undamaged but in a state of chaos and bitter confusion. The foremost sailors of the age, Athenians, whose skills had built them a maritime empire, had been foiled within sight of Attica by a land-loving enemy whose navy they were fond of mocking.

No more. Now, the well-armed Equals who passed the Athenians by as if they were standing still were the ones doing the mocking, an activity which they undertook with voices triumphantly raised, and in some cases backsides exposed. Styphon took no measures to rein in such juvenile displays on his own ship or any of the others. An admiral, Knimos, commanded this fleet, but once land was made, another was to take charge. A man who six months prior had stood in disgrace, on the verge of being branded a trembler, stripped of his property and his rights as an Equal. In the Athenian jail, Brasidas had called him *dog*; now he was called *lieutenant* and had been entrusted with a task on which the outcome of a war may well depend.

Styphon, son of Pharax, would lead this attack.

The Spartan fleet sailed at speed past the squat guard towers flanking the harbor entrance of Pireaus, passing under thick volleys of spindles that managed to take no lives. It sailed across the quiet harbor and landed on the beach where the dry, empty hulls of the Athenian navy sat forlorn on their props and in ship-sheds, tinder for Spartan torches, were that the attackers' intention today; but the hoplites who spilled over the rails of the thirteen experimental ships into the surf and mounted the beach did not stop to burn. No, they only hacked down the few resisters they met and raced up shore into the virtually undefended harbor town.

No orders were needed, and none given. Styphon entered into Piraeus riding a wave of slashing spears and unneeded lambda-blazoned shields, while behind him, on the beach, the oarless ships put back to sea, and a small team of Equals set to their specially appointed task of collecting the masts from the beached Athenian ships. The townsfolk, already alerted to the danger by a shrill trumpet, screamed and ran from their homes to flee in the direction of Athens. A few unlucky ones were cut down as they ran, but the invaders gave no attention to slaughter. Before long, the inhabitants of white-washed Piraeus with its long, straight avenues, learned that hiding in their homes was the safest course, and they did just that, for the tide of crimson and iron that had surged out of the Saronic Gulf this day had no interest in seizing the port. Their black eyes were on a much grander prize, toward which they moved relentlessly.

A band of Athenian bowmen appeared on a rooftop firing straight down, and three or four Equals clattered dead or hurt onto the paving stones. A squad was sent up the stairs in pursuit, and the archers scattered and fled.

This was the heaviest the fighting got. In no time, and with little blood shed on either side, Styphon's troops reached their destination, the northeast wall of Piraeus, and there they were stopped cold by the heavy timber gates blocking the long, straight road flanked by the Long Walls which connected city to harbor.

Several of the small clusters of residents running ahead of the invasion force, desperate to escape, had slipped through those gates as the defenders were slamming them shut, but other refugees, now trapped in swiftly-conquered Piraeus, had to veer left or right, screaming children in tow, to seek shelter within the port. Fortunately for them, the invaders deemed them unworthy of notice. Instead, Styphon's hoplites secured the gate and waited. They waited some minutes, until thirty men arrived from the beach carrying six smooth Athenian trireme masts on their shoulders. Once at the gate, the men set the masts down on the paved street and began bundling them like a sheaf of javelins, using thick ropes brought especially for the purpose. Then they attached sets of chains at even intervals along the huge bundle's length and placed on the end which faced the gate another object borne on the ships from Sparta: a convex bronze drum with a spike at its center and a hollow wide enough in diameter to fit over the six masts. They hammered the drum into place, secured it with nails, then heaved the chains over the leather-clad shoulders of the ten stoutest Equals present and brought the completed battering ram forward to the gate.

In drills in Sparta, men armed with such a ram had penetrated wooden walls the thickness of a typical city gate in seven blows. Piraeus's gate lasted six. The first three gave the double doors a bone-jarring rattle. The fourth and fifth created a crack and made it wider; and the sixth blow,produced a man-sized hole in the wood through which were visible the backs of dozens of stupefied Athenian defenders who now set to fresh flight. Equals poured through the breach unopposed and swung the gates wide to speed the passage of the rest.

The bastions lining the Long Walls were meant to allow defenders to fire missiles outward, but they could almost as easily direct fire within. "Shields!" Styphon cried, but the Equals were already assembling into a tortoise-like formation. The centermost troops took turns bearing the weight of the battering ram, which would be needed again when they reached Athens, held their shields overhead while those on the edges kept them angled out. A hard rain sounded on the barrier, a constant thump-thump of iron heads striking hidebound wood and either embedding there or clattering onto the paved street. As it became clear the barrages posed little threat, Styphon ordered the formation's speed increased, and the thunder of missiles pounding nearly eight hundred bowl-shaped shields rose briefly before tapering off again as they passed each bastion.

An hour into the march, Equals at the fore reported the Athenians in their path throwing up a hasty barricade which it seemed they then meant to set aflame. A force had been picked from among the Spartans to deal with just such an eventuality, and Styphon wasted no time calling it to action. He led the twenty men forward himself, all at a full run, screaming, shields high, spears forward. Faced with that sight, the Athenians scattered like ants, deserting their hasty barricade of wagons and market stalls, throwing their lit torches behind them in the hope the tinder would catch.

It did not, and twenty of Greece's most feared warriors—nineteen after one Equal was laid low by a spindle in the back—became a work crew, using shields as ploughs to shove aside debris meant to block their path to victory. The blockade failed in its purpose, hardly even proving a delay. The Equals' steady progress up the broad, deserted street brought them soon to the end of the Long Walls, to the inner cross-wall from which hung, on two stone pylons, the gates of Athens herself, taller and sturdier than those of Piraeus.

Beneath a shelter of shields, the ram was brought forward and its bronze spike, blunted by its earlier use, was set against the bronze-clad timbers on the small gap where the twin doors met. Three men drew the ram back from behind, the ten wielders set themselves and then, on cue, they heaved. The full weight of six ship's masts struck the doors, which rattled on their hinges but refused to yield. For the second and third attempts, a dozen more men lent their shoulders and arms to hammering the weapon home. The gates of Athens shook again, and a dent appeared in their bronze edging, where the ram's spike forced the doors apart just slightly. Letting loose a great bellow with each heave, the determined sons of Sparta drove the ram five more times into that same spot and achieved at last a break in the bronze, a splintered hole in the wood.

The achievement came at a cost: at least ten of their number slain in the constant hail of white-fletched arrows sent down from atop the sheer walls that towered above them on three sides. But whenever an Equal fell, those around him merely closed the gap in their tight formation, providing first and foremost unbroken cover to those engaged in the back-breaking labor of swinging the great ram.

At last, with a thunderous boom which must have shaken Attica, and a rousing cheer for which the people of Lakedaimon had waited the better part of a decade, the doors of Athens gave way. Its breakers did not waste much breath on celebration, for there yet was work to be done. The city's inanimate wall lay open, but ten paces beyond, visible through the small hole, stood a second wall of spears and set shield-arms yet to be breached. These could not be the cream of the Athenian hoplite class, and their numbers could not have been great, for the bulk of Attica's forces, assuming all had gone to plan, were currently arrayed against Brasidas on the Megarian frontier. Assumption, of course, was the enemy of victory (as the once-contemptuous Athenian navy had learned this day), but events thus far suggested no hitches in the smooth execution of Brasidas's strategy.

The two forces glared at one another through the gap in the door, which after three more crushing blows of the ram became large enough for perhaps four fighters to pass if they packed tight. Neither side wished to be the first to approach, but the defenders held the advantage in that regard, for this was their city and time would only swell their ranks. Doubtless they would pounce the moment four or fewer Equals dared become the first to pass through the breach. All the while the rain of arrows continued, raising a curse here, a groan there. Taking stock of their position and the assets at hand, Styphon devised a plan and conveyed it, over the patter of arrow on shield, to a half dozen men around him, who conveyed it to a dozen more, and within minutes all was ready.

The ram, which had been discarded on the ground, was hoisted again, and this time Styphon was among those who set down their spears and slung its supporting chains over their shoulders. But instead of letting the ram swing free, the wielders hugged it close, and on the count of three, holding shields high, they charged with it through the breach.

The Athenians, as expected, pounced with thrusting spears. The man ahead of Styphon took a blade to the leg and fell, but the rest took up his share of the load and pressed on with undiminished momentum. The Athenians could do nothing to prevent the bronze-crowned bundle of masts from entering their city at an acute angle to the doors. Once it was inside, the holders turned it parallel, using it as a barricade behind which the remainder of the invading host could spill through.

Five of those who had held the ram were slain, but not for nothing. By the time the survivors slipped off the supporting chains, letting the bundled masts crush their comrade's corpses, and drew their short swords, a foothold inside the city was achieved. It would not be yielded. Within the breached city walls, Spartan warriors fought in a mass that swelled like a pool of crimson blood flowing from a freshly opened wound. An Equal in the rear ranks which had yet to join the battle raised a war chant of Tyrtaios, and those around him lent their voices, so the heart-raising sound competed with the insistent shriek of the Athenians' trumpeted alarm.

Well before the last of the seven hundred plus Spartiates had set foot in the city, the defenders broke and fled. Styphon ordered his men not to pursue, but regroup instead by the broken gates. He looked down and made a rough count of fallen Spartan shields: ten, give or take, but there would be time for tallying corpses later. Just ahead and to the right of the broad, paved avenue before them stood the hillside theater called the Pnyx, the seat of Athens's beloved democracy and a place where, by all accounts, a dizzying array of demagogues were wont to make flowery speeches in praise of themselves.

While the ranks were mustering behind him in even rows, Styphon picked out twelve men, told them to gather wood and anything else that could be used as kindling, and he pointed at the Pnyx.

"Burn it," he ordered.

5. Clash of the Star-Born

"Our democracy is our greatest strength!" Nikostratos cried out over a sea of gently bobbing shields, the colorful menagerie of gorgons and lions and lizards that was the Athenian center. Behind the general, closely packed, facing the enemy and moving as he moved, were twelve hoplites with shields held high in a barrier against further attempts at assassination from afar. Demosthenes stood watching among the cadre of aides who were still in shock at the death of Nikias.

"We do not depend, as other cities do," Nikostratos exhorted, "on the skill and virtue of one man, or even thirty, to lead us to victory. If one Athenian falls, strategos or not, another is ever ready to step into his place. Nikias served this city all his life, and gave her more than most, and we shall sorely miss him, but the *demos* lives on, and shall live on! Do not let this shameful display of cowardice on the part of our enemy make you think for a moment otherwise!

"This is Attica!" Nikostratos thrust an arm at the occupied Megarian frontier. "And those blood-drinking vultures have no business being here!" He raised his hand skyward in a fist, and the ranks of hoplites raised a warlike roar in which Demosthenes could not bring himself to participate.

The quarter-hour allotted by Brasidas had expired, and more time besides, with no sign of Thalassia. The likely explanation seemed that she was unaware of the deadline, but Demosthenes could not help but let another, less innocuous possibility enter his mind.

Perhaps Eden, who had known Geneva far longer than he, was right about her. Perhaps a habitual traitor had decided, after all, to save her own perfect skin.

He could not quite bring himself to fully believe that. She would come.

The roar of the Athenian troops subsided rather too abruptly and became a murmur. Someone pointed out into the space between the two armies, and Demosthenes turned to follow the gesture to spy a pair of riders making its way over the field of swaying grass into Attica at a gallop. Without hesitation they came, and even before their identities became easily knowable by sight, Demosthenes knew them. Brasidas carried his shield and the herald's wand which he imagined, rightly or wrongly, rendered him inviolable, even after the shameful slaughter of Nikias. Or maybe his confidence came from who it was that rode beside him: Eden, silken blond locks fluttering over a brightly shining corselet that looked to be composed of hundreds of interlocked iron rings.

Brasidas reined in his mount thirty yards out, at the base of the hill on which the Athenian lines stood. Instead of stopping with him, Eden turned in a wide arc and circled back, never even slowing, as if a boundless energy animated her. Her strange little bow bounced on the flank of her black horse (which she rode well, using stirrups, Demosthenes noticed).

"Where is your champion?" Brasidas cried up the hill.

Having not been informed of Brasidas's earlier ultimatum, Nikostratos, of course, had no inkling of what was meant. His aides rushed to his side, and all began speaking at once in hushed tones.

Demosthenes meanwhile signaled to Straton, the captain of the belly-bowmen, and shared a glance with him that said all was ready. As Chief of Special Weapons, he had decided how the gastraphetes and the fire-pots would be deployed today. He hoped he had chosen well.

He walked slowly, resignedly, to Nikostratos and said,

"Send me."

The general and his circle of advisers fell silent and stared, first at the speaker, then each other. One man nodded, then others, and then all agreed.

"Fine," Nikostratos declared. "Once it is made clear to me what we stand to gain or lose."

"Everything," Demosthenes answered dismissively, then turned his shoulder and headed down the hill with hand on the hilt of his sheathed sword.

Ahead, Brasidas remained perched atop the horse for which he appeared to have no love, and vice versa, while beyond him Eden slowed her mount and wheeled, halting near the midway point between the two armies. Near the limit for accurate gastraphetes fire, Demosthenes could not help but notice.

Descending the hill toward smirking Brasidas, he thought of the promise to Laonome he was breaking. It was not yet a year that they had been wed, and here he was putting city and duty first. There was no doubt in his mind she would forgive him the lapse, yet still, a part of him, perhaps the greater part, wished to turn back even now and race home to her embrace.

Certainly Laonome's welcome would be warmer than that of Brasidas, who chuckled scornfully.

"Left you, did she?" the Spartiate said. "Come to beg for more time?"

"I have come to fight for Athens," Demosthenes said plainly. "Call forth your champion."

Brasidas laughed. "It is not worth her time to dismount. She can put an arrow down your throat from where she is. I am always glad to see my enemies die, but that would just be...disappointing."

"Then you fight instead," Demosthenes suggested, idly,

but not without hope. "On the same terms."

"Save your breath," Brasidas scoffed. "The duel was her idea. If it were up to me, the shield-walls would have crashed already. So if your sea-wench isn't–"

Suddenly Brasidas, who had been gazing down from atop his mount, looked up toward the Athenian army's right. Demosthenes twisted his head to follow the gaze, then turned the rest of his body and watched with a mix of awe and relief as a lone horse and rider careened down the slope.

It was Phaedra, and on her back rode salvation.

The first sight of Thalassia in her Amazon's armor dragged a short peal of quiet laughter from Demosthenes: the laughter of a condemned man around whose neck the garrote wire has just snapped. Just as to such a man, in that instant, to Demosthenes' mind it scarcely mattered whether the sentence of death was lifted or the gods had only granted him a short reprieve; it was relief all the same.

While Thalassia slowed to a canter for her descent of the hill, Demosthenes looked over to see the mounted Spartiate's reaction. Brasidas's look of assurance had faded, and he seemed now to be reconsidering the wisdom of having ventured so far from the protection of his allies, or at any rate from the one ally capable of protecting him from she who approached. But rather than turning tail, he stood his ground. The next few moments would determine whether that decision was to his credit or regret.

From a distance, Eden on her black charger watched unmoving. Undoubtedly her malevolent, cerulean eyes were tracking her enemy's approach. Who knew what thoughts lay behind them? Eagerness for the kill? Or perhaps under her hatred, as was often the case, flowed a current of fear. This enemy had beaten her once.

After an eternity, Thalassia reined in Phaedra just short

of Brasidas and dismounted. She thrust the horse's reins at Demosthenes and ordered him in steely tones, "Return to the lines." Not once did her pale stare focus on either man present, but rather it stayed fixed in the distance on her fellow star-born, right eye peering through the mourning veil of black lace that was Magdalen's Mark.

Though he accepted the horse's lead from her, Demosthenes hesitated to do as she asked. Thalassia seemed to be in no mood for words, even what few they had time for, but he felt the need for some. But what were they? How could one do justice to the feelings she inspired? Stirring in his breast were awe, pride, gratitude, and respect, but most of all he felt sadness that this strange, flawed, infuriating being might shortly be sacrificed to the incoherent rage of a blood-crazed beast.

Thalassia found words long before he did, and they were anything but sentimental.

"I'm here, Spartan pig-fucker," she spat at Brasidas, without sparing him her gaze. "Bring her."

It took Brasidas a few beats to answer. "You will fight at the midpoint between our lines." The barely perceptible tremor in his voice said he was acutely aware of what Thalassia was capable of doing to him.

"If the cunt wants me, she can come and get me."

Brasidas, burdened with no death wish, showed his disappointment in a typical Spartan scowl. He kicked his horse, turned it to face the Spartan lines and departed through the field of waving grass at a fast trot. Thalassia drew her two short swords, one then the other, and stood with legs parted, the twin blades of gleaming Athenian steel forming an inverted lambda with its apex between her knees, eyes locked on her distant, mounted nemesis.

Standing behind Thalassia with impatient Phaedra's

reins in hand, Demosthenes could not see her pale eyes, only a thick braid and the back of her bronze-studded leather armor. Still perched above her ear was the purple blossom given to her on the Dromos.

"Get away," she said without turning.

Yet Demosthenes stood frozen. He wanted to embrace her or at very least say something to express his gratitude, but no words came. Perhaps it was better that way. All he could be to her at this pivotal moment was a distraction.

Half a battlefield away, Eden began slowly to ride forward.

"Look, idiot," Thalassia said, her perfect Attic edged with ice. "I am doing this for Red and Laonome, and that only makes sense if you live. So fuck off already!"

The sound of the names of his loved ones broke whatever enchantment he had been under. Setting his foot in Phaedra's stirrup, Demosthenes mounted, and with one last look down at his city's champion, he kicked the mare to a gallop. At the crest of the hill, where Nikostratos and the rest still stood, he stopped and dismounted. He had expected a flurry of inconvenient questions but was greeted by only a sea of blank faces and mouths hanging partly open.

Strangely, the battle brewing below did not seem to be the cause of their distraction.

With one eye on the slow advance across the plain of Sparta's she-daimon, Demosthenes asked of Nikostratos or any of them, "What is wrong?"

The strategos swallowed hard. "News from Athens."

During the grave pause which followed, Demosthenes noted the presence of a panting messenger and a sweating horse not far off.

"A naval assault at Piraeus," Nikostratos said. "Spartans are within the Long Walls."

The news hit like a hammer blow. When Demosthenes had recovered enough to draw breath, he used it to inquire, "What is to be done?"

Nikostratos gave no answer, and Demosthenes could not press him for one, because out in the swaying grass of no-man's land, the star-born champions of two cities were about to meet.

Eden trotted up, halted her black horse and slid gracefully from the saddle some three spear lengths from the place where Thalassia had rooted herself. In the same fluid movement, she produced a short sword from a scabbard at the horse's haunch, a second from her hip, and took a step forward, leaving her mount to wander. Though it was hard to tell from such distance, a smile seemed to haunt her pink lips. More easily discernible was Eden's mark of Magdalen, a network of dark lines covering the upper right quadrant of her face. Thalassia had said no two were alike, but from this vantage they might as well have been.

Eden spoke some words which, even were they audible, Demosthenes knew no being on earth (but for one other, who slept beneath a mountain) could comprehend.

Thalassia, evidently, was in no mood for words in any language.

She attacked.

From a standstill, Thalassia launched herself panther-like across the few yards separating her from her enemy. She closed the gap in an eyeblink, twin blades rising, but Eden, showing no sign of alarm, dove under the charge, parried one of Thalassia's swords and thrust her own second blade upward, piercing Thalassia's shoulder. The blade punched easily through the armor of Penthesilea to emerge on the other side coated in dark blood, the first of the fight, and it was Thalassia's.

That blow, which would have ended any contest of men, caused not even a pause in this one. Just as quickly as it had entered, Eden's blade slid free. Thalassia's momentum was barely broken, and in a heartbeat she had answered the wound by reversing her right hand's grip on its sword and bringing the blade down, like a priest's sacrificial dagger, into Eden's hip.

The two parted, rivers of blood pouring from mortal wounds, but neither showed any sign of pain or inclination to break off the fight. On the contrary, within seconds they were dealing fresh blows. As before, each was able to parry one of her opponent's blades while the other struck home. Thalassia got the better of it this time, if just. She hacked down onto Eden's collarbone and received in exchange only a stab that glanced off her rib cage. But on the side opposite, Thalassia parried not with her sword but with leather-clad forearm: Eden's blade bit straight through the hide and into her flesh, cleaving to the bone.

They parted, blood-covered like twin sirens freshly slaked on sailors' blood. The pause lasted barely the length of an indrawn breath, and then battle was rejoined. Thalassia went again and again for the collarbone, as if her aim were to hack the blond head from Eden's shoulders. She connected twice, gouging a deep cleft and soaking the flaxen hair in red, but Eden blocked her third stroke and paid her back by running Thalassia through yet again, inches from the navel.

Demosthenes did not look to either side of him, lest he miss the ending of a fight which plainly could not endure much longer. Thus he could only assume that the rest of the watchers on the hill were as transfixed as he by the spectacle, albeit in rather more confusion. Only Nikias might have understood, and if Nikias watched, it was only his bodiless shade.

The champions hacked and stabbed and slashed, and more blows landed than were blocked, and the gore spattered across the plain of Eleusis. Blood flowed in torrents until the two combatants could scarcely be told apart, and still they battled on. Each should have been killed ten times over, yet limbs and blades flew on with undiminished fury, delivering mortal blow after mortal blow. The fighters were beautiful, or had been, but there was no grace or beauty in this struggle. It was no dance, but a whirlwind of butchery. Every so often, one or the other woman shrieked, never in pain but only in belligerence, and the sounds were like those that heroes of yore must have heard in their journeys to hell.

The next few seconds did not treat Thalassia well. Each time Demosthenes managed, by a lock of hair, a glimpse of armor, or pattern of wounds, to ascertain for certain which bloodied combatant was which, it was the champion of Athens who was on the defensive. The tide of the swift-flowing red current had turned decisively in Eden's favor.

Some twenty seconds into the fight, one blade of Thalassia's became lodged in Eden's ribcage–Eden twisted, and the handle was wrenched from Thalassia's grasp. Thalassia began employing her empty left hand as a shield, and in no time that limb became so much meat dangling from her elbow. Thalassia stepped back, back, and back again, toward the Athenian lines–deliberately–and Demosthenes, loath as he was to wrench his eyes away, knew he had to move. He looked to his right to find Straton among the awestruck ranks, and he signaled to him.

Straton, transfixed as the rest on the impossible battle below, already had his orders, and needed only to be snapped out of his stupor.

"Straton!" Demosthenes cried sharply at him.

At the sound of his name, Straton blinked and

acknowledged understanding, then set to shoving the bowmen around him and hissing the code word *makellon*: slaughterhouse.

Thalassia stood unsteadily on one leg which looked as though a great beast had mauled it, which very nearly was the case. She resorted to grappling with Eden, holding tight to her like a wrestler waiting out the end of a round, only there was no respite to be had in this match, just victory or death. It seemed almost certain now that the latter of these would go to Thalassia. Eden hacked down again and again on her staggered foe, cutting every time. After a mad frenzy of slashing, Thalassia's sword arm flopped into the trampled grass, severed at the shoulder. At the same time, Eden got a foot wrapped around the ankle of Thalassia's mangled leg and tripped her.

Thalassia vanished into the grass, but mad Eden, living up to the name of the goddess by whose name Sparta knew her, let up not a bit. Blood flew in a mist from Eden's silent lips as she cast aside one of her swords, took the other in both hands and stabbed down into the waving grass, again and again and again.

Though victorious, gore-soaked Eden had not come through the combat unscathed. Where once she had moved like a cat or a nymph, now she jerked about like a red-painted puppet dangling on invisible strings.

Makellon, Demosthenes prayed, would cut her strings.

As Thalassia was falling and Eden beginning her butchery, Straton ushered the plan, if belatedly, into effect. The hoplites arrayed in front of the line of gastraphetes-wielding archers sank into a crouch to allow three hundred belly-bows, each loaded with two giant bolts tipped with razor sharp Athenian steel, to take aim over their shoulders, helmets and shield rims. Straton, taking aim down the stock of his own gastraphetes, uttered the command to fire, and the hillside filled with the sound of twanging sinews and of wooden shafts scraping iron rails. Six hundred javelin-like missiles let fly from the hill's crest and sliced straight down the grassy slope to converge on the spot where the single combat had just concluded.

A volley like that could not miss, and it did not. In her moment of triumph, Eden was cut down. At least a dozen shafts struck her, some running her through, others ripping great gashes in her limbs, while one opened up a skull that was already so slick with blood, hers and her enemy's, that only a single wisp of long, golden hair remained visible. Butchered, Sparta's champion dropped into the grass alongside the rival she had slain, the rival whose service to Athens shone no less for her defeat.

6. Battle for the Bodies

Demosthenes let no cumbersome feelings slow him, neither ones of mourning for she who had offered up her life (one of them, anyway) for Athens, nor feelings of relief at the elimination of a dire threat in the she-daimon Eden. He spared not even a thought for gentle Laonome and playful Eurydike, no longer safe back home in threatened Athens. He thought of nothing but the immediate task which must be accomplished.

"The body!" he cried out to any who would listen. "Retrieve her body!"

He ran, legs pounding the hillside, carrying him down at breakneck pace. Halfway down, it occurred to him that he might have been well advised to remount Akmon or Phaedra, but what was done was done. He could not turn back now, for not far ahead a small mass of Spartans had appeared. They bore neither shields nor spears, and by their sudden closeness they could only have spent the last few minutes crawling on their bellies through the tall grass of no man's land.

Demosthenes was first to reach the ring of slick, matted grass in which the two butchered bodies lay. He picked out Thalassia by the crown of crushed purple iris petals scattered about her head. Both corpses were riddled with gastraphetes bolts, which also sprang at varying angles from the earth all around, like a miniature forest. Two shafts sprouted from Thalassia's torso while one had passed through her neck, half severing it before burrowing into the ground underneath. Coming up to her, Demosthenes grabbed the bolts one in each hand, yanked them out and set to lifting her. Heedless of the hot gore that immediately coated his skin, he worked hands under and around her.

When he heaved, her well-greased body slipped back to the earth. The oncoming Spartans, eight of them at least, were seconds away, yet glancing behind him, Demosthenes found no equivalent motion in the Athenian lines.

"What are you waiting for?" Demosthenes cried frantically back at them, waving a hand gloved in sticky blood. Seeing him, Nikostratos turned his cheek and put his arms out to either side in a restraining gesture, instructing the men on the hill not to move.

Spitting one of the many curses which, when she lived, had flowed copiously from Thalassia's dirty mouth, Demosthenes tried again to achieve a grip on the corpse. This time he hooked the fingers of one hand under the waist of her Amazonian corselet and wrapped the other arm around the neck, the skin of which felt against his bicep like a slice of rare lamb. He heaved, the body rose up, and blood, if blood was what truly ran in the veins of the star-born, ran in rivulets down his arms, dripping from his elbows onto his thighs and coursing down his breastplate of iron scales.

Thankfully, her enhanced body was no heavier than a mortal woman's. He threw it over his shoulder and, without stopping to look at the charging Lakedaimonians who were almost upon him, he spun and ran.

His first step faltered, sandal sliding on blood-greased blades of grass, and the body slipped from his shoulder. He caught it before it hit the earth, recovered his balance and mounted the slope at a run. He could hear the grunting breaths of the Spartans, and imagined, at least, that he felt their footfalls shake the ground. He could hardly spare a look, but knew they must have reached the battle site by now. One or more of their number would stop and return to Brasidas with the body of Eden, but the evidence of Demosthenes' ears said the rest were chasing after him, and Thalassia's corpse. Their general had no intention of letting Eden's trophy slip away.

He channeled his every drop of strength into his thrusting legs, hammering the earth with each step to ensure firm footing and a strong push up the hill. Up top, at the hill's crest, a sanctuary still too far off, his countrymen began to cheer him on, but still offered no help. Seconds later that changed when Straton pushed to the fore, knelt, and leveled his gastraphetes. A dozen or more archers followed his lead, but all held their fire for fear of hitting the comrade they meant to aid. And so, barely halfway to the safety of the Athenian lines, carrying a load on his back that the Spartans were not, and wearing iron armor to their leather, he knew he would be caught. He cursed himself again for not having mounted Phaedra for this task.

He could think of only one course of action, and he took it: he dove, landing hard in the grass alongside the warm, wet sack which was Thalassia, and as he hit the earth, he heard Straton shout the command to fire. Sharp bolts cut the air over his head, and from downslope came at least one groan. Demosthenes scrambled on hands coated in greasy blood to right himself, rise and draw his sword.

He succeeded in time to face five long-haired Spartans at a full run, twenty paces off and just now drawing their own blades and raising a war-cry. Standing astride the mangled body they came to claim, Demosthenes set himself for the attack.

Before it could come, the earth rumbled with a rhythmic pounding that his ears knew well. His eye caught motion and he threw a glance toward it in time to witness a stream of horsemen: the citizen cavalry of Athens, spilling out from the Athenian right and thundering along the slope.

Two of the charging Spartiates slowed in their headlong rush, fell to silence and hung a moment in equivocation before rejecting their city's warrior code and taking flight. When yet two more fearless Equals opted to turn tail, a fresh war-cry came from behind and Demosthenes risked a second look over his shoulder. A line of spears was surging forth from the Athenian center, in defiance of Nikostratos' orders, charging headlong down the hill to the aid of the countryman whose actions they must have thought crazed. Battles over corpses were fought in the bard's songs, but not on today's battlefields.

The last two steadfast Spartans, realizing they were alone, bent their paths to loop back and flee at top speed, but for them it was too late. The foremost rider of the citizen cavalry rode one down and skewered him with his lance. Two more horsemen pursued the second fugitive, who eventually turned to face them in a futile stand which ended with his body crumpled on the hillside, a pair of lances protruding from his chest.

The four Equals who had fled were run down next, an easy sport given the distance from their lines. But the ones who had quickly borne Eden away were long gone by now, and her body with them.

As Athenian hoplites converged on Demosthenes' position, swarming around to set up a belated defensive wall, the leader of the horsemen brought his mount to a halt a few feet away. The look on the finely sculpted features visible between the gleaming cheek pieces of Alkibiades' helmet was uncharacteristically grave. His glittering eyes mourned as he gazed down on the butchered remains of the body he had lusted after from the moment he had first seen it in his friend's megaron.

"Star-girl." He spoke the made-up word not mournfully, but as if gently reprimanding his playmate.

Alkibiades had only learned of Eden's existence days ago, but had not begrudged his two partners the secret they had revealed to him only when it could be kept no longer. Even now, he remained unaware of the existence of the third of their kind, Lyka. However faithful a friend he seemed to be, however useful he proved himself, there was an indelible blemish upon Alkibiades in the form of an act of betrayal which might now never occur, but would have had Fate been allowed to run its proper course.

Of course, of that blemish he knew nothing either.

"Thank you," Demosthenes said to him blankly. The danger past, he stooped, found his grip at the edges of Thalassia's corselet and heaved her corpse onto his shoulders. Gummed and drying blood caused his arms to itch, while fresh streams of it rolled hot down his neck.

"You want help?" Alkibiades asked.

"I have her."

They started walking together up the hill toward the Athenian lines, Demosthenes slowed by his burden and Alkibiades keeping pace astride his mount. Around them, the men who had rushed to their aid returned to the lines, too, not a few throwing questions which Demosthenes was forced to ignore.

He posed a sullen question of his own to Alkibiades. "How fared your mission?"

Alkibiades tossed his head at Brasidas's host. Pausing and twisting, Demosthenes followed the gesture and picked out against the sky a sight he had failed to notice while engrossed in Thalassia's death and the retrieval of her corpse: three plumes of black smoke rising from somewhere behind the Spartan lines.

"Well done," Demosthenes commented absently. But his mind was elsewhere. Only now, as mayhem faded to quiet, could he begin to process Nikostratos' dire pronouncement of minutes ago.

Spartans were inside the Long Walls.

It meant they had found some way to foil the world's foremost navy, the foundation on which Athenian empire was built. There could be no doubt as to who had helped them to achieve such a feat. Seasons ago, he had seen with his own eyes drawings of strange ships which were an improvement on current designs, and he had rejected them. Yet, even had he foreseen the necessity of making the trireme obsolete, the democracy would have scoffed, and Athenian shipbuilders would have considered even the suggestion an affront.

Not so in Sparta, whose navy rarely ever matched the success of her land forces. In retrospect, the plan of Brasidas and Eden was almost shamefully obvious. He should have seen it. The lumbering *katapeltai* were a threat, certainly, but not the most dire one, and Brasidas's march across the Megarid, the expected path of attack, was not quite a diversion, but almost. And it had worked: nearly every able body that Athens could field stood here, ten miles from the city. Perhaps some or all of the cavalry could swiftly withdraw, but that was a decision for a general to make. And as that bitch Fate, who refused to accept defeat idly, would have it, Demosthenes was not a general this year.

Perhaps seeing defeat written on his face, Alkibiades urged, if somewhat spiritlessly. "It's not so bad. Sure, star-girl is gone, but no more siege engines, right? And we still outnumber Brasidas, even when the Thebans are counted. Probably."

Under his load of dripping, leather-clad flesh, Demosthenes laughed bleakly. "You have not heard."

"Heard what?"

They crested the hill, reaching the spot where a silent Nikostratos and the rest of the Athenian line had turned as one to stare east at a dark line which slashed the sky from horizon to clouds. Billowing smoke.

Athens was burning.

7. The Battle of Eleusis

The sight failed to shock Demosthenes. Perhaps he had seen and learned too much to be shocked anymore. Instead he felt numb as he secured Thalassia's corpse over Akmos' saddle, her sopping, disheveled braid pelting the earth with crimson droplets. He heard Nikostratos issuing orders. They were the right orders, at least: stand fast here, the whole army staying intact on the plain of Eleusis. The other choice was a tempting one, to split the force and send relief back to Athens, but that was likely just what Brasidas wanted. Almost certainly, the moment those maneuvers began, his army would surge across the frontier. The Spartan attackers' ready spears and lambda-blazoned shields would then meet an enemy line in disarray, and defeat for Athens would be all but assured.

There was no choice but to stand firm for now, then fall back to the city only when victory was won here on the frontier. In the best case, if victory were swift, which it would not be, that meant leaving homes and loved ones at the mercy of whatever force had penetrated the Long Walls for, what? Four hours, probably more.

From the evidence in the eastern sky, at least one fire burned already, though the smoke was too sparse to represent a general conflagration. But four hours, four hours spent at arms with backs turned on wives and offspring, was a long time. A great many fires could be set in that time. The temptation to race home and protect one's own was strong, in Demosthenes no less than in any other man. Gods, how he longed to go to Laonome's side, to sweep her and Eurydike onto Akmos's back and take them to safety, wherever that was. But down that path lay certain disaster. The army of Athens would be run down piecemeal and dashed against the very gates it had failed to defend. The horde on the frontier would be the hammer, the city walls the anvil.

All that prevented that outcome now was discipline, and already that was showing cracks. Demosthenes, standing among the commanders on the hill's crest, saw the army begin to unravel well before messengers started bringing news that city-dwellers were falling back from the line, first by ones and twos, and then in droves. Emboldened by that sight, or perhaps giving up hope because of it, or maybe just drawn into the herd in a phenomenon well known to any observer of democracy, others followed. A trickle soon swelled into a flood, and within half an hour the road home was awash with bronze helmets and brightly painted shields moving east in a chaotic but determined swirl.

At Nikostratos' urging, Demosthenes and others of the cavalry rode into the seething mass to try rallying men back to their posts. Some were persuaded, but the greater number were beyond reason. When words failed to stop the tide, the would-be shepherds of men resorted to lashing out with flats of swords, but it was a hopeless fight. The numbers overwhelmed them. Short of killing friends and cousins (as indeed a few raging country-folk urged) there was nothing to be done.

It was the reverse of the first seven summers of the war. Then, it had been the rural citizens whose homes and farms were ravaged while city men led by Perikles urged restraint on them. Now, as then, the city held sway. The retreat was unstoppable. Accepting that, Demosthenes extricated himself from the throng. Over the swirl of heads and spear blades, Alkibiades called out to him, but whatever few syllables he spoke were lost in the din of the bronze snake clattering its way to Athens.

He was persistent, though, and finally Demosthenes

heard:

"Dekelea! Dekelea!"

Alkibiades was right. The mountain town was farther off than Athens, but its freshly built walls presumably remained uncompromised. There was a small risk that the Thebans had already taken Dekelea, and a greater one that they blocked the path from here to there, but it was their only hope. The mass flight now unfolding all but ensured that this day would end with Brasidas the master of Athens. However much it weighed on the heart, which now resided in Demosthenes' throat, to stake Laonome's life, and the lives of a thousand wives, on the chance that Brasidas would show the city restraint, retreat to Dekelea was now the only choice.

Fording the human river atop Akmos with Thalassia's lashed form draped in front of him in the saddle, jostling with each move, Demosthenes rode to where Nikostratos stood alone on the hill. His perpetual cloud of aides and unit commanders had scattered in the effort to restore control, and now the junior general gazed blankly, resignedly out over the plains of Eleusis.

When he reached the general's side, Demosthenes stared, too, for the invasion had begun.

Brasidas's force was on the move, marching double time, shields and glinting spears bobbing above the tall grass, collective voice raised in a slow war chant which belied the speed of their charge into glory.

"Fuck."

The inelegant remark earned Demosthenes a disapproving glance from Nikostratos, whose mood was already foul. Ignoring it, he said to the strategos urgently, "We have no chance here. We must get as many men as we can to Dekelea."

"Too late for that." Nikostratos' knuckles were white on

the shaft of his yet unused ash spear. Drawing a deep breath, he came to life, whirling and setting vehemently to the task of rallying his diminished army.

"We stand fast here!" he screamed. "Stand fast, do you hear me! *Stand fast!*"

There was no telling how many men remained in the ranks to heed his command. Rather than waning, the exodus seemed to be gaining in strength, with more and more men making the late decision to join it in the belief that their cause now was hopeless with the army in such a shambles.

Maybe it was. But it was the chaos itself more than the dwindling numbers which posed the greater threat to Athenian hopes. So greatly had Brasidas been outnumbered when the morning began that even now the Athenian force could not but still be larger than his. But an army was only as strong as its discipline, and that of the Spartans was legendary while discipline this day had failed Athens utterly.

Leaving the general, Demosthenes galloped back down the slope to the road behind the hill, where Alkibiades and a small fraction of the citizen cavalry persisted in the effort to stem the tide of shirkers. The rest of the hippeis had given up and now sat astride their mounts in clusters on the hillside awaiting instruction. Donning his white-plumed helm, Demosthenes gave it.

"Form up on me!"

Hearing him, Alkibiades took up the call. "You heard him!"

Within minutes the bulk of Athens' citizen cavalry had regrouped, and over the snorting and braying of their steeds, Demosthenes belted out his simple orders. A third of their own number, perhaps a hundred men, was absent, he noticed. They were likely far ahead of the mass of men on foot in the race back to Athens to defend their homes. If they rode hard, maybe they would even succeed in carrying away whatever people or possessions were foremost in their hearts. By law the price would be charges of cowardice, the charge Demosthenes himself had beaten months ago. But the only verdict for these men was likely to be that imposed by their own souls, for at present it looked as though it would be some time before any jury again convened to try an Athenian. Demosthenes wanted to curse those hippeis who had gone, but knew that some of his anger came from envy. Perhaps their selfishness was worth the price.

Those horsemen who remained, every one of whom had as much to lose if Athens burned this day, followed their hipparch east and south along the course of the infantry's spontaneous, disorderly retreat. At a place where the road bent sharply and the land dropped straight into the sea, Demosthenes gave a signal. The horsemen inserted themselves into the flow of running and shuffling footsoldiers, cutting off their paths and penning them in like sheep.

"Hear me!" Demosthenes screamed over the heads of the trapped infantrymen. Every second, every word counted, for the human current was relentless and the pressure on its equine dam would build and build. "Look to the sky above Athens," he urged. "Look! Still just one fire! Your homes are not burning! Athens is not yet theirs, but it will be if you continue doing as your enemy wants! You think you run to save your wives when in truth you doom them! Yes, there are Spartans inside the Long Walls. Perhaps many, more likely just a few. Either way, the safety of Athens is not in her walls, it is in your hearts and your set spears, in this army! And as long as this army can kill Spartans, Athens will be free!"

Some of the trapped men seemed to be listening. Others were focusing on finding a way through or around the barrier, only to be rudely shoved back by the cavalry. Demosthenes took one foot from the stirrup and kicked a man hard in the chest. The blow would have sent him to the well-trammeled earth but for the steadily rising pressure at his back.

"None of you are cowards!" Demosthenes said. "You run to Athens knowing there is danger there. But it is the wrong danger, and now is the wrong time. I hold no office this day, but you have elected me twice before as strategos, and I ask you to follow me again now."

Amongst the hurled curses and grunts of exertion, a few voices asked, "Where?"

Demosthenes gladly answered. "To Dekelea! Come with me to Dekelea, and from there we will take back our city!"

Somehow. Possibly.

By now, the river of deserters had swollen into a lake behind the makeshift dam. The riders had already been forced to give ground to relieve the pressure, but now the choice came of whether to let the deserters pass or watch them crush each other to death into the mud. Demosthenes chose the former. The screen of cavalry parted, and the tide it had briefly contained burst forth.

Demosthenes remained in the current, shouting frantically, "To Dekelea! Dekelea!" Alkibiades and others lent their voices, too, so that over the clatter of arms their collective demand, more of a plea, could be heard. They devoted some ten minutes to that thankless endeavor, then regrouped the cavalry a short distance inland

For all the deaf ears upon which his entreaties had fallen, some had heard. By the time the body of footsoldiers clustered around the citizen cavalry stopped growing, it numbered some six hundred hoplites and peltastes. No army at all, by most measures, but it would have to do. Demosthenes was forming them up for the march when a clap of thunder split the western sky.

It was not the thunder made by Zeus, but that made by men: the clash of shield walls. Paeans and battle cries were drowned out by the crash and then by screams of pain and the grunts and groans that marked the start of the pushing match. No Athenian who heard it from a distance could help but whisper a guilty prayer to Pallas on his countrymen's behalf, not even one who scarcely was able to believe in gods. When he had finished addressing the goddess he doubted, Demosthenes sent his miniscule army on its way to the mountains, with ten riders as escort, while six more of the cavalry went ahead at full gallop to round up a work force from among the population of Dekelea and begin dragging as many provisions as it could behind its gates.

Demosthenes, with the bulk of the Athenian horse, remained behind. They took up a position behind the Athenian right wing and there waited for the worst to happen. If and when it did, if the diminished army of Athens under Nikostratos crumbled and fled the field at Eleusis, a screen of cavalry might at least deter pursuit. And perhaps some of the army's tattered remnants could be steered to Dekelea.

Long minutes wore on, the air thick with clashing iron and grating bronze and groans and wails and soaring hymns and coarse insults.

"Those were some fine words back there," Alkibiades said over the echoes of the not-so-distant battle. "And here I thought star-girl came up with all your speeches." Feeling in no mood for chatter, much less levity, Demosthenes made no reply. The youth's exquisite eyes, keen readers of men's minds, fell to the carcass slung over the front of his friend's saddle, and he changed his tone. "It'll be tough if you have to fight with star-girl in your saddle," he remarked dourly. "You should have sent her on ahead to Dekelea."

Demosthenes answered resolutely, without sparing a glance for speaker or object: "She stays with me."

Alkibiades' chestnut mane, darkened by blood and grime, bobbed in understanding.

Any further one-sided conversation was cut short by a triumphant cheer. None among the citizen cavalry were foolish enough to believe that the triumph in question could be that of Athens. No matter how poorly Brasidas's army might have fared, it could not have broken so quickly. Such a swift end to the battle could only mean a Spartan victory.

A lone rider atop a nearby ridge, from which a portion of the plains of Eleusis were just visible, kicked his horse and sped down the hill bearing news which came as no surprise: the Athenian right had begun to turn. Grim minutes later, a clattering sound arose, and the first wave of retreating hoplites appeared, streaming over and around the gentle hills at a full run. Most had their shields, some spears, while others had cast one or both down in the knowledge that speed was now life. No one could blame them. The puncturing of a phalanx marked the end of a battle. There was no point in heroics, no descent into single combat as had been witnessed on the fields of Troy in bygone days. War these days was a test of cities, not of individuals, and today Athens had been judged unworthy.

The cavalry spread thin to act as a screen which might let their countrymen pass and then close up swiftly to block pursuit. As the fighters' retreat brought them within earshot of the line of horse, Demosthenes called to them with his familiar refrain.

"To Dekelea! To Dekelea!"

Men ran by in droves, a thousand of them or more, and they ran with no single purpose in mind except escape. Many were likely headed for their homes in the rural demes to become civilians again, since that's what they all truly were, and simply to pray that Sparta declined to impose the kind of brutal retribution to which the gods and the unwritten laws of war entitled them.

Demosthenes kept up the rallying cry until his throat was raw. Following the lead of Alkibiades, he even began to lie: "Regroup at Dekelea! Nikostratos commands it!"

At last, hot on the heels of their vanquished foe, a band of Peloponnesians appeared, screaming victory. Their shield blazons, Demosthenes noticed immediately and with relief, were not the uniform crimson lambda of Lakedaimon but rather a colorful menagerie of beasts and gods that marked them as men of Corinth or Arkadia or some other Spartan subject or ally. No surprise, since had they been Spartiates, they likely would not have made the mistake of breaking formation to pursue a broken foe blindly into the unknown, perhaps to learn too late of the presence of heavy cavalry, as was the case today.

Man by man, the pursuers saw their mistake, slowed, stopped, and turned back.

"Hold!" Demosthenes told his men. For although the enemy hoplites were in disarray, they were atop a hill and could quickly enough form a wall of spears. These Peloponnesians had tasted victory enough for one day, it seemed, for they chose the path of discretion and withdrew, vanishing from sight down the rear face of the hill over which they had come. After giving them some time in which to change their minds and attack, and Athenian stragglers more time to find their way east, the citizen cavalry of Athens turned their mounts north to take the advice they had been screaming for some time at any of their countrymen who would listen.

To Dekelea.

8. Dekelea

No roads led directly to the mountain village of Dekelea, and so they rode hard through open country, over hills and fields and farms. Whenever they passed a village, they sent a pair of men to spread word of what had happened and ask for weapons and food to be brought to Dekelea as quickly as possible for the inevitable siege. Before long, they caught up with the band of six hundred would-be deserters sent ahead. Rather than racing on by, they kept pace with the infantrymen, as much to ensure they did not change their minds along the way as to protect them from ambush.

Along the way they encountered a trio of scouts of the prodromoi, the light horse, and exchanged news. The Theban cavalry, the scouts reported, had stayed close to the main Theban body, which presently was investing the Attic town of Phyle. It was good news which meant that for now, at least, the way to Dekelea was clear.

At the foot of the steep, pine-covered Parnes mountains, the ground became rough and the going more difficult, but the column did not slow. With no sign of pursuit and not a soul in sight, the sense of immediate danger began to fade. Into the void rushed feelings of loss and despair that were visible in the men's faces and their hollow eyes. Demosthenes tried to keep his own eyes on the mountains, for if they sank to the vaguely human-shaped mass draped in front of him, he began to think of Thalassia as she had been in life, which in turn brought on thoughts of home, of Laonome and Eurydike, whose fates he did not know and surely would not for some time.

In the end, it did not matter much where he kept his eyes, for he thought of them anyway, and the thoughts sat like a lump of lead on his chest. The weight numbed him, preventing him from feeling anything; he only acted. The events unfolding were unreal, dreamlike. But then, what had the last two years been to him if not training to exist in unreality, to live daily with madness surrounding and infecting him and all he touched as surely as the great plague, and as deadly.

As the procession made its way ever higher into the hills, Alkibiades drew up to ride alongside him. He said sadly, "She was the perfect being." His melancholy gaze was on Thalassia's corpse. "Both hard and soft at the same time."

Demosthenes expelled his grief in a sigh and begrudged the ward of Perikles his attention. "Mostly hard," he observed. He lied.

"She had thick armor, to be sure," Alkibiades said. "And some manly traits. But at her core, she was a woman." He smiled. "Just as we all have some woman in us. She was showing hers more and more until–" There was no need to finish. He looked up from her gently jostling corpse and said abruptly, "You must know that she loved you."

Demosthenes left the assertion unanswered.

Alkibiades went on. "She never said so. Just call it my well-drawn conclusion as a student of the human... and *human-like* heart."

"What I shall call it is horse shit," Demosthenes grumbled at him. He had the strange and utterly unfounded feeling that Thalassia could overhear them even now, with cold ears concealed by gore on a head that barely clung to its spine.

Alkibiades' shrug was not one of concession. "Suit yourself," he said. "I'm sure it was coincidence that I always seemed to wind up with bruises shortly after your name came up."

"She picked my wife, for fuck's sake," Demosthenes said,

defying his better judgment by arguing. "And could not have done a better job of it. Right before she moved out."

The self-professed student of the human heart laughed sharply. "Oh, please," Alkibiades scoffed. "You don't see? She got sick of you refusing to touch her, so she put you off limits. The problem with that strategy is that she resembles me in a way. We always want most what we cannot have. Not only that, though. I think she genuinely wanted you to be happy, which is what I call–"

"Shut up," Demosthenes hissed.

"–love."

Bowing belatedly to the rebuke, Alkibiades sighed and changed the subject. Almost. He mused philosophically, "Socrates says love is a form of madness."

The last word rang in Demosthenes' ears.

"I said it first, though," Alkibiades continued. "He borrowed it from me. I wonder how he fared today. He was positioned in the center. I can guarantee you he was one of those who stood his ground."

Demosthenes gave these comments no reply. After riding in silence for some minutes, gazing out at the forested peaks and valleys, Alkibiades renewed his efforts to make conversation. His subject yet again was Thalassia.

"Damn, I wish I could have seen star-girl fight!" he lamented. "Must have been a beautiful sight." As before, he was undeterred by lack of reply. "Do you think she will return?" He answered himself: "I don't. That's how it goes with stars that shine brightly. Or star-girls. Like Achilles, they burn out in their prime and go to join the gods. I intend do the same."

He might have shared further musings, but Demosthenes, staring blankly ahead at the wooded, uneven ground and the horde of aimless, defeated souls shambling over it, finally managed to shut him out.

***

By late afternoon, the gravel-faced walls of Dekelea were in view. Thanks to the outriders, the villagers were expecting the band and met it with food, fresh water and words of encouragement. The storehouses were already stuffed with provisions, the villagers informed, and still more were en route from the surrounding country, but that morsel of good news failed to raise anyone's mood. The hastily gathered remains of Athens' defeated army numbered a thousand by now, but that was not nearly enough. They marched, with stooped shoulders and precious little hope, through fresh-cut gates into the remote, fortified village where they were to make their stand.

Dekelea was hardly more than a waystation on the trade route from Athens to the coast., its unplastered, single-story houses of wood and brick a far cry from what city-dwellers were used to. None knew how long their stay here might last. Much-needed rest might have changed their outlook some, but there was no time for that. For one thing, a barracks would have to be built, which meant felling trees and dragging them in from the surrounding wood. After their ten-mile hike wearing bronze armor in the afternoon heat, men were slumping to the ground exhausted, only to rise again mouthing curses when their leader divided them into work crews for the accomplishment of that task and others. Demosthenes joined a crew himself, and lent Akmos as a draught animal, though not before he and Alkibiades had reverently removed Thalassia from his saddle, wrapped her loosely in linens and laid her out in an old tool shed already stripped of its contents by the work crews.

In the shed, Alkibiades cleaned her bloodied face with a damp cloth, exposing her tattoo-like mark of Magdalen. Her serene features were marred by deep slashes hopelessly packed with trail grime. He stared down at her, bent and kissed her parted, half-mangled lips. "Goodbye, star-girl," he whispered, and rose. "Do you want to say anything?"

"I do not speak to corpses," Demosthenes snapped.

Alkibiades drew up the linen shroud over her face, but as they were leaving Demosthenes' conscience stopped him, and he looked back.

"I have only met two servants of Magdalen," he said to the lifeless shell on the dirt floor. "But I say without any doubt, the one who betrayed them is worth all the rest combined."

With those words of tribute, he left behind the silent, mutilated remains of a thing that the sea had coughed up one day: a seeker of vengeance, a meddler in space in time, a spreader of madness, the star-born benefactor of a city whose defeat her aid had only hastened.

Chaining the rickety door of her unfitting mausoleum, Demosthenes threw his aching heart into making Dekelea an Attic thorn in Brasidas's grasping claw.

9. A Spartan's Duty

A fast drumbeat of footfalls slapped the smooth tops of the walls of silent Dekelea. Demosthenes stood behind the battlements staring southward over evergreens and crags boldly lit by a violet dawn. As the wearer of the sandals pounding the poured stone drew up to him, their rhythm slowed and ceased.

"Hello, Andrea," Demosthenes said, failing to feign good cheer. "Men are trying to sleep. Maybe you could run barefoot."

It was the morning of the third day since the fall of Athens. Two days ago the Spartlet had shown up at Dekelea of her own accord, having taken a horse and ridden from Alkibiades' country estate. Either her Lakedaimonian heritage had bequeathed her a natural military mind or Alkibiades had had been schooling her in the ways of war. Likely both.

"Maybe they should wake up earlier." It was a Spartan answer, and Andrea reverted to her native Doric dialect to deliver it.

Demosthenes permitted himself a dry chuckle. "Maybe so."

"What's wrong?" the Spartlet asked. Her dark eyes missed little.

"Can you keep a secret for just a little while?" Demosthenes asked. "Until I have a chance to tell everyone?"

Andrea's answer was a reproachful glare. Demosthenes had been the target of such a look plenty of times before, but from paler eyes. The behavioral resemblance to her tutor was probably no coincidence. Sighing at the similarity, he shared with Andrea, a child of the enemy, the fresh news which had him so worried:

"Our watchers in Athens say Brasidas marches here

today with an army of six thousand. We are going to be under siege."

"Haven't we been already?" the girl asked. She pulled herself up onto the battlement and settled there with wiry legs dangling. Demosthenes did not bother to offer her a boost, knowing his help would be rejected.

"Almost," he said. He had learned by now not to try to speak to Andrea as he might any other child. "Until now we have had men–and women–slip back and forth from Athens and the coast. We have ambushed enemy troops who try to pass. But now we will have to shut our gates and keep them shut. No one in or out." He frowned. "Alkibiades will insist that you leave."

The Spartlet scoffed. "He can't make me. Anyway, there are lots of women and children here."

"They will be leaving, too."

Andrea spat on the battlements. "Cowards."

Demosthenes inhaled to scold the child, but instead expelled the air in silence.

Andrea did not linger on the subject. "Why don't flies land on Thalassia's body?" she asked. She stared down at her swinging heels as they kicked the poured stone underneath her.

"I told you not to go in there," Demosthenes chided her half-heartedly.

The Spartlet flashed a little girl's version of her Spartiate father's scowl. "You don't know me very well, do you?"

"I do. Too well." Demosthenes managed to tousle the top of Andrea's long hair before she jerked her head away. "I don't know why," he said in answer to her question. "Ask the flies."

"Anyway, Uncle Alky said I could go in the shed," she said haughtily. "I washed Thalassia's body and anointed it and said prayers for her."

Demosthenes said quietly, "That was good of you."

Andrea's mood suddenly sank, and she said with a frown, "She was my favorite teacher."

"You were her favorite student."

Andrea clicked her tongue in reprimand, as her teacher often had done. "I was her only student!" Abruptly she deflated. "I miss her."

"Me too." Demosthenes covered the Spartlet's small hand with his and was mildly surprised when she failed to snatch it away.

She looked up, concern lighting her black eyes. "Any news of Eurydike?" she asked. "Or your wife?" The former was one of Andrea's favored playmates; the latter seemed to have been added to her inquiry in a rare show of sensitivity.

"No," Demosthenes said.

The admission pained him. On the day of the fall, he had sent a loyal man to Athens with instructions to take the two into hiding, but word had failed to come back of either success or failure. With full-blown siege imminent, the outcome now was likely to remain unknown. "They are safe," he said, but it was hope rather than certainty that he voiced.

By the accounts drifting out, Athens had been treated as well as any conquered city could expect. Only the Pnyx and a few other symbolic civic sites had been razed. The democracy had been abolished and mass arrests made of individuals deemed a threat to the new regime. Four generals of the Board of Ten, Nikostratos among them, were en route to Sparta for trial and possible execution, another three imprisoned in Athens. Women and children were safe for now, though that could change with one word from Brasidas.

"Finish your run," Demosthenes said to Andrea, and hoisted her down from the crenelated wall, depositing her on her feet before she had the chance to protest.

Instead of dashing off, Andrea looked up at him. "Since you told me a secret," she said, "I'll give you one, too."

"I would be honored," Demosthenes said, crouching level with her to receive it.

"Uncle Alky likes to think he's Achilles, so he'd be mad if he knew," the Spartlet confided with a note of pride in her small voice, "but I've always thought the Trojans should have won."

With a final sly smile she raced away, sandals slapping the walkway.

***

In wave after wave of round shields bearing the crimson lambda, the dark tide which was the army of Brasidas spilled north. It washed over the forests and foothills and flowed around crags jutting from the green earth. It swamped the broad road from Athens, and by noon it would have lapped at the base of Dekelea's walls, but for the threat posed by about sixty men atop the wall with drawn bows. Some of the sixty were not even archers, but those below could not know that.

Demosthenes stood on the walls, too, watching the army come. Beside him stood Alkibiades and a half dozen sub-commanders of the now-besieged force. They shared no words, for none could matter now. None likely existed which would suffice to convey the depth to which Athens' fortunes had sunk.

Before the waves of enemy fighters had even stopped appearing on the horizon, a lone long-haired Spartiate came forward from the black mass armed with a herald's wand. He stopped in front of Dekelea's gate and called up in a voice barely audible over the din of the assembling horde behind him, "I would enter!"

"Fuck off!" Alkibiades shouted back down.

"I offer generous terms of surrender!" the Spartan came

back, unperturbed.

"Shoot them out your ass!"

"I would enter!" the Spartiate repeated. Then, "You need open your gate only a crack."

After grinning at the Spartiates doubtless accidental pun, Alkibiades turned from the battlements to throw a questioning look at Demosthenes. The ward of Perikles had found time to polish his gear and stood resplendent in his breastplate of enameled bronze.

"Let him in," Demosthenes reluctantly agreed, and wasted no time heading for the stairs.

A cluster of sub-commanders accompanied him to the village's south gate, where they gathered ten paces behind the heavy double doors of bronze-clad timber. Thirty hoplites lined up with their hands on the gate to hold it in place in the event of trickery, and at Demosthenes' command they pulled one of its halves open just enough to let a man pass. The Spartan herald slipped through, and with a creak and a crash the massive door slammed quickly back into place.

The Spartan came forward. Well before he completed his advance, Demosthenes knew his identity. Though he had not seen the face in a year, he was well accustomed to a smaller and pleasanter version of it. Alkibiades recognized the man, too, and was the first to speak his name in cool greeting.

"Styphon."

Forgoing acknowledgment, the Spartiate announced loudly, so his voice echoed off the expanse of pristine wall behind him.

"What you are doing here is pointless! Athens has capitulated, and her new government has ordered an end to resistance." Styphon drew a curled parchment from his belt and tossed it into the dirt, where it remained. "Simply leave your arms and armor behind, and come out. No harm will befall you, and none shall be subject to arrest!"

His ringing words gave way to total silence, which Demosthenes allowed to persist a few moments before answering. He spoke, as Styphon had, at a volume intended to let any Athenian within earshot hear clearly.

"Any who might have taken you up on that offer have already gone to their homes. We keep no man here against his will. So if that is all you've come to say, your work is done."

Styphon was unfazed by the rebuff and by the chorus of muttered agreement which followed. He returned in a more conversational volume, directly at Demosthenes, "You ought to reconsider. The consequences will be harsh, and I would as soon not witness them. Attica has seen enough bloodshed. It is time for peace."

"Then go home!" someone shouted.

Ignoring the outburst, Styphon nodded at Demosthenes. "To you and him"–he indicated Alkibiades–"Brasidas offers exile. Take your families with you and never set foot in Attica again. In exchange, he demands the corpse."

He did not need to specify which.

"Before you reject this offer," Styphon added heavily, "think hard about those who are not protected by these walls."

Demosthenes spat. He felt both fear and anger, but let only the latter show, as he spoke words which he hoped passionately were true.

"I have heard such threats once before, outside the jail in Melite," he said. "They were empty then and empty now. Brasidas knows he will not long command respect if he murders wives and children. That is not the Spartan way. If you are half the man I believe you to be, you will be first in line to put a knife in him when he descends to that."

"You have never known me," Styphon countered calmly. "Even less do you know Brasidas." He shrugged his wide shoulders, then raised the volume of his voice again for all to hear. "You have heard our offer! No one need suffer if you just pile your weapons and walk out. You have one hour!"

He turned his back to Demosthenes and faced the closed gate and the thirty Athenians arrayed in front of it. The faces of those men failed to give any hint of whether or not they were tempted by the envoy's terms.

"There is one more matter I would raise with you," Alkibiades said to Styphon's back. With a show of reluctance, Styphon turned, and Alkibiades called out, his voice soaring over the village, "Andrea, show yourself!"

Almost instantly, a small figure stepped out from behind the thick corner post of a stockade fence attached to a nearby dwelling.

"Come here," her guardian said. His were the only eyes which did not follow Andrea's straight-backed march to his side, where she inserted herself between him and Demosthenes. "Do you recognize this man?"

The Spartlet answered in a voice that belied her stature, "He is my father, and he means to kill us all."

Her guardian smacked her lightly on the back of her head. "Answer the question as asked."

Andrea grated, "Yes."

"You owe your father respect." Then Alkibiades addressed Styphon, whose reaction to the sight of his offspring could not be read. "I ordered her out of Dekelea, but she hid until the gates were sealed. I agreed to let her stay and help however she could, but now that her father is present–"

Foreseeing what Alkibiades intended, Andrea pleaded quietly, petulantly, "No."

"–he can be trusted to take her to safety."

Styphon stood unspeaking. The black eyes beneath his heavy brow failed even to shift down to the defiant face of the girl in question.

Andrea's jaw set. "I won't go."

"You will do your duty," her guardian insisted. He looked hard at Styphon. "If he'll have you."

A heavy silence settled between the gathered Athenians and the lone, stone-faced Spartiate as the latter pondered his decision. A minute later, and still without his black eyes having settled on the girl, he delivered it with a nod.

"No!" Andrea's high-pitched shriek echoed off of Dekelea's walls. She whirled, and her little arms flew up to wrap around Alkibiades' ornate breastplate. "Uncle, please!" She pressed her cheek hard against the bronze.

Alkibiades set a hand on his ward's shoulder, bowed his head and said, "It's Spartan blood in you, girl. His blood. You owe him obedience. Have I not taught you that much? Do as he says. If the gods let me live, I'll see you again when all this is over."

Andrea sniffled, drew a shuddering breath and detached herself from Alkibiades. She hardened her flint black eyes, raised her chin high and met the bracing gaze of her guardian as if drawing strength from it. After holding that posture for several heartbeats, she turned and aimed a blanker stare at the father she barely knew, but so resembled. Then in the steady, shade-like gait of a condemned man walking to the garrote, she went to unblinking Styphon and took a place by his left hand, facing the Athenian contingent. Side by side they stood, Spartiate and Spartlet, but there might as well have been a wall between them for all the notice they took of each other. Maybe Styphon was aware, or maybe Demosthenes only imagined, that behind the little girl's laconic mask, she was choking on tears.

One who knew him well could see the pain in Alkibiades' bright eyes, too, as he sent away the ward he had raised for longer than a year: his little monster, first pupil in the secret school he had hoped to found with Thalassia and his friend and mentor Socrates. But now Attica was under the Spartan heel, his star-girl was a corpse, and wise Socrates had gone down in the Athenian center at Eleusis with a spear in his belly.

Alkibiades' dream was dead, but he steeled his gaze and stood fast with the gentle hand which had been on his Spartlet resting now on the hilt of his sword.

"You have our reply," Demosthenes said to Styphon. "Now go and tell Brasidas that if he wants us, he can fucking well come in and get us."

The undiplomatic utterance prompted a flashed smile, if a melancholy one, from Alkibiades, who recognized the shade of Thalassia speaking through him. Other Athenians took up assailing the enemy envoy with jeers of their own, and so under a hail of curses, Styphon wordlessly turned his back and marched to the closed gate. A pace behind, Andrea followed mechanically, keeping her gaze straight ahead. On Demosthenes' signal, the heavy double doors were heaved open just a crack and the Spartiate slipped through first. After a barely perceptible moment of hesitation, his daughter followed.

The door thumped shut, but before even the iron reinforced timber bars were set back in place, Alkibiades had fallen back from the crowd to stride off into the unpaved streets of empty, hopeless Dekelea alone.

10. Vengeance Is Sworn

The sun was a violent red disc pouring blood over the western peaks when the Spartan army finished arraying itself before the walls of Dekelea. To the south, Brasidas's Peloponnesians were a dark forest of men and spears standing just out of bowshot, while northward, deeper into the mountains, a Theban force blocked the narrow pass through which in peacetime flowed a large percentage of Athens' grain supply. A foreign force that seized Dekelea could choke the life from Attica, and in a never-would-be world, that had happened; here, instead Attica was already in foreign hands and Dekelea the last resort of its defenders.

The doe-eyed leader of those holdouts was dead on his feet, a restless shade hovering in front of the shed which housed dead Thalassia. Would that he needed as little sleep as she did, barely one night out of every six. But Demosthenes was mortal and did need sleep, and he itched, too, all over the scalp under the hair which once had been blond but now was a helm of flat, grime-encrusted tendrils, and on the jaw covered by five days' worth of beard.

Why did he keep ending up here, at her shed? Wherever in Dekelea he was headed, his feet seemed to choose a path that took him past it. Its door was tied shut with a thick rope; perhaps he hoped each time he passed to find that rope hanging broken and Thalassia leaning casually on the wall with her supple neck unbroken.

But the door was always locked, and Demosthenes resisted whatever macabre impulse it was that urged him inside to see if he might find some way to awaken Athens' fallen champion in her adopted city's hour of need. But she had done her part... more than her part, and earned her rest.

"Demosthenes!"

He was standing with his back against the wall of a house opposite the shed, half asleep on his feet, when he heard his name shouted from the walls.

"Here!" Demosthenes answered swiftly, before he could be tempted to remain in hiding and sleep. He forced his legs to bear him out into the open space of Dekelea's main north-south road. There, looking toward the village's south gate, he saw his summoner: Alkibiades, waving him over from atop the wall. Coming alive again, or managing to make it seem that way, Demosthenes picked up his pace and soon was climbing the nearest stair to mount the protected walkway on which Alkibiades waited.

"A party approaches," Alkibiades said when he was within earshot. His manner was strangely subdued, even guarded. "Brasidas is among them."

Demosthenes replied swiftly, "Tell Straton to fill him with arrows, herald's wand or no."

Alkibiades hesitated. "I... don't think you'll want to do that."

Certainly, the habitual blasphemer's reluctance could not have come from any unwillingness to violate a sacred protection. He must have had other reasons, but rather than asking for them, Demosthenes brushed past Alkibiades and sped to the battlements. There, on the rocky ground below, midway between the dark line of besiegers and Dekelea's sheer walls, a spear-studded group of ten or so figures advanced. Squinting to see the band against the sunset, Demosthenes realized that the foremost two figures were unarmed.

They were not even men, but a pair of women, and they walked reluctantly on rope leads held by a Spartiate walking a few paces behind. Sackcloth obscured their heads. The female on the right was slight of build, with a short chiton of soiled linen covering a minimal expanse of her pale flesh. The other wore the long dress of a citizen woman, pleats stretched taut over a bulging abdomen.

As paralyzing terror overtook Demosthenes, Alkibiades appeared beside him and set a hand on his shoulder. He might have thrown it off, but his limbs would not respond.

The advancing party drew to a halt within easy shouting distance. The hooded prisoners' leads were jerked, and the two human shields marching with hands bound in front of them stumbled and twisted, but managed to stay upright. At the party's center was a figure who wore nothing to distinguish himself from any other of the long-haired Equals around him. It was this man, Brasidas, who spoke.

"Everywhere there is celebration at the news of Athens' defeat!" Brasidas bellowed. "The world is set free from the yoke of empire! Nothing that happens at Dekelea today, or any day to come, can reverse the spread of liberty! In that spirit of celebration, I give you one final opportunity to lay down your arms and–"

Rage built up in Demosthenes' tired limbs and spilled over the battlements in the shape of a roar which drowned out the Spartan general.

"Let them go!"

Brasidas aborted his speech. He might have smiled as he gestured to the Spartiate holding the rope leads, who obediently stepped forward and pulled the canvas sack from each prisoner's head. Coppery curls tumbled from one, light brown locks from the other. The two blinked in adjustment to the twilight and cast bewildered looks all around as they came to grips with their surroundings. Finding one another, they clung close, but it wasn't long before their fearful eyes went to the wall, and up it to find the husband and master whom they could not have failed to comprehend, now more than ever, held their lives in his hand.

Demosthenes could not long return their stunned gazes. Guilt turned his shocked eyes instead to the women's captor.

"Release them now! They have no place here!"

Brasidas refused to mirror his adversary's fury. "I will gladly let them go," he called back evenly. "You know the price. Open your gates."

For that moment, Demosthenes stood alone. There were no ranks of defiant Athenians arrayed on either side of him atop Dekelea's walls. There were no walls at all, and no Dekelea. There was only Brasidas and his two hostages.

"You can have me," Demosthenes returned resolutely. "For execution. Just let them go."

"That is not the trade at hand."

"The body you want, too! Have it!"

Demosthenes finally cast off the reassuring hand of Alkibiades when the latter began to utter a syllable of protest. Brasidas fell silent, and for an instant Demosthenes let himself hope that this new exchange was being considered.

That hope was dashed when Brasidas only repeated, "Lay down your arms and throw open your gates."

"I cannot give that order! These men would not listen to me if I did. I lead here only by consent. Take me, and take the body. That is all I can give!"

Brasidas drew the sword from his hip and stepped forward. Demosthenes lunged instinctively, as if he could step off the high wall and stay the Spartiate's arm. But he could not. He was helpless, moreso than ever he had been. All his effort won him was a sharp impact on his hips where they struck the edge of a battlement.

Drawing up behind the bound prisoners, Brasidas poised his blade in the air above Eurydike's head.

"I am not without mercy," he said. "I shall kill only one of them. But which? Most Athenians love their whores more than their wives, I am told. But not you, I think. Am I right?" His sword point drifted right to hang over the bowed head of Laonome. "She has your spawn in her bowels. An heir, if you're lucky, since you will soon be in need of one." The blade slipped lower, stopping alongside Laonome's round belly. "Or maybe I'll just relieve her of the burden."

"Let her go!"

Even as Demosthenes cried out, a Thracian storm knocked Brasidas back a step. Eurydike, whirling, aimed the hooked, claw-like fingers of her bound hands at the Spartiate's throat. Brasidas easily dodged the attack, and a second later the threat was nullified by a second Equal whose thick arms yanked hard on the rope fastened to Eurydike's neck. Her back arched unnaturally, her legs flew out from under her, and she slammed into the earth. Brasidas came forward, laughing, and he loomed over her, putting the point of his sword to her cheek.

A pace away, Laonome raised her eyes skyward. She sobbed, and her imperfect lips moved in inaudible prayer.

"Goodbye, Little Red."

The latter, a pained whisper, came from Alkibiades, who like Demosthenes knew precisely what Eurydike had hoped to gain by her rash action. She had suffered no illusion of being able to kill Brasidas, but rather only hoped to make herself the one he chose to murder.

Yet Brasidas's hovering sword did not cut.

"Styphon!" the polemarch barked, laughing. Only then did Demosthenes realize that one of the party's spear-wielding Equals was Styphon. His face had been averted as though in disapproval. "Do you have any use for this little beast?"

"No, polemarch," Styphon answered stiffly.

Heedless of the negative, Brasidas wrenched Eurydike's rope lead from its holder and thrust it at Styphon. "Take her anyway. Enjoy her. Tame her if you can, kill her if you must."

Obediently Styphon accepted the rope, and Brasidas set his now-free hand on Laonome's neck. She tried and failed to jerk her head away.

"Will none of you raise a hand to stop him!" Demosthenes cried desperately over the battlements at Brasidas's entourage. "What has become of Sparta's honor!"

"You can stop me yourself," Brasidas shot back. He spared not even a sidelong glance to search for signs of mutiny among his men.

Coming up behind Laonome, Brasidas yanked her body in close to his. His hand found her breast and squeezed. Laonome tried futilely to stop him with her bound hands, but her struggle ceased when the edge of a short sword grazed the soft underside of her chin.

"What say you, Athenian?"

"I say why kill her when you can kill me instead!" Demosthenes' answer was earnest and given without hesitation. "Why cut a woman's throat when you can cut your enemy's? She is no threat, but my death means–"

Brasidas's sword arm slid sideward. Blood gushed around his blade and down over Laonome's dress. Her bulbous form slumped heavily into the dirt, spindly limbs flopping lifelessly.

A raw, piercing sound filled the sky over Dekelea, resounding in the space between Demosthenes' ears. Only minutes later, with cold stone under him, abrading his skin as he struggled to escape the tangle of men's limbs fighting to restrain him, did he realize that the source of the persistent sound was his own throat.

Silencing the cry, he broke from the restraining arms and

threw himself against the battlements.

"BRASIDAS!" he roared. "Hear me, murderer, and know this! From this day, I have but one purpose. I will kill Spartans until it scarcely seems worthwhile to lift my arm to slay another! And only then, when your wretched kind is all but extinct, will you kneel before me and become the last! This I swear by every dark god that lurks in the earth! Do you hear me, Brasidas! You have doomed your city!"

Whirling, Demosthenes did not watch or listen for Brasidas to reappear and make reply. He strode off, shoving men from his path and descended the stair from the battlements into Dekelea with but one destination in mind.

On his heels, Alkibiades grabbed his arm. "Demosthenes!"

He ripped his arm from the youth's grasp. "Take command," he bid him.

"No." Alkibiades grabbed him again, with both arms, forcing Demosthenes to a halt. "You are not thinking clearly. I know that you–"

"You know nothing!" Demosthenes broke loose once more and resumed his march. Alkibiades trailed after. "Thalassia lied to you. Before she came, you were fated to be remembered forever, for both good deeds and bad. You want the chance to make it so again? It is yours. Embrace it. As for me, I have never been more clear of purpose."

"*Lied...?*" Alkibiades echoed dully. His steps slowed, and he ceased his pursuit through the dirt streets of the mountain village. "What will you do?" he shouted at Demosthenes' back, to no reply.

Hardly a minute's walk brought Demosthenes to the shed housing Thalassia's corpse. Drawing his sword, he sliced the thick rope holding it shut, and he entered. The small room, lit by shafts of light that seeped through the wall boards, did not smell of death but rather of dirt and olive oil and musty wood. Thalassia's mutilated body lay on the earthen floor of this, her mausoleum, shrouded in a white cloth that was pink in spots where it had soaked through. Kneeling, Demosthenes peeled back her shroud. In the space around her eye, the lines of her Mark seemed to eat the light, as did the great, gaping wound between chin and shoulder that had nearly severed her head. Bridging the gap was the thick single braid, deliberately placed, which came up from behind her head to cross her collarbone and end near her heart.

Andrea had cleaned and anointed the corpse, but there was not much anyone could do to make the star-girl look whole again. She made a grisly sight: head hanging on by a shred of flesh, one arm a dark red stump, and much of her formerly smooth skin sliced to ribbons, such that little skin even was visible. Her appearance was little changed since her death three days prior, but that in itself offered hope, for her body had not gone the way of normal corpses, growing pale and stiff. But for her horrific wounds–which had begun to ooze a sort of clear liquid–Thalassia might have been merely asleep. She was healing, but her recovery would clearly be slow, likely much longer than Dekelea could hope to hold out in a siege.

Thalassia's face was largely intact, and it was to this that Demosthenes addressed his words, delivered as he lay down beside her on the dirt floor.

"You are a weapon," he said, "unlike any this world has known. You chose me to wield you in my war, as you would wield me in yours. *Exairetos,* you called me once in my dreams. *Chosen One.* But I was hesitant. I wielded you badly. No man possessed of a heart should ever wish to wield to its full potential a weapon such as you are. But now... now, I have no heart. Laonome–" His throat clenched around the name, as if to squeeze her tight in denial of her absence. "Laonome has taken it with her to Hades. Unburdened of it, I can do what must be done."

He raised a hand and touched Thalassia's cheek, which was not warm, but neither as chill as a corpse's should be. His finger traced the sinuous, black curves of her Mark. "When you rise again, we shall wield each other and each take our righteous vengeance. We shall become that terrible, beautiful, destructive force of which you spoke on the day you died. I will rip out Brasidas's heart, just as he did mine, and squeeze the blood down the throats of Sparta's ephors. I will see his unburied corpse fed to dogs while his restless shade is raped by Furies. You will strip the meat from Eden's bones and smash her every Seed. Sparta shall be erased from this world, and after it Roma, that future generations will not live under her yoke. And then..." He exhaled through tightly clenched teeth. "And then I shall let myself sink into Hades and rest with Laonome."

He raised himself from the floor and set to preparing for the chosen course of his fate. Some time later, he exited the shed, stripped of the black scale armor with its patch of spun bronze that had saved his life at Amphipolis. His sword remained belted at his hip, and a coil of rope was slung over his shoulder. He dragged behind him Thalassia's body, which he had wrapped tightly in canvas and strapped to a makeshift bier. He walked west with this burden, and his passage did not go unnoticed; word began to spread, mostly in whispers, of poor, bereaved Demosthenes' emergence. It must eventually have reached Alkibiades, perhaps on the new commander's own instruction, for he came running up, dressed in his glittering armor, just as Demosthenes reached Dekelea's western wall.

"Where are you headed, my friend?" Alkibiades asked,

his voice filled with condescension. "I fear you may plan something rash."

"How often has someone said exactly those words to you?" Demosthenes returned, without halting.

"Quite often," the youth conceded. "Usually they are right."

Reaching the base of a bastion, Demosthenes entered and began dragging Thalassia's bier up the stairs.

"You aren't leaving town, are you?"

"Yes. Try to stop me, and I will kill you."

"If you do, the Spartans will kill you."

"I will get past them."

Alkibiades took the dragging end of Thalassia's bier and lifted it, helping to carry her up the stairs. "And what can you accomplish?" he asked. "There are two of you, and one is dead."

"Two are dead," Demosthenes corrected. "And she is Athens' only hope of regaining freedom. She must not fall into Spartan hands. It is too dangerous to keep her here."

At the top of the wall, they lay down Thalassia's body. "I see the folly of arguing with you at present," Alkibiades conceded. "Where will you go?"

Demosthenes sank to the rough surface of the liquid stone, his back against a battlement. "Even if I knew, I would not say," Demosthenes answered. "When and if this town falls, you could be made to talk."

Or you might elect to, he declined to add.

"Very well," Alkibiades said glumly. "I suppose all that remains to say is, 'May Zeus protect you, my good friend.'"

"And you," Demosthenes responded hollowly.

With a smile full of pity, Alkibiades, in his shining armor inlaid with ivory and gold, vanished down the stair to resume command of the tattered remnants of Athens' army.

Demosthenes sat on the wall for hours, now and then choking on tears but mostly only staring blankly, waiting for full darkness to descend, that he might more safely make his escape.

When it came, he secured his rope to a battlement, tied the other end to Thalassia's bier and lowered her down. Then he descended the rope himself, untied the bier and began dragging it west at a run over the rocky ground, making for the thickest part of the wood that surrounded mountainous Dekelea. The invading army would soon fully invest this countryside, dig an encircling ditch, and put the town fully under siege. But Brasidas had only arrived today, and so, apart from a small Spartan patrol that forced him briefly into hiding, Demosthenes found his passage unopposed. He reached the woods and continued into the mountains, into hiding, bearing behind him the weapon with which he intended to achieve nothing less than the total annihilation of the man and city which had stripped him of all in his life that had been good. Although Demosthenes of Athens was dead, he walked on, while from the distance, soaring over the battlements of a doomed mountain refuge, came the raised voices of Spartans singing hymns to victory.

END

The sequel, *Spartan Beast,* is out now. If you enjoyed *Athenian Steel,* please consider leaving a positive review on the retailer website.

Made in the USA
Middletown, DE
03 December 2017